MW01180568

51A

51A

Frank Brennan

6-6-02

Joan W.,

The most useless day of all is that in which we have not laughed.

Now that your stress has been diminished, may you find all of your days: useful.

Frank B.

REN

Library of Congress Number:		2001119784
ISBN #:	Hardcover	1-4010-4066-7
	Softcover	1-4010-4065-9

This book was printed in the United States of America.

To order additional copies of this book, contact:
Xlibris Corporation
1-888-7-XLIBRIS
www.Xlibris.com
Orders@Xlibris.com

Contents

REN

REN

For all the children, everywhere

Do you hear the children weeping, O my brothers
Ere the sorrow comes with years?
The Cry of the Children
(1844) Stanza I

The child's sob in the silence curses deeper
than the strong man in his wrath.
Ibid. Stanza 13

Acknowledgement

For my wife, children, grandchildren and my family for their encouragement and belief in me.

For four lovely ladies: Maria, Eileen, Margaret and Donna whose talent and hard work were a tremendous assist in giving birth to 51A.

For all of the world's dedicated social workers – you *have* made a difference and for it, I thank you.

51 A

Chapter 119, Massachusetts General Laws, Section 51 A

Physicians, Medical Interns, etc., to Report Cases of Abuse, etc.; Immunity from Criminal Action; Privilege not to be Invoked; Penalty.

Any physician, medical intern, hospital personnel engaged in the examination, care or treatment of persons, medical examiner, psychologist, emergency medical technician, dentist, nurse, chiropractor, podiatrist, osteopath, public or private school teacher, educational administrator, guidance or family counselor, day care worker or any person paid to care for or work with a child in any public or private facility, or home or program funded by the commonwealth or licensed pursuant to the provisions of chapter twenty-eight A, which provides day care or residential services to children, probation officer, clerk/magistrate of the district courts, social worker, foster parent, firefighter or policeman, who, in his professional capacity shall have reasonable cause to believe that a child under the age of eighteen years is suffering serious physical or emotional injury resulting from abuse

REN

inflicted upon him including sexual abuse, or from neglect, including malnutrition, or who is determined to be physically dependent upon an addictive drug at birth, shall immediately report such condition to the department by oral communication and by making a written report within forty-eight hours after such oral communication; provided, however, that whenever such person so required to report is a member of the staff of a medical or other public or private institution, school or facility, he shall immediately either notify the department or notify the person in charge of such institution, school or facility, or that person's designated agent, whereupon such person in charge or his said agent shall then become responsible to make the report in the manner required by this section. Any such hospital personnel preparing such report, may take, or cause to be taken, photographs of the areas of trauma visible on a child who is the subject of such report without the consent of the child's parents or guardians. All such photographs or copies thereof shall be sent to the department together with such report. Any such person so required to make such oral and written reports who fails to do so shall be punished by a fine of not more than one thousand dollars.

Prologue

Merrilee and he were in the Hyannis Filene's shopping for clothes for the two girls. Avé was in her carriage and Genie clutched on to her father's hand. The store was crowded even though it was two months before Easter. There had been a thaw and it was like a beautiful spring day.

"Oh, Don. Isn't this coat adorable!"

"I don't know. How much is it?"

"Genie could get two years out of it. And then, Ave."

"How much?"

"Now a nice straw hat and some Mary Janes . . ."

"How much?"

"Look how much I saved by making their dresses."

"How much?"

"It's a Holly Linders and a steal at one fifty."

"A dollar fifty? Not bad at all. They won't stay in business long with prices like that."

"Don! Really! Bring Genie over here and we'll see how becoming this shade of blue is . . . Where is she?"

The child was gone. Both children were gone. As Don looked

across the large areas of the store, he saw the seediest looking man going out the exit, pushing Ave's carriage. Genie was holding his left hand, while sucking a lollipop which she held in the other. He knew in the pit of his stomach that the man was a pedophile. They all had that same look about them. His heart was pounding until it seemed it would either explode or he would go deaf. Merrilee began screaming, "My babies! My babies! Please, somebody, stop that man!"

Don tried to run through the crowded store but his legs wouldn't move. The greater effort he made, the heavier his legs became and the more stationary his body. He could see the man, now, through the wide expanse of store windows. Other adults and children were coming towards the trio touching and embracing his children. He knew them all from his past cases. Child abusers and child victims. Victims who, involuntarily, had lost their innocence. The large group were now hurrying towards a bus in the parking lot. On it, was a bumper sticker that read: 'Keep Families Intact. Kill a DSS Social Worker Today'. Scott Peck was right, he thought. Evil men with oily, slippery skin; evil women with perpetual, false smiles. Abused children abusing other children.

He screamed from somewhere in the deepest cavity of his soul, and, immediately awoke. He lay in a bed of clamminess while his chest repeatedly heaved. Then he began to shake. He pulled the covers up under his chin, and started to cry, softly. Dear Lord, thank you. Better a dream. Slowly, very slowly, he drifted back into sleep. A sleep without dreams. Later, the alarm beckoned. Another day. Please Lord, make the horror less. For all of the children. As the cold shower washed away whatever it could, he decided not to tell Merrilee about the dream. Or that this was the fifth successive one. He didn't realize that no matter how often it would recur in the future, he would never know it was only a dream.

Homefront

"Merrilee?"

"Yes, dear."

"Have you seen my brown belt around anywhere?"

"Genie was playing with it in her room yesterday."

"Oh—"

"Find it, Hon?"

"Mmmm. In the doll carriage with two of my neckties."

"Isn't she a riot?"

"Yeah, a regular four alarm."

"Oh, Don!"

"Only kidding, only kidding. Really, do love you and the girls. Scout's honor."

"Hmmm. Oh, while you're out that way, please see if Ave has finished her bottle. She's been throwing it on the floor lately. Must remember to get some plastic ones."

"About two ounces to go, Gorgeous! If I think of it, I"ll drop into a druggie on the way home and pick up a few."

"Oh would you? You know my memory—"

"Yup. Ancient."

"No, seriously, the last few weeks I've been forgetting to get things we need. Any suggestions?"

"Mmmm."

"What?"

"List."

"What?"

"List,"

"Oh, Don! You won't believe it! I feel so silly!"

"Try me."

"I thought you said lisp and I couldn't imagine how that could help."

"I've just come to a considered decision that will affect our lives for many moons."

"Really? This early in the morning?"

"Come on. Give Daddy a big kiss. Daddy has to go to work."

"Work is comin'! Work is comin'!"

"Isn't she a riot?"

"Yes. A regular four—"

"I know. I know."

"'Bye, hon. MMMMMMMM!"

"Hey, watch out! You know how easily that can get you into trouble. Besides—bad time."

"When?"

"About five days,"

"MMMMMMMM!"

"Remember what I just said?"

"That kind of trouble—I know—You can stand more of."

"What are you, anyway? A mindaholic?"

"A what? Is that another of those new words you're always making up? Next thing you'll know, the world will finally have a Goode dictionary."

"Mmm."

"Don't get it, eh?"

"Get what?"

"Goode Dictionary?"

"Have two now."

"Ugh! G-o-o-d and G-o-o-d-e. Now do you—"

"Double ugh! And you talk about my punny jokes. Get that?"

"Don! Stop! The tears are coming. Genie'll think we're both cracked."

"Mrs. Goode! Are you daring to infer that the head of this home is possibly even a little—"

"Well. Not seriously enough to be committed or anything like that. Perhaps a little Outpatient—"

"Come on! We'd best stop all this nonsense or 'Genie'll think' might just come true."

"What?"

"Do I have to explain everything?"

"No, no. I get it now. Genie'll think we're both."

"Well, gotta go now."

"Without telling me the 'Big Decision?"

"What 'Big Decision'?"

"Oh, Don! Now I'm beginning to wonder about your memory. You said only a few moments ago that—"

"Oh! That decision. I've decided to keep you around—for laughs—forever."

"Don Goode! Am I really a clown? I know with this face and all, one might think so, but—"

"Stop! To me, you're the most beautiful girl in the world!"

"Oh yeah? Then how come you won't let me pick out any ties for you, like in the song?"

"Song? Song??? Genie's right! Ar Reservoir!"

"'Bye, My Love—"

Before they became the All American two-car family, Don was glad of his decision to leave the car every day for Merrilee's use. At first, he thought he would be making quite a sacrifice but, as time advanced, he enjoyed more and more the opportunity of being alone—waiting for the B-bus that took him daily to the office. The trip and the return trip home were almost the only times he was alone. And he used the time well. If something that should be remembered came to mind he would remove the pad and pencil (one of the gifts Merrilee had placed in his Christmas Stocking), from his suit coat pocket and make a notation for future reference. He was quite surprised how quickly the book was filled. For it, he thanked his wife many, many times.

Everyone needs time to be alone, Don thought. Not lonely—they were not one and the same. He considered himself the most fortunate of men. There he was, because of a seemingly unselfish sacrifice, being afforded the opportunity to begin and end his workaday world with the gift of aloneness. How precious this gift of time to prepare himself daily to properly fulfill his avocation and, at day's end, to similarly prepare himself to likewise fulfill his vocation. His so-called "sacrifice" must have been inspired he would chuckle to himself.

Both of his jobs were time and energy consuming he knew, to be done properly. Their two children had come less than a year apart—'Irish twins', they would joke. Ave was just two months of age and Genie, eleven. The doctor had strongly advised the use of rhythm to preserve Merrilee's health. But how she and Don hated it! It removed the spontaneity, and Don sometimes, lamely joked, "When is it our two weeks to go to bed?" He was unaware how deeply this hurt for it was not by her choice. Perhaps if she had been stronger physically, she asked the doctor; he told her it was just one of those things. But he told Don a lot more. Ave's birth had been very difficult and the after-birth had been abnormally small and had to be sent to the lab. He wanted to see Don in his office, alone, in a few weeks' time. Don spent a privately tortuous three weeks after the delivery, imagining the worst. Fortunately, the tests proved negative, but the doctor emphasized how important it was that Merrilee not get pregnant for at least another two years. At the time, Don was so relieved that he would have agreed to anything. Now, whenever he thought how distasteful rhythm was to him, the memory of that day in the doctor's office lessened the pain. And, now having two cars, he realized how more fortunate he would have been with just one. If he thought of something, he'd have to remember to write it down, and more often than not, would forget.

Lunie Tune

Another one of those dreaded evening calls. Whatever happened to the sanctity of the home or a man's castle? But that was the nature of his job, he thought. As bad as the news always was, it was better to know the night before. At least that way, he'd be in the right place in the morning. Life had become much more bearable since he'd learned to think in comparatives. Or to make bizarre jokes about the tragedies. The family that plays together stays together. To scandalize an innocent. What was that biblical allusion about never being born or wearing a millstone necktie? Better the former, he thought. Thank God, he was one step removed from the horror. Being the Department's attorney was better than being a social worker and seeing it all firsthand.

That Lunie was a great worker. How she exercised the control she did, he'd never understand. And that name. Her parents were astrology buffs long before it was fashionable and had named her Lunar. Try as they might, to insist on the given name for their little Cancer daughter, the inevitable happened as well as the jokes that followed. She had tired long ago of explanations and told people she was born in a mental institution and her parents' fellow inmates selected the name. But that call . . .

"Don?"

"Uh huh."

"Sorry for calling you at home. This is Lunie Nelson.

"You'd have to be looney to do the job you do on the hotline."

"That stale joke again? When will you come up with some fresh material?"

"Well, I could ask you if you were Tommy Tune's sister."

"Ugh! This is serious business, Don. I'm at Falmouth Hospital. Brutal rape of a little girl. She's in surgery now. Evidence of semen in the vaginal area."

"Who's the bastard this time? Mother's boyfriend?"

"No. The bio father was the caretaker at the time of what he describes as an accident with a baton."

"Was the baton circumcised?"

"I'll pass on that one. See you in First District Court tomorrow at nine. If you need me before then I'll be in the office starting at seven-thirty. I'll have to start writing up my 51B investigation before Court and I'm waiting here to talk with Dr. Arnold. Couldn't get much out of the mother. She's hysterical."

"Before you go—how old is this victim?"

"I'm not sure. She has a birthday coming up next week. I'll let you know tomorrow."

"I guess her father gave her her birthday present a little early."

"Well, I wish he'd waited and changed his mind. Have a wonderful evening. 'Bye'."

"Bye."

How did these things happen, he wondered. It was easier to understand sickos abducting kids than it was to understand a father raping his own child. But how did it happen—how had this one happened. He would never stop wondering. At least he guessed he wouldn't.

Daddy's Little Girl

"Daddy, please don't hurt me in the pee pee or. . . ."

"Yes?"

"In my bum."

"I only do it to show how much Daddy loves you."

"But it hurts so much and why can't Mommy know? She loves me and she doesn't hurt me."

"Because it's our secret. It will spoil everything if you tell anyone. And Mommy would get jealous. She thinks she is the only one I do this with."

"Maybe she is the only one you should do it with because she's a big lady."

"Yeah. About 220 . . ."

"What's that?"

"Just a little joke. Come on, get into bed. We haven't got much time. Mommy will be back from Grandma's soon."

"Why does she have to go so much and why can't she take me?"

"Because she knows how much Daddy loves you and wants to be with you."

"But if you love someone you try not to hurt them. Mrs. Evans, my teacher, says so."

"You didn't tell her did you?"

"No, Daddy."

"Good. Now start rubbing me and I'll start rubbing you."

"Why does it have to get so big, Daddy?"

"To make you happy. Now spread your legs."

"Daddy, please don't put your pee pee in my pee pee. Please!"

"Come on. This is what Mommy and I do. You want to be a big girl don't you? Why you're going to be five years old next week. I've been waiting for you to grow up. Remember last year when I'd be giving you a bath and rubbed you between your legs? You got to like it a lot."

Later, he told himself he really hadn't meant to enter such a small opening. As he rubbed his body over hers and began rhythmically going back and forth between her little legs he became overwrought. He threw caution to the proverbial winds. He abandoned all thought of anything or anyone except his own pleasure. She screamed and screamed and screamed. He continued on, blocking out all sound except his own grunting. Then it was over. Now he could feel her warm blood running down his thighs. Mercifully, she had lost consciousness. He glanced at the bedside clock, 7:15 P.M. She would be home in less than twenty-five minutes. He had to hurry. He left the sheets the way they were. He got her baton from her room and turned it over and over in her blood. He took more blood and with his fingers placed it on the sides of the baton. Next, he got some large heavy Turkish towels and tied them around her in diaper fashion. The last two things he did was wash the blood off himself and then, he got dressed and waited for his wife. He was in complete control of his emotions. He lighted a cigarette and inhaled deeply. It had been wonderful. Just wonderful.

After her child was rushed into surgery, she finally found her voice.

"How did it happen, Ralph?"

"Flossie, you don't think I wanted it to happen, do you?"

"Your old habit of answering a question with a question."

"I didn't mean that. You know how much I love Cindy."

"Well, what happened?"

"I was in the living room reading the paper and Cindy asked if she could play in our bedroom. We had already had our soup so I told her, sure."

"And—"

"And I didn't know she had her baton and was turning tricks in our bed."

"Yes?"

"Then I heard the screaming and ran in. At first I couldn't see what had happened because of all the blood. Then, Cindy passed out. Because of all the pain, I guess. Well, then I saw it. The baton. It was sticking out of her —pee pee as she calls it. I, as gently as possible, removed it. Then I got the towels and put them on to stop the bleeding. I didn't have time to do anything else."

"Why didn't you call the police and rush her to the hospital?"

"Because, I saw the clock and knew you'd be home within minutes. I thought you'd get hysterical if you saw all the blood and well, with us both gone. So I decided to wait."

"Ralph, why don't you have any blood on you?"

"I didn't do anything!"

"You removed the baton and tied on the towels?"

"Oh, yeah. I guess I must have washed without realizing it."

Florence Fenwick had just about gotten her emotions in check and hoped for the best, when Dr. Arnold approached her.

"Mrs. Fenwick?"

"Yes, Doctor. My husband just went for coffee."

"Dr. Hayes is finishing up on Cindy in surgery. I'm Dr. Arnold. I think she is going to be all right, physically, in time.

"Oh, thank God. Thank you, Dr. Arnold."

"Mrs. Fenwick, the hospital has had to call the Department of Social Services Hotline with a complaint. It's called a 51A."

"Why? Can't the hospital care for my little girl? That's the State, isn't it? I don't want to get involved with them."

"You have no choice. We here, at the hospital, are what are called mandated reporters. We are required by law to report cases of suspected abuse or neglect of a minor child by a caretaker."

"Oh, you mean my husband should have been taking better notice of what was going on in the bedroom?"

"Something like that."

"What do you mean, 'something like that'? You are accusing or suspecting him of being neglectful, aren't you?"

"No."

"You said neglect or abuse, didn't you?"

"Yes, I did."

"Well, there's only physical or sexual abuse, right?"

"Right."

"Now, Doctor, you don't think Ralph inserted that baton into his daughter's vagina do you?"

"No, Mrs. Fenwick. Was your husband the only other person at the home at the time of the accident?"

"Yes, Why?"

"Because we found evidence of semen in Cindy's vagina."

"Oh, No! No! Pleeeasse don't! Nooooooooo! ech-ech—ech—echhh. . . . . . ."

They were still trying to revive her when Lunie Nelson arrived on the scene.

To Court Via Office

Don thought he'd better stop at the office first, to check his messages and see how Lunie was doing on the affidavit for the court case on Fenwick. There was no doubt in his mind that the court would grant a Care and Protection petition and give custody of Cindy to the Department, even though she would be in the hospital for another while. Another child abused - another placement for foster care. But, worst of all, a child whose scars would never heal.

"A partment of Social Services. May we help you? No, she's at service training in Boston. Care to leave a message? Let's check the schedule. Tomorrow, in all day."

"A partment of Social Services. Intake? O. K. I'll ring . . ."

Why does she keep saying 'a partment'? People are going to think we have rooms to rent. Next thing you know a homeless unit will evolve. He looked for Lunie and found her in 'The Great Escape' or conference room to outsiders. Workers came here as a last resort to get court letters and record keeping done without telephone interruption. It was the only place in the two buildings that didn't have a phone.

"How's it going, Lunie?"

"Well. What are you doing here? This is quite an honor. You always go directly to court. Why the change?"

"It is that new policy of DSS."

"Policy? You mean you are actually going to go according to Policy. That's a laugh!"

" Now, now. I may not keep the greatest records . . ."

"You don't keep any records. I saw that matchbook cover you used for your notes during the Smith hearing."

"I won didn't I?"

"It seems you almost always do. Now what's this policy?"

"In all court cases, the DSS Attorney has to check all social workers' court letters and affidavits, revising them if necessary. If not, approving them."

"You don't have enough to do? You have the largest case load in the state."

"I know. But the second part of the policy says that all court letters will be seen by the attorney three days prior to the court date, unless it's an emergency."

"Ha! That's a crock. You see every worker in this office late the day before court or early the day of court, lined up for the poor two stenos to type their letters. And it's because they're too busy. Caseloads are anywhere from three to ten above Federal sanctions. You don't intend to tell the workers do you?"

"Yes. I'm putting out a memo and attaching the policy I received from Regional and then . . ."

"Don. They'll hate you!"

"Lunie, I haven't finished. Then I'll tell them, orally, to disregard the second part of the memo."

"No wonder you're our favorite office attorney."

"I'm your only office attorney."

"You know what I'm saying. I just didn't want you to get a big head."

"Lunie, in this letter you shouldn't say the child was raped. Just iterate what the doctors told you. That way, you won't be putting yourself in an embarrassing position, if it comes to trial. You know, something like, Doctor Hayes reported that semen was found in this almost five year old's vagina."

"Don, you're a genius. Can—oops—before you correct my syntax. . . . may I also state what Mrs. Fenwick said to me?"

"If it's relevant. What did she say?"

"She asked me if it was—I know, subjunctive and it should be 'were', but I'm quoting—possible that Doctor Hayes put the semen there to get her husband in trouble."

"Lunie, put it in. It shows she tends not to believe the child nor the doctors, that she can't protect the child and, ergo . . ."

"The child is at risk! Don, you should have been a teacher."

"I am. And I'll see you in court."

"A quick question, Don?"

"It will have to be. I'm on my way to First District."

"I got this Dad that's in prison. Mom has already signed an adoption surrender. I told Dad if he signs a surrender, this couple will adopt the child but when he gets out, he gets the kid back. He doesn't believe me, so could you speak with him or give me a sworn statement for him?"

"Can't do that Conchita. He has every right to disbelieve you. Adoption surrenders are irrevocable and once an adoption is legalized, it's final. Why did you tell him that? Didn't you check first with your supervisor?"

"No. I told him that because I knew he'd feel better and I thought it would be nice for a kid to go home again."

"Well, in the future, I suggest you check these things out with your sup. If your sup. isn't available, then with the sup du jour. That's sup of the day."

Provocative Four Year Old

He hitched a ride to Court with Melinda Thatcher. She was blunt, but that's what Librans are. More importantly, she was a good worker, made her clients toe the mark and she was kind. Two months before, after a court date, she drove a client to the bus terminal to catch a bus to Connecticut. The body odor was so bad she drove with both windows open, with temperatures at thirty degrees, so she could breathe. When the client, Cynthia Rottenbotham, didn't have enough for her fare, Melinda gave her the last ten dollars she had on her.

"So, Don, I'm going up to the big city tomorrow."

"You know if I closed my eyes I'd swear I was in South Dakota. Whereabouts are ya'll headin'?"

"South Dakota isn't southern United States. I'm going to police division Area B. The whole complex there involves the court and the Police Station, I understand."

"What male worker is going with you? That's a very bad area."

"Someone else said they thought that but when I spoke with the A.D. and his assistant, the bowlegged little greaseball, as you call him, they both said no problem, fine area, no need to tie up two social workers to pick up those thirteen year Nielson twins who have raised more havoc than fifty other kids."

"Did you check with Trudy, your sup?"

"Yes. And she was told the same thing by them, but disagreed."

"I don't think you should go. If the Area Director orders you to go, you should refuse. You'd be on solid ground."

"Don, you're always telling me how tough I am. I can take care of myself." Well, here we are at the magnificent Halls of Justice, Don."

"Linny, if you want justice, this is the last fucking place you'd come."

As they entered the building, several lawyers nodded greetings. Some of the more humorous said things like:

"Hey Don, have you grabbed any little ones away from their mothers today?"

Don responded, "Oh yes, two infants even as they suckled at the breast." Then he hurried down the stairs, where he would wait for Lunie to process the papers in the clerk's office.

"What you got today, Don? Another horror story?" It was Juan Leonardo the probation officer.

"Yup. A father raped his four year old—almost five—daughter and blamed it on a baton. . . ."

He walked down the corridor to peek in the courtroom to see which judge would be sitting. Gina, the beautiful black court officer saw him from the other side and came to the door.

"What are you doing here on a Thursday, Hon?"

"Emergency, Ms. Johnson. Which Judge do we have?"

"None of the regulars is available, Hon. His name is Arlo Fassbinder. I hear he's a real cowboy, Don, so watch your step. Is this a bad one?"

He told her the circumstances and she rolled her eyes towards the ceiling.

"You want me to tell him you're here?"

"No. The paperwork is being completed upstairs. You'll know when Mary brings it down with the petition."

A half hour after Lunie came down for the Juvenile Session, the case was called.

"All rise please. The honorable Justice Arlo Fassbinder sitting. Please be seated."

"Will counsel please identify themselves."

"Yes your Honor. Don Goode, Attorney for the Department of Social Services."

"Would you please fill the court in on this matter."

"Yes your Honor . . ."

"Wait a minute. Where are the other parties and their attorneys? You don't think I'm going to hear a change of custody request ex parte, do you? I wasn't born yesterday."

Gina was right. And he's not even a knowledgeable cowboy.

"Your Honor, if it please the Court . . ."

"It doesn't!"

"If I may, Under Chapter 119, sections 23 and 24, the Court is empowered to hear emergency care and protection matters. The parents will be summoned to appear at a seventy-two hour proceeding. If they do not have counsel and qualify financially, the Court will appoint counsel. Thereafter, a modified hearing will take place to determine whether the child should be returned home. Sometime thereafter, a full hearing will take place to determine so called 'permanent' custody."

"Thank you for the lecture, Mr. Goode. I still don't see how I'm to make a decision when I know nothing about the child or the family."

"Well, your Honor, you have before you a Care and Protection Petition sworn to by the social worker, Lunar Nelson. In addition, there is an affidavit signed by the same person, which is in support of the petition. The background and history of the case which led to this emergency procedure are spelled out there, your Honor."

"I don't know any of the details, the important details. For example: How was this child dressed? Did she act in a provocative manner? You may be unaware of it Mr. Goode, but some of these children are wise beyond their years and many a good man's reputation has been ruined because some innocent appearing child has led him down the garden path and then cried 'wolf'!"

"Your honor, this child is four—almost five—years old. Her father is the alleged perpetrator. No matter what she did, and there isn't any evidence she did anything, nothing could justify what her father did."

"Well, I believe in keeping families together. The state is a poor parent and I am not going to be a party to an unjust disruption of the family unit. You may find some other judge in this courthouse who is half-asleep and who doesn't know enough to ask pertinent questions leading up to the incident and have the state prevail, but I will not tolerate it!"

"Your Honor, are you denying the petition?"

"Oh. Ho! So you can run up to the Appeals Court and let those Apes have a field day with me? Not on your life. I am refusing to hear it. Now take these papers out of here! I have more important work to do."

Later, the clerk called the presiding judge, Kevin Kelly, and explained what had happened. Don and Lunie were ushered into his lobby during his court break and treated royally. What a difference. The petition was granted; a seventy-two hour hearing was set and summonses ordered for the parents. They both thanked Judge Kelly and went to the Clerk's office to wait for the orders giving temporary custody until the seventy-two hour hearing, to DSS.

Later, as Lunie drove Don back to the office he thought aloud,

"See how uneven justice can be? You go before one judge and end up in prison. You go before another, on the same merits, and you walk. They ought to have a scouting course in law school. Check the court and judges therein, before your case comes up. That's how to best serve your client. Either that, or train a machine to administer justice."

"What are you going to do if you have Fassbinder again?"

"Get very, very, sick. . . . On him."

"Thanks for the ride Lunie. I hope my car at Sunoco is ready by the time I leave. They were putting brakes in the front end."

"Why don't you call them, now, from your office. That will make one less thing you'll have to unload, Don. Nothing's worse than not knowing."

"That's pretty good logic for a social worker, who is also a Cancer."

"At least I have a sign."

The car was ready. He decided to walk up, get it, and leave it in the office parking lot. He felt better. Lunie was right. He had unloaded two things. On the way to Sunoco, he thought of an incident in court last year. Thank God, it wasn't Fassbinder or he would have gone to jail. He made an untoward comment in a stage whisper, thinking no one had heard. But everyone had!

"Mr. Goode, are you attempting to express contempt for this court."

"No, your Honor, I'm trying to conceal it."

Judge Strait's chair swiveled until it faced the wall, which was lined with law books. The silence was deafening. Finally, his shoulders began to go up and down. Don knew he was safe for another day. He also learned to decrease the size of his mouth, temporarily.

"Hello Don. Juan Leonardo. On next week's list, do you have Smith, St. Regis and Harding?"

"Yes, I do."

"What's the date you have for the full hearing on Chester?"

"Can you hold until I check. . . . March 17th."

"Is that going forward?"

"As far as I know. I have been trying to get an agreement from their two attorneys. The child's attorney is willing to consent to custody in DSS. But the mother's attorney, Mike Rock, thinks he can win the case."

"With that fuc—excuse me—evidence? Clarence Darrow couldn't win. Is he aware she showed up shitface for the review two months ago. She'd take a step forward and three back. She fell off the bench in the courtroom three times. Her hair was spiked, unintentionally. Somehow she got to her car and drove home or somewhere, and was back the next morning in the First Session on an O.U.I.'

"Juan, it's too bad you didn't have your camcorder with you that day."

"It was at the cleansers with my autograph book."

"Well in that case, I may have to call you as a witness."

"Be my guest, Don. Bye, bye. And, thanks."

Don looked at the next day's schedule. Ugh! Martha's Vineyard, Judge George Washington Worthington presiding. He would have made a great president of Nineteenth Century Fox. Don would never forget his first time on Gull Air. The social worker and he walked out to the tarmac, after boarding was announced. He was expecting a 707.

"Where's the plane, Chris?"

"Right there, Don."

"Where?"

"There."

"You don't mean that itty, bitty thing with the elastic behind the propellers?"

"Well, that's the eight seater. We may get the smaller one coming back."

He always remembered to bring two changes of underwear after that first experience.

George Washington and the Choo-Choo-In

Was it three months ago? It was his first introduction to Judge Worthington and his first full hearing before him. A mother had sexually abused her five year old son and had the child tell the police her boyfriend had done it. The boyfriend, Tom Tully, an unemployed gas jockey, was arrested, arraigned and had the story on the front page of the Island Gazette. It was months before the truth came out. The child told a baby sitter how Mommy plays choo-choo going through the tunnel with him. The sitter notified her brother, a state cop, who notified DSS and the child was removed under an Emergency Care and Protection. After a few court reviews and an investigation by an independent investigator appointed by the Court, the matter was set for trial. The mother, Rose Rappucci, gave the performance of her life. When the Judge asked questions from the bench, she told him she had better things to do. She had to plan for her wedding. She had invited seven hundred and fifty guests to a cookout reception at Gay Head, the Judge was on the list, and she, Rose Rappucci, was to marry Ted Kennedy! Don inquired if there would be any objections from Joan? Had Ted been notified so he could make sure he could fit it into his schedule? Had the hot dogs been ordered? The Judge instructed the witness mother to put these ideas out of her head (she was already out of her head, as far as Don was concerned) and concentrate on what she was doing to earn a living. Rose stated she worked for an hour a week at Helen-of-Troy beauty parlor, sweeping the floor on Saturdays and putting out the trash barrels. Her housing was unsettled at present. She had a cot in the living room of a friend's unheated two-room cottage but was looking around for better things for her and her son because her friend was being evicted for non payment of rent. When she left the stand, she reminded the Judge to show up at the wedding.

Part of the Court's decision was as follows:

> *'This rather attractive, well-dressed mother testified most engagingly. While she may, on occasion, engage in flights of fancy . . . does not make her an unfit mother. She has actively sought and obtained both suitable housing and employment. . . .*
>
> *'It is the object of the Department of Social Services to reunite families. This Court finds that the Department has failed to prove by clear and convincing evidence. . . . unfitness of the parent and cites the following cases . . . '*

After Don read the decision, he wondered what George Washington Worthington would give Rose and Ted for a wedding present. . . . or was this it. His supervisor had him enter an appeal immediately with a motion for stay of execution.

Now, tomorrow, he would be facing Worthington again. This time the mother was a wealthy socialite of the same mental imbalance as Rose Rappucci. And the abuse was the same, now known to the Department workers as the choo-choo-in syndrome. Maybe the Judge saw nothing wrong with that?

Before he left for the day, he checked to see if Melinda's supervisor, Trudy Teller, was around. He was deeply concerned about Melinda's solo trip to Roxbury the next day. Neither Trudy nor the area director nor the area program manager was in the office. And no wonder. It was 5:25 P. M. He got the file on Amanda Faye and her son, Arthur, who had been in foster care for four years. The witnesses had been summoned four weeks ago.

Linny's Cases Explode

Melinda Thatcher groaned after she hung up the phone. She should have gone directly to Roxbury from home to get the Neilson twins, Neila and Nella. How could any mother give those names to her children? It was almost as bad as one of Don's stories about his Army service. His bunkmate was a guy named Bill Leer. His wife gave birth to a daughter. It wasn't so bad that they named her Crystal. But her middle name was Shanda.

Her extension rang again. Yes. Yes. Oh God! Two cases had blown up minutes apart. The first was a mother suspected of suffocating her infant son with a pillow. The second was the six-year-old girl who arrived at school with welts all over her body. She said her mother was passed out on the floor and when she went near her to see if she was all right, the mother's boyfriend beat her with his cowboy belt. Melinda had been pleading with the mother to dump the drifter, to no avail. Cathy Crosby had a lot of needs and would withstand anything for a little attention because she was so insecure and wanting.

The other client, Karo Karlyle, was as slow as cold molasses in January. Of her older three children, two had already been adopted because of the mother's unfitness, which was proven by severe physical punishments inflicted over a long period of time. Now she was involved with Tony Spiro, an alcoholic, in the last stages of alcoholism. A baby murdered! She wanted to cry but she had to save her energy for that four-hour trip, and she didn't have time for tears.

The child's death had to be reported to the District Attorney under the law. That set in motion; she arranged to meet with Karo at 1:00 P.M. Next she turned to the possibility of an emergency C&P on Kimberly Crosby. She conferenced that with Enid, the Sup of the day, as Trudy was giving an in-service training at Lakeville Hospital. Enid approved the C&P; next, she called Martha's Vineyard. Good! Don hadn't started his trial yet. After relating the facts, he gave his approval. She was to call Mary in the Clerk's office to alert her and give the info she needed. The school was to be alerted to hold Kimberly in light of the C&P action. Once it was granted, she could go to the school with the mitt and take custody of Kim returning her to the office for placement. She thanked Don and went to the Family Resources Unit to give background on the child and what would be needed.

She sat and wrote the affidavit for Court. It would have priority over whatever else the two stenos were doing.

Judge Kelly granted the petition setting the date for the seventy-two hour hearing, ordering a summons for the mother and commending Melinda on her excellent affidavit. With the mitt in hand, she went to the school and got Kimberly. The child smiled with relief and then started to cry. She was taken to Doctor Talbot to treat and verify the wounds.

It was after 2:00 P.M. by the time Melinda returned to the office. Area B Police, Roxbury, had called three times. She escorted Kim to Family Resource, had a further talk with her and gave her two Milky Way candy bars.

Oh, God! She just remembered Karo Karlyle waiting at Burger King. She would never have time to stop there. Since the office had its monthly staff meetings there, she was sure someone could seek her out and give her the message.

"Enid, You've got to save my life."

"Well. I don't know if it's worth saving. A social worker who doesn't keep her appointments isn't worth a damn."

"What appointments?"

"A lady—and I use the term loosely—with the unlikely name of Karo Karlyle called about thirty-five minutes ago. Fit to be tied."

"I was just going to ask—in view of my schedule— if you'd contact her at Burger King."

"She said that lunch there is bad enough, she wasn't going to have dinner there too."

"Oh, Enid. Stop. What did she say? What happened?"

"Oh, I just told her you had an emergency and had to go to Boston to pick up two kids and that you tried to call her at Burger King but they said they didn't provide that service, and that you'd call tomorrow if you could."

"Oh, Enid, you devil. And with that deadpan expression, I believed you."

"Well here's your folder on those ugly twins. I stuck the mittimus inside the front cover to make it easier. Good luck!"

"Oh, Enid. I—"

"Never mind I, I, I, if you don't get on that road out there you won't get to Boston 'till tomorrow. Remember, it's not daylight savings yet. Now, scoot! And be careful . . . I grew up in that area. Ba-a-ad!"

"'Bye . . . Oh, about the foster placement . . ."

"Old Enid'll take care of it. I've placed a kid or two in my time."

Parallel To Drowning

How had a farm girl ended up as a social worker on Cape Cod? Melinda thought about how simple her life had been, then. Long, long ago. No complexities. And she couldn't wait to get to college. To get away from the farm. Oh, she loved her parents and her sister but there was a great, big, wonderful world out there. To enjoy. To have fun, fun, fun. And she did. Those four years flew by, filled with as much socializing as possible. It wasn't until the second semester of her junior year that she became interested in social work. And she didn't understand why. She just knew she had to. Mr. Thatcher thought she'd get married early, even drop out of school to do so. Then she and her husband could come back and work the farm. He'd even planned to give them three thousand acres as a wedding present. But things didn't turn out that way. Even now, she was thirty-one and planning to get married in three weeks—three weeks! And there's still so much to do. She liked this long drive to Boston. Soft music playing, no telephone ringing, time to think—without interruptions. She was thinking about her present caseload. Twenty-two clients with children. The case names always went according to the mothers' names. Many times the children had different names and sometimes siblings had different names. Real crazy. In fact, it was the craziest collection of cases she'd ever had at any one time. That Cathy Crosby, for example. She'd had the case for two years. Her children had been in and out of foster care four times because of Cee Cee's emotional and alcoholic relapses. The alcohol abuse amplified her character problems. She sure knew how to pick men who were losers. The latest one was the biggest loser of all. Tex. Was he from Texas? No. Well why do they call you Tex, she asked. Because I'm from Louisiana. Then he would laugh and laugh. She still didn't get that one. Her last visit was too much. Well, her last visit before the beating of Kimberly. Tex had mastered a lot of the social work lingo. Told about his being the second in a sib ship of four. His parents believed in appropriate behavior and if anyone touched them inappropriately they should make a full disclosure and never think of recanting. That he didn't think Kimberly was parentified. She was just trying to take care of her mother. He handed Melinda a sheet with the lyrics, got his guitar and told Melinda that he wrote it for Cathy, who thought it was real sex-x-xy.

He began to sing:

Jambalaya, I'm on fire, me-oh-my-o
Son of a gun, I'll have big fun on the bio.

He was so proud of himself and although Melinda had the words in front of her, she pretended she didn't get his little joke. He said he had a second verse just about completed and would she like to hear it? No, no, she had another appointment.

Poor Cathy. Men coming and going like Grand Central Station. She needed two social workers. One to wade through her myriad problems, the other to build up her self-esteem.

Lorenzo Lockwood. She hadn't been able to get any response for weeks, either by phone or by mail. His wife was a patient at

Pocasset Mental Health. She thought she'd drop by on her way home, the other night. She found the three kids unattended. They recognized her through the glass portion of the door so they let her in. Lolo was out in the woods "getting laid," said the four year old. It seems he had a favorite tree out back. Melinda decided to wait. A short time later, she heard someone running up the back stairs. At first, there was no recognition. Then she realized it was Mr. Lockwood dressed in his wife's clothing, including hat, yelling ecstatically, "I fucked the tree! I fucked the tree!"

Cynthia Rottenbotham. Four children had been removed. The twins were in a pre-adoptive home in New Hampshire. Two children were with Mom's mom. Longest case she'd ever had. Five years. Mother moved to Connecticut. Had three more children. The Court Investigator assigned to do a home study said it was the filthiest place she'd ever seen. Cockroaches all over the apartment, crawling up and down the children, on their faces, in their eyes. The olfactory senses were assaulted by the many pungent odors.

When 'Rotten' (Melinda's affectionate pet name for her) was up last year for one of her Court reviews, she insisted she was staying at the Kennedy Compound because her boyfriend had the same Indian lineage as Ted Kennedy and she was welcome any time. Melinda suggested she call the Compound to make sure there was enough help to tend to her needs. 'Rotten' said no. Just drop her off at the bus terminal in Hyannis. She could walk from there, as she had many, many times in the past. Melinda decided not to press the issue. She was just glad when she got out of the car. But she left something behind. She always did. The odor. It clung for three days.

She was reminiscing about her tenth case when she realized she was near the Franklin Park Zoo. She saw a police officer directing traffic and stopped for directions. He asked if she were sure she wanted Area B. When she explained who she was and what her mission was, he gave her directions and cautioned her to keep her windows up and her buttons down. Within minutes she pulled up to the station, alighted, went back to the car. She had forgotten to lock the doors. She also had forgotten to get gas. That damn fuel gauge wasn't working and it was a new car. Funny about reviewing her life and caseload. It was almost like they say it would be if you were drowning.

"Hi. I'm Melinda Thatcher Department of Social Services. I'm here to pick up the Nielson twins."

"Hi. Sergeant Foley. Glad you're here. They were in the same cell. One punched the living shit out of the other. I think her nose is broken. I'll wait for your associate to come in before I get them out of the two cells. Is he parking the car?"

"I don't have any associate with me. All alone."

"It's a jungle out there. Are you crazy?"

"I probably will be by the time I get to Phoenix."

"You goin' all that way?"

"No. It's a poor joke. That's how frazzled you get in this job. Lead on McDuff."

"Foley. The name's Foley."

Crossing the Cape

It had been a smooth flight to the Island. Don actually opened his eyes and looked down. The pilot had been coaxing him to sit up front beside him. He must have thought he was related to Amanda Faye. That Don was.

In the corridor outside the courtroom, Amanda paced back and forth glaring at everyone as though he/she were the enemy. At one point, Don emerged from the men's room with his fly unzipped. Amanda took great delight in pointing this out saying he was a mean, dirty, old man who had never bothered getting married and having children and who walked around with his fly undone ready to screw anything in sight. Finally, their case was called.

The Judge asked everyone to identify themselves. He noted that Amanda had no lawyer. She said she didn't need one and had already fired two of them. Robert Reed, an Island lawyer, had been appointed to represent Arthur.

"Where is Art Faye?" asked the Judge.

He's on the enchbay, thought Don, regretting his inability to share the joke.

"He's at school right now, your Honor. His presence is not required once he's been identified for the record."

"Thank you, Mr. Reed. You've been most helpful. Proceed."

The Department's case went in very smoothly. The history of the case was traced from the discovery of the initial sexual abuse by M.S.P.C.C. and the various 51As filed by school personnel, neighbors, police and other mandated reporters. The child had been left locked in the car, late at night, while the mother went from bar to bar. The child had been unfed, inappropriately dressed, kept home from school, physically abused by his mother's hand and on one occasion with a stick she found in the street. He had his hair pulled; he was punched, kicked, slapped and thrown to the pavement. The choo-choo-in syndrome was expounded upon by psychiatrists and therapists who had used anatomically correct dolls. These dolls enabled children to express what had happened to them. When the foster mother was testifying she had, in her hand, a letter from Amanda's mother which stated that Amanda had broken into her home, broken her mother's nose and arm, kicked and slapped her, stole a large amount of money and then left leaving her mother on the floor. For these reasons the mother would not be appearing as a witness, as she had in the past, because she was frightened. Before the Court could even pass on the admissibility of the letter, Amanda tip-toed up to the witness, grabbed the letter and tore it to shreds, throwing the pieces up in the air while chanting "Now my mother doesn't even exist." She left the courtroom. Judge Worthington sent a court officer to inform her if she did not return immediately he would rule on the case. With great reluctance, she returned to the courtroom.

The Department rested its case. The child's attorney had no additional evidence to offer.

"Miss Faye. Do you wish to offer any evidence?"

"No, Judge. The state and, in particular, Mr. Goode, have paid off anyone I could have called. I stand before you and throw myself on the mercy of this court and ask you to open your heart to this poor broken-hearted mother. Return my son to me! It is the only way my heart shall ever heal. I'll bet you don't remember what movie that was from!"

"Miss Faye. These are very serious proceedings. If you do not have any witnesses and since you are party to these proceedings, you may take the stand. You do not have to, but you may. If you take the stand, you are subject to cross-examination by these lawyers. Think it over, carefully. I shall give you the time."

"As a matter of fact your Honor, we've been on trial for over two and one-half hours. I was going to suggest we take a twenty minute recess."

"A good suggestion, Mr. Goode. No pun intended. This Court will be in recess."

The thirty-two dollar question (she was only half-there) was would Amanda take the stand. It was so difficult for an attorney to try a case where a person was self-represented. There was too much leeway given someone who was pro se. They didn't have to abide by the rules of evidence because they didn't know them. The Court treated them with kid gloves. No attorney could get away with what the unrepresented party could get away with. Oh well, thought Don, DSS had a very strong case. But then he remembered the Judge's decision on the Rappucci C&P appeal now pending. Motion to stay return of the child was allowed because Worthington knew if he had denied it, that too, would have gone to the Appeals Court and been granted. Like most district court judges, he was afraid of criticism from the higher ups. Especially since the decisions were printed and made available to all members of the Bar. Not a great deal of loyalty there. Only fear.

Don knew he had a lot going for him in this case. The mother was clearly a screwball. The child had been badly damaged, psychologically. She couldn't provide for him. DSS didn't even know where she lived. She refused to say. It was another of those state secrets. If Martha's husband ruled to return this kid, he'd appeal at the earliest moment. So he had all the bases covered.

He felt much better, 'Brains is a wonderful thing' Mama always used to say. Now, let's see what the coo-coo has decided.

"What is your name?"

Judge, you know my na-ame."

"Yes, I do. But we must establish this information for the record. All this is being recorded as required by law."

"Another trick! Why wasn't I made aware of this?"

"My dear. In every District Court in the Commonwealth, all proceedings before the Court have to be recorded."

"But it's just like that social worker, Miss Little. She thinks I don't know it but when I was in New York, she was in a building across the way. And she kept reading my thoughts with a recording machine. I had to keep changing my thoughts to throw her off the track."

"We'll begin again. What is your name?"

"Amanda Faye."

"What is your address?"

"Refuse to answer. DSS is out to get me. Besides I move around a lot."

"Witness refuses to give address."

"You are the mother of Arthur Faye."

"Yes. And I want him back!"

"Are you employed?"

"Refuse to answer."

"Would you describe the premises where you reside?"

"Why? So DSS can match the description and find it?"

"You're making it very difficult for the Court to give you consideration of caring for your son. Could you give me an idea of something you've done that shows you are a responsible person?"

"Well, Judge. I hope this impresses you more than it did DSS. I told them many, many times. Mother and I were flying to London. Now, I don't know whether it was the food or not because I never eat on planes. But, anyhow, it's like a movie really. The pilot got sick. That wasn't bad enough, but then the co-pilot got sick. Well, we weren't about to let a plane load of people go down into the cold Atlantic, so mother and I flew the plane across. Naturally, I was the pilot. But mother was very helpful. Just her sitting next to me, gave me so much courage. When we landed safely at Heathrow, a huge cheer went up from the passengers. Now is that being responsible or what?"

"Do you have an income that would allow you to support your son?"

"Yes, I do."

"What is it?"

"Refuse to answer."

"Would you write it on a piece of paper for the Court?"

"Yes."

"Your Honor, my brother attorney and I object to such a procedure. The Court cannot consider, secretly, evidence from one party to a procedure."

"Mr. Goode, I can do as I damn well please."

"Please note my exception."

"And mine, too, your Honor."

"Yes, Mr. Reed. So noted."

The Judge read the figure on the paper. She so wanted to impress him.

$100,000,000,000,000,000,000,000.29

"Is there anything further you wish to tell me before you're cross-examined?"

"No, Judge."

"Mr. Reed, proceed."

"Yes, your Honor."

"Miss Faye. It is Miss, isn't it?"

"No. It's Ms."

"When is the last time you visited your son?"

"I told DSS, I think it's harmful to visit him. I want him home."

"When?"

"As soon as possible."

No, when did you last visit your son?"

"Do I have to answer, Judge?"

"Yes."

"About three years ago."

"Do you have a visitation arrangement?"

"Yes, but it's supervised."

"Why is it supervised?"

"Because I tried to take him off the Island—got as far as the boat, too. Damn police stopped me. How can you steal something that already belongs to you?"

"No further questions."

"Mr. Goode?"

"Yes, Your Honor. Miss Faye did you insert your three old son's penis into your vagina?"

"Well, if I did, it would be better than inserting yours!"

"How often did you have intercourse with your son before he was removed? From your home, that is."

"We had no heat. I was trying to keep us both warm."

"If you were trying to keep warm, why were you both naked on a narrow cot, when the social worker from MSPCC arrived at your home?"

"She's a liar. We were both wearing skin colored night clothes."

"You heard her testify and you chose not to cross-examine her on that area?"

"I could tell the Judge knew she was a liar! There was no need to cross-examine her."

"Why did you keep your child home from school?"

"He was already bright enough, and they weren't teaching him anything except to make up stories about his mother, and trying to get him away from me. I saw the way they taught him how to study me. He watched my every move. So, actually, I kept him home so he wouldn't play into their hands."

"When the MSPCC social worker arrived at your home that morning or had been there a short time—she said you were drinking an amber colored liquid; what was it?"

"It was medicine, prescribed by my doctor."

"And the doctor's name?"

"I don't remember."

"No further questions of this witness, your Honor."

"Mr. Reed? Anything further?"

"No, your Honor."

"Miss Faye? Do you wish to call any witnesses?"

"As I said earlier, Judge, Mr. Goode and DSS have paid off all and any witnesses I could call."

"Then you have no one else you wish to call?"

"No, Judge."

"Let the record indicate that both counsel for Department and for the child have nothing further. I assume that also includes anything by way of rebuttal evidence?"

"Yes, your Honor."

"Yes, your Honor."

"I would like to see both counsel in my chambers. Miss Faye, where you are representing yourself, I would include you, except that this conference has nothing to do with the evidence in this case. Is that clear?"

"Yes, Judge."

"I might add further, that I am taking this case under advisement. The Court's written findings will be issued as soon as possible. Copies will be mailed to each attorney and to Miss Faye at whatever address she indicates. Naturally, appeals may be taken by any party claiming to be aggrieved. Mr. Goode is well versed in this procedure. I'm sure he'll be most generous with the information that may be needed."

"Will the court officer announce the recess and direct counsel to my chambers?"

"All rise. This court shall be in recess."

The bastard. The rotten bastard, thought Don. He's trying to saddle me with that screwball, Amanda. She'll be calling my office at all hours, saying, "The Judge said . . ."He's just pissed because of the Rappucci appeal. Fortunately, he had ordered the trial tapes before the Judge got wind of the appeal. Everything was there from Rose Rappucci's own mouth. Employment, one hour per week. Living quarters: a cot in the living room of an unheated cottage of a friend who was being evicted for non-payment of rent. He'd waltz to a win on that one.

Ingrid, the Wop and the Judge

When they entered the Judge's chambers, he had a very pained expression on his face. His expression was one of such distaste that would be found on the face of someone who had a piece of excrement stuck to his upper lip.

"Gentlemen, there is one thing about this case which I find very troubling. I'm hoping you are able to clear it up. I know some young people retain their own names when they marry and, while I don't approve of that, I suppose the fact of the marriage is paramount. The confusion that results on bank books, mortgages, deeds and other family matters are not my concern. You know, I came to the conclusion recently that life is very simple. It's people who complicate it. As a result, we're surrounded by incompetence."

I don't know about surrounded, thought Don, but definitely, head on.

"Well, enough of that. My question, gentlemen, is that since the foster mother does not share the same name as the adult male in her home, please to tell me that they are married?"

"No, your Honor. They're significant others."

EN

"Mr. Goode, I am shocked at someone of your standing permitting people to live in sin, virtually, and further to place a young child in the midst of such moral inturpitude. Is there such a word? No, no. Don't answer. The word isn't important. Is this child to stay there, Mr. Goode?"

"As far as I know. I don't handle placements. If you have some concerns you may call them to the attention of the administration."

"So much for the concerns of DSS! Mr. Reed, you are the child's attorney. Are you intending to call this disgrace to the attention of the administration?"

"No, your Honor. I've visited the home and I've talked to young Arthur. I was very impressed with the home and the foster mother and, more importantly, Arthur is very, very happy. His schoolwork has improved greatly. He has friends where he was a loner before. I credit that to leaving his mother's care and entering foster care. Particularly, this house."

"So you and DSS are in league with each other, and against me?"

"No, your Honor. I state my position independently. I wouldn't be much of an attorney for any child if I did otherwise."

"Very well, gentlemen. Before you go, I wish to share with you my own deep, personal beliefs. Call it my philosophy if you will. I find that today's young people have no values. No morality. No moral judgments. Everybody is sleeping with everybody else. No thought is given to instilling proper values in children. And after much thought, gentlemen, I have concluded the source of it. The beginning. I lay all of the blame at the feet of Ingrid Bergman. Things were just fine before that. People did a day's work for a day's pay. Most people were virgins until they entered the marriage bed."

Don began to shake involuntarily. He didn't dare look at Bob, because he knew he had a similar type of humor and both of them would lose it.

"Yesiree, gentlemen, if Ingrid Bergman hadn't deserted her husband and child and run off with that wop to Stromboli, things wouldn't be the way they are today. To desert a family for two and a half pounds of salami and a lifetime of spaghetti is unconscionable."

Don had drawn blood by biting his lower lip inside. He was about to burst.

"Mr. Goode, are you feeling all right?"

"No, your Honor. May I—excuse—"

"Certainly. I understand. Go right ahead. This conference is over, anyhow."

"You know Mr. Reed. Sometimes recognizing a tremendous truth can just knock you off your pins. Come to think of it, you don't look too well, either."

"It's those pins, your Honor, it's . . . excuse . . ."

He ran from the chambers and met Don in the men's room. They laughed until the tears came.

"Ingrid Bergman! Ha-a-a—a-a"

"Wop!" "Stromboli—Ha-a-a-a-a-a"

With a little more time, I could convert those two. He smiled as he removed his robe. I believe I had those two sensitive chaps close to tears.

EN

Smoke Gets In Your Eyes

By the time they left the police station, it was after seven o'clock. Nella and Neila insisted on checking their valuables one by one before they would even consider 'signing off'. Sergeant Foley helped carry the twins' belongings to the car. And it's a good thing he had insisted. Five black teenagers with a name across the back of their jackets were around the car trying each door. Thank you Sergeant Foley, thought Melinda.

"Come on you guys. Move along."

"Yes sir! It's the po—lice."

They did a step'n fetchit stroll moving their shoulders, heads and other body parts back and forth. Sergeant Foley offered to have a police officer follow them out to a safe area in a station car but Melinda declined, saying she knew the way now. They'd be in a car. How safe can you be?

Several blocks away, the car came to a stop. The starter was working. What gives, thought Melinda? Then she knew. Empty gas tank. She remembered passing a gas station a block or so back. She carefully instructed the twins not to open the windows or doors for anyone. They were out of gas and she'd be back in about ten minutes. When she got to the station, the attendant was a middle-aged man, who was most sympathetic. He told her she would have to leave a five-dollar deposit for the container and three dollars for the gas. She said she'd be back to fill up her tank. He advised her against it, noting it was nighttime and there were a lot of people, especially young people. Guns, knives, dope. Life meant nothing to them. If she should be in the area at another time, whoever was on duty would refund her five dollars.

"Lady. Get out of here as fast as you can."

"Thank you."

As she got closer to the car, she could see five young blacks surrounding the car. They were the same people that she had seen outside the station! Now she could see the name on the back of the jackets, 'Saints.' They sure didn't look like saints. They were motioning towards their privates and shouting to the twins.

"Open the door, mother. Honkie baby we got something for you!"

"Excuse me, I ran out of gas. I work for the state. You probably saw me coming from the police station."

She thought that would frighten them. It didn't.

"Here mama. Let me pour that in the tank for you!"

After thanking him, Melinda bent down to console the twins. As she did, the contents of the can were dumped over her head and body. It was blinding her as it ran into her eyes. She knew enough not to rub them. It would merely force the gasoline in further. She staggered. She couldn't see where she was. Then she heard what she thought sounded like a match being struck. No, it must be her imagination. Someone was throwing something at her. Finally, she could see out of one eye. At her feet, she saw two kitchen matches just about to go out. Oh God! Don't let this happen to me! I'm getting married in three weeks! Please, dear God! Please!

Suddenly, it felt like the hottest day of summer. Then she was completely on fire. She screamed. She threw herself on the street and began rolling back and forth. There was too much gasoline. Then she smelled the burning flesh. Her flesh. The last thing she remembered before she died were the five 'Saints' standing in a circle, urinating on her.

One of them got a brick, and broke the car window, unlocked the doors and he and the others dragged the twins toward Franklin Park.

The neighbors pulled down their shades. No one called the police. Sergeant Foley, on his way home, came upon the scene and immediately radioed for an ambulance. But, of course, it was too late. The twins were found the next day roaming Franklin Park nude and mute. It would be several months before they would be able to communicate with anyone.

The Boston Globe gave five lines to the story on page seventy-three between giant ads for warehouse sales and auctions. But word got around and irate telephone callers nearly burned out the Globe's switchboard. The story was moved to page one with an apology on the editorial page. That's where Melinda Thatcher belonged: The Front Page.

The Coward's Way

"But Noel, how are you going to say that at the emergency staff with Trudy sitting right there?"

The area director with that smug, half smile he adopted for troubling situations responded:

"Because I have the file with all the figures for the M.S.P.C.C. meeting this morning. The contract will take at least one and a half hours to review. And then, you know, nobody's ever satisfied with the first drawn contract. There'll be suggested amendments. It should keep her busy most of the morning. And out of here. Now, Manny Gomes, don't you think I'm brilliant?"

"That depends on who 'her' is."

"Why, Trudy Teller, of course."

"Yes. You are brilliant. I'm bad, but I couldn't think of something like that. I'd get too nervous and start to st-st-stutter."

"Let me get her down here."

"Trudy, Noel. Could you come down here for a minute. Good."

Her eyes were red-rimmed. She had the sniffles and tears were still running down her cheeks.

"Trudy, you've lost your best worker and I. . . ."

:EN

"Worker, hell! She was my best friend!"

"Oh. I wasn't aware of that. Anyway, Manny and I want you to take this file over to M.S.P.C.C. and go over the contract with them, the figures. See if you can work out some kind of tentative agreement. Tentative, not permanent. We can smooth it over later."

"When?"

"Now."

"Oh Noel! Don't ask me to do that today. Besides, it's Manny's function."

"It's not a request, Trudy. It's an order. We all have to make sacrifices for the good of the agency." He placed the folder in her hand just before she ran out of his office crying hysterically.

"Manny, the meeting won't start until she drives out of the parking lot. Wait a few minutes and then saunter out by the front desk to make sure that she's gone."

"O.k. Noel. Your wish is my command. So long as you get us out of this jam."

"I've been playing these games for a long time, Manny and I've learned that all agencies work the same way. By the time Trudy hears what went on at the staff meeting, the source will be one or two people at a time. If she comes to us, those other people must have misheard. Eventually it will die down. You want to be an Area Director some day, don't you? Just follow my moves."

Manny went out front to check. Trudy's car could not be seen. But just to be sure he turned to the receptionist.

"Placenta, has Trudy come in yet?"

"In? She's been in and out. Left here a few minutes ago crying her eyes out. I guess she and Melinda were close."

"Best friends, I understand. I just wanted to offer my condolences, personally and privately, so don't mention our little conversation if you happen to be talking to her."

"Don't worry Manny. You know me. Mum's the word. But you men really get me. Your sensitivity is something I can't phantom."

'Phantom'? She must mean 'fathom' but needing her at the moment, he had no intention of criticizing her. He'd just throw a meaningless phrase at her.

"Thanks kid. I owe you one."

"That won't be necessarily necessary, Man."

He and Noel walked over to the emergency staff. The meeting room was filled. Many of the workers had been crying. Noel and Manny walked to the small desk at the front. Noel began.

"Let us bow our heads in a moment of silent prayer for our dearly departed co-worker. Her last case, where tragedy occurred, was handled just as independently as the rest of her caseload. Manny and I sent for her. We told her she was going into a high crime area and considering her goal being the Area B Police Station, expressed the thought that we wanted a male social worker to accompany her. She was adamant. She said no one had ever done that on any of her other cases and why start now. I pleaded with her to . . ."

"Begged," added Manny

"Reconsider. She refused. Why even Manny offered to go with her to protect her. Right, Manny?"

He was carrying this too far. Manny put his head down and closed his eyes. He began to tremble. Not because of what had happened to Melinda but because it could have happened to him. His middle initial should also have been 'C'.

"I'm going to suggest as part of the healing process, that we break up into small groups. Try not to be in with others of your own unit, if possible. You'll be discussing it there I'm sure, for a long time to come. Enid is making two pots of coffee. Lunie and a few others went to get muffins and donuts, compliments of Manny and me. I know we may not seem to express our feelings and appear detached. Don has said it's because we're both Aries. But remember, it's lonely here at the top but someone has to lead." He excused himself because of all the work he had to do.

Neither Manny nor Noel mentioned their meeting with Trudy the day before Melinda left for Boston.

And neither Manny nor Noel were aware of Melinda's conversation with Don the day before her ill-fated trip to Area B Police Station.

Teddy Bare

In the next morning's edition of the *Cape Cod Times,* a front-page story would have far reaching effects. Ted Mitchell, well-known psychologist and sexual abuse expert was indicted on forty-seven counts of rape, sexual assault and indecent assault and battery. Most of the victims had been referred to him by DSS social workers, who believed in his ability to help victims. These child abusers always seemed to place themselves in positions where they'll have access to children. Everyone has heard the jokes about the Boy Scouts. The sad part of it is that abusers are in every field where they can access children. Many times it's a position that is generally recognized as one of trust so there are only a few steps from that trust to a violation of it.

When Don entered the office and went from unit to unit giving messages about court dates and witnesses he became aware of a silence. No soft music was playing. No good-natured kidding. No talk of experiences the night before. And strangely, no laughter, no telephones ringing. A cloud of depression just hung there.

He motioned one of the workers into the record room at the

end of the building and closed the door.

"What the hell is going on here? Did someone else die?"

"Sort of" responded Aubrey Jones newly moved from New York City.

"What do you mean, 'sort of'?"

"Well, like the death of innocence and trust. You get the *Cape Cod Times*?"

"No, the *Boston Globe*."

"You stay right here, I'll get it for you."

She stayed while he read the article.

Don was thunderstruck. He had had Ted Mitchell testify in several cases of sexual abuse by a priest, school teacher, school custodian, police officer, neighbor, parent, significant other, older children, siblings and on and on. Had he also sexually abused these children while helping to prove their abuse by others?

"And this is the reason for the office depression?"

"Yes. They feel as though they've been victimized too. I hadn't referred any child to him. But only because I'm new. What do you do in a situation like that? You ask another worker or supervisor to recommend someone. And you rely on that recommendation which is sincerely given. Now everybody's feeling part of the pain those poor little kids are feeling. And the responsibility lies with this office. Or we think it does."

"Oh my God! How do you dissipate a cloud like that?"

"Look. Before you correct me—or my syntax—is that what you call it? —You're the one who lifts spirits around here with your crazy humor. If you're not going to Court today, why don't you go to your office and come up with something. Make sure it's way, way out. That only we, in the office, can appreciate. People outside would think we were crazy. Now, may I have—notice I said 'may' and not 'can'—my paper back. Anyone ever tell you that you should have been a teacher?"

"Yeah. I've heard that once before, I believe."

Don walked through the museum quiet of the office, praying for an inspiration. It came.

The refrain would be from an old melody, 'Sixteen Tons'.

TEDDY BARE

Now East is East and West is West.
Spice is nice but incest's best.
Search high and low for every thrill:
If your father don't get you, then your therapist will.
You're just not acting right
You act out every night
Something's gone wrong inside your head
It's time for you to see Doctor Ted
Refrain: If your father don't get you, then your therapist will.
They took me down to see the Doc
Waited in the office just watchin' the clock
He took me in and locked the door,
'Sofa's at the cleaner's, just lie on the floor.'
Refrain: If your father don't get you, then your therapist will.
This is the treatment, I don't tell no lies
Ted means spread right up to your thighs
If you want permanency gluing
Don't you tell no-one, that you took a screwing.
Refrain: If your father don't get you, then your therapist will.

He made copies for everyone in the office and distributed them in each mailbox. Then he sat in his office and waited. It took almost an hour for anything to happen. Then, a short laugh. Eventually, guffaws. People started coming to his office door to thank him. It was bizarre, but it broke the spell of depression. He would continue to be known for diffusing tough situations with humor both in his own personal situations as well as in DSS matters. Like: "therapist" a combo of two words.

Later that day, Don checked his mail box. There was a memo from the Area Director and the Area Program Manager.

To: All Staff
From: Noel C. Peel, Manny Gomes, APM
Subject: Melinda Thatcher

EN

At the behest of Central, our Regional Office is conducting an inquiry into the untimely death of Melinda. We expressed our feelings at a recent staff meeting, and even though the memo we received suggests that, any of the staff write directly to that office, we are requesting any responses that are made be made to us here at the local level. In that way, we can correlate efforts and reduce the possibility of duplication. As you may be aware, Mr. and Mrs. Thatcher have sued the Department and the Commonwealth in the amount of ten million dollars for wrongful death. Each of you will remember our position stated to you at the staff meeting, and about that lovely lady's determination to maintain her courageous independence.

NCP

MC; sb

Regardless of the memo, there were two people in the office who would be contacting Regional directly. Trudy had already been in touch with Mr. and Mrs. Thatcher who had planned to come on for the funeral and to consult with the attorney they had engaged by phone, to begin legal action. What Trudy told them may have been the impetus.

In his next appearance at First District, Lunie gave Don the court original and his copy of the letter in the Antonia Marshall, C&P. Don always read court letters carefully.

"Hey Lunie? You're requesting a dismissal of the C&P? How come? Two weeks ago, you told me here was a child who'd never go home. She was a danger to other children. She needed close monitoring and should stay in foster care as an only child and continue with therapy. What the hell happened in two weeks?"

"Well, Don. I don't mean to sound condescending, but we decide what's best clinically, not legal."

"Oh, Lunie. Cut the shit! What happened?"

"Well. She ran home and didn't want to go back to foster care. And she'd keep running, if she did."

"Hell. They all do that. They all want to go home again no

matter what's happened. They believe everything's their fault. That's no reason to dismiss."

"Well, my supervisor, Neal, and I discussed this very carefully and came to the conclusion after six years of foster care, we should move towards a return home or engage in permanency planning."

"What permanency plan was considered?"

"Jesus, Don. You sound as if I were on the witness stand and an enemy of the Department."

"That second part may not be too far fetched."

"There was no p. p. discussed. We decided, clinically, to send her home."

"Well, I hope you can live with whatever happens."

"I'd never be able to provide services if I were to worry about what may happen down the line, Don."

"Okay, but. . . ."

Six months later thirteen-year-old Antonia Marshall scalded a six month old baby to death by submerging her in 140-degree water in a bathtub of the motel where both resided. Why? Because the child cried and Antonia felt she should be disciplined as she was, as a child. Sometimes being made to sit on a toilet all night because she wet her pants. Or having the sharp ends of pencils shoved into her ears by Mother Bertha sometimes known as 'Big', in order to get the child's attention, or correct her deficit span.

One Flew Into The Cuckoo's Nest

Within a week of the story breaking, Lunie signed herself into a private psychiatric hospital in Brookline, Massachusetts. The question then would be, whenever anyone called her name, how many others would turn around?

Lunie's supervisor, Neal Arthur, was exceptionally quiet and subdued for many months thereafter. The Department really shined on this one. Nola Bellafatto and the Intake Unit refused to accept or process a 51A although the Area Director ordered it in hopes of protecting Antonia and any other child to whom she might have access. Three months later, Antonia attempted to suffocate an infant by placing a pillow over its head. The child, in a coma, was flown to Children's Hospital in Boston and after five days regained consciousness, and could breathe without the aid of a machine.

As in such cases, what the office called 'The Death Squad' from Central descended on the Cape and Islands area office. They were more confused by the time they left. Here was an Area Director who gave an order that a 51A be put in place but who couldn't say that he had because he was impotent when it came to the Intake Supervisor, Nola Bellafatto. You mean for three months you never followed through with a murder? Noel decided it was best not to mention it. Or he thought it was best. His brains were really fried. Most of his daily 'intake' was alcohol. As a result his judgment was increasingly poor, impaired or unreasonable. He was unable to give sensible answers to the D.S. and, of course, all this would be written up by very factual people. Demises in state government take longer than the private sector but they do take place. And in his case, as they say, it was just a matter of time.

Phil Facey and Irma Friendly were driving back to the Central office. The other two investigators from the Death Squad, Rachael La Plante and Rick Antonio had left a half-hour earlier. There was little conversation in the car until they reached Duxbury.

"Irma, was it my imagination or was Noel the Coward half in the bag?

"I wouldn't say half, Phil. Three quarters or perhaps all."

"How does someone like that get to be an area director?"

"The Peter Principle. Remember the Lateral Transfer? You go from being incompetent as a director of one agency to being incompetent as the director of another agency. I have a friend at D.A.R.E. who said that after three years without the Coward they're just beginning to come out of the tail spin in which he put them."

"But why did the Area Board make such a choice?"

"Politically, two real losers were Noel's only competition. It was all pre-arranged by Senator Morton Streeter. And Phil, look at it this way: In an age when mediocrity is at a premium, he didn't stack up too badly. At least he wanted the job so much, he managed to stay sober for a while. When he got it, he told someone it was the first time he had been able to save because of the much higher salary."

"A lot of good it did him. His days are numbered. One thing the Commish hates are dead kids who are highly publicized."

"And another hate. Lawyers.

The Face That Never Launched a Single Ship

Don hated this drive to the Central Office in Boston. He hated driving. Period. Well it was better—there goes that alternative again—getting up at 5:00 A.M. to shave, shower, dress and eat in time to leave his driveway by 6:00 A.M. to arrive in Boston by 8:00 A.M. even though the meeting wasn't scheduled until 9:15 A.M. The alternative? To sleep in until 6:30 and then act like a speeded up movie, hit all the traffic, become discombobulated by cars aiming at you if you stayed in the same lane, arrive late and find all the parking spaces taken and no free meters. Gosh, life was simple, it was people who complicated it. Isn't that what the brilliant judge, George W. Worthington, said?

Don drove in at 8:10 A.M. to a smiling lot attendant (it was early). He mentioned he'd be leaving a little after noon, slipped the guy a deuce and asked to park near the exit/entrance. Now this dreaded meeting with the new Commissioner. He hated meetings more than he hated driving. He exited the elevator at the tenth floor and walked the corridor to the meeting room.

"Hello, Don." It was Sylvia Symmes, former secretary to legal at the Brockton office.

"What a transformation, Syl. You look beautiful!" (he didn't mention the forty odd pounds she'd obviously lost).

"Do you think I look better as a blonde or as a slim blonde?"

"Yes."

"Ah, still the clever grammarian."

"Are you happy here, Syl?"

"I was until about four weeks ago."

"That would roughly coincide with the Governor's appointment of the new Commissioner. Is she nice?"

Sylvia drew her forefinger across her throat.

"That bad?"

"Worse, as you are about to witness."

"You coming back to Brockton? They'd welcome you with open arms. You're the best legal sec they ever had."

"Thanks, Don. But it told me . . ."

"Wait a sec, sec. What do you mean 'It'?"

"You'll see soon enough. Anyway, I was to stay here at Central or I was to leave, voluntarily, in thirty days. If I didn't I was to be fired. Nice person, eh?"

"But what are you going to do?"

"I've taken a position as a manager of a Dunkin' Donuts. So, the next time you see me, I might be looking like the old 'Syl'. With all those free carbs lying around, who could resist?"

"Syl, I'm sorry. I know a lot of lawyers in Southeastern Mass. I could ask around . . ."

"No thanks but many thanks, Don. Now enough about me, I want you to have some fresh coffee and Danish. It' wouldn't let me get Dunkin' Donuts even though they promised me a discount. Eat and drink before those legal barracuda arrive en masse."

"O.K."

"I'll be busy for a while, Don, but if you're free for lunch . . ."

"Can't today. Going to see one of the social workers in the loony bin in Brookline . . ."

"O.K. I understand. Now, scoot!"

Someone he didn't recognize was signaling that the meeting

was about to begin. The room was filled with lawyers from around the state.

"Ladies and Gentlemen, the Commissioner of the Department of Social Services: Myrna Malcon!"

Applause.

Oh, God, thought Don. She's the homeliest man or woman I've ever seen. He hoped she was competent because she obviously had no heart or spiritual qualities. And she was angry! Who wouldn't be if they looked like that?

"Thank you. Thank you. I know you're all busy, busy, busy, so I shall (good syntax, thought Don) try to not keep you too long. I wanted you to know whence I'm coming from (bad form, thought Don). He almost had his hand raised to say 'Shouldn't that be from whence I'm coming'?', when he took a closer look at her eyes. They were tiny beads of blue ice-cold blue—and very close together behind those thick glasses. There was a wart on her forehead and one on her nose. Her hairline was lower than Rita Hayworth's before the studio edict of electrolysis. There was no warmth emanating from either her voice or her body. Don cancelled his interruption.

"What I'm hearing, is that social workers and lawyers are at odds. Not getting along at all. I'm ordering that stopped. As far as I am concerned, the social worker makes the decision on whether a 51A goes to court or not."

There were audible gasps in the audience.

"Item number two. I am pushing all of you to go out and complete your 210 adoptions. There is only one lawyer in the entire state who has completed eight 210s and he did them in one day. If he can do that so can each of you. I don't want to tell you his name but he's from Cape Cod and we all know they sleep until noon down there, go to the office for an hour and then knock off for the day—"

"I beg your pardon. I'm from the Cape and Islands Area Office, Sir, and it isn't quite 9:40 A.M. and I'm here in Boston. I arose at 5:00 A.M. this morning. Are you suggesting I completed those 210s one morning in my sleep or maybe mailed in the Department's cases to the Probate Court?"

"So you're Don Goode, the attorney who has 'done good'. You even get along with social workers, administrators, judges, court personnel, foster parents and clients. My remarks were not meant to include you."

"But I'm the only attorney assigned to the Cape Office. And I'm the attorney who did those 210s to which you made reference . . ."

"You're also very courageous, I've recently discovered."

"I'm speaking only to the truth."

"Yes, you and Plato."

"To which office is he assigned? I'd like to meet him." Roars of laughter.

"Enough. We must carry on. As you know, there are presently six Legal Divisions. My expert from the private sector and I agree that the same work could be done by three legal divisions, eliminating at least six administrative positions and some staff in legal. I hope to implement this plan in a minimum of three months, a maximum of six. . . ."

"Just a minute!", screamed a voice from the rear. It was Lou La Penta from the Berkshires, a hot-blooded half-Italian, half-Spanish who held nothing back.

"Are you a lawyer?" again he screamed.

"No, but I have an MBA from Suffolk", she purred, stalling for time in order to make a decision. She had never been so aggressively confronted before.

"Just who the fuck do you think you are?!"

She didn't respond.

"You walk in here off the street, with a job you got because you knew Governor Dukewell's wife—who I'm sure felt good standing beside you—and all of a sudden you're going to reduce staff in legal and you don't know a fucking thing about its problems nor does that asshole you hired from the private evidently very private sector."

A very soft applause began in the back and swelled to a moderate degree.

She could always fire him later. Now was not the time. There was something about him. He looked like a Spanish Clark Gable. More volatile, perhaps. He was obviously very popular with the other lawyers and as much as she hated lawyers because of Kevin O'Meara, she couldn't risk alienating a large number of them. She was where she was because of political pull. But so were many of them.

"Well. That's a good point and well taken. I promise you that no action will be taken until an in-depth study of legal is taken and until other meetings have been held with you. During the future meetings, I want each of you to feel free to express yourselves. You need not be as vocative as 'Berkshire Lou' however . . ." Laughter. Even from Lou.

"I'm pleased that we were able to cover as much ground as we did. I had hoped to go until 1:00 P.M. but I completely forgot a meeting with the Governor's committee on Human Services, which I hope will result in raises for you long overdue, as well as for social workers. There's plenty of coffee and Danish left. Feel free to remain and chit chat. I know some of you don't get a chance to see one another very often so take advantage of this opportunity and be grateful you didn't need to listen to me until 1:00 P.M.

"And, oh, I nearly forgot. Mr. Goode, I'll have my secretary make a search for the office that houses Mr. Plato and convey his whereabouts to you."

"Thanks. If it's overseas do I get an opportunity to travel on the Commonwealth?"

"If you and Lou get close, if you aren't already and I suspect you are, I'm sure both of you could travel anywhere on your own power."

More laughter. Then she was gone. A certain lightness filled the air.

"Lou."

"Don."

The two shook hands and with their left hands give a side closed Burt Lancaster-punch to the upper bicep.

"Talk about 'Dante's Inferno'. Wow!"

"You did all right yourself. You and that bland Irish exterior while you insert the knife, calling her Sir."

"It."

"What 'it'?"

"No. What is it?"

"Don!"

"Lou!"

"Oh shit. I suppose it's another one of your latent references that even the F.B.I. couldn't solve."

"Anyhow, I'm proud of you and your courage even though you're not a mother."

"Mother? Courage? Awful, awful. It's about time you and I went out and hoisted a few."

"Only if it can be done at Hung Flung Chou in Brookline. One of our social workers slipped over the edge and I'm going to visit her on the way back. With our meeting being shortened, I have some extra time. If that's O.K. with you."

"Don, I'm not going to Brookline and then backtrack to the Pike. How about an early lunch. On me."

"That's what you said the last time and I ended up paying."

"I know. That's why you have to let me get on the inside of the booth. Then I can't get away. Unless I wait for you to go to the piss house."

The Looney Lunie

He was glad that effen meeting was over. What a bitch and a half. He had heard that in the previous administration the new Commish had been a deputy when a serious policy disagreement developed between the Department's General Counsel, Kevin O'Meara, and her. The Commissioner sided with O'Meara and because of the Deputy's inflated ego she felt compelled to resign. Now, appointed Commissioner by a new administration, she hated all lawyers (one or two throughout the state would escape her wrathful vengeance). Poor O'Meara. She fired him three times in the space of one week. She kept asking him to come back, only to fire him again. After the third firing, he got the message, and refused to come back.

Don hoped he would be able to safely hide out at the Cape office, crossing the bridge only when he had to, for staff meetings in Brockton. With the largest caseload in the state, he didn't need the added stress of someone who could have coined the riddle: What do you call a thousand lawyers chained together at the bottom of the sea? A good beginning.'

The parking lot attendant was signaling to Don that there was an open lane for him. He pulled slowly up to the gatehouse, paid his fee and eased out into the traffic on Causeway Street, drove by the Registry of Motor Vehicles and onto Storrow Drive. He exited at Kenmore Square went up Boylston and out onto the Jamaicaway. He hoped Lunie appreciated all this, knowing how much he hated to drive. It seemed in the City, other drivers aimed at you, while on the Cape, (absent the summer), it was almost a pleasure to drive.

Lunie had been a patient at Bournewood, a small, private psychiatric hospital located in South Brookline, for six weeks. No one had been able to obtain any info about how she was doing. The hospital was unaware she was divorced and that it should have been contacting her children for any releases of information and not her ex-husband (who had tried to strangle her on one occasion). Don would insist on seeing her, stating that he was her attorney (hospitals hated that breed almost as much as the new commissioner).

He needn't go into the fact that it applied only to her status as a social worker. Department attorneys were forbidden to give any advice in private matters or of a legal nature to any Department employee. In fact, they could only give advice to members of their own immediate families (with prior approval by the Department). Oh well. He stopped at the gate, stated his business and after a telephone call, was told to go to the administration building and park in one of the visitors' spaces. He was to ask for a Doctor Murphy.

"How long have you known Lunar Nelson?"

"About three years."

"What did you observe about her that could have caused or added to her emotional problems?"

"That she worked too hard, that she also worked the Hotline nights, that she internalized many things rather than trying to develop a detachment. She thought she could solve everybody's problems even though her own personal problems were of such magnitude as to seem incredible. Her sense of humor seldom saw the light of day. But it was there. I witnessed it and tried, on occasion, to encourage both its expression and development."

"You seem to think a sense of humor is vital to a whole, healthy person."

"Well, in this field, Doc, when you see cases of infants being swung by feet and their little heads being bashed against kitchen counters because they had the temerity to cry while the father was trying to watch a sporting event on TV or when you see a two month old whose head has been forced down a hopper with the toilet flushed over and over until the last bit of life has ebbed from the body"—the doctor blanched—"if you do not develop a sense of humor, if you do not laugh, no matter how bizarre it might appear to others not in the field, you do one of three things. You resign. You pretend these things aren't happening or you crack up just like Lunie did."

"Do you think Lunie's psychotic?"

"I don't know. I'm not a psychiatrist, but she couldn't have functioned as well as she did or been as effective as she was, were she psychotic."

"If you are correct, what do you think caused the psychotic behavior?"

"She told me how little sleep she was getting. Being on the hot line on a busy night, none at all. I remember when I was in college; there was a notice on the bulletin board for volunteers for an experiment in sleep patterns. I didn't volunteer but my roommate did. They divided into two groups. Group 1 was allowed, during the week of testing, to sleep without interruption. Group 2 had their sleep interrupted. Whenever the eyelids of the volunteers fluttered (indicating dream time), they were awakened so that very little, if any dream time was permitted. At the week's end, Group 1 were normal and exhibited normal behavior. Group 2 (my roommate included), exhibited psychotic behavior."

"Very interesting. Did you ever consider becoming a psychiatrist?"

"No, I did wish, at one time, to become a psychologist, but I took the LSATS to keep a friend company and to give him some confidence. I did well enough to qualify for a Class A Law School."

"And your friend?"

"He didn't make it. I should qualify that. An ex-friend."

"If Lunie's lack of dream time caused her behavior, she's been getting plenty of rest here, why would her behavior continue?"

"I don't know if drug-induced sleep affects dream time. There may be an excessive amount, since drugs are not natural or there may be a minimum amount. In any event, she may feel safe here. Nothing can hurt her or invade her. No security like a good, private, psychiatric hospital. And to be on the receiving end of lots and lots of attention. Lunie is a Cancer, and a great actress. You may want to consider that."

"Nice little armchair psychology, Mr. Goode."

"Sorry, Doc. I get carried away sometimes. Same sign as Lunie. Wait I didn't mean that literally."

"Let me ring for the attendant. You won't be allowed more than fifteen minutes. After you see her you may wish to cut it even shorter. Oh, here's the attendant. Do come again soon, Mr. Goode. Perhaps if you come often enough, you'll solve all the problems in our little community."

"Ouch! Was I that bad?"

"Actually, you have a rather benign appeal. For a lawyer."

"Well as long as it's not malignant."

"You're young yet."

"Thanks. See ya, Doc."

Bastard!

Lunie was in a padded cell. Don was admitted, told to press a red bell if anything went wrong or if he wished to leave earlier. The heavy door was locked behind him. Lunie was sitting in a chair with her arms extended in front of her, looking at her hands with fingers extended. Don approached her, gingerly.

"Hello, Lunie."

She didn't look at his face but only at his outstretched arms.

"Oooo. You have fingers, toooo."

"Lunie, it's Don. Please look at me."

"Not until you give me the password from the President. He's the only one I trust. You say that you're dawn. How do I know you're not really night, which represents evil." It was all said in a monotone, without feeling.

Don filled up and the tears ran down his cheeks. Lunie wasn't looking at his face so he just let it happen. After unknown minutes of absolute quiet, he dried his eyes. Just as he was about to ring the bell he heard the attendant's key in the lock. Someone was behind him. It was Lunie. What stealth! As the door was being opened, she pinched him in the bum.

"Get your ass in gear, kid!" she whispered.

It was 3:00 P.M. Oh how he hoped to get home while it was still light. Like Jean Simmons, he liked to be home before dark. But what to tell the office staff about Lunie. For most of the visit she seemed to be in Kansas with Dorothy and Toto. Yet that parting gesture. And comment. Had he heard it correctly? He really hoped he had. If Lunie wasn't looney, she was stalling for time. She needed to heal. That one baby's death and near death of another infant, she might feel responsible for. And that was no easy burden to bear. For anyone.

Nice to see 'Entering Barnstable' (Barney Frank's preference was 'Dennis'). He would skip going to the office and go early in the morning. Only ones working now were the four-day-a-week staffers. And there were not too many of them. Even so, they all knew he was going to try to visit Lunie and would settle for any news. No, he would have to 'get his ass in gear,' first. For Lunie's sake.

Suffer the Little Children

Funny how little traffic there was at 7:00 A.M. With luck, he'd be at the office by 7:30. He couldn't believe the call—another night call— (it could have been Lunie on the hot line if she weren't—oh, what's the use?)—two parents abandoned five children in a house with no heat. The children had ripped the oven door off to heat the kitchen by the gas stove. The youngest child, a boy, was under two years of age, and untrained. There were four dogs in the house. The children slept on mattresses on the kitchen floor. Each Saturday, the parents would drive by and throw a carton of food in the driveway. (It would later be learned they were living in a nice, immaculate home in Yarmouth. With them, was Mrs. Sheinfield's son, Ethan, eighteen years of age. He was having some emotional problems and the noise of the other children bothered him so his mother and stepfather thought it best to remove him from the source of conflict). The children had been living in these conditions for three months. There was dog shit all over the floors. Parents like this should be locked up, thought Don.

He pulled into a space in the office parking lot. Seven twenty-nine. So far, so good. Let's hope the Investigator's report and the court letter could be whipped into shape by 8:50 at the latest.

He approved the court letter for typing at 8:30. It had priority, so there shouldn't be any problems. There's my friend, the phone. Sometimes, my enemy but more often than not, mi amigo.

"Don Goode, here."

"We've never met, Mr. Goode. My name is Ivana Rossi. I'm an emergency care provider. Last night the Barnstable police and your social worker, Chris McLean, brought two children, Abel and Karen Sheinfield, to my home. Abel is not quite two and Karen is six. It was my son's birthday. In light of all the joy, this terrible tragedy. My daughter called me to the bathroom. This little tyke had on five pair of pants. His lower body was covered with urine and feces. He has scabs all over his penis, between his legs and on his backside. Karen was not as bad. The pipes had frozen in the house. She would take any material she could find and wrap it around her as underpants.

"This morning I went to the house to see if I could find any salvageable clothing. Instead, I found why they weren't using the bathroom. There was a dead rat as big as a cat in the hopper. He must have been trying to get whatever water was left. Does this help DSS' case at all, Mr. Goode?"

"It certainly does. And call me Don, please."

"Will you need me in court, today?"

"No, Ivana. Not today. But when it comes to a hearing, yes, definitely. May I take your number for my file?"

"Yes. 771-0630."

"Thanks, again."

"Chris, —Don. I just had a call from the emergency placement. I think the info should be included."

"Oh, Don. Do the letter all over? I just couldn't. Really, I couldn't."

"How about by way of addendum . . . at 8:30 this day, the department received . . ."

"Don. I just couldn't. I'm worn out. I've been up half the night . . ."

"Okay. Okay. I'll do it myself." If I don't do it, it's another regret for my bag of regrets.

While the addendum was being typed, Don walked into the Intake Unit.

Always Nice to Talk with Laverna

"What kind of horrors do you have for me today?"

"Don, you know we have nothing but dream cases for you." It was Laverna one of the Unit's best workers and one who had the best sense of humor.

"Here's a beaut, just came in. Foster parent in Brewster makes a kid stick a potato in her mouth, douses her with ketchup, licks it off, and then rapes her. He was chosen the Cape and Island's outstanding foster parent last year."

God, he thought. If we're being attacked from within, how are we going to survive? Better buy another gross of band-aids.

"And for those who hold the clergy in the highest esteem" . . . it was Laverna again." . . . A priest in Chatham has been giving mouth to you-know-where-resuscitation to three altar boys over a two-year period and then telling them he felt a little unconscious in the you-know-where and to please return the favor. This was a parish blow-by-blow description. One of the kids had a brother, three years older, who was found dead two years ago. Last time his parents saw him he was on his way to an overnight with the same priest at the rectory. Father says the D.A.'s office told him you could never convict a priest."

All those stories Don had heard in the past. Were they true? The Church was paying off parents to avoid bad publicity. It assuaged its conscience by deceiving the semi-outraged parents into believing it was in the best interests of all, for the abused children to receive therapy and it reassured parents that the priest would also receive therapy. Instead, the priest was quietly transferred (sometimes to a 'better assignment') and, once there, would work his way into a position of trust with young boys, and the vicious circle would continue. Didn't they know that child abusers would insinuate themselves into any position in order to gain access to children? He shuddered to think how many he may have met and had not recognized. Even worse, abusers are never cured.

"And here's one about a teacher at D-Y. Offered to give a beautiful fourteen year old cheerleader special assistance after school so she could go on cheering. Well, he gave it to her, and she ain't cheerin', Don - she's cryin'."

"Please, please Laverna, are any of these going to Court today, is what I meant."

"Maybe the priest case. Still being typed. The others are 51As that have to be investigated and supported before a decision on a C&P is made. My sup, Nola, will inform you."

"Well, I always check in her office. But, it's dark and empty."

"Yeah. She was out late last night with her girlfriend."

"You mean boy . . ."

"I always say what I mean and mean what I say."

"See ya, Lala. I chose a sweet la la palooza in thee." Don made an attempt at singing. He didn't succeed.

Adopted: At Long Last Love

Well, well. A happy ending. He wasn't sure those things happened in this business. But here Don was enjoying himself at an adoption party for Lola and Maria Kenyon (nee Cesspo). Family and friends and those from DSS who had a direct hand in helping, first with the Care and Protection case and on through the adoption, were invited by Marge and Bill Kenyon to the party. Don had never attended one (never knew they existed), but accepted the invitation even though Merrilee and he were having weekend company. The Kenyons worked so hard at being good parents. They had no natural children because Bill had been exposed to Agent Orange in 'Nam. They were afraid of what might result.

The bio parents, Chai Ciocco and Tony Cesspo were a case of a union between a sadist and masochist. Technically, it should have been ideal. Tony liked to inflict massive doses of physical and emotional pain (as his father did to his mother) and Chai liked to receive it. She must have. No matter how much it hurt or how unable she was to recognize herself in the police photos, she kept going back for more.

The Cesspo-Ciocco-where there was no marriage the DSS case name would go under the mother's name but in this case it started as the "Cesspo Case" (and remained so) the family first came to the attention of the Department when Chai was found wandering the streets with Lola and Maria. It was late at night, she didn't know where she was and the girls were crying. When questioned by a Dennis police officer, she was unable to respond. She was drunk and had bruises on her face and neck. Clumps of hair had been pulled out of her head. The more she tried to respond to the officer's questions the more hysterical she became. She, and the girls with her, were taken into protective custody. Since any police department is mandated to report, the DSS hotline was called. Lola and Maria were placed in an emergency home while an emergency Care and Protection Petition was sought in Court the following day.

After nearly five years of foster care and three placements, Lola and Maria were finally adopted. It was an open adoption, meaning they could still have contact with their parents and brother, Tony, who would remain in the custody of his father.

After two years of therapy, while hiding at the battered women's shelter, Chai finally broke away from Tony. The last 'incident' was enough to repel anyone. Even Chai.

Tony, Chai and little Tony were living in a cottage for the winter. He accused her of drinking again and started punching her around. Little Tony was into the lighted fireplace. When his father went to rescue him, Chai slipped out the back door and ran to a friend's cottage two streets away. She was in the middle of her story when he found her. Chai's friend, Ellen, later told the police it was the worst beating she had ever seen. Work boots kicking, closed fists, knees, fireplace poker. As she lay on the floor in too much pain to move but before her two eyes closed, she looked up and saw Tony with little Tony beside him.

"Tony, don't ever forget this minute. This is the way we treat women. This is the way all women should be treated."

He took out his penis and urinated on her face. Oh, God how

it stung the eyes. She prayed that they would close before any more pain came. When he finished, he turned to Ellen.

"If you want to continue living, you didn't see anything. You were out for a walk."

To protect Ellen, Chai said she would testify. The case was set down for trial three times and summonses were issued for Chai. She was in hiding, trying to save herself. Ellen had disappeared.

Tony? He found another victim. There was a recent article in the Cape Cod Times about a woman brutally beaten. Near death. Will she testify? Don awoke to present reality, thanked the Kenyons, said his good-byes and headed home to his own company.

Going to the Dogs

"Hi, Juan."

"Don. Always nice to see you. It's always good news when you're around. You're here on those parents of the year? The Sheinfelds? Haven't seen them as yet. Barnstable police are looking for you. Judge wants to know if you're going to have the children I. deed today. If not, why not? DMH wants you to take custody of Antonia Marshall—you know the baby murderess—even though she's in one of their facilities—Gaebler—I think. Are you ready to argue that Motion today? Or did you not receive any prior notice which is a favorite tactic of DMH? I believe there were one or two other things. Oh, yes, Ivana Rossi called. She can have Abel and Karen Sheinfeld here this A.M. to be I.D. Doesn't want you to lose the case because they weren't here. Oh, Judge Kelly says you were supposed to furnish him with those custody forms the Feds are insisting on being completed in order to reimburse the state for foster care payments. Did you forget? Oh. Your office called. Did you want the case of the priest who hummed too many hims today or Friday?"

"Juan, I said 'Hi'. You know, h-i, not h-i-g-h, Juan?"

"I do ramble on, don't I? You know once you get the hang of this English language, it's difficult to . . ."

"You mean you can't stop spic'-ing it?"

"Oh, a man after my own nationality."

"Hi Gina. Whom do we have today?"

"Hi, Hon. Hensley's supposed to be coming down. That's the last word I had."

"Oh shit. I hope he can stay awake. Someone told me those coke bottle glasses he wears were definitely made in Italy. The printing on the glass says 'Please open other end'."

"Don . . . Hon . . . Pleeease! When he came in last week with his toupee on crooked and you kept pretending to blow it off, I had to get up and leave the courtroom. I was spastic. Nothing like that today. I'm the only court officer in Juvenile and can't afford to leave the courtroom. O. K.?"

"O.K. O.K. I see you're wearing that silver bracelet your husband gave you. I was telling my wife about it. She thought it was so clever. Handcuffs. One open, one closed."

"I nearly died when I opened this on our anniversary. I gave him a tie which he'll never wear and he gives me a sterling silver bracelet. Last year it was a gift certificate to Wendy's Ah, men. I'll never understand them."

"That's the way I feel about women. Mystery is one thing but to not even have a clue. I mean, after a number of years you recognize moods but as to causes or reasons, forget it. They say one thing but mean something totally different and then they get upset because you don't understand what they really didn't mean. Know what I mean?"

"No, Hon. Listen, this case you have—is it really as bad as everyone says?"

"I don't know what everyone says, but it would be a safe bet to say it's even worse."

"Social Worker? Here?"

"Chris McLean. Upstairs filling out the papers. Mary said

she'd bring them down from the clerk's office when they were ready."

"Hon? Why do people have children if they're going to treat them like dogs? Excuse me, worse than dogs."

"I don't know. There are a lot of childless couples out there who would make wonderful parents. If only there were some way to connect the two groups before the damage was done. Or, maybe, the damage has to be done before there's an opportunity to connect."

"Hi Mary. Hi Chris."

"Hi Don. You're all set. I put the folder on the clerk's desk. God help those kids and God damn those parents.

"Thanks, Mary."

"For what, Don? Bringing down the folder or calling the Creator for both help and damnation?

"Yes."

"Oops, Gina. I think the Judge is awake."

"How can you tell?"

"He just picked up his slippers and Cape Cod Times which were just outside the door of the lobby."

"Don? Do you ever stop?"

"I have a right to remain sane, don't I?"

"I guess. I guess."

"Don, have you seen the parents? I had the Barnstable Police serve them with a notice early this morning."

"But Chris. I heard they were living in Yarmouth. Did you have their address?"

"No, but Barnstable P.D. said they would find them. I guess a neighbor had a number to call if anything unusual happened and the kids couldn't take care of themselves. Can you believe it? Can you believe it?"

"Now, now Chris. There's nothing wrong in living with dogs. As long as you know that if they're sleeping, you let them lie."

"Thank God for your sense of humor, Don. You have no idea how many times I felt I was sliding over the edge and your humor saved the day. As a matter of fact, I have a Chins case on this morning. Very serious. Boy, 11, set fire to the foster home. Caused sixty thousand dollars damage. Needless to say, no one will take him. I want the Court to order a criminal complaint and then commit him to the Department of Youth Services. I have worked so hard on this case and have met with one frustration after another. Please, would you help me? The Area Director said I should ask you."

"Well I normally don't take Child in Need of Services cases, Chris. And I wouldn't at the request of that idiot Area Director. But for you, y-o-u, I'll do it. You should know in advance that Judge Hensley is a Pisces. I doubt if he'll make a decision other than a non-decision. Just wait and see what he does with this Greyhound Case. Just note his area of concentration. Regardless, if it makes you feel more secure I'll sit in on the Chins case. What's the kid's name?"

"Hy Flambeau"

"Cut the shit, Chris. No one has a name like that. Especially in this situation."

"Don, I kid you not . . ."

" . . . Yeah, you and Jack Paar."

"Don, His name is Heinz Flambeau. They call him Hy."

"As German as a French flamethrower. Oh, gosh, it reminds me of another Chins. I believe the worker was Lynn Holster. She had a client, 14-year-old Billy Duarte. Just couldn't get up for school. Bright, too. Kid was on the verge of going into foster care (which he hated). Lynn asked me to intercede because he wasn't fodder for foster. I couldn't resist. Not in helping but in humor. I asked her who was with Billy. She said Mrs. Duarte. Deadpan, I insisted she get the father and one other sibling into court. She said it wasn't appropriate but asked me why. I said so I could sing: 'It don't mean a thing if it ain't got that swing. (And then I'll point to each member of the family) Duarte, Duarte, Duarte, Duarte! He didn't go into foster care. Someone told me later that the Judge overheard my singing and determined that was punishment enough."

"Hon, the parents are here on Sheinfeld. You ready?"

"Yeah, Gina. They have a lawyer?"

"Hon. You have no idea how expensive it is not keeping up two houses like that. They can't afford a lawyer. It's only you highly paid state attorneys who can run two homes and afford a lawyer. Oh, Don, I crack me up! And remember what I said about the toupee. The further we both stay away from that the better."

"All rise. Judge Horatio Hensley of the First District Court at Barnstable presiding. You may be seated."

The Judge had a pinched mouth and his dark eyes, almost black, darted around the room, as he stooped forward. His very thick glasses made them seem larger than they were. Behind his chair were a number of bookshelves, which housed the Massachusetts Reports of the Supreme Judicial Court and the Appellate Court. In addition, were the Massachusetts General Laws annotated. These were updated on an annual basis. New laws, and if any, cases, in all areas of the law first became known through advanced sheets. When there were enough of them, they became the next highest volume of each set of reports. In addition, the various decisions were broken down into fields of law and a pocket insert gave the latest changes, if any, in the different areas of the law. The previous year's insert was discarded. (Some judges and clerks were timid about discarding because it seemed like a desecration of the law).

"Mr. and Mrs. Sheinfeld . . . do . . . you . . . have . . . your . . . lawyer?"

Don didn't dare look in Gina's direction.

"No your Honor. I was working but was laid off. My husband hopes to start at Burger King next week. If he passes security."

"What . . . kind . . . of . . . security . . . would . . . he . . . have . . . to . . . pass . . . for . . . Burger King?"

"Maybe they mean secure in himself as a person, so he can do the job. I don't know, your Honor."

EN

"Hmm. Temporarily . . . I'll . . . find . . . you . . . qualified . . . for . . . Court . . . appointed. . . . lawyer . . . Is. . . . there. . . . a. . . . conflict. . . . between. . . . you?"

"Oh no, your Honor. He's my fourth husband and we get along great."

"No, Mrs. Sheinfeld . . . I meant . . . in. . . . your . . . legal . . . positions."

"Oh no. We both plead not guilty."

"Well . . . this . . . is. . . . an. . . . emergency . . . hearing. Following . . . this . . . will . . . be . . . a seventy-two hour . . . hearing with . . . your lawyer . . . Who's on the . . . list . . . to . . . be . . . appointed?"

"Antoinette Perry, according to probation's records your Honor."

"Thank you . . . Mr. . . . Leo . . . Nardo. When you people . . . leave . . . today . . . see this probation . . . officer . . . He'll . . . give . . . you . . . Miss Perry's. . . . address . . . and. . . . telephone number."

"Your Honor."

"Ye—es"

"About the children?"

"Oh yes . . . yes . . . yes . . . Whom . . . do . . . you . . . have?"

"My list shows Michael Rock, your Honor."

"Good. Not you Mr. Goode . . . I . . . need . . . to . . . get . . . more . . . young . . . lawyers . . . involved . . . in . . . these . . . cases. Well, I. . . . need . . . to . . . hear . . . some . . . evidence, Mr. Goode."

"Yes, your Honor. Officer Alnut, take the stand please."

"Has . . . this . . . witness . . . been . . . sworn?"

"No, your Honor. If the Court finds his testimony sufficient, he may be the only witness today."

"Are . . . the . . . other . . . witnesses . . . corroborative or collective?"

"Both, your Honor. But I don't believe it is fair to the parents for the Court to hear all the evidence without their attorney being present. Just enough to support the temporary custody order for seventy-two hours. After all, your Honor, it isn't as though these children had been in their parents' custody to begin with."

"Good point . . . Mr. . . . Goode . . . heh, heh, heh."

"Raise . . . your . . . right . . . hand . . . I said . . . your . . . right . . . hand."

"This is my right hand, Judge."

"Oh yes . . . yes . . . You're facing . . . me . . . so it's . . . the . . . opp. Let the . . . record . . . indicate . . . that . . . Officer Alnut . . . has . . . been . . . duly . . . sworn."

The clerk so noted on the case manila folder.

"Proceed, Mr. Goode."

"Would you kindly state your name, address and occupation."

"Samuel Alnut, Barnstable Police Department, Phinney's Way, police officer."

"How long have you been a police officer?"

"Seven years, sir."

"Directing your attention to yesterday, at or about 5:30 P.M. did you have the occasion to go somewhere?"

"Yes."

"Where?"

"With other officers, Brown and Townsend, I went to number 5 Gully's Gap, Barnstable."

"How did you happen to go there."

"We received a telephone call, sir."

"Did you make certain observations upon your arrival?"

I did, sir."

"What observations did you make?"

"There were five children ranging in age from two years to ten years. They had on dirty, wrinkled clothing. The youngest smelled strongly of urine. There were mattresses on the floor in the kitchen. The door to the oven had been removed. There were dirty dishes crusted with food in the sink. There were four broken windows. There were four large dogs on the premises. There were dog feces everywhere, on the mattresses, all over the floors. There was a huge rat dead, frozen in the only hopper in the house."

Were there any adults present?"

"No sir. We asked the children . . ."

"Just . . . a . . . minute . . . officer . . . before . . . you . . . go. . . . any . . . further . . . do . . . you . . . know . . . what . . . kind . . . of . . . dogs . . . these . . . were?"

Everyone in the courtroom was stunned. He had zeroed in on the pedigree of the dogs as the important issue instead of registering outrage at this type of abuse and neglect.

"No, your Honor. I'm not a dog fancier."

"Well, I . . . am . . . sort of . . . describe. . . . them for me."

The officer was furious. It didn't take a Ph.D. to know he was dealing with incompetence.

"Well, your Honor. Each dog had four legs, a tail, a snout, teeth, two eyes and two ears. The two male dogs had additional equipment."

"No. . . . no. . . . I . . . mean . . . the lines . . . things . . . that . . . would . . . put . . . each dog . . . in a . . . certain . . . class.

"You . . . have . . . no. . . . answer?"

"No, your Honor."

"Did . . . you . . . take . . . the . . . dogs . . . into . . . custody?"

"No, your Honor. We figured the children were of primary importance."

"Tsk . . . tsk . . . that's . . . too . . . bad. . . . it. . . . might. . . . affect. . . . the. . . . outcome. . . . of. . . . this. . . . case."

"You mean, sir, that these five children weren't abandoned because we didn't arrest the dogs."

"It's possible. . . . possible. After. . . . all. . . . every. . . . dog has. . . . his day. . . . heh. . . . heh . . .

"Are the. . . . children. . . . going to . . . be. . . . identified. . . . for. . . . the. . . . Court?"

"Privately, your Honor. At another time. The trauma in this case is quite severe."

"Mr. Goode. . . . you don't. . . . believe. . . . in re. . . . uniting. . . . the family? That's the whole. . . . purpose of the statue. . . . Ms. Johnson would. . . . you. . . . please. . . . get me. . . . Chapter One. . . . nineteen on. . . . the. . . . shelf. . . . behind. . . . me?"

"Yes, Ho—your Honor." Gina couldn't look at Don, having almost addressed the Judge as 'Hon'.

She ran her fingers across the different volumes until she came to 119. What she didn't realize was that the open handcuff on her bracelet had caught onto a clump of the judge's postiche. As she thrust her hand forward to remove the wanted volume, the toupee came off. She handed the judge the volume and wondered what the fuzzy thing was against the side of her hand. She held her wrist up and for the first time she realized what had happened. The judge sat there more than barefaced as his hairpiece swung from Gina's arm.

"Stay. . . . there. . . . Miss. . . . Johnson. I. . . . may . . . need . . . your . . . further assistance."

"Yes, your Honor." A sigh of relief. She had been given the gift of time.

She finally untangled the bracelet and as the Judge handed the Chapter 119 volume back over his head, she reached for it while replacing the toupee at the same time. Now it was on sideways. The judge didn't seem aware. There was controlled hysterics facing the bench.

"You. . . . don't. . . . intend. . . . to. . . . suspend. . . . visitations, do. . . . you, Mr. Goode?"

"No, your Honor. The department would not do that without notifying the court, except, of course, in an emergency."

"When. . . . could. . . . the. . . . children. . . . be brought. . . . in. . . . to be. . . . identified?"

"I'm scheduled for a full hearing in Wareham District Court on Monday, your Honor. How about next Tuesday?"

"Fine. I'm. . . . going. . . . to. . . . give. . . . temporary. . . . custody. . . . of these . . . children. . . . to . . . DSS. . . . until next Thursday. . . . I know . . . that's. . . . more. . . . than. . . . seventy-two hours. . . . but. . . . it might be considered. . . . a. . . . serious. . . . case. . . . The parents'. . . . attorney and the children's attorney. . . . will. . . . need. . . . time. And . . . will. . . . someone . . . connected. . . . with. . . . the. . . . case.. . . . try to. . . . find. . . . out. . . . more about. . . . those dogs.. . . ?"

"Thank you. . . . Next case."

"Your Honor?"

"Yes,. . . . Mr. . . . Goode?"

"Chris McLean has to be at the Department's Plymouth Office involving a case where she is servicing two of the children in a family and the Plymouth office is servicing one of the siblings. I was wondering if the Court could call her Chins case, Heinz Flambeau, out of order?"

"O.K. . . . O.K. . . ."

"Regardless . . . of. . . . your. . . . request. . . . Ms. McLean. . . . I will not. . . . order. . . . nor have. . . . I. . . . nor will I. . . . in. . . . the future. . . . a criminal. . . . complaint. . . . out. . . . of this. . . . Court"

"Your Honor. This boy has caused sixty thousand dollars worth of damage to the foster home. Word of that has spread faster than the conflagration itself. No foster home will take him. His parents don't want him. The Court gave custody to DSS. We do not have a placement for him. You say you cannot order a criminal complaint?" She was doing better than Don.

"Ms. McLean. Why don't. . . . you. . . . have. . . . the. . . . foster parent. . . . apply for. . . . a. . . . complaint. . . . You have. . . . to. . . . learn. . . . to be. . . . de. . . . ci. . . . sive . . . about. . . . things."

"I have learned to be decisive about things. The foster mother has applied for a criminal complaint. The application has been denied because the idiot juvenile officer, Pedro Arnaz, told the clerk there was no crime because he forgot to give the boy his Miranda warnings when the boy had already voluntarily confessed. Now the poor victim's insurance company will not make her whole."

"Oh. . . . I. . . . didn't. . . . know. . . . that. . . . But. . . . I'm. . . . sure. . . . you. . . . can. . . . find. . . . a. . . . placement."

Chris began to cry. She couldn't even attempt to control the tears. The judge called a recess and invited both Chris and Don into his lobby.

"Now, now. . . . Ms. McLean. . . ."

"Don't you Ms. McLean me, you asshole! You're wearing that fucking black robe and you're supposed to dispense justice? I'll bet you don't even know how to spell it. I bring these kids in here and tell them they're going before the judge. And they draw you! What a laugh and a fucking half." Through it all she was in hysterics. Don had never seen so many tears. He had always told Chris she was a repressed Leo. Well she certainly wasn't repressed today. And so forceful. Finally the judge had Gina let them out the back door which led to the corridor. She was still sobbing and had run out of Kleenex. Don happened to have a new linen handkerchief which he had bought in Ireland. He gave it to her and told her to keep it. He was so grateful for what she had done, but today's outbreak was a portent of her leaving the department.

Before leaving for Plymouth, Chris collected 'flaming Hy' and brought him to the office in South Yarmouth where a fruitless search for placement would continue. As hopeless as a case appeared to be, the Family Resource unit would continue to look. Once Hy's background was mentioned to a prospect, as was required, that placement ended. Hy spent the night sleeping on the floor of a supervisor's office with two volunteer foster parents watching him until the start of office hours the next day. It gave Don small pleasure to tell this result to Judge Hensley when he asked, three days later.

Three weeks later Chris resigned.

Fostering a Strike

Don couldn't believe it. The president of the Fitchburg Area Foster Parents support group was calling for a strike. There were more than two hundred eighty-nine foster homes in that area. That was bad enough, thought Don, but she was asking foster parents throughout the state to support her request. They were demanding the return of 'Mikey' to a foster placement. He had been removed one day after school, without going back to the foster placement. He was eleven years old and had lived most of his life at the placement since he was an infant. First, the Department supported the removal but punished the administrators involved because of the way in which the removal had taken place. Now the foster parents were demanding the reinstatement of those who had been demoted. To further complicate matters, Mikey has been in five different placements since being removed, while yet another child had been placed with the same foster parents.

What will happen if the strike takes place? The foster parents will continue to foster those children already in their care but will take no further placements. If only one child a week was placed in DSS custody by each district court, that would be two hundred eighty cases per month, thought Don. He knew the figures were high but it was fascinating to ponder the power people had. Provided they knew how to use it. Even if DSS used outside agencies and their facilities, it would still fail miserably in providing care for children. Thank God, the foster parents weren't contemplating returning the children they had. They were acting a lot more responsibly than the Administration of the Department of Social Services.

Another Feather in Tonto's Cap

Noel was in a dither. His usual state when any problem arose. If someone came to him with a problem, before it was fully explained, his two arms would shoot up, and he'd respond, "Not my department. Not my department." People were wondering if he had one. A department. When asked 'whose department,' his response was always along the lines of, 'Now you have a good head on your shoulders. I know you can figure it out. Besides, can't you see how busy I am?' He would be sitting back in his swivel chair, feet on a totally empty desk, a glazed look in his eyes and picking his nose. He would have been picking his bum had he been standing (he used to alternate) but sitting, it was inaccessible. He imagined (he had a great imagination) he was providing exemplary leadership and guidance.

But present was a problem he could not relegate to another department. Oh God, how he hated it when he had to make a decision. If only he could get someone to make it for him. Then it would go away. And he couldn't be blamed. He was in enough hot water (no pun intended) with the Death Squad and the Antonia Marshall scalding-death case. The report hadn't come out yet. What should he do? Tonto East, a Boy Scout Leader and foster parent was allegedly studying the asses of three foster boys he had in placement. If one boy was washing the dishes, the other two would observe Tonto staring at the boy's ass. And only at his ass. The next night, the next boy's turn at the dishes. The same thing. One of the boys awoke during the night and felt someone massaging him; as he began to move and turn, he saw Tonto leaving the room.

Two days before a 51A report was filed, a neighbor came running out of his house, wrapped in a towel. He was almost on top of Tonto before Tonto realized it. He quickly put down the binoculars, which he had trained on the neighbor's bathroom window, which faced the tub. Tonto, on his porch, gave him the sufficient elevation to view the neighbor's lower anatomy. As the neighbor screamed, Tonto kept insisting he was adjusting the binoculars because the scouts were going out bird watching. Not really convinced, the neighbor calmed down and went back to his house. However, he called the Intake Unit of the office. Since Nola was out that day, it was screened in and was ready for assignment to one of the investigators. That is when Noel stepped in.

He convinced the acting sup of Intake, Manny Gomes, that Intake was much too busy and that it was a very sensitive case and perhaps a worker from another unit should be assigned. He handpicked Maureen Dubin and stressed over and over certain points and things for which she should look. In other words, he gave her a map. She, so naive, so innocent, thought he was telling her to do a great job. Let-the chips-fall-where-they-may type of thing. She returned and told him she was going to substantiate the 51A. Noel was horrified. Told her not to write up anything and to leave all her notes with him. After thanking her, she was excused. Noel looked around until he found a worker who was willing to unsub the complaint. Tonto went on as a scout leader, foster parent and voyeur. Noel went on thinking of his great contribution to society by keeping one of the best foster parents ever.

Little Man, Big Liar

It was 2:30 P.M. and Friday—thank God, Manny thought, hoping he could get away without any more blunders. He was sick about Central's coming investigation regarding Melissa Thatcher's death in Roxbury. Noel didn't seem concerned at all. Manny told him that he wished he could lie as easily and as convincingly. Noel opined that all it took was practice. Lots of it. He said he'd been doing it since he was four years old. He told his parents and later his teachers whatever he thought they wanted to hear. Oh sure, there were the occasional slip-ups but once he realized he was going in the wrong direction, he quickly altered course with, ' . . . but what I really and truly mean is . . . '. It worked like a charm. And now he was perfect. A perfect liar. Not a goal that many seek to achieve. He was very much like *The Incredible Charlie Carew* a book by old time movie actress (The Maltese Falcon), Mary Astor. The book was hailed by psychiatrists all over the world. Charlie and Noel were not responsible for anything. If an emergency arose, a fast exit was made. If there were no exit, heads were buried ostrich fashion, hoping someone else would make the decision. And if something went wrong,

EN

very quickly deny responsibility and point the proverbial finger. Manny's phone rang. Oh shit! What now?

"Manny, this is Bill Argent at the Attleboro Youth Shelter. We have here one, Prudence Valentina."

"Yes, I'm familiar with her record. What's up?"

"You or Noel or both lied to us. We've just received copies of two psych evaluations done prior to her coming here. Are you familiar with them?"

"Wait. Wait. Wait. Just a minute. I'm no liar."

"Does this mean that Noel is?"

"Well, he can speak to that himself."

If I could only find him. He's probably on his fourth Heineken in the cafe behind the building. That was his daily lunch. No food. Just beer. And even if I could find him, Manny thought, it would be impossible to get through to him. This sounded like something serious. Naturally, Friday afternoon. My bowling league starts at six. Oh shit.

"Manny, are you still there?"

"Yes. Yes. I was just collecting my thoughts. . . ."

Hope this combined with Melinda's case, doesn't lead to collecting unemployment.

". . . . Could you hold a minute till I get Prudie's record?"

"Yes, I'll hold. Only because I have to in order to detonate the bomb."

"Oh." They're going to throw her out. Someone is going to have to go from Yarmouth to Attleboro, back here and then what? How in hell are we going to get a placement on a Friday afternoon for a screw-up like Prudie?

"Yes, Bill. Have the record in front of me. Everything in this office is an open book."

"With missing pages and reports?"

"Bill! I've worked with you on a number of cases and have always thought we treated each other fairly."

"Manny, I'm beginning to have second thoughts on those other cases. This one is so blatant."

"How?"

"Manny, go past the assessment, her first ten placements to just before her coming here."

"Yes?"

Those two psych evals, according to their dates should be or should have been on her record that you sent here. Are they in your record?"

He knows. I can't lie about their existence but I can lie about something else.

"Yes. Yes. I see them now. Dr. Adams and Dr. Blanche. What about them?"

"Manny, those reports never came here with her record!"

"Bill, Bill. Why didn't you call me? It was just an oversight. You know how busy this office is. And we're understaffed. It was probably some secretary making copies. You know how it is."

"Manny, are you familiar with the content of those evaluations?"

"Bill, I pride myself on knowing every single case in this office."

"Then you're aware that Prudence Valentina should never be in a group home, should never be in a foster home with other children, should just be a single placement because of the danger she presents to other children, that she's constantly acting out sexually, encourages violations of other children, has sexually abused children, enjoys being cruel and seeing other young children suffer?"

"Why yes, I'm aware of those items you ticked off."

"Then why the fuck did you send her here?"

"Now, Bill. No need to fly off the handle. You got it all off your chest. Now I'll wish you a pleasant weekend and we'll part still friends, I hope."

"Friends? Friends? You fucking asshole! We're putting Ms. Valentina outside the front door, if you're not here by 5:00 P.M!"

He thought he'd better see Noel to alert him. Not that it would do any good. Sure enough, Noel was seated at his desk, feet on it

EN

left thumb up his left nostril, voice raised to the Regional Director;

"Mary Quincy, I did cooperate with the Death Squad" She told him she didn't like his answer, his evasions, his excuses and that he was treading on very thin ice.

"Mary, if you think all I have to do in this busy, busy office is sit here on a Friday afternoon with my feet up on the desk and picking my nose, you have another think coming."

It was too much, even for Manny. He ran down to the kitchen and let out a roar. Without missing a beat, he set about screwing some foster parent in earnest. Like with Prudie Valentina for the weekend, and knowing Noel would be of no help.

"Can I speak with Jeanette La Lima, please."

"Just a moment . . . Jeanette, for you . . ."

"Hello."

"Hi, Manny Gomes from the Cape and Islands office. You're getting pretty high-falutin'. You have a secretary now?"

"No, Manny. That was Susan Pans, mother of my foster child, Annie. She just got off the 7:00-3:30 shift at Falmouth Hospital. I don't know if you are aware that she is a nurse."

"Yeah. Someone mentioned that to me. The father is a long haul truck driver?"

"That's correct. Listen, I have a lot to do before hubby gets home. What's up?"

"I hope you realize you're probably our most outstanding foster parent (Noel always said to flatter the shit out of them) and I absolutely wouldn't bother you except this is an emergency. Yours is the thirteenth call I'm making."

"Manny, cut the b.s. Just be up front with me. If my answer is going to be 'no' it's going to be 'no' no matter what you say."

"Okay, Okay. This is just until Monday morning. A nice, sweet fifteen year old girl whose short term group placement ended today."

"I've worked a lot with group homes in the past. Where was it?"

"Now, now, Jeanette. Confidentiality forbids my mentioning it."

"I thought the Commissioner said foster parents were entitled to just about everything if it helped to foster a child."

"Well, yes I agree, providing it is a long term care. But this is just for the weekend."

"Manny, if I'm going to seriously consider this—even for the weekend, I need to know certain things."

Why doesn't she shut up and take Prudie? What could possibly happen? Didn't she know he had to go bowling? It was the semi-finals. Oh, God.

"Okay. What do you want to know? Do you want me to have a social worker bring the record over to you (Noel said to promise them the sky and they'd settle for a patch of blue)?"

"Manny, we've known each other for years. You know that won't be necessary. It's just that my foster child Annie Pans is only twelve years of age and innocence personified. I don't want some sexually advanced teenager tinkering with her fragility. That's why I have to ask these questions."

That's it. That's it. Make our team lose. They're counting on me. What time is it? Oh Jeez. It's 4:40 P.M.

"Let me get the record." It was still on his desk. He hadn't been to the gents' room since noontime. What a relief.

"Okay, Nette. Shoot."

"If I had a gun, I would."

She asked about trouble in other placements. None. She asked if there were any evaluations showing any disorders or possible threats to younger children. None. Manny kept the record on his desk closed so he could answer from selective memory. What the heck, if his memory was faulty or he misremembered, that wasn't as bad as telling an outright lie. Was it? She asked if the child was on any medication. None. Actually she was on Thorazine, an anti-psychotic med. All Manny could think of was his Bowling League. As soon as Aubrey James was ready to leave Attleboro with Prudie, she called Manny at the office and he gave her Jeanette LaLima's address. He drove out of the parking lot at 5:00 P.M., happy that he wouldn't be late for his bowling league. He was glad that Aubrey had been in the office. It had been Melinda Thatcher's case. He smiled to himself. Obviously, she wasn't around.

Falling Behind and Catching Up

Noreen Hartman was a very dedicated social worker. She tried to follow all the rules. One of the rules she found physically impossible to do, was the writing. She made all her home visits, she got whatever was coming to 'her' children. The clothing vouchers, the medical passports, the transporting parents to and from visits, supervising visits where necessary, in the office or churches or wherever, to and from court—she loved going to court—despite the wasted hours spent in waiting for one's cases to be called. She loved it because of Don. She thought his irreverence towards what was considered sacred was a screech. She remembered her trepidation the first time she had to go to Court. She was literally shaking. It was her first time in Court for DSS but it was also his first time. The difference? He wasn't shaking. On the outside, he said. By the time her case was called, he had her laughing so much that tears were streaming down her cheeks. The judge wanted to know if she wanted more time. Don later said it was a poor pun. She fudged and said she had an allergy. Well it really wasn't fudging. She was allergic to Court. Later, they went out for coffee with James Blender another social worker who was very much laid back. Well, naturally. He was an Aquarian. They had a lot of laughs talking about zodiacal signs. Especially the exaggerations. Don remembered things from the book *You Were Born on a Rotten Day*. It was a nice beginning. Nearly all the Court personnel were helpful. Not obsequious but very respectful. A hell of a lot better than those jungles in Boston. Please spear me, ugh!

Well here it was 7:30 A.M. and Noreen was off and writing. No Court, no home visits. She requested to be excused from supervision. When she stated why, no objection. If she could stay until 7:00 P.M., she'd make a pretty good dent in the writing. Thank God for diaries. How could anyone remember things without one? 8:30 A.M. Two records up to date! Twenty-two to go. She was going to reward herself with a large coffee from the Little Peach next door.

"Reenie, you have quite a bit of mail out there. Coming out of the box." It was her supervisor, Trudy Teller. A little sadder and more subdued since Melinda's death.

"I'll get it a little later. Want to finish this coffee for the caffeine and do two more records. You know, the writing thing."

"Yes, I do. I've seen your records and I know you're a good social worker because I'm your sup and you know all your cases. But if anyone else looked at your records what would they surmise?"

"That I don't do the work I know I do. Trudy, would you check these two and see if you can sign off on them as being done?"

"I would be only too pleased to do so. And you have no idea how much better this is going to make me feel."

"Glad to oblige."

Noreen with much diligence completed all her writing for a two-month period in two more records. She was down to twenty! Work is salvation. Work is salvation. Coined by some bum on the dole, no doubt.

Gosh, these large coffees contained a lot. Her cup was cold

but still contained one-half. She went to the kitchen and put it into the microwave that they had all pitched in to buy. The greatest miracle. Her husband thought the dishwasher was a close second. It made the chores they divided much easier.

Now for the mail. She had neglected it for the past few days because she was so occupied outside the office. She had to carefully remove some pieces simply to avoid tearing. Then she got a good grip and was able to remove the bunch. Back to the desk. In two trips. She thumbed quickly through. There was nothing there to indicate that her rich uncle had died and left her all his money. There were psych evals on clients, three mileage checks (yippee), invitations to new service center openings, and a lawsuit against her for three million dollars (would you settle for three cents?) and on and on. What's this? A letter from Jeanette La Lima. She had just made a home visit on Thursday last. That Annie Pans was so sweet. An angel, really. She hoped she would never change. But knowing life and youth—.

'Dear Nonnie,

I didn't know who else to write this letter to. But since you are Annie's social worker and I feel close to you, I figure it would be to you. Are you acquainted with one of your Agency's kids by the name of Prudie Valentina? I think she was one of Melinda Thatcher's clients and was taken over by James Blender, but James is on vacation, so an Aubrey James dropped her off here Friday night, and came back an hour later with her anti-psychotic medicine.

I said I would take her for the weekend because she had just finished a short term placement and there was nowhere for her to go. This, of course, was only after Manny Gomes had assured me that she had no serious problems, posed no threat to Annie and was on no medication. After prying some information from Prudie I called Attleboro Youth Center early Monday morning. After that, I wrote this to you so you would have it on Tuesday morning, your usual day in the office.

The information I received put me in a state of shock. I wish Manny had been honest with me. He seemed in a hurry to get out of the office Friday afternoon. The information was also received after the damage was done.

Prudie asked if she could take Annie out for a walk Friday night. I agreed because my husband's relatives were coming for a visit. Prudie said she was used to caring for younger children and had a lot of responsibility in her own home.

Sunday afternoon I noticed some bruises on Annie when she was going in the pool. I was very gentle in questioning her because she seemed to be in a daze. She told me that both Friday and Saturday she was raped by three older kids. On Friday, the boys were maybe 19 and were propositioned and encouraged by Prudie who I now know is dangerous to younger children, and should never be in the same home with them. She threatened to kill Annie before they got home Friday night at 9:45 P.M., if she told anyone anything. Saturday, after dinner, she threatened her again, to kill her, if she didn't go out with her. They met three different boys—about—twenty and Prudie asked them if they wanted to get laid by a virgin, meaning Annie. They went behind the bathhouse and she made Annie take her clothes off and then cheered as each guy took his turn telling each one to 'pump faster'.

Nonnie, my heart aches for poor Annie. I just want to ask you one question:

Why did Manny do this to an innocent child. Because he may as well have been there as a participant. Why? Why? Why?

Sincerely, Jeanette L.L.

P.S. Please call or come out. I don't know what to do. I kept Annie home from school. Do I tell her parents who knew she was 'safe' here?

Noreen began sobbing. Just then, Manny came into the unit for an appointment with Trudy.

"You no-good bastard! You rapist! You liar! You ought to be

castrated!" She ran to the copier and copied Jeanette's letter. She broke into Trudy's conference with Manny and placed the copy of the letter on Trudy's desk, giving Manny a copy at the same time.

"Just look at what this no good rotten bastard has done!"

"Now just a minute, young lady. Everyone knows what an upright and honorable person I am. And plenty of people would like your job."

"Then they can have it! We'll see what the Commissioner thinks of you!"

"Noreen we will discuss this within the office. Then it shall be decided what needs to be done. Is that clear?"

"Yes, Trudy. . . . it's just that. . . ." She began crying again and ran from the office.

EN

The Safe House

Maureen Dubin went on a home visit to Vangie Noble and her son, Ignatius, Jr., age 4. She knew she shouldn't do what she planned to do but she was disgusted with the Court's decision. Vangie had been beaten at least thrice weekly by Big Ig, who was a former wrestler. She had lost four front teeth, suffered a broken pelvis, clavicle, and both arms and five concussions at various times over the past two years. Although she had restraining orders and Big Ig violated them, he was never prosecuted. Two psychologists had stated that the best interests of the child lie in placing him with his mother and that any visitations with his father should be supervised. Then how could the Court order the child to be placed in the custody of his father—even his name should have given the Court a clue: Ig Noble—and visitation with the mother be supervised? Some personal connection with the judge? Well, Maureen would do what she had to do.

"Vangie. Hi."

"Hi, Mo. What's up?"

"You have time to pack a few things. The Court gave custody to Big Ig, as of this coming weekend."

"What?! Oh my God! My baby with that animal! Never! Never!"

They packed as quickly as possible, taking a few of little Ig's favorite toys (he would be called Nate from now on) and waited for it to get dark so that traffic would be light.

"Vangie—here's a long blond wig I want you to wear and this pair of glasses with window glass. Nate can lie on the floor in the back. I'll take your belongings down to the car while you put on the last tea—not supper—in this burg."

"Actually, Mo. I've always wanted to be a blond. Heard they had more fun."

"That's it Vangie. Keep it light. Keep smilin'."

When everything had been put in the trunk, they sat for tea.

"Now, Vangie, I've typed a list of telephone numbers for the Eastern Seaboard. The first three numbers—the exchanges—are reversed. O.K.? When we leave here I'm driving you to a safe house in Rhode Island. They will make connections for you. You may never need this list but should you get lost or separated, use it. Don't worry about the cost. Call collect. You will say, "This is Mrs. Smith, is my mother there?"

"Oh Mo, couldn't I say this is Mary Noble, backstage wife?"

"No! Who the hell is 'Mary Noble'?"

"Oh, my grandmother told me about old radio shows that were on. You know, in the last century?"

"Finish the tea. It's dark out."

"Come on Nate. Time to go."

"Couldn't I please have my name back—Iggy—although I never really liked it. I'm the only one I know with a name like that."

"Maybe at a later date. Listen Nate. My father went to a Mission High School with a kid whose nickname was 'Iggy'. Today he's a famous lawyer. So who knows what the future holds for you."

"Thanks, Mo."

They drove the backside of the canal over the Bourne Bridge

and up 495 to the exit that would take them to Providence. On the outskirts of Providence they took a sharp right to a long driveway. Maureen had already made her call. They came to a tall gate and Maureen blinked her high beams four times in succession. The gate opened and fifty feet further on they saw about a dozen flashlights beckoning them. Women and children of the safe house. Maureen helped unpack the car, kissed Vangie and Nate goodbye and wished them well.

"We could never thank you enough, Mo."

"Will you come to see me on visiting day in prison?"

"I'll bring a big cake with you-know-what in it."

They both laughed and Maureen, knowing it was time to go, drove off. She was back on the Cape in an hour and twenty minutes. Very little traffic.

She was too exhilarated to be tired. If the Courts dispensed justice, they'd be no need for 'safe houses'. And when they didn't, wasn't God's Moral Law superior to man's law? She hoped she'd never get caught. Her argument wouldn't hold up in man's court. She tried not to think of the consequences. This was her tenth time. Later, she fell asleep with a smile on her face.

Crack Baby

Somewhere in the distance, a telephone was ringing. Why doesn't someone answer it, thought Maureen. It couldn't be mine. I've only been asleep about five minutes. Finally she came to and groped for the phone.

"He-ll-o."

"Maureen Dubin?"

"Ye-e-s?"

"Time to be a little do-be. This is the Hot Line Supervisor calling. You're next in line for subbing for Lunie Nelson. You are to go immediately to the hospital. Crack baby abandoned by mother."

"Wait a minute. Lunie's never sick."

"Never say never Harry the Truman always said. It's a long time in between."

"Well, yes. Now I remember. I got a half day off for saying I'd sub. Who thought then that Lunie'd get sick. I've got to get my name off that list."

"You do that, honey chile. But once you take that time off you have to substitute at least once."

"Got it—damn!"

"'Bye, b—"

"Wait! Which hospital?" Dear God let it be Cape Cod.

"Falm—oops, another case. It's Cape Cod."

"Thank you, God."

"You must have the wrong connection."

"Not you! God wouldn't do this to me."

"Then why thank Him?"

"You did it to me. I'm thanking Him it's Cape Cod Hospital."

"Oh. Well, don't forget to write the case up and don't forget to file an Emergency C&P in 1st District tomorrow.

"I hope I can contact Don Goode, our attorney."

"Don Goode?" Don't worry about him. He's like horseshit. All over the place."

"'Bye."

"'Bye."

She dragged herself out of bed and for the first time looked at the clock. She'd had about two and one-half hours sleep. Like in the Army. Never volunteer. She couldn't forget that advice in a hurry.

The nurse at CCH handed her a summary of the case. As soon as she started to read, her eyes misted over: For the child. Crack baby. Mother 18, father unknown. Second child. Previous preg at 15. Delivered baby in toilet. Eighth grade ed. Baby's head size of a plum. Arms and legs like matchsticks. Two pounds wght. Two fingers one hand, three on the other. Probs. kidneys, bowels. Cries constantly, Mo. left hosp. two days after del. two weeks ago. Has not returned. When the mother was asked how she would pacify the crying baby she said the latest was to rub coke on the baby's gums. And the baby, 'he get high and go for a ride!'

"How can you stand it Miss Holmes?"

"We just look at it medically, Miss Dubin. The mothers get de-toxed in jail. We de-tox the babies."

Maureen turned away biting her lip.

"Miss Dubin, don't worry about a placement. This child needs us, needs medical attention. We called in the 51A because the law requires it."

"But the child was, according to the records, born two weeks ago."

"I know. And that is when it was called in. Would you like to see a copy of our written report to DSS?"

"Yes. Not that I doubt you. That creep on the Hot Line sounded like someone had rubbed coke on his gums and that none of it spilled."

Reading the report, it was clear a timely report had been made. He gave her the wrong info. He started to say Falmouth Hospital so that was where the case probably was. Where could she hide. It was 3:45 A.M. She could go to Melinda Th—no that was definitely out. Lunie's kids were skiing in Aspen with their father. Lunie had given her a key to keep an eye on the place. And she had checked at least twice a week. What a brainstorm. Three minutes away. She hoped the kids had left some munchies—she'd even settle for peanut butter.

"Thank you Miss Holmes. I'm going to hide out at a friend's home."

"Good. You need to hide out some place when you're dealing with people like that. Not to worry, if that eejit calls, no matter what time it is, I'll tell him you just left."

"Thanks, again. Maybe we could have a cup of coffee together sometime."

"Kindred spirits?"

The eejit called at 5:15 A.M.

"She just went out the door; sorry." It's nice to be part of a good conspiracy.

EN

Character Disorder

The Wynn family lived in an exclusive section of Centerville among neighbors who were mostly professionals. It didn't take long for those responsible people to notice the neglect of the children. The youngest, Bridget, was eight months old, the next in line of ascendancy was Todd, age 4, and the oldest who was parentified was Thomas, almost ten. The parents would go off for weekends or days without the children. During one of their absences, Thomas tried to drown Todd by holding his head under water in a wading pool. The child's earlier screams had alerted the neighbors who walked to the edge of the property. They had been reluctant to go near the house because of the Wynns' coldness toward them. When they saw what was happening they pulled Thomas away and pulled Todd out of the water. He was blue, almost purple. Mouth to mouth resuscitation revived him. Mrs. Wynn was called that night to be told that Todd was at a neighbor's. She was furious. They were never, ever to interfere again with her children. Boys will be boys. Clearly, it was time for a 51A.

When Laverna Andrews from the Intake Unit rang the Wynn's bell and said, "I'm from the State and I'm here to help you," Mrs. Wynn showed she had a sense of humor and could actually smile. She took an instant like to Laverna, even to the point of saying "Could you sing a few bars of Boogie Woogie Bugle Boy without your sisters?"

"If I started singing, you'd start running and then where would we be?"

"Apart."

They both laughed. Laverna listened to her story, taking a family history. How old were you when you married? When? Where? When was the first child born?

"Oh, my, married at sixteen, mother at seventeen. You were still a child yourself. Explains why you want a social life now."

"Mrs. Wynn are you all right?"

She nodded, "I'm okay. Please call me Lynn."

"Is there something you want to tell me?"

"No, I don't want to tell you but, yes, I am going to tell you but I don't want you to record it. Is that all right?"

"Yes." She put her pen and pad down to give Mrs. Wynn her full attention.

"When I was sixteen years old, I was going home from a friend's house. There was a brief section of woods near my parents' home. It was just turning dusk. I saw a gang of young guys, perhaps sixteen to twenty standing near the woods, drinking beer. I decided to skirt the woods and go home the long way. I moved way over to the right of this fairly wide dirt path—wide enough for a truck going one way. As I drew opposite the gang they started teasing me because of my weight. Like, 'How about the first verse of 'God Bless America, Kate?' I ignored them and increased my speed. Before I knew it, they had surrounded me. I started to scream. Someone covered my mouth. They carried me into the woods and ripped off my clothes. Then they began raping me. I started to count each one so I could tell the police. I passed out after fourteen. When I woke up I was in the dark woods all by myself. I salvaged whatever hadn't been savaged and made my way home. Do you know what my father and mother said when I told them what happened?"

"No. What?"

"My father said that I must have encouraged them, led them on because people don't behave that way. My mother said that you can't thread a moving needle."

"My God! You never told the police?"

"With support like that from parents, what good would it do?"

"But did you get pregnant?"

"Yes. Two weeks later I met Kevin at a friend's home. We started dating. A month later we got married. I had told him the whole story. He knew I was pregnant. Said he didn't care."

"So he's not Thomas' father?"

"He is legally. Our lawyer said if Thomas was born during 'coveture', whatever that is—am I saying it correctly?—he's presumed to be legitimate."

"You have a smart lawyer. I hope you always have him."

"Well I'm not exactly married to the Mob, but he and Kevin are friendly."

"What's his name?"

"Perhaps I shouldn't tell you—don't tell Kevin—his name is Sid Silver, out of Brockton."

"Silver. Didn't I read something about him in the paper? A missing child. A son, I think. . . ."

"Yeah, you probably did. All kindsa stories going around. One says, he didn't do what he was told to do, so the Mob kidnapped his kid. Kept him for a while. When Sid didn't follow through, they killed the kid. Did an awful job on Sid's wife. I hear they're getting a divorce."

"Do you believe the story, Lynn?"

"About the divorce, yeah. I would feel the same way. About the rest: A story is a story is a story. Pretty good for a high school drop out, huh?"

"You have a lot of native intelligence so."

"Wait a minute. No Indian in me. Of course, I did lose count after fourteen . . ."

" . . . Don't let anyone shortchange you. See, the humor? Cultivate it."

"Didn't know you could grow it."

"Well, you can, internally. It's all in your perspective."

"The way you look at things. See!"

"Excellent, but back to business. Do you think you could agree to what is known as Protective Day Care for Todd. The Department may want to know."

"You think he'd be safer with strangers than his own family?"

"Possibly. If Thomas resents him for some reason . . ."

"Of course he resents him. You never heard of sibling rivalry?"

". . . . Yes, of course. But that rivalry shouldn't be expressed in eliminating, permanently, the competition."

"You're right there. Was he really purple? Did he need mouth to mouth?"

"That's what the report said. At this point there's no reason to disbelieve the source, Lynn."

"No reason? Do you know that everyone on this street hates our guts? Has since the day we moved in. The high and mighty. Teachers, Lawyers, Accountants, Doctors. Have you talked to any of them yet?"

"No, I haven't. With me, a parent comes first. Parents and children belong together, except sometimes. And even if it is necessary to separate them, the family members should be reunited as quickly as possible in order to prevent further harm, and to preserve family life."

"You are one helluva smart broad."

"Thank you. I'm just trying to prepare you for what might happen. Barring what I hear from others, I'm going to recommend for consideration that, in my opinion, Todd could remain at home if the family accepts services and follows the service plan."

"What is it going to be?"

"I don't know. That—if the 51A is substantiated—would be up to the ongoing social worker assigned to your case. What happens is the worker does an assessment of the family, the child in question, the other children, their strengths and weaknesses. Then a service plan is drawn up to address those problems in order to make the child or children safe, and hopefully, to give the family a better life. If you agree, you sign the service plan. It's like a contract. If you neglect part of it or forget part of it, the social worker will get you back on track. If you disagree with the service plan or any part of it, you will have a conference at the office with the worker, his or her supervisor and you may bring your own attorney if you wish. Then you try to work things out. This is based on the 51A-51B not being considered an emergency. If it is considered an emergency—I do not make the decision—then the child is removed, put in foster care and you and your husband, together with your attorney, are entitled to a seventy-two hour hearing before a competent judge . . ."

"Where are they going to find one?"

". . . . who will determine whether the child shall remain in care or be returned to his parents and a date is set for a hearing unless the Court finds no grounds and dismisses the petition."

"You spout off that stuff like you know it by heart. How the hell long have you been working for DSS?"

"Do I look as old as a waitress at the Last Supper? Well, not quite that long, but long. I came over from the Department of Public Welfare when DSS came into being on July 1, 1980."

"Doesn't this work depress you?"

"It certainly does. We deal in human tragedy every day. But once in a while, there is a happy ending. A family is put back together again, children want to be with their own. Just as you and I. And when that happens successfully, as rare as it is, it seems to make the job worthwhile. As you said earlier, it's how you look at it. Now, Lynn. Do you have any questions? Is there anything at all I could do for you?"

"You mean that, don't you?"

"Umhmm."

"I've never met anyone as sincere as you. There is something you can do. It's after four. We've gabbed so. Have a couple of belts with me. Okay?"

"I'm not sure I know—if you're referring to tea, yes I'd love some."

"You're more perfect than I thought. Don't drink, haven't seen you smoke."

"I do have a 'belt'—as you so quaintly put it—almost every night when I get home. Need it. Once in a great while I'll light up. But rarely. I never drink during work hours and never drink and drive. My license is my job."

"Never had a few pops and then drove a car a little woozie?"

"Of course I have. I think everyone who's older and drinks has driven under the influence, when it was fashionable to do so. Now, however, it's a serious crime. Would you like to be incarcerated? Lose your license? Hurt somebody?"

"Fuck the establishment—excuse me, I know you're a real lady, I'd just drive without a license. Lots of people do, you know. Or maybe, you don't. I wouldn't want to hurt myself, my kids or anyone else, understand, but whether you have a license or not doesn't matter."

"Whether you're drinking does. It definitely affects one's perception."

"Yeah, I guess I know you're right. I just don't want to drink and not drive. Part of my make-up, I guess."

"Well, admitting it is a tremendous step forward. You can work from that point. Listen, I must away. I thought I'd be going back to the Yarmouth Office but no chance of that now. I've enjoyed our visit, Lynn, and I wish you the best."

"Thanks, I hope your wish comes true and thanks for everything else. I'll try to improve my perception of things."

EN

"If you do, you'll be a lot happier. Bye."

"'Bye. Thanks again."

Now that is the kind of client she would like to have had as an ongoing social worker. Lots of promise. Uneducated but far above average in native intelligence. A hint of character disorder and great resistance to authority (because her parents disappointed her?). Still, she was workable. And when the changes took place, a tremendous degree of satisfaction. Well she may as well forget that. She was an investigator in the Intake Unit and, as such, she had to maintain detachment. Otherwise, she couldn't function as she was supposed to. One of Don's words: 'function'. She had to restrain herself when she first heard him use it in Court: 'And just what is your function?'. To hell with Court, to hell with work, to hell with Don. She hoped he couldn't hear her. Sometimes he was uncanny. Well she was off the clock. She'd stop at Parker's for a quart of gin and dry vermouth. She could almost taste those martinis. Oh, and don't forget the lemon (she had olives). She was out of those. Did Parker's have lemons? Parker's had just about everything that went with alcohol. T.G. I. F. She let out a hoot.

Doo Doo Occurs

Another blue Monday. Think in comparatives, Don. Well, he didn't have to go to Wareham and he didn't have to go to Martha's or 'Tucket in one of those God awful tiny planes with the elastic behind the props. He thought he would never get used to them. At one time he used to drive to Wood's Hole and take the Island Queen boat or whatever the name was—and the social worker would meet him at the dock on the other side. But the all-knowing DSS figured it took too much of his time. Away from it. So now he flew. Many times he could complete his legalistics in the morning, be back at Barnstable Airport a little after noon, go to the office and get in four more hours of work. Smart Department. But he was running out of underwear.

He had to attend this morning's office meeting to share the Central Office's new procedures on copies of Department records. That meant listening to Noel. Remember: It is through the imperfections of others we achieve our own personal sanctification. Shit. He might be saying the same thing regarding me! Well, maybe he'd let me talk first. No such luck, he was already talking and there was no one else in the room. Don turned to leave.

"Don, don't go. I was just warming up. I might lose my voice if I don't."

We'd never be that fortunate. You're saving all our souls, Noel.

Where'd they all come from. Or correct syntax: From whence did they all come? The meeting room was filled to capacity in record time. Oh well, some people liked to suffer.

Noel droned on and on ending with the story of the first time he had to speak in class at college.

"And as you know, today I could talk a hungry cat off the back of a fish wagon. It was not always the case. That first time in college—and I'm glad I stuck it out. As I got up I was so nervous I developed diarrhea. I said to myself: Do I excuse myself or do I brave it out? The mess kept running down my legs but I continued talking. I. . . ."

"Wow! Shit coming out both ends."

" . . . That isn't funny, Don. I'm trying to help the people in this office by. . . ."

"By sharing your shit with them?"

"No, Don. By showing them they can overcome any obstacle."

"Even if it's liquid?"

"Well I can see I'm not going to be allowed to continue without interruption so I'll have to let this end in sudden death."

"Like you did to Melinda Thatcher?"

"For your information, Don, Investigators from Central Office have made a thorough investigation of the facts—F-A-C-T-S-not rumors, and have vindicated both Manny and me. So there!"

"That 'ain't' what they told Trudy and me."

"That's absolutely ridiculous, and you know it. What do you know about it? "I only give statements to responsible people. And I've been asked not to share with you or Manny what transpired."

Actually I was told not to share it with anyone else.

"Well I never! Going behind the Area Director's back."

"I'm sure they wouldn't have, if you were giving your first talk."

"Wha-a-t?" Noel abruptly left the room. His face was crimson.

Don stood up and walked to the podium.

"Rather than have you ask a hundred questions, go on and copy the records the way you have been. Show me the copy before it goes out. I'll tell you what needs to be redacted. Basically it's any legal input from me to you and things which could be damaging, emotionally, to a child. I'd like us to err on the side of the child. To protect them. To avoid legal input—in the future—just avoid putting it in the record. Unless, of course, you have to.

"I'd like to stretch this out for three or four weeks but I just don't have enough shit to go around." Then he held up his pointer and middle fingers a la Churchill. But it didn't mean victory. Just double of anything you wanted. Like, Noel's an asshole! Two fingers.

Don walked back to his office and then began a series of conferences with the different units.

When he walked into the Intake Unit he sensed a difference in the atmosphere. Either a giant boo boo had been made and a visit to or from the Regional and/or Central offices was in the offing or there had been some devastating news about someone in the office or someone in the 'family'. He learned soon enough. It was the latter. Nola Bellafatto was pregnant! How could that be? She was a Lesbian who hated men, and had a girlfriend of long standing. She looked like a truck driver in drag and walked like a cowboy who had been riding too long. She made occasional hits on the women in the office without much success and had had many long conferences in her office with Placenta, the receptionist. No one knew why. One position had nothing to do with the other. Nola didn't just hate men. She seemed to be angry with everyone and treated her workers like turds. Was it because she had never come to terms with herself and her sexual preference? Did she hate it when she saw and heard very feminine social workers describing their escapades? Escapades that she had never had nor ever would have. Don wondered.

"Congratulations, Nola. I never knew you had it in you. I mean. . . ."

"I know exactly what you mean, Don. You don't think I'd let a chauvinistic pig like you near me, do you?"

"But . . . then, how. . . ?"

"Artificial insemination. That's how we leses achieve motherhood these days. We don't need men!"

"You sure as hell need what comes from a man. That will never change."

"And men need mother's milk, do they not?"

"There's a substitute for that. There's no substitute for spermatozoa."

"You almost sound educated, today, Don."

"Well I didn't get my degrees by writing to the address on the back of a matchbook cover like you did, Nola."

"My son will show all of you men up!"

"You know the sex already."

"Yes. Ultrasound."

"Well I can think of two frustrations he'll have."

"Yeah, what?"

"He'll try to marry a woman just like his mother, and . . ."

"And, What?"

"And the other frustration is never knowing his father and having to send a necktie every father's day to a syringe at Boston Lying-In Fertility Clinic or wherever you had it done."

"Enough of this mutual hatred. . . . by the way, Don. Do you hate me because I'm a les?"

"No, I hate the rotten things you do to other people on a daily basis. If you were kind and giving and helpful to others, and a les, that wouldn't make any difference to me. I'd like you. Probably very much."

"Why, Don. I can hardly believe my ears. I could have saved myself a trip to Boston!"

"Wait a minute. Wait a minute. Not that much."

"Oh, shucks. And I thought we were making progress. Wait till I call the new APM. Then we'll review the latest 51As to determine if they should become C&Ps. The new Area Program Manager, as you shall see, is tall, dark and handsome."

The Man from King Solomon's Mines

"Don, this is Keeshu Walker, the new APM. He just started yesterday so he's getting his feet wet. We'll have to do it by the numbers."

Well he was tall enough to be a guard outside of King Solomon's Mines. And dark? He qualified there. Not handsome. Very ill at ease. Almost in pain in being there. God help him. This was a choice left to the area office, itself. That is Noel and Manny. Ordinarily, the job would be posted throughout the state so that those with the proper background and training might apply and be interviewed. Not in this case. Don would learn that Noel and Manny went out and recruited a man totally incompetent in the field of social work. Better to serve their own ends? To go on successfully torturing certain workers who questioned their bad judgment?

The meeting that should have taken one-half hour to review the latest cases took three times as long. Everything had to be explained in detail in order for Keeshu to understand. He was a duck out of water. And Don would bet he wished he was back in his own soothing, warm, comfortable milieu again, instead of this embarrassing hot water.

"Don, how do you like the new APM?"

"Thanks a lot, Manny. People are going to be thanking you and Noel for a long time to come. I mean, even upper management."

"Oh. That's nice to hear. . . . I think."

Don continued his tour of the other units, legally addressing the problems that were presented. He liked nearly all the workers and supervisors. Many times, if the workers were encouraged with certain questions, they saw the solutions themselves. He guessed they just wanted the encouragement of someone outside the unit. Why that would carry so much weight Don never understood. Did it instill confidence?

By now it was 12:55 and Don had received a call from Court on an adoption hearing in Barnstable Probate Court. A Dennis Police Officer and his wife had taken into foster care two brothers, now ages eight and five years. That was three years ago. The bio mother and father had disappeared. At the adoption proceeding the previous Friday, the Court was about to approve the adoption when in walked the father in splattered clothes and shoes, pleading with the judge to have a visit with his sons and, hopefully, to be able to take them back. During a brief recess, Don walked over to Marion Lifka, the social worker, and softly said, "Unless I miss my guess, he's a painter".

Judge Rachael Daniels ordered a visit to take place and for the parties tentatively, to return on Monday afternoon at 2:00 P.M. The foster parents and the bio father were to meet at Burger King on Saturday afternoon.

The foster mother was so angry, she turned on Don.

"It's your fault. All you state lawyers stink. I should have hired my own lawyer!"

Rembrandt Relents

The first session of the Probate Court was on the second floor of the building that also housed the Registry of Deeds. All the parties were present, including the biological father, who approached Don.

"Mr. Goode? As you know, I'm the boys' father. They wouldn't have much to say to me. Told me their foster parents were their real parents because they were the ones who took care of them. I don't know why I let my wife talk me into running away to Florida. Then she ran away with a shoe salesman and whatever money we had. It took me all this time to work my way back here. Whatever odd jobs I could get I took."

"Did you have the address of the foster parents?"

"Yes. And there was no excuse for not writing, not even at Christmas or birthdays."

"What do you propose to do?"

"Well, I went to see the parish priest Saturday morning, told him the whole story and he says to give up the kids if I really love them. I can't provide for them and have no home for them."

"Maybe if they want to see you in the future, visits could be arranged. Would you want that?"

"I think that's all I'm entitled to want. . . . now."

"We'll see what can be done."

"Thank you, Mr. Don. I mean Mr. Goode."

"It's the thanks that count."

"Your Honor."

"Yes, Mr. Goode"

"The biological father met with the foster parents, the prospective adoptive parents, on Saturday afternoon. The parish priest with whom he met on Saturday morning, told him to assent to the adoption. He's had a visit Friday night, not very promising, with his sons, and all he wants now your Honor, is to maintain some sort of connection. Nothing forced, nothing regular but if his boys want to see him, he'll be available."

"It looks as if you've pulled another rabbit out of the hat Mr. Goode. And the Court appreciates it. You have performed outstanding services in behalf of the state for this Court and I'm sure, other Courts. (Oh, oh. Someone must have told her about the foster Mom's comment. The Judge, as an Aquarian, wasn't too free with compliments). I just hope all these foster parents for whom you intercede appreciate you as much as the Courts do.

"Mr. Fenton. It shall be entered that parental rights in this case are terminated.

It shall also be entered that there is to be visitation between the biological father and the children in question provided that the children so desire it."

"Now I wish to thank you all for your co-operation. You probably see that it is only 2:45 P.M. But on top of the judge's desk, in chambers, are perhaps two dozen more folders, awaiting decisions. So if you don't see a judge sitting at his or her bench, it doesn't mean they've gone home or are asleep in their lobbies. It means that they are attending to their other myriad duties and responsibilities to make certain that justice is done to the best of their abilities. Thank you."

"Thank you, your Honor."

The Judge left immediately for a hairdressing appointment.

As they walked to the outside corridor, the foster mother rushed up to Don.

"Oh Mr. Goode. I'm so sorry. I didn't realize how good you are until Judge Daniels' comments were made in court. You don't stink anymore!"

"Probably because I took a shower this morning."

"That was great Don! Can I buy you a cup of coffee?"

"Marion, you may if you wish. You can if you're able."

"How do you remember all those rules?"

"Parochial school education. That's where I met my first D.Is."

"Oh. Well, let's walk down to the Picadilly."

"Okee dokey."

"I'm still screaming about your guessing the bio father's occupation last Friday. I think I've told ninety percent of the office."

"It was just a lucky guess."

They were at the door of the deli.

Slow Boat from China

She was glad about her decision to begin divorce proceedings against her husband in New York. It was nothing factual, more perceptive than anything else. You know, how sometimes you can perceive certain things with no basis in fact. Well, in this case she could perceive something but she didn't know just what it was. She and China—that was his nickname—his given name was Irving—had had some knockdown, drag out fights. Sometimes he'd be gone overnight, sometimes for two days, and sometimes he'd have Becky with him. Say he was going to take her for a walk and not return. When she pressed him he'd say he was doing volunteer work at 'the clinic' to help emotionally disturbed children who had been sexually abused. Ruth Diamond-Gold stood up to her full height of four feet, eleven, and demanded to know what kind of place was that for their three year old daughter. She was becoming reclusive where she had been so outgoing. She forbade any more excursions. Since she had cut down to twenty-two hours on her interior-decorating job after giving birth to Becky, she was sure she could control any more unauthorized outings.

She'll never forget that day. The office at Living Anew had called. Two of the decorators were out sick and they had a prospect. A 'live one'. Bonus for her if the deal went through. She'd have to check with Mrs. Holton to see if she could sit Becky until China came home. It was now 3:00 P.M. China should be home by 5:30, 6:00 at the latest. Mrs. Holton was available, so off she went. It took some doing but she finally convinced the prospects that her suggestions were not only practical but beautiful and costly.

It was 7:15 P.M. when she returned to the empty apartment. China must have had to work late. Mrs. Holton must have taken Becky to her apartment to prepare dinner for her own family. Well, she was being paid so Ruth began removing things from the fridge and the freezer. Thank God, she thought, for man's greatest invention: the microwave. Saved hours and hours of labor. When she decided what they were to have she collected items in an orderly fashion and called Mrs. Holton.

"No, she isn't here. Mr. Gold came home shortly after five and said he had volunteered at some clinic. I said I couldn't keep Becky beyond 7:30 or so because I was going to Bingo. Mr. Gold said he didn't expect me to because he had planned to bring her to the clinic. Some doctor there had enjoyed Becky's visits so much that he wanted her father to bring her."

"Did he say where the clinic was, or its name?"

"No, Just that it was outside the city with fresh, clean air. Much healthier environment for the children."

"Oh. Well thank you. Did Ch—my husband pay you?"

"No."

"Well I'll drop a check in your mailbox tomorrow. Okay?"

"Fine. No prob."

"'Nite."

"'Nite."

She had felt ravenously hungry. Now she had no appetite. She went to the liquor cabinet, contemplating a triple, if she could get it down. Then, she removed the cap from a bottle of

Glenlivet, the aroma assaulted her senses and she felt nauseous. She replaced the cap and put the kettle on for tea. Normally for just one cup she'd use the microwave. Now she decided that a pot of Earl Grey would be the thing. It seemed like it was going to be a long night and it was best to have a clear head. Decisions had to be made. When they weren't back by 11:00 P.M., she took two Excedrin p.m. and went to bed. But not before she selected the names of three attorneys who specialized in divorce. She was so drained, physically and emotionally, that as soon as her head hit the pillow she was asleep. A sleep without dreams.

The alarm went off at seven. She realized she was still the only one in the apartment. Instead of bounding out of bed, she arose slowly, went into the bath, turned on the shower, returned to the bedroom for clean underclothes and after selecting a wardrobe, returned to the shower. She soft boiled an egg—her mother used to call them googie eggs—had one slice of wheat-thin and a strong cup of coffee.

Then she called her father. She wanted to get him before he left the house. No one, including he, knew where he would be at any specific time. He started with a trial retirement. Couldn't stand it. What were those eejets doing with my company? Then he tried working Mondays and Fridays. Ruined his weekends, he said. The last Ruth had heard he was working Tuesday, Wednesday and Thursdays, with an occasional long weekend trip to Barbados or Nassau.

"It's Ruth. Is my father there, please?"

It was the cook. She always insisted on hogging the incoming calls. And if that paralleled what she did to the food, it was no wonder she was the size she was. Another candidate for Kate Smith's job.

"Yes, Ruthie, baby", she purred. "On his way out the door." She always said that even if he were in the shower.

"Daddy. I've decided to divorce China. I hope you don't mind."

"Well, it's about time. Never understood why you married

that bum in the first place. The only thing you had in common was religion. What is it the sociologists say? Marry someone whose background is as similar to yours as possible. Well you can't say you weren't warned."

"But you and Mom never said anything when I told you . . ."

"Did you see us smiling and whooping for joy? I actually contemplated not wearing my yamulka during the ceremony hoping that would invalidate the marriage."

"But Daddy, why didn't you say something?"

"You can't tell other people how to live, least of all your own children."

"I'll try to remember that."

"So how much do you figure you'll need. The reception alone cost $25,000, a divorce can be as much or less, what do you say?"

"I'm just calling these lawyers this morning, Dad. I honestly never thought about costs. I was thinking more about get away money."

"You know or ever hear of a lawyer working for nothing? You get what you pay for in this world, kiddo. I'll send you a bank check for fifteen grand. Better yet, I'll have it phoned to Chase right now. Give the lawyer as little as possible. You give those legal eagles too much and they sit on their haunches because they have nothing to produce for, or should that be 'for which to produce'?"

"Thanks Dad; I'll keep you informed."

"If your runaway plans develop a hitch, you can always come back here." He didn't say home.

"No. This is my problem. Under no circumstances would I return home."

Thank God, he thought.

"And I heard what you just thought, Dad!"

"How in hell—oh—I—had something caught in my throat."

"Yeah. Like the truth. See ya."

"'Bye."

She settled on Attorney Jerome Dunbar to represent her in the divorce. One of the first questions he asked was whether she thought the child had been kidnapped by her father. She didn't think so, but if they didn't return by tomorrow evening, she was going to notify the police. She was pleased his retainer was only $2500.00. There would be more than enough getaway do-re-mi. Just as their conference was concluding, she decided to advise him of her plans. Why pay a lawyer if you don't tell him what you intend to do, and then follow his advice?

"I strongly advise you against that. You can fantasize all you want but separate that from reality."

"But there's something drastically wrong . . ."

"What?"

"I don't know what. I just know there is something wrong. Very wrong."

"Listen, Ruth; may I call you that?"

"Yes, please do."

"Since your husband is presently away with the child, I can request an emergency hearing, petitioning that you get custody when the child is located. Because of the circumstances, I can request that you be allowed to leave the state but and it's a big but, you have to agree to return here to New York for any future hearings. That, barring some future revelations about your perceptions concerning the child, is what I can do for you."

My God, she thought. An honest lawyer. And bright. How the hell did that happen? Well, he was young yet. And he was mine!

"That's okay with me. When do we go to Court?"

"Let me call the Register of Probate's office. See if they can squeeze us in this p.m . . . Hello . . . Jer Dunbar here. Listen, here's the scoop . . ."

The judge was furious at China's behavior. Did that augur well for future hearings? Ruth hoped so. They got everything they asked for, including a separate support order and permission to leave the state.

"Thanks, Jerry. That was wonderful."

"Aw, shucks. You know, sometimes the practice of law is a lot easier when you don't have any opposition?"

They both laughed and parted company. She had all the court documents in an envelope in her bag including copies for China.

When Ruth arrived at the apartment it was very quiet. She was glad. She packed, mostly essentials, for Becky and her. She hoped she could get the other things, including furniture, later. She called Mrs. Holton and asked if she could leave the suitcase in her apartment for a short period of time. Mrs. Holton sent her son up to get it. He said it would fit nicely in their reception hall. Ruth promised Mrs. Holton a full explanation at a later date. Next Ruth called the garage three blocks away to have her tank filled and oil checked. She hoped to be by either later tonight or tomorrow to get the car.

They came through the door a little after 5:00 P.M. China looked seedy, almost shabby. Becky appeared to be in a daze, almost ashamed to look at her mother. She was wearing the same clothes she had on two days ago. But they had been washed. And ironed! That means she had her clothes off at some point. She almost screamed but, remembering her plans, thought it wiser to be discreet.

"I wonder if you two are as hungry as I am."

"Well, I am, Ruth. What's cooking?"

"Well if I had known just when you'd be returning, I would have prepared something special."

Too strident Ruth, soften it. How about take out? Perfect. "How about take out?"

"Aw, Ruth. They're so busy at this time, they wouldn't deliver before ten."

"True China, true. Wait a minute, I've got it! If you go in person and order, you'd be back in two shakes of a lamb's tail."

"Time translation?"

"Oh, about 30 minutes. And since I got a bonus and you've

been doing all this baby sitting —I'll pay."

"Great. Can I get a six pack for me and some wine for you?"

"You get whatever your little (and I mean little) heart desires."

"Gee, Ruth. I love it when you're like this."

Enjoy it while you can a—hole.

Before she called the taxi, she left copies of the Court papers on the kitchen counter. China was to make support payments directly to the Probate Family Officer. On top of the papers Ruth placed their framed wedding picture.

After waiting ten minutes, she took Becky by the hand and walked down the stairs to Mrs. Holton's apartment to get the suitcase. They waited inside the foyer. Ruth remembered to drop the check for baby-sitting in Mrs. Holton's mail slot.

The taxi pulled up and double-parked outside. Even though the traffic was heavy, it took only eight minutes to get to the garage. Ruth paid the gas, oil and garage fees. She told the attendant she didn't know when she'd be back so they could rent her space to someone else. No problem with that in New York City. There was always a list of waiters to fill any spaces, which became available. She strapped Becky in the back and eased down the exit. They would stop halfway to Cape Cod for something to eat. Becky talked in her sleep. Ruth wasn't sure but it sounded like 'no ice cream cone, no ice cream cone.'

After crossing the Sagamore Bridge (the Bourne area seemed deserted) she headed for the Hyannis Exit 6. Happy memories came flooding back. All those summers the family spent in Centerville, Osterville, Harwich and Brewster. Her mother preferred the lower Cape of Orleans, Eastham, Wellfleet and Truro. P-town was too, too much. But Daddy said, no, he wanted to remain in civilization. Perhaps a day trip to the hinterlands now and then, but not to stay. They still had a good time.

Ruth eased out of Exit 6 and bore right on Route 132 to Route 28. It seemed odd passing all those closed stores, restaurants, and bars: Parkers, the new Mall, K-Mart, Filene's, Jordan's,

Mitchell's Steak House, Windjammer, Strawberries, T. J. Maxx. She crossed over the railroad tracks and continued on 28 until she reached The Irish Village. Well, he'd never think of looking for a daughter of Hadassah there. Her plan was two or three days here at the most until she found a rental. Off-season should be easier. A short distance away from the Irish Village was a real estate office, which would be the first stop in the daylight.

She had to ring the bell for the manager to respond. He looked agitated until he saw the child and the New York plates.

"Sorry, we weren't expecting anyone this late. Next time, you give me a call. Be much easier."

"I'm the one who should be sorry. I didn't know who to call because I didn't know who might be closed."

"Open all year, Ma'am. We just keep a small block of rooms—20 or so—heated, for rental. Otherwise, all profits would be burned up in heat."

"Oh, I see."

"How long're you plannin' on stayin'?"

"Three nights at the most. I'm looking for a rental."

"This has got to be your lucky day. I have a nice little place at the end of that road over yonder. Not big. Four and a half rooms. But you can see the ocean from the back porch."

"Well, I may not be here for more than three or four months. I'm not sure. And I was looking for a furnished place."

"Look no further. It's furnished and it's heated. I don't aim at makin' you sign no lease. Just gimme a coupla weeks notice afore leavin'"

"This sounds too good to be true. When can we see it?"

"Well, my wife'll want to git down there by mornin' 'n scoot any cobwebs away. How about eleven?"

"That would be wonderful. Now about our room?"

"First story or second?"

"Second, please."

"Okay, room 29. You can just pull your car over here near the stairwell. Then come back here. We got a little kitchen behind the office. You must be starvin, comin' all that way. I'll make some sandwiches and coffee."

"Why thank you, Mr. . . . ?"

"Nickerson's the name, ma'am. Well knowed on the Cape for many years."

"Thank you Mr. Nickerson. See you in a few minutes."

"Don't you be delayin' none. No point in having the bread go stale."

Ruth told Becky, who was still half asleep, that she would be right back. She ran up the stairs with the suitcase and opened the door of 29. It was immaculate. As in most places, the parking area floods would go off at 1:00 A.M.; maybe earlier off-season. In the meantime there were drapes which covered the picture window facing the lot. There were two queen size beds and the room was tastefully decorated. She put the bathroom light on. Just great! It was squeaky clean. If Mrs. Nickerson could do that to the rental cottage, there's no question she would rent. She loved the area. It was convenient to everything. She left the lights on, got Becky and noticed the ringing sound in the car. Those keys again. She removed the keys, locked the car, took Becky by the hand and walked over to the office.

"Cheese'n turkey's all I got. I thought there was more of a selection, but those kids. The ones who work for me, I mean—never did have any of our own—they'd eat you out of house and home. They have three meals here and, and I'm thinkin' eat afore they get here and after they leave. An' two of 'em skinnier'n a pole. Never understood that."

"I believe it's due to the fact that they're growing in two different directions while at the same time chemical and hormonal changes are taking place in their systems."

"That sure is a mouthful. You a doctor or nurse or somethin'?"

"No, just widely read, I guess."

"You sure sound educated to me. Go to college?"

"Well, yes."

"What fer?"

"Just because everybody was doing it. I majored in Eighteenth Century literature and minored, if you can believe it, in interior decorating."

"Hot damn! Don't care nothin' about that eighteenth stuff, but my wife and I, we was thinkin' 'bout doin' somethin' with the cottages. They're eight of them. Be interested?"

"Well, I'll like to see them to see what 's involved. What kind of a challenge the job presented. I don't do any structural changes . . ."

"Don't expect you to ..."

" . . . but I could recommend some basic changes if it would improve the overall look."

"You have any experience with this stuff?"

"Yes. Five years in New York. That's what I did."

"Why'd you leave? Or is that none of my business?"

"Yes."

"Smart gal. I like that."

Becky was dozing in her chair.

Mr. Nickerson leaped up, startling Becky.

"An' now for the resistance piece . . ."

He was standing over Becky, bending over slightly.

" . . . How would you like Nick to get you an ice cream cone?"

Ruth had never heard such a curdling scream from Becky. Then she started to cry.

"No! No! No! No ice cream cone!"

She was sobbing hysterically. Ruth apologized to Mr. Nickerson. Said it must have been the trip. That she was expecting a four year old to be carried along by her momentum.

Thanking Mr. Nickerson, she carried Becky out of the office and up to her room. Before she would let go of her mother, she looked around to see if anyone else was in the room.

"Are the doors and windows locked Mommie?"

"Yes, sweetie. They are."

"Can anyone get in this room?"

"No, I don't think so.

"Will you stay with me, Mommie?"

"Yes, I will."

What had happened to my beautiful daughter, who was so outgoing, who was never afraid of anything? Would it require therapy? And, how much? The child was deeply disturbed about something. She was exhausted. She'd think more about it tomorrow. How she hoped she could find the key. No matter how distressful it was, nothing was worse than not knowing.

Mr. Nickerson scratched his head. First little 'un he'd ever met who didn't like ice cream cones.

Having had another p.m., Ruth slept soundly. She wasn't sure whether the effects were psychological or not. Some people tried the new p.m.s, and swore they didn't sleep a wink. No matter, she had slept well. No dreams she could remember. If Becky had had nightmares she hadn't heard her. She was still sleeping. Ruth was too tired to shower before going to bed. She felt so cruddy after the long drive but you had to have priorities and sleep was the most important thing at that time. Now she enjoyed the shower even more. And to shampoo her hair with the new Paul Mitchell preparation felt luxurious. When she finished she looked at her watch. That can't be right. Eleven. She opened the drapes to double check her watch. Was it time for glasses? The beautiful sunshine confirmed the first observation.

She wanted to run to the office for a recommendation for brunch but after last night's outburst and her promise to Becky, she didn't dare. Then she noticed a wall phone near the front door, obviously for use within the compound. She lifted the receiver and within seconds, Nicky (as she was to begin calling him later) was on the phone.

"Yup, Mrs. Gold. How can I help ya?"

"Becky is still sleeping, but I was wondering if you could recommend a place for brunch."

"Sure can. Joseph's is just up the street. Could walk it in about seven minutes. Beautiful day. Been out yet?"

"No. I didn't awaken until just before eleven. I can't remember when I've slept that late in years."

"Must've needed it. Oh by the way, Gris, Griselda that is, or to be modern, my woman, is down at the cottage now. Got a late start. Could you wait till three?"

"Absolutely. I don't feel like rushing with anything today. Especially, after the circumstances under which we left New York. No, don't even think of asking. Maybe when I know you better. Not now."

"Furthest thing from my mind. MYOB is a philosophy everybody should adopt. By the way, even if you don't take the cottage or the job or both, you won't be charged for an extra day here. Check out time is normally eleven o'clock. Ain't no line of people waitin' to git in here, so if you decide to leave . . ."

"You're so sure I'm taking the cottage, aren't you? You little devil! Oh, could you get me a number in New York and another in Danbury, Connecticut? I'll give you my telephone charge number."

"Easy as pie; any preference as to which is first?"

"Yes. I think I'll speak to my law—ah, the New York number, please. And could I give your number for any messages to be left for me until I get my own number?"

"Cottage phone is still on. And also, I can ring you there from here. So. . . ."

Another 'so' left hanging. Perhaps she shouldn't be so judgmental and have the confidence he had. Only difference was he had seen the place. Many times. She hadn't. Not even once.

"Okay. I'll give your number. But don't think I'm taking the cottage because you think it's wunderbar."

"Is that French or German? I knowed I shoulda stayed at school whenever I talk to someone like you. Talk 'bout confidence."

"It's German and it means wonderful and there was a song by that title from a Broadway show with, I think my father said, Patricia Morrison and Alfred Drake. In fact, I think it may have been my grandfather who told me. And I also think you're pulling my leg."

"'Tain't possible. Must be someone else. Besides, got short arms."

Becky was awake. A good reason to end this insanity.

"Becky's awake. Have to go. Please call when you get through on those calls. And thanks."

She finished her calls and while bathing Becky, noticed a series of bruises on her body and especially in her crotch area. She decided not to say anything right then. They walked up to Joseph's, had a delicious brunch which was very reasonable and walked back to the I.V. It was a little after one-thirty. No need to visit the realtor down the road. Not yet, anyway. She decided to walk beyond the I.V. to see what the little shops were offering. Not horrors, she hoped. She had enough of those for a while.

She came back loaded down with good buys. The merchants were glad to see someone like she coming. They were trying to clear out as much as possible to avoid storage. There were drastic reductions, more than fifty percent off, in many places. And the items were all first quality. She had practically completed all her Christmas shopping except for China and Becky. The former would receive nothing and Becky, she liked to save two days, just for her. Although her family was Jewish, they had always celebrated Christmas. Even had a stable. After all, her father used to say (probably still did. Bad habits are hard to break), "The Holy Family are relatives of ours." China didn't see any humor in that. In anything, for that matter. As far as she knew.

She charged everything on an American Express Gold Card. His. China's Gold.

Just at three, Nicky drove them to the cottage. Mrs. Nickerson, Gris, was coming out the front door with an array of cleaning implements: brooms, mops, pail, rags sticking out of a plastic bag and a box containing all types of cleaning agents.

Nicky introduced Ruth and Becky to his Gris. Up close, she was a striking woman with beautiful skin and a very pleasant manner. After she knew her a while (was Nicky's certainty contagious?), she would recommend a different hairstyle and some make up tricks. It would make her almost breathtakingly beautiful. Ruth thought: it just wasn't homes and apartments she made over. Whenever she met someone she had out her mental check list called 'Anything You Can Do I Can Do Better'. Thank heaven she didn't have to compete with Ethel Merman's rendition of the list or song. Ear shattering.

After a brief visit, they entered the cottage. It was immaculate. There was a cathedral ceiling in the living room which had a fireplace. On the other side of the fireplace was another fireplace in the next room, which could be a family room or another bedroom. There was a fire in each fireplace. The bedroom was not large and had twin beds and adequate closet space. There was not a speck of dust anyplace. Ruth was pleased. The kitchen was the big surprise. Every inch of wall was covered with beautiful birch cabinets. A nineteen cubic foot refrigerator, frost free with ice water and icemaker was between two of the cabinets and had shelves over it for cereal and cracker storage. There was an ambassador General Electric stove with oven below and above. In a corner of one counter was a microwave with turntable. There was a small narrow closet with brooms, brushes and a trash receptacle. A double aluminum sink stood between the dishwasher and another cabinet. There were two cabinets above the sink. To the left of the sink was an enormous picture window that showed the back porch and fifty yards beyond, the Atlantic Ocean. Ruth rushed out the back door onto the porch, drinking in the beautiful surroundings and smelling the fresh, salt air. She was so pleased and happy she didn't know whether to laugh or cry. She went back inside.

"Guess what?"

"You'll take it."

"Is that a question?"

"No. It's a declaration."

"How'd you know that?"

"I said I was uneducated. Not stupid."

"Oh. Oh, where's the bathroom?"

"Outside."

"Nicky, you stop—Right this way." There was a small hallway off the kitchen which led to the bedroom. Ruth couldn't imagine the size of the bathroom. It must be tiny.

When Gris opened the door and switched on the light and fan, Ruth was flabbergasted.

"Corridor used to be much wider. We also took six or seven inches from each room so it wouldn't be noticeable. And va vavoom. A good size bathroom."

It was like something out of house beautiful. Ruth approved of everything in it, which was rare.

"Who did the designing, Mrs. Nickerson?"

"Look. Or, listen, I suppose. Call me Gris. Everybody does. One of them fancy interior decs did. Cost a pretty penny, too. But you get what you pay for. This here shithouse will be standin' when the house is gone. Nicky says you be one of those people. We got some dough ahead and want to do over eight cottages during the off-season, so we can get more money in rentals. I figure one or two summer rentals and we've recovered our dough and paid our taxes and utilities. Sounds like a good investment to me. Whatta ya say?"

"Well, I'm interested, but I would like to see the other seven before I give you an answer. If they're anything like this, there's no problem. "

" They're not. This is the best of the lot. The others are not insulated or winterized but they be sound structurally and are real pretty, in a rustic way."

"How rustic?"

"Well we could be chewing the rag forever and gainin' nothin'. Why don't we let you get settled and in a week's time we go take a look see. Okee dokee?"

"Okay. If I go back to stay in that motel room, I won't be able to sleep. Could Becky and I move in now?"

"Sure thing. I made light suppers for you which can be eaten now or later this week. They're in the fridge. Two minutes in the microwave should do it. I left some coffee and tea bags, rolls, cream and milk. Cereal—I hope Becky likes raisin bran—is on top of the fridge. Bottle of wine for you in the fridge plus a couple cans of beer. Don't know if you drink it or not."

"You're so kind and perceptive. How did you know I'd take it? The cottage."

"Damn fool if you didn't. Don't look like a damn fool to me. A lady. Real lady. They's always knows what's good for 'em. Besides, I know you'll be a real help to us. And everybody benefits."

"Everything's happened so fast. Yesterday I didn't know where I was going. And today it doesn't make any difference."

"Yer learnin' gal. Sometimes you just have to stand still and let life happen to you. You just stay put, now. Relax. Open that wine. Nick and I'll bring your car and things down. Least we can do."

"You do one more thing for me and my heart will burst."

"Oh, pshaw. Where're the car keys?"

"Oh, in my bag. Here."

They were back in less than twenty minutes. It was already dark. Nick carried in the luggage and decorating paraphernalia, that Ruth always kept in the trunk of her car. Gris was carrying a small roasting pan, covered, with the handles of a shopping bag over her left wrist. She set the pan on top of the stove and removed the cover. In it was a Perdue oven stuffer, stuffed. She moved the chicken onto a platter, opened a can of Kelly's Irish Potatoes and a jar of Aunt Nellie's Onions and a jar of Del Monte small carrots. She set the bake dial for 300 degrees, filled the baking pan with the contents just opened and set the pan in the oven. Then she opened a can of cranberry sauce, sliced it, placed it in a bowl and refrigerated it.

"I can't take anymore of your Christian charity. I have to tell you, I'm a Jew."

"You be a Jew? Nick collect everythin' up and put it in the

vehicle. We made a big mistake!"

They all started to laugh then, just like old friends.

"Gris, with all you did today, when did you find time to roast a chicken?"

"Made the stuffing last night, stuffed the chick afore I came here, that's why I got a late start, and used that new fangled timer to start and stop the bakin'. The rest is canned goods, as you plainly saw. That other stuff in the fridge will keep for a week. You can have it anytime. Didn't know if the chicken would be cooked."

"Will you join us for dinner? Please?"

"Nope, Nick and I have a whole raft of carrot and celery sticks that need eatin'"

"I thought we'uz having spaghetti and meat b—"

"Shh. Now just shush up. Don't you know nuthin' 'bout bein' a martyr?"

"Well," They were out the door.

Ruth found a candlestick holder on the kitchen counter. In one of the drawers, she found a variety of colored candles. She chose a blue one which seemed to resemble peace, and placed it in the holder. She found a white tablecloth in one of the storage drawers that had four napkins on top of it. She set the table carefully placing an artificial daisy in a bud vase. Their first meal in their new home. It had to be special. For Becky's sake. For her sake.

The meal would be perfect if they had just a little gravy. When she was spooning the vegetables out of the roasting pan, there it was. Gris had made gravy and left it on the bottom of the pan to season it even more. How is it you can know someone all your life and not know them at all? And how is it you can meet someone a day or two ago and know them very well? There are givers and takers in this world and for every giver it seemed there were three takers. Nick and Gris must have been giving all their lives to become so good at it. They made others happy. No, not happy. Content. She was so content now; she felt she could spend the rest of her life here. Here. On Cape Cod. If anyone had mentioned that to her five days ago, she would have thought they had gone over the edge. We remain basically the same but our lives change so drastically. How is this possible? She cleared the dishes into the dishwasher, after rinsing them. She would use the miser wash. A little Yankee ingenuity. Well if Jews could be Yankees, she was sure she would qualify. After all, Gris said—or was it Nick—that she was a real lady.

She made sure the doors were locked. Then she tiptoed into the bedroom and quietly removed a nightgown from the suitcase. Becky slept peacefully in the next bed. This contentment must be contagious. She quickly said her prayers, thanking God for their safety. She was asleep before her head hit the pillow. Little did she know that her newly established contented life would fall apart tomorrow.

She awoke at 7:00 A.M. with glorious shafts of sun streaming through the bedroom windows. Becky wasn't in her bed. Probably in the bathroom. She fished a robe out of her luggage, put it on and went to the kitchen to plug in the coffee maker. As she stood at the picture window, looking at the sun playing its lights on the beautiful Atlantic, she noticed something moving to her right. It was Becky swaying to and fro. She walked out to the porch.

"I see you have your jacket on, but it's a little too cool for a nightdress this time of year on Cape Cod."

"Oh, Mommy. It's so beautiful here. I hope we can always stay here. Can we? I was doing a dance to the sun god, like the Indians did in that movie."

"We can want certain things—or think we do— but our lives change from time to time so it's not possible to say you can stay in one place forever. You have to keep adjusting your dreams."

"I think I know what you mean, Mommy. You can't always have what you want. Or what you think you want."

"Something tells me you'll be a great lawyer when you grow up. Now, how about some breakfast?"

"Yay. How about some french toast?"

"I'll see if we have the ingredients. We have a lot of shopping to do today."

She also had to pick up thank you gifts for Gris and Nicky. What a wonderful couple.

Where does the time go? Later, after two hundred dollars worth of food purchased at the Stop and Shop, gifts for the Nickersons (who would never be mistaken for the Bickersons), returning to the cottage after a quick lunch at MacDonald's, putting the food away, thinking about dinner, putting all the clothes away, carrying the luggage up the pull down stairs for storage, she was exhausted. She knew the more time consuming chores she got done, the easier each day would be. She might even be able to relax. Gris had given her a T.V. booklet put out by the local Cape Station, earlier. She glanced through it and was surprised at the variety of programming for a small station. She really got excited about something that was scheduled for 5:00 P.M. It was on interior decorating with a panel of experts about whom she had only read. Another gift from Gris, she thought. She started a spaghetti sauce (Becky's favorite was spaghetti) and mixed the hamburg for meatballs. She also wanted to try these new turkey sausages. Eighty percent fat free and supposedly very tasty. Also very large. She'd have to remember to cut up Becky's after it was on the plate. Otherwise, the sausage would get too cool. Then she remembered Gris had said the set was old, so it was best to warm up the set if you wanted a good picture.

She left Becky playing with Ken and Barbie dolls (were they too old for her?) on the living room floor in front of a nice warm fire. She hadn't had time to make a regular fire so she lighted a burner log which was pretty and gave the appearance of warmth. That Stop & Shop had everything.

4:40 P.M. and everything was in the pot. She planned on eating around 6:30. She was going to make her own garlic bread but bought a loaf already made up. Much easier. It's in foil, just

EN

follow directions. She was catching words here and there from the T.V. Child. Abuse. Physical. Sexual.

"Becky, it's warmer here in the kitchen. Why don't you bring Ken and Barbie and their friends out to the kitchen table. I'll make you a small cup of cocoa."

Just then, Becky screamed. She continued screaming. "Nick-Nick. Take away. Take him away. No ice cream cone. No! No! No! No! No!"

Ruth picked her up in her arms turned her head from the T.V. screen. Now the child was crying softly. Ruth noticed a Dr. Nicholai Nicholas. The announcer was saying he was head of 'New Beginnings' a facility outside of New York City which specialized in treating children who were victims of sexual abuse. It also accepted unpaid volunteers to work there and who could bring their own children to observe the wonderful work that was being done at the clinic. Arrangements could even be made for overnight accommodations for volunteers and their children, out of gratitude for their unselfish assistance.

So that was where China worked. She was sure of it. Now to find out what happened. She shut off the T.V. She could watch her show another time. The station had frequent repeats. Becky was her priority.

In the kitchen as she poured the cocoa, she saw how rigid Becky was. It might be like pulling teeth, but this child had to reveal what happened. She might never fully recover, but she had to make it through today and tomorrow.

"Becky. You know that Mommy loves you and will always love you no matter what has happened or will happen."

She nodded.

"And I can tell something awful has happened to you. When these things happen, children believe it's their fault. But it's not. Children may become innocent victims. But they are still innocent."

"Do you want to show me, with your doll, Ken, what Nick-Nick did to you?"

She nodded again, picked up the doll, stood him on the table and took down his pants. She licked the area where his penis would have been. Ruth was in a state of controlled rage.

"How many times did it happen?"

"A lot."

"Did anyone else ever do this to you?"

"Yes. Daddy."

"How many times?"

"More than Nick-Nick."

"What did he say?"

"That he wanted me to lick his ice-cream cone."

"And what happened?"

"Sometimes something came out but it wasn't ice-cream"

"Did Daddy say anything?"

"Yes. He said he should have put it in the freezer."

And I would have gladly slammed the door shut on it.

"Oh, and he told me it was our secret. Not to tell anyone. Especially you."

Somehow they got through dinner. But not without incident. When Ruth put the turkey sausage on her plate, Becky started screaming. Ruth quietly removed it and her own as well. For the rest of her life she will be scarred. It's a good thing I don't have a gun. Or a long range A.B.M.

After she said prayers with Becky and told her she loved her and always would. She returned to the kitchen, leaving the hall light on. Poor, poor child. She had thought about therapy before, now there was no question about it. The sooner the better.

It was her fifth glass of wine. She didn't care at that point if it were her fifty-fifth. She kept going back in her mind over her life with China. Since Becky was born. He'd be baby sitting and she'd go out on a job. When she returned, the first thing she'd check would be Becky. How many times had it happened? Her diapers would be on differently. Had he changed her? No, no, never he said. She noticed red marks in the vaginal area. Had he changed her, or noticed anything? No, nothing. She never cried or woke up, he said. Hindsight is always 20/20.

Why hadn't she gone to see a sexual abuse expert? Many times they could tell, even in infants. Why hadn't she gone? Do you suspect your husband, the child's father, someone that close? Well now she was learning fast. It's almost always someone close, a person of trust, someone who has the child's confidence. The younger the child the more the secret was kept. The more exalted the position of trust, the less chance of effective revelation, especially when the child feels he or she is responsible. That they, the children, made it happen.

Tomorrow she would call the Department of Social Services. Then her attorney. Last and, most difficult, her father.

She went to take another glass of wine but the bottle was empty. She heated some warm milk instead. The roller coaster of emotions. Nothing could have been happier than yesterday. Nothing could be sadder than today. Like the old Frank Sinatra song, 'That's Life'.

"Apartment of Social Services. May I help you?"

"Yes. I want to report a case of sexual abuse."

"A moment, please. I'll give you the Intake Unit."

Ruth recited the facts regarding Becky.

"Well, it is not an emergency . . ."

"It's not? I think it is."

"What I meant was the perpetrator presents no immediate threat of harm to the child. The child is in a protective situation with you, her mother. We'll respond in ten days. May I have your telephone number and address, please. And by the way, I don't know if there'll be any court action taken because of where the alleged crimes took place."

Ruth gave her the address and telephone number.

"What do you mean 'because of where the alleged crimes took place'?"

"Well, I don't know whether we have jurisdiction in Massachusetts when the actions took place in New York. I'll check with our attorney, Mr. Goode, and let you know."

At least it was a 'good' attorney, thought Ruth. Perhaps Ruth could call her lawyer and have the two of them connect.

"At any rate, Mrs. Gold, we'll be able to offer you any services that are available to help the child through this difficult period."

"Thank you. I expect to be hearing from you in the next ten days."

Laverna Andrews hung up. Another beaut for Don. He'll be thrilled that I thought to mention his name to Mrs. Gold. She wondered if her in-laws were referred to as Old Golds. Naw. Probably didn't even smoke.

Don Juan in Heaven

James Blender was an excellent social worker. He was also prolific in affairs of the heart. He knew, in the biblical sense, nearly every woman in the office. Everyone he wanted to know. Those remaining were too old (never too young) or grossly unattractive. But even they were willing. The female populace referred to him (behind his back) as 'la machine'. He could go all night without, somehow, demonstrating any warmth. Never a kiss or a hug. It was as though he had stepped back and watched the acts take place.

"Now that's detachment" cited Olive Newton.

"You never worry that he's going to ask you to marry him," said Rita from Family Resource.

"Marry him? You don't have to worry that he'll ask you out to lunch."

"That's right, Elvira. And dinner? Forget about it. I'd settle for a cup of coffee even though he'd forget his money and I'd end up paying. Again." It was Sally from Ongoing.

They were in hysterics until the door to the kitchen opened and there stood James Blender as big as life. And almost as big as his—No, no, Sally. Musn't think such things. At least not on the State's time.

"James! Why we were just talking about you."

"It must have been pretty funny Olive. I could hear you out front by Placenta's desk."

"Is she still saying "Apartment of Social Services'? You just wait. As Don says we'll have a homeless unit before long."

"Well, Elvira. She said it three times while I was standing there."

They all laughed.

"Say, I have a new, heavy date this Saturday night. Have any of you got any free passes for movies this weekend?"

They all laughed again.

A Valentina for the Judge

"Judge Holden, this is Keeshu Walker, DSS's new Area Program Manager, and thank you for seeing us."

"How do you do Mr. Walker." They shook hands.

"In how many offices of DSS have you worked to earn such an exalted position?"

"None. The Regional office let us recruit someone from the community," said Noel.

"Oh, I always believed that one had to have a great deal of experience in social services to get a position in management."

"Ordinarily, that's true. But Manny Gomes and I convinced upper management that this would not only work but would cement relations with the community."

Should I pull that old joke of Don Goode's? About the woman comrade in Russia falling into the cement which was being used to erect a memorial in honor of Stalin and shouting 'Solidarity forever'? The judge thought better of it. Besides, these two seemed devoid of humor.

"I was surprised you wanted to come on a Monday. Don Goode, your attorney, is here on Wednesdays, as I am sure you're aware. He could have sat in on the meeting. A very valuable lawyer to DSS. Always does a top notch job."

"Wednesdays, you say. Hmmm. No other days?"

"Mr. Peel of course there are other days. Emergency cases. Other C&Ps can wait for his regular day. Emergency medical needs can be brought any day by motion."

"Keeshu has a medical emergency."

"What's wrong with you, Mr. Walker?"

"Oh, no. I didn't mean that, your Honor. One of his cases. Prudence Valentina's on an anti psychotic medication. Keeshu thinks it should be reviewed."

"Oh, really? Well those things are normally brought to our attention by counsel for one of the parties. In the Valentina case, I believe there are three lawyers. Since you are requesting a medical review, you will not receive any notice. Let me ring the Probation Chief. —Oh, Jack, always nice to hear your voice. Could you run down your assistant who has the Valentina case? Have him send notices to the attorneys for a medical review only, to be held on —just a moment—When gentlemen? (Noel motioned two days. The judge lip synced 'never') two weeks from Wednesday gentlemen? Yes, Jack, for the seventeenth at 10:00 A.M. at the request of DSS. A pleasure doing business with you, Jack. Thank you. Gentlemen, I hate to cut this short but I have some decisions to make in some other cases. Thank you." They shook hands.

On the way back to the office, Noel insisted on stopping by the Yardarm for a few Heinekens.

"You gonna tell Don about the date on the case?"

"Now Keesh. You heard the judge's instructions to notify the lawyers. We don't want to be stepping on anyone's toes by doing their job, do we?"

"But, he's our lawyer. I know I'm new but it seems to me just common sense to tell our own lawyer."

"You just stick with me and do things the way I do." The Heineken was having its usual effect. Deadening the brain cells.

On the seventeenth, Don had four cases in Orleans District Court. Or thought he had. Three lawyers approached him wanting to know what the medical review on the Valentina case was all about. It took him fifteen minutes to convince them he knew nothing about it. The probation officer approached.

"Hi Reggie. What's the story on Valentina?"

"Don't know, Don. Your Area Director and that new guy—you know the one from King Solomon's mines—met with the Judge a little over two weeks ago. I don't know what was said or what transpired but I nearly got my ass chewed out by the Chief for not being on top of my cases. Not knowing there was a medical need that should be reviewed. I feel sorrier for you than I felt for myself. I can see you're in a quandary and it's difficult for you to hide your feelings."

"Thanks, Reg. I'm going to call the office."

"Is Noel or Keeshu there?"

"No, Don. It's Placenta. Would you like to speak to Manny or is it in venereal to you?"

Invenereal? This dame ought to start her own dictionary.

Yeah, get me the little grease ball.

"Yeah, get me the little—man."

"Manny Gomes here."

Shit. He knows who he is.

"Manny, this is Don. I'm facing a very serious problem here at Orleans Court."

"Well, call your supervisor at Regional. I don't solve legal problems."

"It was caused by management, as most problems are. Do you know anything—about a medical review on the Valentina case being requested by Keeshu and Noel on a visit to Judge Holden a few weeks ago?"

"Yeah. Yeah. I know something about that case."

"Is it a state secret?"

'No. No. Keesh and Noel are at an in-service training for management."

It won't make any difference. They should have put a 'mis' in front of the last word.

"Is the telephone number a state secret?"

"No, and you are a pain in a horse's neck."

And you're the other end.

"If it's not too much trouble would you have one or the other call me, here, as soon as possible. Preferably, before Court is over. Thank you."

Well, well. In the midst of all this furor, coming down the corridor was Aubrey James with her loping gait. A gait that should be reserved for something pleasurable, not for going to Court.

"Hello, Don."

"Hi, Aub. I wasn't aware you had a case today. If you do it's not on my list."

"I'm replacing James Blender on the Valentina case."

"Light shines on yon marble head. Then you must know what the medical review is all about?"

"Nope. Read my Court letter. But don't blame me."

"I used to sing that song."

"'Nope' or 'read my court letter'? Oh, oh, What a dunce, 'Don't Blame Me'."

The letter was brief. She had been assigned the case that morning, had never met the clients and was requesting a continuance in order to familiarize herself with the case. The matter was continued. Neither Noel nor Keeshu called. He saw Manny in mid-afternoon at the office but no mention was made of anything. These cases were difficult enough to review and try. It was impossible when you were being torpedoed by your own side. Two days went by with no word from Noel or Keeshu. Well, they asked for it. At first, he put the memo in his head in sections. For laughs. Then it got rather serious. Then he put it on paper. Perfected it. His last instructions to the head secretary on Friday was to cc it to office supervisors and the Regional Director. Even though it was to be so stated, Don's instructions were not to send it to the Regional Director, Mary Quincy.

Going for the Jugular

To: Noel Coward Peel

From: Don Goode

Re: Debacle on Rock Harbor Road, Orleans District Court

My name is Don Goode. I am a lawyer. I have been assigned by the Commissioner of Social Services to the Cape and Islands Area Office. My function is to provide legal services in all related matters pertaining to this area's Department business.

I had hopes that after three years, a vague smattering of what I do here might have penetrated, even by osmosis, your intellect so that you might begin to even understand what I am about.

Two weeks ago Monday last, you paid a visit to Judge Holden at Orleans District Court. Thinking it was a courtesy call to introduce a new member of our staff, he invited you into his lobby. When the meeting devolved into a case conference on the Valentina Care and Protection matter, the Judge called the Chief Probation Officer, Jack Smithers. You indicated that the case be called forward in two days. When the Judge declined, it was set for two weeks from the following Wednesday. I believe you termed it a 'medical emergency'.

A Judge is forbidden by the Canon of Ethics to discuss any matter pending before him/her unless all parties are present. The child and parent in this case are represented by two different attorneys. The parties have distinct rights which are to be protected at all costs and not violated by the intrusiveness of others.

After you left the Courthouse, Probation Officer Reggie Case, who services this case for the Court was severely criticized by Mr. Smithers for not knowing about this 'situation' and for not being 'on top' of this cases. He had never been called by anyone. He is very angry at you. When I appeared in Court this past Wednesday I was besieged by Messrs. Case, Arnstein and Haggerty (the latter two attorneys having been ordered by the Court to appear because the Department had advanced the case because of an 'emergency'). I, your own attorney, had never been notified. I had never been consulted for legal input nor had the case ever been conferenced with me. I knew nothing and conveyed as much. In a controlled panic, I called the office. Neither you nor the new APM was available. In conference, I was told. No telephone number. I left instructions to be called asap. To this day I have not heard a word from anyone in management.

When Aubrey James, social worker newly assigned to the case, appeared with a letter requesting a continuance as she had never met with the family and knew as little as I did about any emergency, the effect upon all of us was one of being dumbstruck (you must have a little behind on your visit). Except, of course, the Valentina family. They were never notified. We are all very angry at you (the child, Prudence, has continued in the legal custody of the Department and could have been removed at anytime without prior Court action, if at risk).

I strongly advise you to confine yourself to the area office, and do your misdirecting there. True, that would continue to embarrass, frustrate, anger and depress the staff, but, at least, the contagion of your bumbling and ineffectiveness won't spread to other outside areas where some of us have succeeded in building good relationships and a good image for the Department over a number of years.

This is not the first time that your misguided mismanagement has interfered with my function, causing great embarrassment for both the Department and me. But I'll tell you this: It had better be the last or my next stop is 150 Causeway Street.

DG: tb cc: Mary Quincy, Regional Director

Supervisory Staff

The purpose of the memo was to scare the daylights out of Noel. To bring him to his senses. To get him to think before he acted. His errors were becoming more and more severe. One of the most efficient supervisors the office ever had, Carol Allbright (even her name indicated her ability) went to lunch with Noel the day she was leaving DSS's employment.

"Noel, if you don't begin to support the workers in this office you're going to have to import a therapist to come in and give therapy to the workers so they'll be able to go out in the field and give therapy to the clients. Am I getting through to you?"

"Sure. Oh, Miss, I'll have another Heineken."

That Friday Don waited for Noel's call. He was at Edgartown District Court that afternoon. No call. Finally, he called the office. Any reaction? None. When he went into the office on Monday, he found a memo from Noel handwritten on the second page of his memo to Noel.

Don-

Would you please discuss any issues you have with me before you write angry, inaccurate memos and send them out to staff and management?

If you had taken the time to do so you would have saved yourself some embarrassment and gotten to the facts of the situation.

I have kicked the matter upstairs to Regional, but I will be glad to discuss the matter rationally with you at any time. However, at this point I think we should include your supervisor, Mary Quincy and Keeshu Walker.

Noel C. Peel cc: Supervisor and Mary Quincy

P.S. Don you would make better use of your time if you concentrated on building bridges in this office instead of walls.

The stupid bastard! He sent the memo to the Regional Director. Another nail in his coffin. Talk about being self-destructive. He must hate either his life or himself. One could better understand the latter.

Thereafter, the many questions that arose as the result of Noel's actions in the Valentina case remained unanswered. All that resulted was a veiled cross accusation. Like Charlie Carew, Noel was not responsible for anything, and, therefore, was free from any wrongdoing or guilt.

The Eyes of Karen Black

The weather had been almost sixty-two degrees for days, and here was one of those crazy snowstorms! It had been forecast for three days, but no one wanted to believe it was actually coming. Maybe the forecasters were wrong. They had been before.

By eight o'clock in the morning, eight inches had been dumped on ol' Cape Cod. Don started humming the Patti Page hit of a hundred years ago . . . 'If you're fond of sand dunes and salty air . . . '

"Don, it's not all that bad. You keep telling others to think in terms of alternatives. Why don't you?"

"Yeah, like what? It could've been rain."

"No. You might get a day off. I have the radio dial set for the cancellations on QRC."

"That's a laugh. The state would expect you to rent a dog sled. Hmm, come to think of it, I haven't seen any husky dogs on the Cape since we moved here."

"Ouch. That is bad. Wait! Wait a minute. Governor Michael Dukewell has ordered all the state offices closed. Apparently it was warmer earlier but now sheets of ice have formed under the snow."

"No sheet. Oops! Yes, sheet. How about some pancakes and turkey sausages and freshly brewed coffee, Merrilee?"

"Coming right up, my lord and master."

"Daddy, build a snowman! Daddy, build a snowman!"

"Yes, Genie. Two snowmen. One for you and one for Avé even though she won't be able to go outside. Maybe she can see it through the window. What do you say?"

"Say yes, yes, yes, yes!"

"This is delicious, Mer. Why can't we have it more often?"

"Because you don't want to take the time. I don't know what you do about lunch but dinner is the only meal I see you actually relax. Perhaps having a few dry bourbon manhattans help. I don't know. What do you think, Don?"

"A few dry bourbs would relax an elephant. But getting back to today. It's like being on Death Row and getting a reprieve. Just think, those cases in Barnstable will go over to next week. Yipes! The only men I have to contend with today are made of snow. If they give me any shit, I'll turn the hose on them."

"Don Goode! Please, the children. Isn't it Freud who said everything we see, hear and experience is stored in the mind. It was Freud, wasn't it?"

"Oh, Mer. Who gives a sh—"

"Don, I'm going to call your mother."

"Ooooooo. Lady going to tell mama."

"Keep it up and you'll have a lot of regrets at the children's nap time."

"You mean—"

"Never mind what I mean. . . ."

"Come on Genie. You and Da will get our snow clothes on."

Let's see. It's not quite nine. Nap time around one-thirty. Sure. He could make five snowmen in that time. With the proper motivation, of course. Was he having early Alzheimers? What was the motivation? He began to get that honeymoon look on his face. Very soon they would be closer than Karen Black's eyes.

EN

My Heart Belongs to Daddy

"Nora, you don't expect to be going out in this storm, do you?"

"No, Harve. I always put on high boots, hat, muffler and the rabbit coat my parents gave me, so I can stand by the front door."

"Your attempt at humor has just failed me. The Governor has closed all the state offices. Even my boss, Catholic Charities, has closed our office."

"Listen, I have a client, a battered woman that I've brought a long way. I told her I'd meet her at Dunkin Donuts in Tall Ass—ten minutes away. She's the type who shows up and finds I'm not there—she's rejected again. It might just be enough for her to slip over the edge again. Besides, she has no phone."

"Are you sure she'll be there?"

"No. But that doesn't make any difference. It's my not being there that's important."

What the hell did she just say? Well, he was learning. If a woman meant what she didn't say, she really meant it.

"Will you promise to call if anything goes wrong?"

"I can't. You didn't give me that cellular phone I wanted for

Christmas. But if there's a phone nearby, I'll call."

"Noreen, if she isn't there, are you coming right back?"

"No, Harvey. I'm going to the office to get some records to work on. I'm not going to fall behind like I did before."

"Supposing the office is closed."

"Believe or no, they actually trusted me with a key."

"What the heck is tall ass?"

"One of Don Goode's bad jokes. High Anus."

"Oh."

"Would you like me to go with you?"

"I wouldn't like."

"Do you have your mittens?"

"No. I have those nice mink lined leather gloves my parents gave me last Christmas. You know those ones I've always wanted, that I dropped a million hints about?"

He was going to have to pay more attention. Instead,

"Well, I wouldn't want to frustrate your parents. And what would you do with another pair of leather gloves?"

"Grow another pair of hands?"

"Enough. Enough. I can't distinguish between when you're serious and when you're serious."

She couldn't hurt him. Even for his own good. And hers. He was implacable. She knew he loved her deeply. Like a father husband. She already had a father. It was always like 'Don't step in puddles.' ' Don't talk to strangers!' Who were stranger than the clients of DSS? 'Don't fart in Church.' 'Chew your food sixty-six times.' 'Always excuse yourself when you belch!' And on and on.

"'Bye."

"I'll be waiting for your call."

How many decades older will you be when you get it?

The client wasn't there. One of the counter girls knew Noreen. She should. Noreen and her upper Cape clients were her best customers.

"Have you seen Madame X today?"

"I could say as opposed to Y and Z? But I don't have to.

None of your clies been in today. Listen, Nor, supervisor didn't make it in. Very few customers. Ton of coffee. Please, have some. On us. You deserve it."

"All right, I will." Don would've said 'shall', except to express determination or definiteness. Then it's 'will' for first person or 'shall' for second and third. She wondered if he knew just how much he had affected the office in so many ways.

"Now, fresh blueberry muffins made this A.M."

"You're too kind."

"Sometimes. It depends on who the other person is. I can be a real bitch. Believe me."

"I believe you."

"Wait a sec. You don't have to agree so quickly."

"Just kidding. You react the way that's best for you as long as it's true and you don't hurt someone. Well, badly. You know what I mean. It's all in the intent. If you don't intend to hurt, you seldom will. Have I lost you somewhere?"

"Do I look lost? I didn't participate because I love to hear you talk. You'd be surprised how much I've learned when I've overheard you with your clients. It's helped me a great deal in my own life."

"As long as you don't repeat or expose the clients."

"That's a crime, ain't it?"

"Oh you! I'm getting out of here before they throw a net over me. Or you. 'Bye."

"Bye, Nor. Thanks."

As she drove to the office, she thought there were so many people begging for help out there. Wanting to resolve problems, so that their lives would be better, happier. They just needed someone to show them the way. It was a simple case of mathematics. There weren't enough helpers. Too many helpees.

As she pulled into the parking lot of the office, she saw only one other car. It was Noel's. He avoided work as much as possible and now that he could be justly excused, he was here. Alone. He was alone everywhere.

"Thank God you're here Noreen. It's just the two of us to man the office, to steer the Ship of State through life."

I'm a woman.

"Noel, I went to meet a client. She has no phone so I couldn't check her availability for this morning. I just stopped by only to get some records I've been working on, so I won't fall behind."

"Noreen, I want you to man the switchboard. I'll be in my office. I only want to be disturbed for the most urgent telephone calls. Do you understand?"

"Noel, the Governor ordered all state offices closed because of the storm."

"Listen. He can order the State House closed if he wants to. This is my office and I'll decide whether it's closed or open. Now, are you going to take over the switchboard or not?"

She had a plan.

"Well, let me put these records in my car for later. And oh, I just remembered I have some goodies left over from the meeting two nights ago. Perhaps you can help carry them in?"

"Oh, sure."

When she saw his eyes light on the ten bottles of Heineken left in the case, she knew she was home, safe. In about fifteen minutes.

"I'll leave this beer in my office for safe keeping. You can put the rest of the goodies in the kitchen."

She did and left. Without saying good-bye. If there was any flak later, she'd say he must have her mixed up with someone else. He couldn't remember anyway. The memory cells are the first to go.

On the way home she stopped and bought Harvey a gift. A frilly apron. Miss Dunkin Donuts thinks she can be a bitch?

When the Moon Hits Your Eye

What a break. It was Wednesday. That meant Orleans District Court. Ten minutes from Don's house. Some heavy competition today. Mother had spent twenty-eight days in de-tox and had been alcohol free for two months. Mother's attorney, Mike Rock, was demanding return of the child as of today. Social worker Debbie Payne had some reservations. She said twenty years of heavy drinking isn't resolved in three months. The child, a sweet fifteen, was Edna LaMer. She had been diagnosed at birth as fetal alcohol syndrome. Fortunately her limbs eventually grew to be the same length but she suffered from an attention deficit and deep fears of her mother's drinking bouts. Like almost all the other children in DSS care, she loved her mother and that feeling was returned. She was beginning to accept that it was a disease over which her mother had little or no control. Like cancer.

Debbie Payne said that within the last two weeks in two separate late night calls, the mother's speech was slurred and rambled on and on. She didn't understand questions Debbie put to her and would answer in a totally different vein. "Like your old joke,

Don, A guy, having had too much to drink is stopped for going the wrong way down a one way street and the officer says: didn't you see the arrow back there? Hell, no, I didn't even see the Indians."

"The mother told me that when she was sixteen, her ambition was to drink Canada dry."

"What kind of alcohol does she consume? If you know"

"Don, she'd drink piss if she thought it had enough alcohol. And what about Edna? She's been sexually abused since she was three years old. All of the abuse inflicted by the mother's boyfriends. You know, get the old lady drunk and have a go at the kid. Can you imagine the kind of emotional baggage she's going to have to carry the rest of her life? Unfortunately, it's not like a blackboard you can erase and start all over. Those scars become so ingrained they'll last through her whole life. I don't know about eternity. The jury's still out on that."

"Deb. I had no idea you felt things so deeply."

"You think only lawyers have a license to feel deeply?"

"No. A license to steal, perhaps. At least, that's what some of them act like."

"Don, I don't want that child returned today. We need a lot more evidence of her being safe."

"Why not use past experience to establish unsafeness?"

"What do you mean?"

""The fact that she's been sexually abused since she was three and the mother's inability to protect her own child because of her alcoholism. Do you have a psych eval showing that?"

"Yes. I left a copy in your mailbox yesterday. Didn't you get it? I was sure you'd stop by from Barnstable Court on your way home. You usually do. That way you could've reviewed it last night."

"Kelly kept us on trial until six-thirty. About three-thirty he said he was going to finish the case if it took all night. That announcement considerably reduced the amount of cross-examination by the attorneys for the child and the parents.

Can you imagine leaving a seven year old and a two year old and going on a ten-day vacation to Aruba? If I'm taking care of my two, I'm afraid of going out to the deck or the yard. Even when they're napping."

"Well, this job has made you more aware of all the things that can happen. Just remember, Don, children somehow survive in spite of the parents. Look at Edna, at least on the surface. Class president, second honors, cheerleader and lots of friends. She's one of the few tragedies who doesn't have 'victim' stamped all over her. I think that's how she survived."

"You never cease to amaze me, Deb. Now may I have that report so it will sound as though I've lived with it? Do you have a copy for the mother's attorney? Edna's attorney called in sick, but her position is that Edna not be returned."

"No, Don. I was leaving that up to you. I just have the one."

"No prob. I'll have them run off three copies in the Probation Department. They can keep one for their records. Make it more official. Or makes it appear more official."

"Don, the way *you* think never ceases to amaze me. I'm going to make a quick visit to Aunt Kate. The ladies room, before you ask."

Debbie had always found underpants an undue burden, especially in the warmer weather. So who was to know? She did tell a couple of friends in the office. They just laughed it off. Typical behavior for a Gemini. They told her not to get involved in any accidents or she sure would be embarrassed, hyphenating the word and adjusting the pronunciation slightly.

Don committed the eval report to memory. It was only five pages. Then he saw Michael Rock. Had he received a copy of the report on Edna? He hadn't.

"Well, here's a copy for your file."

"Wait a minute. You don't think you're going to submit this to the Court without Dr. Aronovich being present?"

"Yes, that is my intention. As is customary, a copy has already been given to Probation."

"That's a cheap shot, Goode, and you know it."

"That's a good shot and you know it. We're here today on your motion to return custody to the mother. Solely on that issue, this report may be reviewed by the Court to determine the best interests of the child. And, incidentally, how do you know what's in the report if you're seeing it for the first time? In fact, if you haven't even read it?"

"Well I . . . I assume it's favorable to DSS if you're submitting it . . ."

"You'd better ask around about my reputation. I'd submit it if it said the child should be returned home and if it supported your contention. Incidentally, haven't I seen you with Aronovitch at lunch at the Windjammer and the Dolphin as well as several times in Probate Court?"

"That's slanderous! Saying that the good doctor would stoop to giving me confidential information to help me on a case."

"Mr. Rock, anyone would have to stoop to get to your level. —See you in Court."

"Wait! I just realized you never accused the doctor of giving me the report. I was in error."

"Methinks the lawyer doth protest too much."

"Wait . . . I . . . what I meant was . . ."

Don left him with mouth agape and entered the Courtroom to establish some continuances on other matters.

"Now Mr. Rock, is it the Court's understanding that your contention is that Mrs. LaMer has been fully rehabilitated and therefore, the child in this case, Edna, should be returned to her mother's care?"

"That's correct your Honor. The doctors have given her a clean bill of health and they feel she's perfectly capable of caring for her fifteen year old daughter, Edna."

"Does Probation have reports from all the doctors?"

"No, Judge Holden. It does not."

"Does Probation have a report from a single doctor which supports the return of Edna to her mother?"

EN

"No, your Honor, it does not. It does have another report, however, but I'll let Mr. Goode speak to that. I understand the Motion for Return of Custody, is the mother's through her attorney, Mr. Rock."

"Quite correct, Mr. Case. Mr. Rock would you please hand the Clerk-Magistrate the doctors' reports to which you have made references. Thank you."

There was complete silence. There was no movement in the Courtroom.

"Mr. Rock, are you having difficulty locating the reports? Perhaps this would be a good time for the morning recess. Ten, fifteen minutes at the most." Judge Holden stood up and left the bench.

Michael Rock was quite pale. Guillotine pale. He was unable to even pretend to be looking for the non-existent reports. Funny how he could rant and rave about Dr. Aronovitch's written report being inadmissible on the issue of return but he could mention non-existent reports to support hurrying the child home. That was perfectly all right. He could see no conflict in his corruption or misstatements of the truth. Lying is what it was. And he would justify that because his clinical professor at Law School told his group that it was okay to lie or misrepresent because the clients were poor. No wonder the legal profession was held up to so much disparagement. It probably would never recover.

"All rise. Justice Holden Presiding."

"Now, Mr. Clerk-Magistrate, may I have those medical reports regarding Mrs. LaMer?"

"I don't have any your Honor."

"Mr. Rock, have you still had difficulty locating them? Perhaps if you refresh your memory. When and where was the last time you saw them?" He was moving in for the kill.

"To tell you the truth, your Honor . . ."

"It's come to that?"

"What I mean to say is, I don't now have my medical reports or have I ever seen such reports . . ."

"I must be losing my memory. Would the clerk please play back from the tape, Mr. Rock's statement on his motion. That way, I trust we'll all know where we stand."

"Yes, your Honor."

The clerk increased the volume on the play back so no one could doubt what had been said. Because of the increased volume, it appeared even more blatant, more heinous.

"Well, Mr. Rock, did you not lead this Court to believe that 'the doctors have given her a clean bill of health and that she is capable of. . . ?"

"Well, your Honor that is what my client told me. I did not mean to mislead the Court, deliberately."

It was getting worse, but not as bad as it was going to get. Thanks to Debbie Payne.

"You don't think it would have been more appropriate to state to the Court, 'my client tells me that her doctor . . . ' And then, before today you could have checked with her doctors to obtain statements from them? What are the names and addresses of these doctors? I'll have Mr. Case call them and order reports for the Court."

"I don't know your Honor."

"Do you think you might take a few steps behind you and ask your client?"

"Yes, your Honor . . . She doesn't remember."

"Were there any such doctors?"

" . . . Yes, she thinks so, your Honor, but doesn't remember their names."

"Mrs. LaMer, please stand. Now Mr. Rock, what is her overall health picture?"

"Excell—she tells me excellent. She's getting between eight and ten hours sleep a night. She's eating regularly and she feels in tip-top . . ."

Just then Mrs. La Mer turned three or four times in a circle and flopped on to the floor. Court officers rushed forward with water. She appeared to be unconscious. Debbie Payne waved

EN

them all away to keep air passages clear. She had taken an intensive First Aid course and knew what she was doing. With her back to the Court, Debbie knelt down over the still form of Mrs. LaMer. As she did so, her dress hiked up and she leaned forward over the body. Her dress hiked up even more. Don cast a glance at Judge Holden whose face had turned crimson as he viewed the scene. What he saw wasn't moon over Miami. More like Moon over La Mer.

In three or four minutes, consciousness returned. This was one case he had won without uttering a word. Edna LaMer would continue in foster care for another while. Rock tried to approach his car in the parking lot, but Don drove on by like he hadn't seen him.

Dead Babies

"Noel! I've never seen you in a tie before. You look handsome and footsome! Shoes! I've never seen you without your dock footers."

"Placenta. It's docksiders. They say blue photographs better for the camera; hence the shirt."

"What has that got to do with anything, Noel, Noel. I always think of Christmas when I think of your name. Not the Coward part of it. But anyhoo, what's with the cameras bit?"

"I'm going to Court on the Antonia Marshall case."

"Why? Doesn't Don handle the Court cases? I've been here a year now and I've never seen you go to Court before."

"Oh, yes. Don'll be there. I'm going to lend support to the two workers from the new Homeless Unit, who were working with the families."

"I must sound like a broken record, Noe, but why the clothes and what's the camera angle?"

"On me, I hope. Dead babies make a lot of news and I might be on T.V. In fact I'm leaving early so I won't miss the T.V. people. I understand they were over at the Rainbow's End Motel the day the story broke." He stretched his neck and brushed imaginary wrinkles from his tie.

"You think I'll dazzle 'em, Placenta?"

"With a razzle, Noe. With a razzle."

"Ta, ta. If Don asks for me, tell him I've already gone."

"He won't."

"Why do you say that?'

"Because the only time he stops here is to approve emergency C&P letters. Otherwise, he goes straight to Court from home."

"How'd you learn that in just a year? I've been here three and I didn't know that."

"It's all in the reflexes, man. All in the reflexes."

Reflexes?

"And smart brains."

While You Were Away From Your Desk

Lynn Holster had gone home to Charlton for her father's funeral. While she was absent, Noel received a call from a D.M.H. worker, Louise Lou, who stated that Lynn wasn't making any effort to locate a Ms. Harriet Haversham and her three month old son, Sue. Ever since she was little, Harry remembered Johnny Cash singing 'A Boy Named Sue'. She vowed if she ever had a boy that would be his name. No word yet on how the kid would feel.

Without thought or consult with the DSS record on Lynn or her supervisor, Jim Smythe, he dashed off one of his afternoon letters to the effect that 'I am sending Manny Gomes, our APM and Aubrey James, two top notch personnel, one a manager and the other probably our best social worker to handle the matter. I further apologize for Ms. Holster's performance (or lack of it, as it appears), and for any inconvenience this may have caused you. Please rest assured that this office is open to any criticism from other agencies or areas for it is only in that way we shall be able to fulfill our statutory obligations. Thanking you again for calling this to our attention,'

Most sincerely,

NCP cc: Manny Gomes, APM

Aubrey James, S.W.

Manny Gomes was out of the office the day the letter to Ms. Lou was sent. Otherwise, he would have convinced Noel, or tried to, that Lynn Holster was one of the office's most important assets. When he returned the following day and checked his mail and saw the 'cc' he nearly flipped.

"Noel are you crazy! All your response memos state the same theme: If you had bothered to check the facts. . . . Why the fuck didn't *you* check the facts? Were you too lazy to walk twenty feet to the record room and read the worker's contacts in the history? Did you check with Jim Smythe who knows his cases? Couldn't you have said, 'I'll look into it and get back to you'? Why do you get an idea and rush forward with it without ever questioning whether it's appropriate or even the right thing to do?"

Manny was displaying some of the potential he had for leadership and fairness, long since almost completely evaporated.

Through glazed eyes, Noel said, "Well people have a right to complain . . ."

"No one can or will dispute that. Don't you know why they call that screwball from DMH a 'lou-lou'? She has made one hundred and fifty-eight; this makes fifty-nine complaints to this office, alone. I'm surprised the administration of DMH who had quadruple that amount of complaints, legitimate, against her, hasn't opted for making her a client instead of a worker. In fact many of their workers have been former clients.

"What kind of flowers do you think I should send Lynn?"

"Noel, have you heard anything I've been saying?" Then he noticed a six-pack of Heineken barely under Noel's desk. Three of the bottles were empty, while a fourth was half empty. At that hour, 10:30 A.M., the smell of beer was strong. Manny knew it was no use. He turned to go.

"I was thinking of red and white carnations, Man."

"I was thinking of Four Roses, Noe. It would be appropriate from you.

To: N. Coward Peel, Area Director

From: Lynn Holster, Social Worker

Subject: Harriet Haversham Case Correspondence to Louise Lou, DMH

I returned from my father's funeral yesterday. Thank you for the four roses. However, they do not lessen or remove the sting of pain I felt, and am still feeling, upon reading a copy of your letter to Ms. Lou, a copy of which she was kind enough to send me. Your letter has now become part of the permanent record in the case while the content of Ms. Lou's telephone complaint appears nowhere nor was its veracity ever questioned.

"If Aubrey James who came to work here less than three months ago, is top notch does that make me bottom notch?

"Ms. Lou has made close to one hundred and sixty complaints about workers in this office in the past seven months. In how many of those other cases did you also send letters and replace the workers with 'top notch ' people?

"I have been a devoted social worker for more than ten years with nary a legitimate complaint about me or about my work. So why do I suddenly become fodder for the Area Director's cannon? An Area Director, who never made an attempt to read the Department's record on this family or never made an attempt to conference the case with my supervisor, is the one who should have been in the cannon.

"A review of the record would have shown eighteen attempts over a two week period to contact the mother just before I received word of my father's sudden death. A conference with Jim Smythe, my supervisor, would have confirmed the contacts or their attempts.

"You should never, ever, have to apologize for my performance. The only performance you have to apologize for is your own. When you have an Area Director who should be a client, it is time to move on. I resign." cc: Mary Quincy, Regional Director

Another nail in Noel's coffin?

What Nice Smiles

Julie Harris had worked only three months in the Kodak 'I am a Camera' booth in the T. J. Maxx Mall, but she loved it. Customers all seemed nice, except one who gave off what she describes as "creepy vibes." He brought in a large order, over two hundred prints to be made, a few to be enlarged.

Time went by very quickly in the booth with all the entries she had to make on outgoing and incoming film. She had to record all the data on personal checks that department stores did, but surprisingly, most people paid in cash. One could drive up to the booth and complete the transaction without getting out of the car. Some times, there were customer errors on the envelope container but she'd learned to catch those quite efficiently. Rarely did an error slip through and if it did, she was able to correct it when the lab called. The reason was that she kept her own personal sheet of 'Ins' and 'Outs' so it was like a double check. Came in handy, too.

What was this? The largest envelope containing the largest order that she had ever seen. And expensive, too. One hundred and fifty dollars. She wasn't going to take any personal check on that. After all, the check limit was fifty dollars. She turned it over to see the customer's name. It was the creep! Ralph Lenz. She thought there'd been a mistake in the bill so she unsealed the flap and took out the order. Oh my God! There, before her, were pornographic pictures of a little girl, no more than six and a boy about three or four. Every imaginable sexual pose was contained therein. She thought she was going to get sick. She was already dizzy. What should she do? Well, what she had witnessed was obviously a crime so . . . she picked up the telephone.

"Barnstable Police, operator."

"Is this an emergency or a call for assistance?"

She thought if she said 'emergency', she'd get help faster.

"Hello. Are you still there?"

"Yes, Operator. It is an emergency."

"Barnstable Police Department, Officer Reardon speaking."

She told her story.

"That booth is unprotected, isn't it?"

"Yes, officer, but why. . . ?"

"If he went to the time and trouble and expense and risk of those pictures, he wants them. Badly. I will have someone there within minutes. I want you to hide the envelope. I want you to compose yourself. You're obviously very distraught. If he arrives before the cruiser, try to be light and carefree like you usually are."

"How would you happen to know about that, Officer Reardon?"

"I dropped some film off last Tuesday. It was early and CVS hadn't opened yet. Now I'm glad I did."

"Why is it that you are glad?"

"Well I wanted to come by when I pick up the film and ask you for a date."

She was trying to remember what he looked like. There was his film right behind 'R'.

"I never date police officers."

"Why?"

"Oh, it just seemed like the sophisticated thing to say."

Oh. Oh. The Creep was at the window. Dear Lord, please help me.

"Hi there! May I help you?" She left the phone off the hook.

"Yes. You probably don't remember me, but I left off a large order about five days ago . . ."

"Do you have your stub, sir? Sometimes it makes it easier." Actually the numbers were for comparative reasons. Julie filed her orders alphabetically.

"N-n-n-n-no . . ." She was going up and down on the racks, while his order sat directly in front of her on the desk-shelf she used for writing transactions.

"You say it was a large order?"

"Yes. Over two hundred prints."

"Wow. And were there any enlargements?" She was hoping Officer Reardon was listening. Not only was he not listening, he had the Lieutenant relieve him. He was on his way.

"Oh yes, some. Why?"

"Well, sometimes, I've observed, if you have an order and then enlargements from pictures in the order, it takes longer than if you had sent a negative to be enlarged. Why I don't know."

"I'm really anxious about those pictures . . ."

I'll bet you are.

" . . . Could I come in and help you look?"

"No, no, no. That's against company policy."

Where were the police when you needed them most?

El Creepo was going to the other side of the booth. He was quite tall and would see the envelope. What should she do?

"Oh, Miss, there's a large envelope on that desk in front of you. That may be my order. Would you check the name and numbers, please."

The price! He wouldn't be able to pay.

"I don't believe it! Right in front of me. Probably because it was so large I couldn't fit it in with the other listings."

"Probably. How much?"

He had the weirdest smile on his face. His chin was almost greasy. He looked like a child abuser.

"One hundred and fifty dollars, Mr. Lenz."

"How'd you know my name?"

"Well, you wrote it right on your order form, sir."

"Oh, I meant to write . . ."

I'll bet you did.

"Well, I only have a hundred and twenty-five on me. Can I give you an I.O.U. or break up the order, or . . ."

"None of the above, sir. You'll have to come back when you have the rest of the money."

"Wait a minute . . . my wife, Marnie, is in the car. She might have the rest of the dough."

Where were the police?

There was a voice on the other side of the booth.

"Miss, I'd like to pick up my film."

I'd like to pick you up, too, you hunk.

"Name, please."

"Reardon, James and your phone is off the hook."

"Those police are slower than cold molasses in January . . . wait a minute. Aren't you.. . . ?"

"The same. I came to save fair maiden. I've been within ten feet of this booth for the last seven minutes."

"But why are you dressed like that?"

"In civvies? Didn't want to scare the rat away."

"What's going to happen, now?"

"He's on his way back here now to get the film. There are two cruisers standing by."

"What can I do?"

"Take the money and give him a receipt. Tell him to check the order to make sure it's his. That way he won't be able to deny it later on. Like, in court. I'll be on the other side of the booth."

"You're pretty smart. For a cop."

You're pretty good looking too. I hope you repeat your offer about a date. How could she have forgotten a face like that?

"Back so soon, Mr. Lenz?"

"Stop calling me Lenz. It's a stage name. Here's the one hundred fifty. Now don't tell me there's tax on top of that."

I would have if Reardon, James wasn't on the other side of the booth.

"Now sign here for having received the order, and, oh, a new company policy . . ."

"What now?"

" . . . Check the order to make sure it's yours and that it's all there."

"It's all there. Don't worry about it."

"Please, sir. My job. I don't want to lose it."

Was she carrying this too far? She hoped Reardon, James—that's what she would call him—appreciated her award winning performance.

"Are you going to be looking over my shoulder?"

"Absolutely not, sir." She stepped back a few paces.

Reardon, James, on the other side of the booth, could hear everything. He was trying not to laugh out loud. This gal was a great fencer. He liked that. No namby pambies for him.

Ralph Lenz, with pupils dilating, and almost licking his lips was making guttural sounds as he pored over each picture.

I didn't react that way, thought Julie.

It was time to close the booth, but Julie didn't want to rush Mr. Lenz.

"Worth every penny of it, Miss. Every penny."

You may not feel that way in a few minutes.

Lenz turned to go and then his head spun around.

"Did I just hear a squawk from a walkie-talkie Miss?"

"Oh I was just disconnecting the outside speaker. We're told not to leave it connected all night. Does something to the connectors. . . ."

Good girl, Julie. Good girl. Reardon, James smiled.

As Lenz started towards his car, a cruiser came from each direction. There was no way he could run. There were some trashcans in a line, but he couldn't bring himself to dispose of his treasure even though he would be relieved of it shortly by the Barnstable Police. Evidence in two cases. The Criminal and the Care and Protection.

"You off for the night, Miss?"

"Julie Harris. Yes, I'm through."

Please, please ask me for that date. Keep it going, Julie.

"And you?"

"Yes. I was going to work until seven. But your call relieved me of going the full ten rounds today. Thanks. I'm very grateful."

"That's it? You're going to say you're grateful and let it go at that?"

"Whoa. I told you I was shy. If you make the first move, maybe I'll acquire the confidence I need."

"What do you think I've been doing? Running around the pole? It isn't even May."

"I'm sure that means something, but I draw a blank."

She took a deep breath.

"Maybe if I invited you to the Windjammer for a drink.. . . ?"

"Heck, I was trying to screw up enough courage to ask you the same thing. You're two steps ahead of me, gal."

Steps? Did you say steps? Try yards. And why wouldn't you expect that from any woman?

"We'll pretend that you extended the invite, Reardon, James. That should make you feel better."

"It does and I'm glad you're such a generous person, too."

And smart. And clever. And love being in your company. If you only knew that a woman could be saying one thing and thinking another.

Jim ordered a Heineken beer (a potential area director, thought Julie). After she ordered a white wine she excused herself and went to the ladies room. What a fright she must be. She got as close to the mirror as possible. Well not too bad, considering the day. She tried, always, to carry a toothbrush, face cloth in a plastic bag, combs, brushes, and assorted make-up. It was a heavy bag to tote around. Do women get hernias and men get hisnias? After brushing her teeth, washing her face and applying some make-up tricks she'd learned in a beauty course she had taken, she took about fifty pins out of her hair and brushed it to a lustrous sheen, remembering to bend over to brush the back underpart and then to quickly flip it back. Who's the pretty girl in that mirror there? What mirror? Where? Now if I had only told him my name was Maria and he told me his name was Tony, we could put on a show and save the local high school. She hadn't touched that wine. Had she? She couldn't remember having felt this exhilarated before. But she'd better get back to Reardon James or there wouldn't be any wine. It would have evaporated.

"Excuse me, aren't you Tony?"

"You have the wrong person, Miss. Or is it Ms? Or Mrs? My name is Reardon, James. Jesse was my great great grandfather."

"I've found it! You do have a sense of humor. You could be arrested for concealing a dangerous weapon. You haven't touched your beer. Or is that your second?"

"Actually it's my seventeenth. I'm waiting for a friend. You'll have to move when she gets back from the Ladies' Room."

"When did she go there?"

"'Bout two days ago."

"Sorry about that, Reardon. It's just that I felt so cruddy and I wanted to make myself a little more presentable. For you." Score one point, Julie.

"Julie? My God, is that you? Do they have a beauty parlor in the Ladies' Room?"

"Rear, please. Now is that your very first beer?"

"It is."

"Why?"

"'Cause I was waiting for you. Waiting and waiting and waiting. Actually, now that I get a closer look at you, it was worth the wait. I can't believe I just said that."

"See. It's really easy. Once you forget about yourself."

"True. I was concentrating on you. Wow. This is fun!"

The waitress approached the table.

"Are you people planning to eat? If so, are you ready to order?"

Reardon waved her away and told her not yet but ordered another round, which would be the most beer he'd ever had in so short a time.

"Do you have a car?"

"Not with me. I've been strapped financially since quitting my former job four months ago. Before you ask, my roommate, Marion, from DSS usually comes and picks me up after I call her. I'd better do that now. There's a wall phone by the rest rooms. What time do you think we'll be finished here?"

His heart sank.

"Never, I hope."

Like Virginia Slims, you've come a long way, baby.

"Well, how do you expect me to get home?"

Score two points.

"Well I have a license, a car with a full tank and a great sense of direction. All the essentials."

"But you haven't even asked where I live. Supposing I said P-Town?"

"I was hoping you'd say Alaska."

"Reardon, are you sure that's only your second Heineken?"

"Scout's honor, Kemo-sabe. Did you hear why the Lone Ranger isn't speaking to Tonto?"

"No. Why?"

"He found out that Kemo-sabe meant shithead."

The two of them began to laugh, uncontrollably, so that other patrons were turning in their direction. And Reardon was so drunk with happiness he kept laughing and laughing. The lid was finally off. He didn't care what other people thought of him.

"Reardon! What has happened to you?"

"You. You intoxicate me!" And off he roared again into convulsive laughter, so much so that the contagion of his laughter spread to other tables. Other patrons began laughing, not really knowing why. A half hour later he appeared to be rational. In the meantime, Julie had called Marion Lifka and told her she had a ride, but did not know what time she would be home. Just leave the outside lights on.

"Have you met someone? If so, who?"

"Can't talk right now. My future, I think. 'Bye."

"What was your former job, Julie?"

"Social worker, DSS. Before you ask, I left because of burnout. I was losing myself. And no one should ever do that."

"You left to save yourself?"

"Correct."

"That takes a lot of courage. Did you like the other people at DSS?"

"Most of them. Some A—holes in both management and the work force. Most of the people work very hard. That's why it kills me to see the Boston Globe do a number on DSS. It simply doesn't know what it's talking about. There are always grounds for error. Ever notice how many errors the Globe makes? Every day it devotes a special column to its errors. Not that it takes any responsibility for them. It's usually due to errors in transmission, communication, etc. That was quite a mouthful for me."

"For you, yes. For anyone, yes. Do you realize you'll have to go to Court, the criminal case I mean, on the creep? And possibly on a Care and Protection."

"When you were giving me all those instructions, I assumed it was for evidentiary purposes."

"Wow. You know a lot, don't you?"

"Well, we had an excellent lawyer at DSS. Don Goode. Do you know him?"

"Yes. Hell, he was just over to the station this afternoon with Manning Hill, the juvenile officer. Man, I couldn't believe he had been here all this time and had never seen the new facility. Goode thought the station was still over by the Bus Terminal. Guess someone forgot to take the sign down for a long time. He's quite a guy. Had us in hysterics with his jokes especially about lawyers and judges. Won't repeat them 'cause you're a lady."

"I hope you always feel that way, Reardon, or do you want me to call you James or Jim?"

"Actually, I didn't like it at first, but I do now. Kind of classy you know, like a Yankee with his mother's maiden name as his first? Stick to the 'Reardon'."

"It's a good thing you're not a D.I. Step to the Reardon."

"Ugh. That's bad."

"Well, no one's good all the time."

"That's what I'm counting on."

"I'll pretend I didn't hear that. I'm starving. How about you?"

Reardon motioned to the waitress who took their orders.

Falling in Love

She directed him to take a right coming out of the T.J. Maxx Mall. When they got to the light at Christmas Tree Crossing, she told him to continue on Route 28.

"Why are we going this way if you live in P-Town?"

"I said, 'what if'. . . ."

"Oh. Did you have a good time tonight, Miss Harris?"

"Considering the company, and all the fencing I had to do, yes."

"Come on. And you're telling me to develop a sense of humor?"

"Well. All's well that ends."

"Isn't there supposed to be another well, there?"

"Yes. I put it first."

They drove in silence, feeling no need to talk, but each assessing the evening, each other, their contentment.

"Take the next right and go to the end of the road."

"Are you kidding? Those homes are all palatial."

"I guess it's time to tell you I'm an heiress. The Harrises of Harrisville, Pennsylvania. I really don't have to work for a living.

Parents are in the iron and steel business . . . My mother irons and my father steals."

Reardon was going off again but caught himself.

"Now where?"

"Left. It's the third gate on the right."

"This car can't fly, babe."

"My name's not Ruth."

"Are you from another time? Planet?

"Click your high beams four times, hesitate, then twice more."

The massive gates opened. They drove up a long driveway passing stables and what appeared to be a ten-car garage, up to the main home.

"Holy shit. If you're not the second story maid, you are an heiress. I'm way out of my league if it's the latter."

"You're way out of your league if it's the former. Now before you get ticked off, I'm neither. I'm a housesitter."

What a relief!

Julie saw a shadow pass one of the shaded windows so she knew Marion was still up. It was just before midnight and Marion was usually abed no later than ten-thirty. Curiosity has gotten the better of her.

"Would you like to come in? For coffee?"

"Aw, Jeez Julie, why'd you have to modify that?"

"Because I'm a modifying person. Did you prefer that I exaggerate and then be disappointed?"

"No. I want you just the way you are," he sang.

"My, my. The Cape has an awful lot to offer. Singing cops and all. Actually, you have a very pleasant voice. Lots of resonance. Any theatrical experience?"

"Camp shows and, of course, the Policemen's Ball." Had he been injured in the line of duty? She decided to skip that. For now.

"Well, shall we?"

When they got in the house they discovered that Marion had already made a pot of coffee, and was sitting in the breakfast room with everything that was needed including homemade brownies and cookies.

"Marion, this is Reardon James."

"Is that with or without a comma?"

"It's an inside joke. On me."

"Well of course it is. We're inside."

"Gemini? I'm surrounded by air tonight."

"Well, I'm just barely a Cancer on the cusp of Gemini."

"That would explain it. At least to my satisfaction."

"Reardon, this is my dear friend and roommate, Marion Lifka."

Reardon shook her hand. "Another heiress? No, no. Strike that. Inside, outside, I am putting myself in the middle."

What a strange person, thought Marion. Aquarian?

"I love this room. Look at the moon shining on the crashing waves." Her eyes were extraordinarily bright and luminous.

"Is it a full moon, Mar?"

"Why Reardon? Are my fangs showing?"

"No. No. Just reaching."

You certainly were.

"Well you two, I'll just clear up these dishes and be off."

What's the present tense. No, no Jim. Only with Jule.

"'Night."

"'Night."

"What's next?"

"Bed." The minute she said it—

"I was too shy to suggest it."

"Go on being shy, Reard. I have to work tomorrow. How about you?"

"Yeah. I might be able to get off early. They owe me some comp time."

"We've been having trouble operating the gate for departing guests—you are departing—electrician's supposed to be coming tomorrow. I'll have to let you out, manually."

"How about womanly?"

They stood on the porch and watched the beautiful manicured lawns and other surroundings in the still night.

"It's beautiful here, Jules. It blends perfectly with the rest of the night."

"You're so poetic for a wax man . . ."

"Wait. I get it! 'To wax poetic' . . ."

" . . . Very good. Now if you want to kiss me good night, I have a simple rule."

You mean you've kissed another man? I can't believe it, but I'll stand on my head if you want me to.

"Like what?"

"Hold your hands behind your back."

Anything. "Okay."

She put her left hand around his neck. With her right, she began massaging the back of his head. Then she kissed him full on the mouth. The sensation was incredible. Everything she did made him want her more and more.

"There. How was that?"

"Rewarding but unjust."

"Why so?"

"You can put your arms around me but I can't do the same."

"Reardon. Now why would you want to put your arms around you?"

"Because I'm cute."

Very cute.

"Okay. One more kiss but that's it. You may put your arms around me and kiss me until we count to five. Understood?"

Anything. Anything. He nodded assent. He couldn't waste energy or words.

She pushed him away.

"Wait a minute! What do you think this is—Christmas, New Years, your birthday? I counted up to twelve and you were still going strong."

"I was on one and three-quarters."

"In the car. In the car."

You really are cute, though.

When they got near enough to the gates, she told him to stop.

"Oh, boy! More?"

"No. I don't want the gate to hit your car."

He turned around and placed his hands on her shoulders.

"Listen, Jules. I don't understand how all this happened. It's like being on a roller coaster and having no control. I love you more than anyone or anything I've ever known. More than Christmas, New Years, Holidays. Even my birthday. When we kiss, I believe you're returning my feeling. That it's mutual. Other than that, I really don't know where I stand with you and, as they say, not knowing is one of the worst things to befall mankind. Can you give me a hint? No, I don't want a hint. I want to know straight out how you feel. How about it?"

She took that cute face in her hands. The property lights enabled clear vision. She said she would tell him two things.

"No one I've ever met means as much to me as you do and if I don't see you tonight . . . I'll kill myself."

"Yippee!!!!!"

"Are you cheering for number one or number two?"

"The whole situation. And I'll be there tomorrow night because I wouldn't want to be responsible for another human taking his life. Unless, of course, it's the creep or someone like him."

"You mean the only reason you'll be there is because you don't want me to be a suicide redhead."

"What the hell is that?"

"Dyed by her own hands."

"Talk about reaching . . ."

She watched him drive through the gates and down the road, then a screech of brakes. Some kind of animal? Wait! He was backing up at a pretty good speed. He screeched on the brakes and jumped out of the car, leaving the door opened. He rushed up to the gate. He looked like he was going to cry. He put his hands on the bars.

"Julie. On my mother's honor, I promise I'll come to see you every visiting day!"

Then he was gone. She laughed as she floated toward the house.

Why couldn't tonight be tonight?

He was gone only about twenty minutes and she missed him already. She put out most of the downstairs lights and went to her room, undressed, put on her nightgown and turned down the covers. Just as she was about to get into bed, the phone rang. She reached for it on the first ring so Marion wouldn't be disturbed.

"Hello? Hello . . ."

She was about to hang up thinking it was a wrong number or, worse, some kook. Then she heard someone singing. Singing? It was Reardon.

"Goodnight Sweetheart, till we meet to-day-ay.
Goodnight Sweetheart, time to hit the hay-ay.
Dreams enfold you, in each one I'll hold you
Goodnight Sweetheart, Good ni-i-i-ght."

Before she could comment, he hung up.

Why me, Lord? Why me? Thanks for arranging for our paths to cross. It was time to hit the hay-ay. She was sound asleep within seconds.

It Could've Been Someone Else

A four year old girl and a three year old boy, abused by their own father. Mother and father divorced. Children were abused on visitation with the father at their paternal grandmother's house. Vaginal scarring on the little girl. Unnatural acts on the little boy. Ruth Goldberg of Intake was the investigator. She was told to bring three report copies to Barnstable District where Don expected to meet with the father's attorney. The emergency Care and Protection had been taken out three days ago and was returnable today. Don had been on trial at Wareham District Court when the emergency arose, leaving Ruth to go to Court by herself to obtain the mittimus giving custody to DSS, at least until today. It would be a lot longer than today, thought Don. Mother was in Drug Rehab. Mom's sister had physical care of the children, which continued to be agreeable to DSS. According to the petition and Court letter on file in the Clerk's office, the parents were Eugenie and Amos Haskins, both aged thirty-two. The children were Lavinia, aged four and Antone, aged three.

Don began to wonder what was keeping Ruth when down the

stairs she bounded, hair flying, in typical heavy footed Gemini fashion.

"Hi, Don. Here are the papers, as requested. May I go?"

"Uh-uh. At least not until I speak with the father's attorney."

"But I already testified before Judge Kelly in his lobby three days ago."

"I know and that was sufficient to obtain temporary custody until today. The parents have a right to be heard."

"In spite of what the father did?"

"In spite of what the father did."

"Jeez, this is a great country. What am I supposed to do? I have an important meeting in Hyannis, or Tall Ass as you call it and have the rest of the office calling it."

"Do you have a number you are able to call?"

"Well, yes. But what good will that do?"

"Tell them you're in Court on an emergency and your attorney is trying to have you excused and that you'll call back as soon as you can. Okay?"

"Don, did you go to school to learn to think like that? I'd like to enroll."

"On the lighter side. Any new developments with your family on your intent to marry a Catholic?"

"Actually, it is a little lighter. You always say to infuse humor into a tense situation and it helps make it more bearable. For everyone. Night before last I came into their house—my home, their house, they always say—singing a paraphrase of a Nellie Forbush song in 'South Pacific'. 'I'm in love, I'm in love, I'm in love with a wonderful goy'. Thank God they both have a sense of humor. That really broke them up. Later, while taking a shower, I overheard my mother singing, "She's in love, she's in love, etc. It isn't that my parents don't like Kevin or a person with a name like Kevin O'Malley. They think he's a wonderful person. He's just not a Jew. They're very strict about that."

"Well, Ruth, you know what they say about time."

"Yes. It heals all wounds."

"And hopefully, it wounds all heels."

"Speaking of heels, Don, Amos is standing by the soft drink machine. And Andy isn't with him. Where can I use a phone?"

"It's 'may'. Go into Juvenile and ask Laurie. She never says no."

"Excuse me. Are you Mr. Haskins?"

"Yeah."

"Could you tell me where your lawyer is?"

"Oh, Jim Callas said he'd be in the third session.

"Are you Goode, the welfare lawyer?"

"No, I'm Mr. Goode, attorney for the Department of Social Services."

"Is that the thing on my case?"

Don looked to see where he was pointing.

"Yes, it is."

"Can I have a copy?"

"No. It's confidential. If your attorney wishes to give you a copy, that's up to him. I cannot without a Court Order. I'll be back after I speak with your attorney."

"Have you seen Jim Callas, Gina?"

"No, hon. Not today. If he shows, I'll send him down. It's really dull up here without you and your cases, Don, but the Chief Court Officer makes out the assignment sheet. Maybe I'll be down again next week. See you."

"Your attorney isn't upstairs. If you see him please come into Juvenile so we can arrange a hearing. I have some other cases on now . . ."

"Wait a minute, how'd they know I'm the one that did it? It could've been somebody else."

"Fingerprints rarely lie."

"They took prints. Nobody told me that."

Don walked over to the entrance to the Juvenile waiting room.

Ruth was still on the phone trying to convince whoever it was on the other end that she could not leave.

"Don, that Nola is such a bitch."

And a half.

"She doesn't think that her Intake workers are subject to the same rules and regs as the other workers in the office. I think you are the only one she's a little afraid of."

"Probably that I'll hold up a cross and cause a miscarriage or is it Mr. Carriage?"

"Don, plea-a-s-e, I'll think of these things during supervision, and break up. You have no idea what a monster she can be."

"Ever see Bride of Frankenstein? She plays the male role. Without a dooky."

"Dooky? What's a dooky?"

"You know the main thing that makes men different from women. Your people throw away part of it, shortly after birth."

"Oh, Don. You are certifiably crazy. Oops, here comes Amos with a white Andy."

"Hi Jim. I tried to catch you upstairs but no one was throwing you."

"I'll pass on that one. May I see you in one of the conference rooms?"

"No, Amos. This is just for attorneys."

Don told him the story and gave him a copy of the Petition and Court letter.

"He said you mentioned something about fingerprints?"

"A joke, Jim. A joke."

"These are pretty serious allegations."

"Sure are."

"Well, this bum hasn't given me a dime up front, as yet."

"Always the best reason for continuances."

"Can you continue these things?"

"We have before, by agreement. You don't see a need for a 72 hour hearing now but you reserve your right to one in the future. Legal custody continues in DSS, physical care in the aunt, Imelda Preble."

"What's a good continuance time?"

"Six weeks, usually. Until after the independent court appointed investigation is in."

"Can you recommend a fair investigator?"

"I could Jimbo, but I don't want to call all the shots."

"Listen, just about everybody knows how fair you are. I would have no objection."

"Okay, we'll see if the Court comes up with someone. I don't like to be the advocate for a particular investigator. If I'm asked, by all means I won't claim the right to remain silent."

"Good enough Don. And thanks. Could you ask Amos to come in so I can show him his death warrant. Why the hell do guys do things like this, Don?"

"I've been asking myself that question since I discovered these things happen."

"Oh, Ruth. You can go to your meeting in Tall Ass."

"Oh, Don. You don't know how relieved I am not to have to go back to the office and listen to a harangue by Nola. Be grateful for little things. Unless you're a guy, goy.

"Bye."

Sock It To Me

Off for a full hearing in Nantucket, with two changes of underwear. At least Don didn't have to worry about the social worker being delayed. He liked the new practice of two social workers, one each living in Nantucket and Martha's Vineyard. It was much more sensible and less costly to DSS. This way the workers could be in touch with their supervisors via phone and trek to the office once a week for staff meetings.

The flight was delayed because of heavy fog. It gave Don a sense of power, because the Court had to wait for him because he was powerless to be there. Did that make sense? He decided to review the latest abuse and neglect statistics reported in the Times. Every year there are 1700 cases of child abuse reported in the Cape Cod area alone. No wonder I'm tired. Child abuse and child neglect happen every day in every part of the United States. Every day, on average, four children die from such actions. In 1991, 2.7 million cases of neglect and abuse were reported nationwide. Despite widespread public education and years of media coverage, the numbers are going up, not down. In Massachusetts there were 28,000 cases of substantiated child abuse or neglect. My God, Don thought. Those are 'subbed' cases. How many cases did DSS have to investigate? And for this we get shit on by the press? No wonder workers are depressed and respond to his necessary bizarre sense of humor.

They were calling his flight. Now if he just kept his eyes closed and/or didn't look down. Again he asked himself, how long is an eighteen minute flight? It's an hour and a fucking half. That's how long it is.

Another brutal case. Would there ever be one that wasn't?

He was reviewing the reports, medical, police and social worker's. Poor kid. Gratefully, the plane landed.

"Don, we have the young lady who was the summer neighbor that called the police. Do you wish to speak with her now?"

"Yes, Sergeant Mason. I do."

In she bounced, hair like Veronica Lake over one eye, which she kept pushing back either with her head action or her right hand. Definitely an air sign.

"Hi! I'm Abby Gilday. My father is a lawyer, I'm from Connecticut. My father is, too. He paid my fare here. I mean, it was his money. Poor little Maheet. Is he all right? I mean, I haven't seen him since the police came and took him into custody with DSS. Do you think we have a chance of winning? I mean, I hope so. Are the parents going to be here? So upstanding looking and prim and proper. I mean who would do such a thing to such an adorable child? Honestly, one wonders what the world is coming to. Did they tell me your name was Don Goode? I mean, I was going to ask my Dad if he knew you, but you're much too young. Unless, of course, you had a lot of notoriety. Have you had a lot? I mean of notoriety."

Don held his hand up.

"Ms. Gilday, when you run down, does someone rewind you?"

"No, no. What a silly question. As a matter of fact . . ."

Don held his hand up again.

"Please, we haven't much time. I don't know whether you've

ever testified in Court before but it can be quite restrictive, especially on direct examination. On cross, there's much more leeway."

"No, I haven't, but . . ."

"Please Ms. Gilday . . ."

"Can't you call me Abby? Everybody does. Or don't you like the name?"

"My mother's name is Abby. Abigail, actually."

"So's mine. Can you beat that?"

"Now listen, Abby. I think it's best if you tell me in narrative form, everything that happened."

"I thought direct was very restrictive and you could only answer questions that were asked. No narrative."

"It is, Abby. In the Courtroom. But here, outside, you can tell me everything."

"Outside? But we're inside the building."

She was beginning to lose some of her charm.

"Outside the Courtroom!"

"Now you're angry at me. I can tell."

"Yes, and I'll be ready to retire before I finish this case. Before I even start it!"

"Well, this is what happened . . ."

She told Don about Maheet, aged four, being left alone. Both of his parents worked and were part of some religious sect that required them to dress up every day as though they were going to church. When they arrived at the workplace, they would change into their laboring clothes. Miriam worked in a laundry, Allah in an auto repair shop. One day when Abby was walking down the corridor to her apartment, Maheet opened the door and smiled up at her. His face beamed. She asked him to get permission from his parents to come over and play. She had things for children from the day care where she worked. He said they weren't home, but they'd be back by six. That's when they started their games in his parents' absence. Maheet would come over and play until 5:45 P. M. and Abby would scoot him home. One day his father arrived at 5:30. Abby had the apartment door opened.

Allah saw Maheet happily playing with the toys but didn't seem upset. When he called, Maheet dropped the toys and ran to his father. It was after that Abby noticed the boy not being around. Or not appearing to be around. She knocked on the door a couple of times but there was no response. About a month later, bursting with curiosity, she started knocking on the door when she noticed the door wasn't completely shut. She knocked harder and, as was her intent, the door opened. She gasped. There was Maheet with something stuffed in his mouth. His hands and feet were tied. He was tied to the chair and the chair was tied with clothesline to the window lock. His body was covered with bruises. Some new, some old. Blood was trickling down his shiny ebony skin. Abby tried not to cry, so as not to frighten the boy. She gently untied Maheet and removed what was in his mouth. A pair of socks, stuffed there so no one could hear if he cried out. She made a cursory search and found some clean clothes and some old sneakers. The first thing she did was call the police when she got to her apartment. She handed him a sandwich she had made for her own lunch but changed her mind about eating. Then she poured him a glass of milk, all the while talking on the phone.

"Yes, Sergeant Mason. I understand about being busy in the summer, but if they did this to him, what will they do to me?"

"What time do they usually get home?"

"Around six. But they could come earlier. Please call the state worker . . . I can't remember her name, but I met her at a party a few weeks ago. Please, Sergeant."

"What's your number there? Okay, lock your door and don't answer it till you hear my voice. Is that clear?"

"Very clear. Thank you."

She tried to entertain Maheet so he'd be distracted from his wounds. His situation. But every few minutes she noticed him looking at the bruises on his body. What kind of person could do this to an innocent child? To anyone? The phone rang. Abby jumped.

"Abby, Sergeant Mason. We'll be there in ten minutes. Just wanted to ease the crossroads of your mind."

"I was going to say how poetic but that would take time and I don't want to delay your arrival any longer than is absolutely necessary. In fact, I. . . ."

"'Bye, Abby."

Abby told Maheet he would be taken somewhere where he would be safe while help was gotten for him and his parents.

"You are a kind lady and I know you would never do this to me. But I was punished every day because I left the house and was trucking with a white lady."

She gently put her arms around him.

"I'm so sorry Maheet. I never intended this to happen. I thought your parents would be happy that you were involved in constructive play with a teacher from day care."

"Well that ain't all, Miss Abby. I was also punished because I didn't clean the house and do the laundry and the dishes. It was more fun being with you. But if I could go backwards, I wouldn't."

Sergeant Mason had Arlene Hunter, DSS social worker with him and another officer.

"Oh my God! How brutal!" Mason was one tough cop but his eyes started filling up.

Arlene Hunter decided to take over.

"In cases like this, it's best to have medical assistance. The doctor at the hospital will be able to tell—and testify later—whether the wounds were inflicted. In that way we are able to protect the child's future."

"Good idea. Maheet, we're going to take you to see Dr. Jonas. Okay?"

"Yes, Sergeant but I want Miss Abby to come with me."

Good, thought Arlene. He trusts her. She can keep him distracted while I look for a placement. Hope to hell it's not off island.

The five of them arrived at the hospital in the cruiser. Dr. Jonas who had worked on an emergency all night was just about to leave.

"What have we here, Sergeant Mason?"

"One of the worst cases of physical abuse I've ever seen. I know I'm kind of insular, working on the Island but I can't imagine a kid undergoing more torture and continuing to live."

"That bad? Miss, bring the child into examining room three, please. And remove his clothes. Nurse, I think we may need the camera. I know the law requires us to take pictures, whenever possible."

"You must be a tough little guy to withstand all that torture. Can you still smile?"

Maheet grinned broadly. I'd like to get my hands on the son-of-a-bitching father. Now, now. You are a doctor sworn to heal. Be kind. He talked to himself, like that, for weeks afterwards. It helped him maintain some semblance of emotional balance. It also helped seeing how quickly Maheet healed, physically. The hearing would be in six weeks. He was glad he had taken the pictures. Then the Judge could see the horror as he had seen it. What was it about a picture being worth a thousand words?

The hearing was closed as in all Care and Protection cases. The big surprise came when the parents' attorney, Luigi Avanti, revealed that Maheet was not the biological child of the Joneses. A petition for adoption was pending in the Probate Court. Maheet's mother, Evalinda Lindall, was in Court. Why? To tell the Court what wonderful parents the Joneses were?

Don would have to wait until the Joneses put in their case to learn what Ms. Lindall had to say. The Commonwealth always went first. And last in closing arguments. It opened and closed. Just like a door. After Abby Gilday, Sergeant Mason, Arlene Hunter and Dr. Jonas testified and the photographs were introduced in evidence, there was no doubt about the outcome.

The only witness called was Evalinda Lindall. And she was reluctant. Didn't want to take the oath for religious reasons.

She told of how much she loved Maheet but when she met the Joneses at a religious service in Pennsylvania and found out they were unable to have children, and were quite taken with Maheet; she decided to let him go because that's what God wanted.

She could tell they were good people and would be good very good, to Maheet. She thought of him often and still loved him dearly. And she could always have other children.

Don did two things. He handed her the photographs. She gasped. Then he asked her a single question.

"Have you seen Maheet since you landed in Nantucket?"

Her eyes clouded over.

"You don't understand."

"No, I don't."

The Judge, Enrico Pinza, took the matter under advisement, as was customary. He would make written findings within ten days as required by statute. If he found for the state's case, the burden would be on the parents to institute changes in child caring before Maheet could be returned. If he found no grounds for the Care and Protection, the petition would be dismissed and Maheet would be returned home. Please, Lord, don't let it be that. It will mean another appeal. They'll be calling me 'Appeals' Goode. And the name is apt to stick.

The following week, the Grand Jury indicted Allah Jones on several counts of assault and battery, some with a dangerous weapon. Rather than face the certain outcome of a trial, his attorney plea-bargained with the assistant district attorney and Allah was sentenced to six months in the House of Correction. Not long enough, thought Don. Not long enough. How about six years.

The finding from Judge Pinza arrived in the mail. DSS had 'permanent' custody of Maheet. Case is to be reviewed in three months to determine if there are any changes in home and in parental attitude. If any visitation takes place, it is to be supervised. Don could live with that. Don called Arlene to inform her. She asked Don to please call Sergeant Mason. He asks all the time about the outcome. She'll notify Jonas.

"Sergeant Mason, please."

"Mason here."

"Goode here."

"Please Don. Tell me, tell me, tell me."

"We won. Well, Maheet won."

"Great! Thanks, Don. Anything I can ever do for you, just let me know."

"I'm letting you know now. Will you call Abby? I would, but I haven't got five hours to kill."

"Very funny. Sure I'll do that. I'll just cut her off at the pass. No prob. 'Bye. And thanks."

"'Bye."

Nice To Talk With You Again, Laverna

"Don, have I got a bag of goodies for you! You DSS lawyers have all the luck."

"Yeah, Lala, and it's all bad. What's up? Or dare I ask?"

"For starters. On that priest who hummed too many hims, we have forty-two complaints."

"D. A. referrals, I hope. When is the diocese going to do something? Anything."

"Onward and downward. Woman, 38, former teacher at D. Y, and presently a tutor. She forced a twelve year old boy to have sex with her. He was being tutored in her home."

"He sure was."

"Wait Don. In a five-month period, it happened seventy-three times. The kid made a mark in one of his notebooks every time it happened."

"I think we're missing something here. Did it improve his grades any?"

"No one has said. Boy finally moved in with his divorced father to avoid the tutor-teacher. Her name's Carla Carlsburg."

"How phonetic. He probably wanted a younger woman."

"The police raided Tony's Restaurant on 28 in South Yarmouth. The owner, Warren Slaw, admitted to hundreds of sexual episodes with males under the age of 14, before January 20, 1986—episodes beyond the statute of limitation. He also turned over 120 pornographic videotapes, half of them involving children. He didn't realize the police were there on a complaint of Tim McCall, now 18, who told police he was sexually abused by Mr. Slaw hundreds of times in 1986 and 1987. His brother, Michael, who was twelve at the time, was killed in front of the restaurant while in Mr. Slaw's care in 1981. The parents have just learned that the kid's blood alcohol level at that time was .20. An older brother, Bart, now 25, says that Slaw molested him and Michael and regularly supplied them with alcohol."

"Slaw could get a job at Phillips Exeter. This is a D.A. referral."

"Already done, sir."

"A Gene Holston, recently discharged from the Army, shook his three month old son to death. Says he had a hangover and wanted to watch a game on T.V."

"Do they have color T.Vs. in prison?"

"A Day Care owner, William Malloy, has been accused of one hundred cases of rape. Nice little day care in Brewster."

"They should string him up and. . . . ."

"I know. I know. Cut them off."

"Arthur English, Episcopal priest in Orleans raped his twelve year old stepdaughter. It may have been going on since she was nine."

"This is one about which you don't want to get ecumenical."

"You called that one, Don. A fifteen-year-old Tibetan girl says she has endured six years of pain and torture at the hands of Rev. Jack Matchy, a Unitarian minister. First he would rape her digitally. When she got older, he gave her the real thing."

"Are you sure you don't have any rabbis in your bag of goodies?"

"Not yet."

"A Sunday School teacher indecently assaulted six of his students. He's sixty-four years of age."

"Give me that old time religion."

"He has four previous convictions for child molestation."

"Fifteen year old male raped by his grandfather who traded alcohol for sex. That came in yesterday. The kid committed suicide last night. Grandfather was going to tell people boy was gay. Just wanted to cheer you up, Don."

"Thanks Lala. You're such a good sport."

"And one more, Don. For today."

"I don't think I can take it, Lala."

"We're only given that which we can take. Besides syntax, isn't that part of your philosophy?"

"It was. I'm beginning to wonder that is it any wonder?"

"You sound like that old time singer, Joni James."

"Not vocally."

"Well, the Barnstable Police called . Remember Katie Sears, missing for twelve days?"

"Don't tell me she's. . . ."

"Nope. Alive and well. Well, sort of. Living in the Barnstable Police Station."

From a tip they received, police went to an old farm dwelling on 6A in Barnstable, I guess the former owner put in a bunker during the A.H. Bomb scares. That's where she was found. The A.D. sent James Blender out to investigate. You can't get much better than that. If he subs it, and I'm sure he will, she's going into foster care. The bunker may be better than the hovel she was living in. Oops, sorry Don. In which she was living. James should have some nice stories for you. And it's off to Court tomorrow for an emergency C&P. Lucky you."

"Who owned the farm? An uncle?"

"No. A guy named Bill Appetito. Very close family friend."

"Well, at least he's not a priest."

"Dropped out of the Sem just prior to ordination."

"And I was only kidding."

I See You're Out Of The Bin, Lunie

Lunie was home. For the weekend. Don had some shopping to do at T. J. Maxx and Marshalls. It would be great seeing her. Again. Outside the nut farm. He finished about 7:20 and headed for Lunie's house. There must have been fourteen cars parked on the lawn and in the driveway. He pulled in two houses down the street. So much noise. It was nice her family was giving her such a big welcome home.

Don rang the bell several times but got no response. He decided to try the door. It opened on about forty people having a great time. Loud anyway. Not one of Lunie's kids seemed to be present. Perhaps they were in the kitchen. He eased his way through the crowd. Many of them spoke to him. Why did they all look so familiar? He had always made a practice of not speaking to DSS clients outside of the office or Court. If they spoke first, he would respond. Oh my God! These were Lunie's clients! As he got to the apron of the kitchen, he heard her familiar voice.

"Three large pizzas. One plain, one pepperoni and one pepper. And three cases of Bud Lite. Same address as the last order. You still take Mastercharge don't you?"

Don turned to go. As he walked to his car, he heard footsteps running behind him. He turned and stopped. It was Lunie.

"Too good to share a piece of pizza and a beer with your old friend, Don?"

"You know I never drink and drive, Lunie."

"Well you could have at least spoken, before you left."

"I could see you appeared to be quite taken up with your clients."

"One of whom was kind enough to tell me you had been there and left."

"Lunie, you know you're not supposed to socialize with clients. Supposing one of them gets stopped later tonight, or has an accident on the way home and says she got the alcohol at her social worker's beer-and-pizza-welcome-home-party from the looney bin?"

"How are you spelling that bin modifier?"

"You know how I'm spelling it."

"Well, thanks for coming to see me. Not now,— then, Outside of my kids, you're the only one."

You're welcome. Take it slow, Lunie. You're supposed to be winding down, not up."

"Okay. Okay. As usual, you put things in perspective."

Don turned to go and as he got to his car he heard Lunie again.

"Hey, Don. Did you keep your ass in gear?"

"I think so." He gave her the Nantasket wave, shaking his ass from side to side.

Well, outside of the inappropriateness of the social gathering, she seemed a lot better. Maybe she was still trying to drown out memories of Antonia Marshall. Those are difficult memories to successfully submerge. They keep surfacing. Well there was one thing that didn't have to be drowned. A bright prospect on the horizon. Noel's hearing before the Commissioner was in three weeks. He wondered if they knew where to start. Anyplace. Anyplace.

K-K-K-Katie

Don met James Blender in the Clerk-Magistrate's office. He had been waiting about ten minutes for Mary to complete typing the necessary forms for the emergency Care & Protection on Katie Sears. He handed Don a copy of the Department's letter to the Court, giving the background, present circumstances and request for temporary custody until the 72 hour hearing could be had, after the parents were notified. It was concise and excellent in every way.

"Will the child be i-deed today, James?"

"I assume so. She's still in the protective custody of the police. The D.A. wants a thorough medical exam, before releasing her to DSS."

"They won't have much choice about releasing her if the Judge gives us custody. Could we agree to a medical. I believe it's in the child's best interest. What's your thought on it?"

"I agree. Of course I'm not an Intake Worker and you know that that les, Nola, hates anyone usurping her authority."

"Well since you were following the orders of Noel, the A.D.

you could assume permission to accede to the request of law enforcement. That's what the Jebbies would tell you."

"I've always admired the Jesuits and their powerful way of thinking, so I'll concede. Ah, excuse me, 'accede'. You have more vocab than any guy I ever knew. By the way, Don, speaking of Nola reminded me of a good one I heard last night. Not dirty. Just clever. Do you know that if you're bi-sexual you increase your chances for a date on Saturday night by a hundred percent?"

Don howled.

"Great. I've already committed it to memory, for retelling."

After James signed the papers, Mary said she would check to see which Judge would hear the petition. Just then James Reardon and another officer, Lisa Brown, entered the clerk's office looking for Don and James. They had little Katie with them.

"Perfect timing Seamus. Mary's gone to check which Judge will be honored by our presence."

"Don, say hello to Katie Sears. Katie this is the lawyer I told you about. The one who is going to see that you're safe. He's a good man."

"How do you do, Don?"

He noticed deep red marks on her wrists.

"Very well, Katie. And you? Has this bozo been putting hand cuffs on you?"

"No sir. That was another bozo. Bozo Bill."

"Lisa, Katie has to go to the Ladies' Room. That's one place I can't accompany her."

"I do not. I'm nine and I know when I have to go."

"Listen Katie. We'll be going in to see the Judge very soon and I wanted to make sure you didn't get nervous and have to leave the hearing."

"Oh, in that case, I'll go. I mean really 'go'."

"Don and James. I know you both know your business. But the D.A. is insisting on a complete medical."

"When did he wake up?"

"The First Assistant. Same name as yours. That should mean something."

"Does. That Don is always numero uno. Well, it's James' case. James?"

"I'll accede to a medical."

"Does that mean you'll agree?"

"See Don. What did I tell you? What good is the greatest vocab if you can't communicate with anyone?

"Excuse me, Don. There's a client of mine I've been trying to contact for months. She's standing in the main lobby."

"She's either a defendant or a defendant's witness in a criminal case."

"Thanks Officer Reardon. When you two need me you'll know where I'll be."

"Don do you remember a former social worker, Julie Harris?"

"One of the lights of the office. I think if she realized how much she inspired others, she might have stayed. Left quite a void. Roommate of Marion Lifka."

"Mother Marion would be more like it. Watches over her like a hawk. Waits up if she's out on a date. . . ."

". . . . with you."

"Don, did she tell you? What does she really think of me. I need reassurance."

"We have very little control over how other people feel. Just take it a day at a time. Don't be wishing your future away. You'll miss the here and now. You're both 'air' so that's as good a beginning as anyone could want."

Across the clerk's office, Mary was pointing toward the first session lobby and mouthing the words 'Judge Kelly'. Thank you, Lord. Justice would be dispensed.

Judge Kelly's secretary led them into the inner lobby. The Judge was already seated behind his desk.

"Always nice to see these two fine officers. And Mr. Blender, a pleasure. I had no trouble understanding your Court letter. . . ."

". . . . Thank you, your Honor. I did it at home last night so we wouldn't delay the Court this morning."

"That's dedication. And, of course, the succinct DSS lawyer, Mr. Goode. No wasted words there. And who is this pretty young lady? You must be all of fifteen or sixteen. . . ."

"No, only nine."

"Oh my. I'm going to make a note, through the Clerk, that you're here and you've been identified as Katie Sears. Now, this nice lady is going to take you down stairs and buy some candy for you in the machine. Would you like that?"

"Yes. Do they have chocolate mints?"

"I believe they do. But, if not, I'm sure you'll find a pleasing substitute."

"Mr. Goode, my clerk informs me that there are T.V. newsmen and cameras out in the parking lot. You don't intend to speak with them , do you?"

"All these cases are confidential your Honor. I never have and I never will violate that confidence."

"Good, I'm glad to hear that. And it was difficult for me to ask that question of someone of your proven caliber. It's just that I thought there might have been a change in policy. One of my Court Officers has informed me that Noel Peel, your Area Director, has spoken at length with the media, even to giving the name of the proposed foster placement and its address. I will not permit this. This is a very sensitive case and this child has been through quite enough. Do you have the name. . . . I want the top person. . . . and telephone number of such a person?"

"Well, since you asked your Honor. The Commissioner (should he give the Governor's name instead?) is Myrna Malcon at 1-617-227-0900." He looked at James who rolled his eyes heavenward. And just a few weeks before his hearing. Goodbye, Noel.

"Mr. Goode. What do you propose as the best way out of the building? I'll have four Court Officers accompany you."

"I was going to suggest the side exit just beyond the Second and Third Court Sessions, up the path to the left. That's where James and I usually park. Very few spaces, but a lot less confusion."

"Excellent. And now Mr. Blender, time for you to shine. . . . once again. I need to make some notes in my diary.

"You write that this child, at the age of four was on the street, unsupervised, dragging baskets of dirty clothes to the laundry.

"At the age of six, she was truant from the first grade, out in the street at all hours, unwashed and skimpily dressed.

"At seven she had no friends and was teased by other children as the 'cockroach kid'.

"At eight she was abducted and placed in a bunker cell where she spent her ninth birthday.

"Her abductor was a family friend, Bill Appetito, age 44, who Katie called 'Uncle Bill'. and who took her to toy stores and game arcades. Mr. Appetito responded to the police presence on the property (as the result of a tip) and led them to the bunker where they found Katie chained to a wall.

"From the time she was four until her abduction, Katie was seen with her little wagon bringing all the dirty clothes of the occupants of her home to the washeteria with detergents and bleach.

"Martha Sears, Katie's mother, has never married and doesn't know who the father is. Last spring, the mother accused Bill Appetito of sexually abusing Katie.

"Now, Mr. Blender, you swear to all this?"

"Yes, your Honor."

"Temporary custody of Katie Sears to DSS until next Tuesday. I won't put down a time since you won't know when your case will be called.

"I'll issue a summons for Martha Sears, the mother. Mr. Goode, do you wish to recommend counsel to be appointed for the child and the parent?"

"I try not to get involved with that your Honor. It's better if it's arbitrary. Perhaps it could wait until Tuesday. Since today is Friday and with the mails being the way they are, attorney notices may not be received until after Tuesday. Anyway DSS is amenable to any continuance either counsel may wish."

"We'll wait until Tuesday for appointment of counsel. Anything else?"

"I might suggest your Honor, that you make as part of the Court Order, that the child not be placed in the home divulged by the Area Director."

"Good idea, Goode. I've wanted to say that for a long time. Hope you don't mind. Get Miss Johnson, please."

Gina stood there shaking her head at Don.

"What was the name and address that Coward gave to the press?"

She reached for her small memo pad. "Elvira Madigan, 151 Pitcher's Way, Hyannis."

"If I call 150 Causeway now, Mr. Goode, will I get Ms. Malcon?"

"I don't know, your Honor. She travels the state a lot. That's why I suggested the Court Order."

"I just thought the way you rattled off that telephone number, you two were really close. Like telephone contact two or three times a day."

"Yeah. We're really close, Judge. Really close."

Who the heck had he been smart enough to contact? Judges have all kinds of sources, many of them eager to get on their good side. If they had one.

Don was walking them to the car. So far so good. No reporters. When they reached his car, James strapped Katie in the back seat, then turned to thank Don.

"I hope you realize how much we social workers appreciate you. When I was with Welfare, we were left to sink or swim on our own. No attorneys. Now the judges treat us with deference. Because of you. Sometimes they even laugh if something's funny now. As for example, do you know Sandy Napoli? She stayed at Welfare."

"No, but I talked with her when DSS came into being. I had to track dates and times and Courts to know where I should be. I was handling CHINS cases as well as C&Ps, 210s and 23cs. Quite a handful."

"Well, Don, Sandy had two CHINS on a Mary Smith. Obviously a mistake on someone's part. She told Judge Strait that he had double CHINS. He told Sandy that his weight or physical appearance should be of no concern to her. With a straight face. No pun intended. You see, Don. You've managed to humanize them. Somehow."

"The CHINS?"

"No. I'll give you one more guess."

"James, I got a call just before I left home this morning. They didn't want to tell you by phone. It's bad news. Michael Pompeo committed suicide last night."

James began to cry silently so he wouldn't upset Katie.

"H-H-How?"

"With his father's police revolver."

"Did that bastard follow the advice 'You gotta hand it to him'!"

'I don't know any of the details. Just the result."

"I swear we had just turned a corner. He was really stabilized. Had a cute girlfriend, was going to school regularly."

"Oh, there was something about a girl. She broke up with him. Told him her parents didn't want any slant eyes around their house."

"My God! The very thing that bothered him most. She went right to the heart of the matter. A Korean import adopted by two Italian-Americans. Father six-two, mother five-nine, Michael five-four. The parents had given up on him a long time ago. The father was a tough talking and acting Brooklyn Cop who thought he could whip anybody into shape, even after he was retired. You wonder, Don, if these bi-racial adoptions ever work out. God knows, about eighty percent of the same race adoptions have problems when the kids reach pre-teen. Everyone wants their own parents. Or wants to know why they can't. I swear that's why

DSS evolved that new policy about assisting kids in finding their parents or approving open adoptions where the bios continue to have contact."

James was a true Aquarian. The way he saw things was 99 and 44 hundredths percent clear, at least to him. And he developed it on his own because you can't tell an Aquarian what to do or how to do it. Aquarians were always able to recognize one another. Amazing. Amazing.

"I wasn't going to tell you this now, James. Maybe later. But now is the hour. When Jeff, the spineless wonder, was Mike's social worker, he sidled—you have to sidle when you don't have a spine—up to me in Court one day.

"Don, you maintain that you're not exceptionally bright but that you do have a great deal of common sense and people often confuse the two. Well, with my bi-racial adoption gone sour—you know Michael Pompeo—do you have a word of advice? Preferably more than a word."

"In very low tones, I said, 'I think if we can get this kid to like Italian food, we've won half the battle'."

"Even Jeff, spine or no, saw the humor in tragedy. And I hope you do, too."

"I do. I do. Thanks, Don. You coming right back to the office? Don't want to face Noel, alone. You always said 'A united front'. . . ."

"And I still do. But I must file some pleadings in Probate. Today's the deadline. Why don't you take Katie to a Dairy Queen and I'll meet you in my office in the back building."

"Okay. Good idea. I won't use Judge Kelly's addendum. Now if you run into some lawyer, don't stay gabbing."

"If he's not an Aquarian, there's no prob."

"Ouch."

"Well, we have been standing here for two and a half days, haven't we?"

"Yeah. We may as well go back in for the 72-hour hearing. Now."

"See ya."

"'Bye."

On the way to the Dairy Queen, Katie disclosed that 'Uncle Bill' had bought her a doll, took her to a convenience store for soda and chips and then to his house where she played a video game, 'Home Alone'. Then he started kissing her and she was in a cave. He said he was going to kidnap her. He told her to make a recording to play to Aunt Linda. That a man kidnapped me and he had a knife. He would handcuff her and put a chain around her neck. He touched her 'down there' on several occasions.

And this was the child whose whereabouts Noel wanted to make public? Asshole!

James had just gotten into Don's office with Katie when Don came through the door.

"Perfect timing." Don took off his coat and put his attaché case on his desk.

"You have the Court Order, James? I mean, specifically regarding the foster placement?"

"I do."

"Then let's go see the A—hole."

James held up two fingers. Wonderful. It was getting to be contagious.

But the trip was not necessary. In the door came Noel with a woman, middle aged.

"Shirl, have you seen Don or . . . Oh there you are! Katie this is your new parent. She is going to love you so much. And I have a wonderful surprise for you. Would you like to be on television? They're all out front. Waiting to greet you. We'll have Mr. Goode holding up the Court Documents regarding custody. Then we'll have James Blender and me. . . . name's Noel Peel. . . . handing you over to Elvira Madigan, then you'll go to her car. The whole staff will be outside. I've been rehearsing them. They'll start singing the old song—I'm sure you've never heard it, or maybe you have—can you guess?"

"Is it 'The Cockroach Kid'?"

"Absolutely not! It's 'K-K-K-aty'!"

"I used to stutter like you but I took speech lessons. You ought to. It really helps."

"No. No. That's the way the song goes, dear."

"Noel, there's something we have to discuss. Would you send Mrs. Madigan to the other building?"

"Well, all right. I just thought she could use this time to get acquainted with K-K-Katy." He laughed hysterically.

"Noel, the Judge doesn't want Katie to go with Elvira Madigan. In fact. . . ."

"No way, Jose. It's set in cee-ment."

"Noel, there's a signed Court Order that she is not to go with Elvira Madigan. It even gives the address, Pitcher's Way."

"What does he know about placements or Mrs. Madigan, who's a personal friend?"

What do you know about anything? And you have no friends.

"Why is he opposed?"

"Because it's a very sensitive case. He does not want the child publicized. And you gave the name and address of the placement. To publicize yourself."

"Well I can tell them to overlook it."

"It will be in the Cape Cod Times tonight and tomorrow."

"Nothing and no one is going to make me change my mind."

"Then James and I are going to abduct Katie."

"You want to make an issue of it, Noel?" James was seething.

"You mean physically? Absolutely not. I just want the two of you to know I consider this a mutiny. And it could cost you your jobs."

"For saving a child from an a—hole like you? An N.C. P.?"

"What have my initials got to do with it, James?"

"They stand for nin-com-poop, don't they?"

Just as James was losing it, the telephone rang. Shirl answered.

"Yes? Yes, he is. May I ask who's calling?"

"Don, for you. It's the Commish," she whispered.

"Hello. Yes, a signed Court Order. . . . No, he refuses to follow it. . . . says the Judge doesn't know what he knows. . . . yes, at risk. Family's crazy too. . . . Do I think the media would. . . . they're here right now. . . . I could never guess who or how. . . . no, he announced it publicly in front of the courthouse. . . . Channel 8, I believe. . . . Yes, he's right here. . . . well, I think you better tell him; he never listens to me. . . . Noel, the Commissioner."

"Yes, Myrna, baby. . . . just overreacting. . . . was I a witness in the case this morning? No. . . . I was just going by. . . . Yes, I know I live in Dennis and the office is South Yarmouth. . . . Did the media know me from before? No. No . . . Why did they ask to interview me? No, I didn't have a sign around my neck that said 'DSS Area Director'. . . . I don't know why I was chosen. . . . Have I ever divulged a placement before, publicly? Of course not!. . . . Then why was this case different?. . . . Maybe I fell in love with the cameras. . . . Yes, I'll see you in a few weeks. . . . Yes, with my attorney. . . . Yes, we'll find another placement. . . ."

"Well, Don and James, you may have won the battle but you haven't won the war. James, bring Katie over to Family Resource to see about a placement."

"I will when the press is gone."

A few minutes later, the walk outside sounded like a herd of wild animals. It was the press and cameramen. Guess who sent them over? Did he think Don and James would be fools enough to be interviewed? One fool is enough. Don locked the door. From one vantage point he looked across at the rear door of the other building. He saw Noel smiling, rocking back and forth on his hush puppies, picking his nose with the fingers of one hand and his can with the other.

Three Little Rats Sat Down To Spin

Why had Noel and Manny told only Jim Smythe, Hal's supervisor, about the information they had received from the Central Office's Investigation Team? The team had substantiated two complaints of sexual abuse by Hal on two former clients who were now clients of D.M.H. The workers at D.M.H. thought it very kind of Hal Ambrose to visit Ginny and Cissy twice a week at the shelter. It wasn't until three months later that both Ginny and Cissy disclosed the sexual abuse.

Since they were considered incompetent with respect to protecting themselves outside or inside the shelter, the Director of the shelter notified the Central Office of DSS.

Three people in the area office knew—four including Hal—and no one else. He was allowed to continue contacting his clients some of whom were in foster placement with clients of other social workers in the office. A very dangerous situation.

Lunie had previously filed a complaint that Hal had come to her home, in her absence and tried to seduce a fifteen-year-old girl who was living there. Noel and Manny yawned. It wasn't until Hal started offering to try to close certain Court cases if the mothers would go to bed with him, that Central Office sent down another team of investigators. Before that occurred, Jim Smythe, Manny and Noel introduced Hal to the various communities as DSS's expert in sexual abuse. Literally, it was true. At an open staff meeting, with the locally elected senator and representative, Jim Smythe said he was proud to show the advances made by the Cape office in having its own expert in sexual abuse. Noel sent releases to the Cape Cod Times and the Island Gazette encouraging those who had been victims of sexual abuse to take advantage of Hal Ambrose's expertise. It really wasn't clear who the advantage taker would be.

Then one evening, Hal broke into the apartment of one of the secretaries and raped her. She wasn't very attractive and, funny thing, she ended up liking it and him. It didn't make any difference that she recanted, the investigators had enough, and were able to hammer another nail in you-know-who's coffin.

Noel was ordered by the Commissioner to fire Hal. He almost refused to do it, but Manny convinced him his demise would be even sooner if he failed to do as ordered. Manny had a few friends in upper management who convinced him that a lateral transfer would be in his best interest. Otherwise both he and Noel were going down. That loyal, bow-legged little greaseball spent no time in knocking Noel and rendering wild stories about his incompetence. Well, maybe they weren't 'wild'. When his transfer came through, he tried to convince people that it took less time to get to New Bedford than it did to South Yarmouth. From Falmouth?

Don tried to buy de-greaser as a bon voyage present but it just wasn't big on the Cape at that time of year. They must save it for the summer and convince people at each of the bridges that at least one application is necessary before going any further.

Ah, well. The Cape's misfortune is New Bedford's misfortune. He's just a loser all around. There was a lot of refinement in the Cape office. But those workers in New Bedford were tough. They had to be with the case loads they all carried. Quality as well as quantity. They took no shit from their clients. They took no shit from the Area Director or the supervisors. They'd take no shit from the little greaseball. They'd eat him alive.

Joe: I Did It For You, Manny

Two weeks before Manny was scheduled to leave, an emergency 51A was called in by Falmouth Hospital regarding a father who was a career Army Sergeant in the process of a divorce. He stated he took his three-year-old daughter out for an afternoon visit. She told him "mommy hurt". He lifted her bangs and saw two severe lumps. He asked her how "Mommy hurt" and she told him she'd pull her hair and kick her in the face. He was sick. He thought the best place to take her was Falmouth Hospital. He didn't want to take her to the Base Hospital because he was embarrassed.

As he sat in his uniform with Tanya, waiting to see the doctor, he noticed different people in the emergency room smiling and waving at Tanya. And she responded. What was going on?

"Mr. Manzi? I'm Doctor Talbot. Nice to see you again, Tanya. You're in much better shape than you were two months ago. What is the complaint now?"

"Mommy hurt. She kicks." She pulled back her bangs and showed the lumps to the doctor.

"Well, at least, she exercised a little restraint this time. Mr.

Manzi, how much longer are you going to put this child's life in danger?"

"I haven't a clue as to what you're talking about doctor."

"Where were you two months ago?"

"I was out of the country for approximately four months. Just returned two days ago. Now, do you mind telling me what happened? I'll do anything to help my daughter. I'm here, ain't I?"

"I'll get the photographs. They're far more eloquent than I could ever be."

"Photographs? I don't understand."

"You will. You will."

When the doctor returned, he handed an envelope to Ted, and said he'd be back shortly. He took Tanya by the hand into one of the examining rooms.

Ted opened the envelope and slid out ten pictures. His mind began racing. He didn't want to look. But he forced himself. It was like a Mack truck had hit him in the stomach, going ninety miles an hour. His baby, almost unrecognizable. Eyes swollen so badly that you could not see the irises or the pupils. Her face was so bruised that no white showed. Her lips were five times their normal size.

Just before he hit the floor an orderly grabbed him.

As a result of the 51A called in by Doctor Talbot, Laverna Andrews was sent to investigate. Both Manny and Nola were out of the office that day.

Tanya would stay with Ted's mother, at least until the seventy-two hour hearing. She was a working person and would love to keep her but was unable to do so. Ted was trying to make arrangements to see if the Base had day care provisions with an opening for Tanya. It didn't look too promising.

As was customary, Don had the office copy all of the DSS documents that he would be introducing in evidence. Then he distributed them to the other three attorneys. The Judge, also got copies. The Originals were too precious to be left outside the office.

When he checked the previous 51A, investigated by Joe Carnivale, he discovered that it was unsubbed. When he looked at times and dates, he discovered it was unsubbed before it was fully investigated. Under 'reasons given', there had been no medical input, he had not seen any photographs. He had not even viewed the child who was in I.C.U. The fix was in. How do you do something like that to an innocent child and look yourself in the eye in the morning while you're shaving? How do you send a child back into a situation that may result in death? You provide no services for the offender or the family. You're sending the message that what happened was okay and that if it happens again, don't worry. We'll take care of you. And, why? Because, obviously, you know someone in management who would have the balls to do something so outrageously corrupt and still go around smiling and bowing and pretending to be up for beatification.

Don swore he would find out. Swore it. Well, he was going to be very surprised. And it didn't take long. Not long at all. It would happen on the day of the seventy-two-hour hearing , which had been delayed ten days at the mother's request. When people deal with corruption in an agency, they automatically assume, the whole agency is corrupt.

On that particular Tuesday, Don arrived at Juvenile, armed with the photographs. He had summoned Doctor Talbot but left him on telephone call with the promise that he could arrive within forty minutes after he was phoned. Joe Carnivale was also summoned. He had avoided talking to Don. Don had shown the photos to Nola and demanded to know how the 51A could be unsubbed without any medical input. She just shrugged in her cute, masculine way and said she would discuss it with Joe. What could be worse than treason in your own ranks?

"Are you the lawyer for DSS?"

"Yes, I am."

"I'm Karen Roselli's mother, Katrina Joseph."

"Oh, hi."

"Could I speak privately with you?"

"Regarding the case?"

"Yes."

"Don't you think you ought to have Mike Rock, her lawyer, with you before you discuss anything with me?"

"Absolutey not. This goes way beyond that."

"Okay. There's a conference room over there in the corner. You secure it before anyone else does., and I'll be with you in a few minutes. You're really sure about Mr. Rock?"

"I'm sure."

Don read over Laverna's court letter. Great. She put in about the previous incident, the 51A that was unsubbed. The investigator, Joe Carnivale, hadn't mentioned any medical contact in his report even though the child was hospitalized for eight days.

"Great, Lala. Just great. Would you give copies to the attorneys? They're in the conference room next to Juan's office. I have to talk to a witness."

"Sure thing Don."

"Well, Mrs. Joseph, What's up?"

"I have been trying to speak with Manny Gomes since this thing happened. He just doesn't return my calls. Has he gone high hat these days?"

"He's much too short for that. He's transferring to the New Bedford office of DSS."

"Aw shit! He was my connection with DSS on the Cape. I have a lot of family and friends who get involved with DSS from time to time. Manny's always come through for me. Do you know what I'm saying?"

"I think I'm beginning to."

"Good. I hate to pussy foot around. If Manny could have Carnivale dump that other case, why are we here? This one is far less serious. Just a coupla kicks. Builds character. That's the way I brought my daughter up. Nothing wrong with her is there?"

"I don't know that much about her. What I do know is that

she has been brutalizing a three year old. I suppose if she kills the child you'll say 'Well the kid shoulda behaved'."

"You think it's that serious? That Karen treats Tanya the way I treated her."

"It has been established that children learn best by example. That abused children become abusers."

"Jeezus! That makes sense. Why didn't Manny tell me that and have the Court order Karen to get help? My parents kicked the shit out of me and from what my mother told me, she got the same from her parents."

"I suspect that's why DSS came into existence."

"You shoulda been a teacher."

"I am . Every day."

"I want you to tell Manny he didn't do right by me. That even though our families have been close for. years, he's a useless little squirt. I know some people in New Bedford. I think I'll have them take him out."

"What good would that do?"

"It might save some kids' lives."

You got that right.

All attorneys agreed to the introduction of the DSS records with some minor exceptions. Then Joe Carnivale took the stand. He had the original 51B of his prior investigation. Before it was read all four attorneys perused it especially the final paragraph showing the reason for unsubbing the 51A.

"Don—"it was Peg Denmark the father's attorney, whispering, "He's added a sentence. There wasn't any room so he went up the side of the paper." The report now read 'And after medical consultation at hospital and especially with Doctor Talbot'. Don couldn't believe his eyes; neither could the other attorneys. They and the Court had copies without the alteration.

Judge Cronout suspended the hearing and asked counsel into his chambers. Carnivale was an unbecoming shade of gray. Wonder why?

"Mr. Goode. Are you endorsing this obvious fraud?"

"I am not."

"I thought not. That's never been your style. What do you wish me to do?"

"I believe you should examine him with a view towards perjury. At least, tell him that. I believe someone at the office told him to do that."

"Any other suggestions, lady and gentlemen?"

"Well, I have a question your Honor."

"Yes, Mr. Rock. Shoot."

"Don, do you realize this is putting DSS in a very bad light. What is your purpose?"

"My purpose is protecting children. As far as bad light is concerned, there are shit bums everywhere. Even in the legal profession."

He looked Rock directly in the eye. You know I mean you.

"Mrs. Denmark, you look perplexed."

"Your Honor, my look must be in sync with my feelings. I cannot believe anyone could be so bold. And knowing we have copies of the report as originally filed. Other than that, I'm speechless."

"Mr. Beaulieu you represent the child. What are your thoughts on the matter.?"

"Judge, if I didn't know and respect Mr. Goode as much as I do, having worked with him on other cases, I would say DSS is a sham. It is not involved in protecting children. It is involved in selling results to the highest bidder. Those are my thoughts or would be if I didn't know Mr. Goode."

"Well, you all have had input which shows you are invested in the case. I am going to examine Mr. Carnivale. I have not decided what to do about the perjury. I shall decide that when I hear his answers. Back to the Courtroom. I'll join you in a few minutes."

Probably had to take a leak.

"Commisssioner Malcon? Judge Cronout at Barnstable Juvenile. I have a very serious situation here, involving one of your employees."

He outlined the case to her with all of its serious implications.

"When do you think the alteration was made, Judge?"

"I don't know what his answer will be on that, yet. As per my instructions in all Care and Protections, Mr. Goode furnished the Court and all counsel with the DSS reports and records that he thought he would be using or introducing in evidence, over a week ago. That's what made the alteration so telling. We all had copies of the records on file at the Cape office before the new addition."

"Whew! I can't believe this has happened. If there isn't any reasonable explanation, throw the bastard in jail. I'll mark the matter for our investigation to be started in the next few days. And thank you, Judge Cronout. I appreciate your call and further, I'll let you know the outcome. 'Bye'."

"Now Mr. Carnivale, I believe you can see the issue here. We all have copies of your report that we were furnished over a week ago. Was that a true report made by you to DSS two months ago?"

"It was at the time."

"You mean when a new 51A was filed on the same child, with injuries caused by the mother and substantiated by Laverna Andrews of your office, it caused you to reconsider your report?"

"Yes, it did, your Honor."

"Why?"

He had no answer.

"Did someone tell you to add to your original report?"

"Yes, your Honor."

"As Mr. Goode might say, 'is it a state secret'?"

"No,"

Good, Don thought; it's going to come out. At the direction of Manny Gomes, backed by Nola.

"Well, who?"

"My supervisor, Nola Bellafatto, and I met with Don Goode

late yesterday afternoon and he told me to do it."

The rotten lying bastard. The hell with 'pants on fire'.

"Tell the Court everything you say Mr. Goode said to you."

"He was very angry that the first 51A was unsubbed. . . ."

"Excuse me, Mr. Carnivale. Would the clerk show the witness the photos taken by Doctor Talbot of the child? Thank you."

The Judge pretended to be busy looking at papers but he kept glancing at Carnivale as he winced and groaned at each picture.

"Now, Mr. Witness, are those photos fair and accurate representations of the child, Tanya, as you saw her during the investigation you were conducting?"

No answer. His face was flaming. He was on the ropes.

"Did you understand the question?"

"Yes."

"Well, you're under oath. Please answer the question."

"I never saw the child."

"Ne-never saw the child? Isn't that required by law?"

"Yes, but I was so busy, I. . . ."

"You weren't too busy to unsub a very serious case, were you?"

"No, your Honor."

"Now that it's been established that the true culprit is Mr. Goode, tell us: Was it Mr. Goode who told you to unsub the 51A before you even investigated it?"

"He wasn't aware of what was going down."

"If he had been, it may not have gone down.

"Getting back to the conversation in Mr. Goode's office, you say he was angry about the first 51A being unsubbed. I believe you said 'very angry'."

"Yes."

"Now tell me how he expressed that anger, what he said?"

"He asked me how I could possibly have unsubbed the 51A, with no evidence in my report of medical input."

"And what did you interpret that to mean?"

"To add something that would show that there had been medical input."

"But did Mr. Goode say that?"

"No, my supervisor, Nola Bellafatto, told me that was what he really meant."

"Do you think that committing a fraud on this Court in a matter in which he had no involvement, would make Mr. Goode feel better or that the child would be less at risk?"

"No."

"Did you, in fact, contact any medical personnel or Doctor Talbot for their input?"

"No, your Honor."

"Ms. Johnson? Would you call for a male court officer?"

"Yes Ho—Judge."

"Ten days in the Barnstable House of Correction for blatant perjury. I want copies of the tapes of these proceedings sent to the Commissioner of DSS. Mr. Clerk. Is that understood?"

"Yes, your Honor."

Joe Carnivale sat there stunned. He began to shake. Going to jail for doing what his supervisor told him to do. Manny telling him to unsub for one of his friends and Nola, that fucking dyke, telling him to alter the record and nothing would happen. Well fuck them. If he were going down, it wouldn't be alone.

"Your Honor, I know you're not going to change your mind but I'd like to say something."

"Go right ahead."

"It was my supervisor, Nola Bellafatto, who told me to alter the record. She said nothing would happen. And if it did, to blame Don. Say it was faulty memory or a misunderstanding. I'm no good at playing that game."

"Well, that is encouraging."

"And your Honor. It was Manny Gomes, the APM who told me to unsub the first 51A He said it was for a friend of his, and friendship always comes first. Even before children.

"That's absolutely true, Judge." It was Katrina Joseph, Karen's mother. "Manny did it for me."

What an interesting turn of events.

Judge Cronout was wavering about Joe Carnivale's ten-day jail sentence. He decided to let him to go to jail. He'd call tomorrow and have him released. He deserved at least one night in the slammer. But he wouldn't tell anyone his plan until tomorrow.

"Don?"

"Yes, Nola."

"Joe C. never came back from Court. Did he, by any chance, mention he was going out on an investigation?"

"No. And he won't be coming back to the office for approximately ten days."

"Ten days! He would never choose to do a thing like that."

"Perhaps not, but it wasn't his choice. Judge Cronout sentenced him to the House of Correction for ten days for perjury. You and Manny should be hearing from Central in a few days. Judge Cronout said he spoke with the Commish."

Nola's hair, which she had dyed black to match her soul, made her skin look whiter than it was. She staggered the few feet to her office. Even a kiss and a hug from her girlfriend wouldn't make her feel good, at this point.

No Jail Shall Sever Your Ties

Don was finishing a Review of his last C&P for that day. He was scheduled to fly out to Martha's Vineyard for the Court's afternoon session. Judge Hensley had graciously consented to hear his matters before the other pending juvenile cases.

Gina Johnson entered the courtroom.

"Yes. . . . Miss. . . . Johnson. . . . you. . . . .have. . . . perhaps. . . . a. . . . message. . . . from. . . . Garcia. . . . heh. . . . heh. . . . heh."

"Not quite, your Honor. My Chief says to inform you that Billy Lopes was arrested on a default warrant and is in the Juvey Lock-up. By way of further info, Billy's father, Leland, is in the first session and he was. . . ."

"Not interested. . . . Miss Johnson. . . . Get. . . . Billy. . . . in here. . . . and ask. . . . his father. . . . to come. . . . down. . . . here. Any problem. . . . with that?"

"Well, Judge, he really doesn't have much of a choice."

"Of course. . . . he. . . . does. . . . It's a. . . . free. . . . country. . . . isn't. . . . it?"

"Yes, but I don't think. . . ."

"We. . . . all. . . . know. . . . that. . . . heh. . . . heh. . . . heh."

"What I meant, your Honor, was that the father. . . ."

" I. . . . don't. . . . care. . . . Just. . . . do. . . . as you're. . . . told. Now . . . Mr. Goode. . . . do. . . . you. . . . think. . . . DSS. . . . can. . . . place. . . . Billy. . . . if. . . . it. . . . doesn't. . . . work. . . . out. . . . with. . . . his.. . . . Dad?"

"I really don't know. I do know that placements are rather tight. It is my understanding that Billy has run from five placements, either to live on the street or to look for his father. His mother abandoned him three years ago. James Blender, the social worker, had to take Billy by the apartment to show him everything was gone. He just couldn't believe it. Would your Honor wish me to call DSS and ask about a possible placement?"

"No. . . . Mr. Goode. . . . I had. . . . forgotten. . . . how. . . . tragic. . . . this situation. . . . is We. . . . have. . . . so. . . . many. . . . cases. . . . its hard to. . . . remember. . . . them. . . . all. . . . I think. . . . Billy. . . . wants. . . . his father. . . . and . . . the. . . . father. . . . has. . . . got . . . to. . . . be. . . . made. . . . to. . . . understand. . . . that. . . . he. . . . has . . . to. . . . let. . . . Billy. . . . know. . . . that. . . . he . . . loves. . . . him. . . . They. . . . belong. . . . together. . . . I'm going. . . . to dismiss..DSS. . . . custody. . . . and return. . . . Billy. . . . to. . . . his. . . . father's. . . . care."

"But your Honor, I thought the father was sent—. . . ."

"There. . . . you. . . . go. . . . Mr. . . . Goode. . . . sounding. . . . just. . . . like. . . . Miss Johnson. . . . although . . . her. . . . voice. . . . is. . . . a. . . . little. . . . deeper. . . . than . . . yours. . . . . heh. . . . heh. . . . heh . . . and. . . . she. . . . has. . . . a. . . . much. . . . darker. . . . tan. . . . heh. . . . heh. . . ."

Billy was brought in, shortly followed by his father, Leland, who had cuffs and chains around his ankles and wrists. Both of them sat in the front row with a Court Officer on either side of them.

"Judge Horatio Hensley presiding. All stand. Please be seated." The Judge was not wearing his thick eyeglasses.

"Now. . . . Mr. Lopes. . . . Are. . . . you. . . . out. . . . there?"

The Court officer closer to Mr. Lopes said he was there and pointed to him.

"Now. . . . Mr. Goode. . . . Attorney for DSS. . . . told. . . . me. . . . Billy . . . has. . . . run. . . . from . . . . five or six. . . . foster. . . . placements. To. . . . me. . . . that. . . . indicates. . . . a. . . . desire. . . . to. . . . . be. . . . with. . . . his. . . . own. . . . family."

" . . . but, your Honor, I am in no position to care for Billy, if that's what you're getting at."

"That is. . . . precisely. . . . what. . . . I'm. . . . getting. . . . at. He. . . . that's Billy. . . . needs. . . . you. . . . and. . . . you. . . . need. . . . him. . . . Now. . . . I'm. . . . going to. . . . dismiss. . . . custody. . . . in DSS. . . . and. . . . return. . . . him. . . . to. . . . your. . . . care. . . . .I. . . . want. . . . both. . . . of you. . . . to . . . stick. . . . together. . . . through. . . . thick and thin."

Yeah, you're thick and I'm thin, thought Leland. He knew it was useless to protest, especially since he'd already been sentenced to 30 days.

"Have. . . . a. . . . happy. . . . life. . . . together. . . . I. . . . wish. . . . you. . . . the best. . . . Anything else today. . . . Miss. . . . Johnson?"

"Yes, Judge. The entire juvenile list. The D.A. has been waiting. You agreed to take Mr. Goode's cases first so he could get to Edgartown District Court for the afternoon session."

"So . . . I . . . did. . . . so. . . . I. . . . did. . . . It. . . . just. . . . seems . . . so. . . . late."

"It's only 11:40, your Honor."

"Really?. . . . where. . . . is. . . . the. . . . clock?"

"On the wall. Same place it always is. Wait a sec., I'll get your glasses."

"Oh is. . . . that. . . . why. . . . I. . . . couldn't. . . . see Billy. . . . or. . . . his. . . . father. I. . . . remember. . . . taking them. . . . off. . . . to. . . . clean."

And then couldn't see them.

When the Court officers, who by now were in hysterics as were Billy and his father, arrived at the Barnstable House of Correction, which sits on a hill behind the Courthouse and overlooks Barnstable Harbor and Sandy Neck, the admission guards refused to let Billy share a cell with his father. Tongue-in-cheek, the Court officers insisted and the Sheriff was called. After much good-natured kidding, Billy returned to the streets and his father began circulating a petition to send Judge Hensley to Bridgewater for thirty-five days observation. Every single inmate at the House of Correction signed the petition.

Dear Solicitor

Dear Jim,

As my attorney, I thought you should be advised regarding the material I think will be the subject of discussion at the Commissioner's hearing a week from Tuesday. I really appreciate all your help and this is meant to bolster your defense as well as refresh my own memory.

1. Lindsay Binnochen, age 3. This was a case of neglect by a mother married to a serviceman. Before any hearing, even a 72 hour hearing, I wrote across one of the forms, which were sent to Regional, 'Possible 210'. I was taken to task by both Don Goode (our lawyer) and Scott Gordon, social worker. I guess the attorney for the parents made quite a thing of it in court that we were trying 'to steal' a child for adoption before there was any hearing or any proof of unfitness. I know the commissioner was pushing for adoption and I was trying to make points. I apologized profusely to both Goode and Gordon, so that should take care of that. Unless, of course, they're out to get me.

2. Melinda Thatcher. Social worker who was doused with gasoline in Roxbury and burned to death. They're trying to say that Manny and I wouldn't send a male social worker with her and that this might not have happened. Well, let me say, and you can ask almost anyone in this office, we had a staff meeting where we told the workers that we offered to send someone with her. And, I think, even Manny Gomes offered to go with her. However there are two malcontents in this office, Goode and Teller, who have been talking to investigators and telling a completely different story. One of those is that we (Manny and I) plotted to keep Trudy Teller out of Melinda's memorial staff meeting by sending her to one MSPCC budget hearing when it was Manny's job to go. True. It was. But Management decided that the memory of a dearly departed and dedicated social worker was more important than a budget hearing. Word around is that Goode had a conversation with Melinda the day before she left and told her not to go. Told her to refuse a direct order of management. He's the one who should be having a hearing. Melinda's parents are suing DSS for ten million or something, but I don't know if that is important or will even be raised at the meeting.

3. Antonia Marshall, age 13. This child, also subject of a C&P, which had been dismissed, murdered a six month old baby by submerging her in 140 degrees hot water. I thought I told Intake to take in a 51A, but it never happened and I didn't follow through. A few months later, Antonia tried to murder another baby by smothering it with a pillow. The child was flown to Children's Hospital in Boston and, fortunately, was revived five days later and able to breathe on her own again. Unfortunately, our office was swarming with state police who couldn't understand why a 51A wasn't taken in after the first incident in order to protect young children from Antonia and to protect Antonia from herself. I didn't push the 51A because I may have intended to and then forgot. Goode says I told him to tell Nola that there was to be a 51A on the case. But it never materialized. Later, the Death Squad from Central descended on the office. I remember, it was one afternoon. I seemed unable to answer their queries. I think they left in an angry mood.

4. Lynn Holster, Social Worker. If only Lynn had come to me, first, I think this could have been avoided. A call came in from a DMH worker, Louise Lou (I found out only later, that they say she's a real Lou Lou), complaining about Lynn. Well you know how busy I am, like to act on things right away, no delay. I sent a letter out and I guess, in retrospect, you could see it could be misinterpreted. You might actually think I meant Lynn was incompetent or not 'top notch'. I still haven't apologized to her because she had the audacity to send a copy of her memo to Mary Quincy, the Regional Director. God knows, she has enough copies of memos from different sources. And a beaut from Goode. Except, he didn't send it. I did, thinking he had sent it.

Oh, I did send Lynn four roses because her father was being waked and buried close to the time I was sending out the letter to Lou Lou. Or was it after?

5. Tonto East. One of the best foster parents DSS ever had. I do not know how they got this information. This outstanding Boy Scout leader was accused of studying the anatomies of foster children (all boys, at his request) especially their asses. A neighbor sees him with binoculars studying him in the shower. He runs out and screams at poor Mr. East who says he was making sure the binocs were clean because of an upcoming scout trip. Neighbor calls DSS. I sent Maureen Dubin, social worker, who supported the complaint. I figured she had misunderstood my directions, so I sent out another worker, who unsubbed it. Do you see anything wrong with this?

6. Prudence Valentina. This was a Care and Protection case in Orleans D.C. I took Keeshu Walker, great guy, our new APM to meet Judge Holden. While we were there, somehow the question of Prudie's medication (anti-psychotic) came up and, well, I guess things got out of hand. The case was put on the calendar in advance of its scheduled date, lawyers were notified, etc. It's just amazing how the Court system works. Just amazing. Anyhow Keesh and I, naturally figured the Court would be notifying Don Goode and the family, but I guess either we were wrong or it fell through the cracks. I guess there was a lot of confusion at Court that day. Keeshu and I were at an in-service training learning how to be better managers. That's why a frantic Don Goode couldn't get through to us. Understandably, he was upset. But he still shouldn't have sent that memo to staff supervisors and Mary Quincy. Wait. He didn't send it to Regional. I did. I just remembered.

7. Katie Sears, age 9. This has been blown all out of proportion. I happened to be going by the Court House and I saw a crowd and T.V. cameras. Well, naturally I was curious. I knew there had been a lot of publicity about the kid being found in the bunker the previous day. So a guy says is there anybody here from DSS? Well, you wouldn't want me to lie would you? So I raised my hand and they hoisted me up on the platform. What's my name, position and so on. Well since I had selected a friend of mine, Elvira Madigan, to be the foster parent, I gave her name and address. Now that's not Katie's name and address; it's Elvira's. And that's my out on that one. Of course, back at the office, the Commish calls and cross-examines me. Me, the Area Director. Can you believe it? She sounded like Don Goode. And if anyone tells you I set the media on them, they're lying. You'd think I was some kind of publicity hound.

8. Hal Ambrose, Social worker. It's true that Central Office investigators substantiated two complaints of sexual abuse against Hal. So Manny and Jim and I kept a secret (We knew Hal wouldn't be telling anyone). It is rather personal, isn't it? I mean, put yourself in Hal's shoes. There are those who would say, that he was visiting clients in homes where they had foster children and there might be a need of protection. I firmly disagree. And as for palming him off as the Cape and Island's Expert on Sexual Abuse, well he was. One might say what's good for the goose. I know the news releases said I was encouraging anyone who was sexually abused to take advantage of Hal's expertise. Well that's a figment of someone's imagination. I refuse to bite the bullet on that one, Jim.

Other complaints involve a work plan which I believe was set out unfairly because of an employee grievance. The monitoring report was done for inappropriate reasons. We did not meet the percentages across the board but we made good faith effort and improved.

There is the matter of Mary Quincy's unethical behavior. She has met with community people to discuss my performance without informing me, ahead of time.

Truth to tell, Jim, I think this all has to do with the fact that I fired Hal Ambrose, who was molesting clients. That decision was overturned either by her or someone higher. He was re-instated and allowed to resign. I was not informed until after the fact. He has since been employed in another social service position with another agency and brought to court on similar charges.

There's a lot more, Jim but I don't think it's necessary at this point. I'm not really sure what they have in mind for Tuesday. I may end up firing them!

Thanks again!

N.C.P.

Jim Gavin sat in his Hyannis office shaking his head. He had just finished reading Noel's self-damning indictment. What he wondered about was reminiscent of the USS Caine. Why hadn't Noel mentioned the hundreds of keys and the missing strawberries?

A Toss Of The Coyne

"Don?"

"Yes."

"Charlie Coyne. Been trying to get you for several weeks."

"Ever leave your name and number?"

"No, 'cause I generally don't know where I'll be."

"Well, you can't expect me to answer a fathom call, can you?"

"Did you say 'fathom'?"

"Yeah. It's an 'in office' joke. Not worth explaining."

"That's a relief. Listen. You don't send a memo to an Area Director, declaring he's an idiot or incompetent. . . . until you first check with me. . . . to make sure the allegations are accurate."

Hurray for Charlie, my supervisor.

"And you don't send a copy to the Regional Director without checking it out with me, first."

"I didn't."

"Well it says here 'cc to Mary Quincy, Regional Director'."

"I know what it says, Chuck. I told the sec not to send it. To hold it back. I wanted to shake him so badly that he would come to me. To see if it were possible. . . ."

"Shouldn't that be 'if it was possible'?"

". . . . no, subjunctive takes the plural form even when the subject is singular."

"Oh. Go on."

"To see if it were possible to work something out. Draw guidelines. I wouldn't do that to someone. Put them in hot water unless there were no other choice. You know me. I had a lot of fun writing that which should show it wasn't vindictive or malicious."

"Well, then how in hell did the memo get to Mary Q. at Regional?"

"He sent it."

"Then he's an idiot."

"What did Mare think of it?"

"She said it was completely accurate. Thought it also was a real humdinger. By the way Don, I've been wanting to tell someone off. Could I borrow the memo?"

"Of course."

"If there is one thing that could change the Area Director so he could change things down there, what would it be?"

"A complete cell transplant."

"You mean that?"

"I mean that."

"Well on to other things. I have to do your evaluation."

"When are you coming down? Afternoon is usually the best time. We could have a late lunch."

"I'm going to do it now. Would you agree to all 'excellents' and one 'good'?"

"Sounds appropriate to me."

"You mean it? You're not going to hold out or appeal for all 'excellents'? You have the largest case load in the state."

"If I do, all the more reason not to have all 'excellents'. It's not realistic. In fact, Carlos, I'd settle for all 'goods'. Except in 'record keeping', that should be 'poor'. I'm so busy, I don't have time to do all the writing."

"This a bad connection. I didn't hear what you just said."

"I said. . . ."

"I heard you, but I forgot what you said. That's what I meant to say."

"Can we change the subject? Like, anything new about raises?"

"Good news. The Commissioner's budget sailed right through the legislature. She did it all by phone. Didn't even have to appear. What do you think about that?"

"Come on, Chuck. What do you mean 'what do you think about that'? She obviously threatened to meet with them face to face. That's why it sailed through."

"Jeez, Don. I never thought about that. And more than likely, it's absolutely true.

"You know ever since Region 6 moved into Causeway Street, two floors below the Central and Commissioner's offices, I always avoid the back staircases. Especially around October 31st."

"You talk about my irreverence? I think I caught it from you."

"Now, now Donnie. You're putting the cart before the horse."

"And the horse looks like whom?"

"This is beginning to sound like treason. I'll call when I hear anything more definitive on the raises. Meanwhile, check out any memos with me because I want to be in on them. Okay? Oh, the most important. Almost completely forgot. Do not file any motion to recuse a judge without checking with me. If I'm not available, call Central."

"I assume you're referring to Hensley. He didn't seem to mind."

"He didn't, eh? Called the Commish. Wanted you removed."

"The rotten bastard. Here he was giving custody of a beautiful sixteen-year-old girl to her divorced father in Japan, whom she hadn't seen in ten years, without any evidence of his fitness before the Court. Just a letter requesting custody. And the lawyer representing the father was totally corrupt. At the lunch break, he was waiting outside Hensley's lobby. They went to lunch together. I had a C&P with him once where the physical condition of the house was an issue. He took or had taken pictures of the interior of the house next door and introduced them as the home of the children. Fortunately, a sharp social worker noticed the front door opened the opposite way and an initial on the lower storm door grill as that of the next-door neighbor. Lawyer said he was just demonstrating the layout of the house. Can you believe it?

"After the trial and after the kids were removed, the father disappeared. Had a wooden leg, as I recall, so he couldn't run anywhere. Has never been seen or heard from since. Rumor has it that it was foul play."

"Maybe he didn't pay his legal fees."

"And, as far as Hensley is concerned, a legally blind client of DSS works at the Holiday Inn. When she finishes they allow her to use the pool. One day when she had climbed down the ladder into the pool, a hand grabbed her ass. She screamed and the assistant manager came running into the pool area."

"How does a legally blind lady identify a Barnstable Court Judge?"

"The assistant manager saw him climbing out of the pool. No one else was in the area. When the woman asked him who it was, he told her that it had happened several times before and, since it was a judge, no one could do anything about it. And, oh yes, he left his postiche in the pool. Name and telephone number sewn in it."

"What the hell is a 'postiche'?"

"A toupee. I'm surprised at you. You with your Xaverian education."

"Do you mind if I pass this information on to the Commish? Believe me, it won't be in person. Memos are the thing."

"Heck, I don't mind."

"Will this assistant manager hold up, if it's necessary?"

"Yup. He's my cousin."

"Good gawd. I'll call you. Still no recusing unless you can't locate an advisor and it's deemed an emergency. Fair enough?"

"Fair enough."

"See ya."

"'Bye."

REN

Martini To Cronout Shatters The Lenz

There was to be a hearing on a motion to suspend visitations in the Lenz case. The attorney for the child, Chuck Igo, was the moving party. Judge Cronout set the hearing for 2:00 P.M. Don raced from Wareham Court where he had had two emergency Care and Protections. Custody was granted to DSS in both cases, which were serious enough to sustain removal to foster care but the court, and wisely so, granted liberal visitation. Judge Rocco Martini was a firm believer in family unity and togetherness. He did not remove children lightly. You had to prove current unfitness. Don had drummed that into the heads of the social workers. They were coming from a social service aspect, while he came from what was necessary from the legal standard of proof. While he found it easier to control potential cases in his own office, the other offices that went to Wareham District Court would pass on the validity of a C & P and Don's first involvement was when the case was in court either by initial application or a 72 hour hearing. If he saw no case, he would tell the worker but would still present whatever evidence that was there. Inevitably his judgment proved that it had foresight, because the petition would be denied because the legal standard of proof could not be met.

Don arrived at Barnstable District at 1:55 P.M. Close call. He went down to the Juvenile Session, which was located in the basement area of the Courthouse and got a diet Pepsi from one of the machines. Nice and cold, it tasted good. Not much of a lunch but he could afford to lose a few pounds.

"All rise. Judge Paul Cronout presiding. Please be seated."

"I have before the Court, a motion to suspend visitation. That is your motion, Mr. Igo, I take it?"

"Yes your Honor, it is."

"Mr. Goode, are you in agreement with this motion?"

"I am , your Honor."

"Mr. Rock, you represent the parents. Are you in agreement or are you in opposition?"

"I'm strongly opposed."

"Very well. Before any witnesses are called, indeed if it is necessary to call any witnesses, Mr. Goode with your remarkable memory, would you briefly trace the history of this case to the present time, so it is fresh in all of our minds. In that manner, we can address the current issue in a more refreshing way Mr. Goode?"

"Yes, your Honor."

Don stood and traced the case from Mr. Lenz' first encounter with Julie Harris at the Kodak Booth to Ralph's arrest and eventual finding of guilty in the District Court with a suspended sentence, the removal of the children both of whom were in the same foster placement, the health of the children, that they were thriving on the order in their lives, the fact that Mrs. Lenz was sexually abused by her father as were each of her sisters with the knowledge and consent of their mother. Mrs. Lenz in turn married an abuser, as is often the case and he, then, abuses the children they have together.

"Subsequently, because of two incidents that occurred, Mr.

Igo brought the motion that is presently before the Court. Thank you."

"Thank You, Mr. Goode. Very well done, indeed."

"Your Honor, I think what is taking place before this Court is outrageous, a travesty of justice. I demand to be heard and will not sit by while Mr. Goode makes all kinds of self-serving statements and unilateral assumptions to prove his case."

"Is this your motion, Mr. Rock?"

"No, it is not, your Honor."

"Do you have a motion before the Court today?"

"No."

"Well, unless they've changed the rules of procedure, it is customary for the moving party to speak first."

"Is that why Goode stood up and gave us all that drivel?"

"Mr. Rock, if you were in the Courtroom—and awake—you would have heard the Court request of Mr. Goode, a summary of the case for the benefit of all of us, you included. Now if you don't like what was said or the way it was said for legal reasons, you may address your concerns after Mr. Igo finishes.

"As far as Mr. Goode's proving his case: everything he has stated is presently before the Court, whether by way of records kept in the usual course of business, affidavits, the Court Investigator's report or psychological evaluations. Did you not receive copies as other counsel have?"

"Yes, I received them your Honor."

"And, did you read them?"

Rock didn't respond. How could anyone defend the actions of two pieces of shit like this? And his representation of the parents was by request. He represented one child, Todd Wynn. Thereafter, he requested to represent only the parents. Did he think the innocent children were the real culprits? Bet a dollar to a donut, after all his attacks, he walks out of here and asks me to have a cup of coffee like nothing ever happened. Oh well. Chuck was talking and talking more forcefully than ever before.

"Your Honor, for these parents to treat as a sham or as a joke, the terrible hurt and embarrassment these children have undergone, is beyond my understanding or the understanding of any reasonable person. To give each of these children cameras for their birthdays defies the imaginations of sane people. All the serious pain and hurt emotions have been because of a camera. Thoughtlessly—and perhaps it wasn't thoughtless but by design—remind them and to call into their consciousness, emotional scars before there is even an opportunity at healing, flabbergasts me.

"I earnestly implore this Court to suspend all visitation at least until such time as a convincing psychologist says that the parents are rehabilitated and the children are out of harm's way. Thank you, your Honor."

"Thank you Mr. Igo. Mr. Goode, do you wish to address the Court or merely assent, as I believe you indicated earlier?"

Sounds like the Judge has an appointment in Taunton.

"No, your Honor, I'll merely assent."

"Let the record show Attorney Goode assents to the motion.

"Now we have Mr. Rock. Mr. Rock?"

"I had a great deal to say, your Honor."

"You certainly did!"

"I meant 'more' your Honor."

"Oh, you didn't say 'more', did you?"

"I guess not. At any rate, while not assenting to the motion on suspension of visitation, my clients just asked me not to speak to that issue. They will continue with counseling and feel certain that within a short time, they will be rehabilitated. Thank you."

Abusers are never rehabilitated. Nor are rotten lawyers.

"Very well then. For obvious reasons, I am granting the motion to suspend visitations while at the same time encouraging the parents to get the counseling they need. And as their counsel, Mr. Rock, indicates, maybe it won't be long before they have been rehabilitated and, hopefully, reunited with their children."

"If that's all, we'll call a close to this session. I have an appointment in Taunton at 4:00 P.M. Thank you, all.

REN

"Oh by the way, if there is some progress made by the parents, I expect this matter to be marked for a full hearing. Actually, if there is no progress, it should still be marked for a hearing before too much time elapses. We want the evidence, whatever it may be, to be current or fresh, if you will. Thank you, again."

If You Live, Age Brings Wisdom

Lynn Wynn refused to cooperate with the Department's service plan. Laverna Andrews had convinced the ongoing supervisor, Enid Evans that Lynn was workable and should be given the opportunity to prove it without losing custody of her son, Todd. Enid assigned Maureen Dubin, newly transferred to her unit. If anyone could empathize with mothers and their problems, it was Maureen. But such success was not to be. Lynn had solidly aligned herself with Laverna and, in so doing, was following the path of a person with a character disorder. Find a single person you completely trust and no one else can approach you successfully.

But this made her unworkable even for someone like Maureen Dubin. She failed to keep appointments, refused to let Maureen in the house while she stood at the locked storm door at the appointed time. Flat out refusal, by Lynn, of any kind of therapy or parenting classes, led to Maureen's request for a legal conference on the appropriateness of a non-emergency Care and Protection. Thomas, 10, was at his grandmother's so any fear of his murdering his brother, Todd, was held in abeyance.

REN

Two days before the conference, a 51A was called in late in the afternoon. A woman motorist was looking for a street in the Wynn's area when she came upon a child filthy, dirty in the middle of the street, skimpily clad in very dirty clothes. She pulled to the side of the road, went back and picked up the child. She asked her to point the house where she lived. The woman knocked and rang several times. A loud voice directed her to the back entrance. She found a light switch inside and called out.

"What the fuck do you want? I threw my back out and it's killing me."

"I found your daughter in the middle of the road. She looks like she hasn't had a bath in a month."

"You put Bridget down on the kitchen floor and go out the way you came in. And kindly mind your own fucking business."

You haven't heard the last of me you vulgar woman. She called the police and DSS.

It now became an emergency Care and Protection. Bridget was removed that night, with police assistance. It was then learned that Todd was also at his grandmother's with Thomas. Both Todd and Bridget would be on the petition requesting DSS custody. Todd was covered with bruises head to toe. He would cower if anyone went near him swinging their arms or walking briskly.

In his Court argument, Sid Silver, attorney for the Wynns, lost his train of thought.

"So when she called me—called me—called me, I told her to get a lawyer."

Don couldn't resist.

"She should have followed your advice."

"Very funny, Mr. Goode. And I suppose you think splitting up families is also funny."

"No. But protecting innocent children from uncaring and neglectful parents is important. Not funny."

The Judge ordered the return of Bridget to the Wynns. Thought she was not at risk, but he gave temporary custody of Todd to DSS. He strongly urged the parents to get help for Thomas and involve themselves in some form of family training so they could better understand the dynamics of family life where each person can function individually and all persons could function as a family unit. He should have been a social worker. Don wondered if he were looking for part time work. He would certainly be happy to recommend him.

Maureen, Laverna and Lynn were chatting in the corridor.

"This gal is the greatest. I wish she were my worker"

"Lynn, there's only one of her. Not enough to go around. We all think she is great."

"Well, she's the only one I trust. You can keep Todd till he's eighteen. I ain't co-operating with DSS."

"Now, Lynn. Remember that nice chat we had about perception and how that and honing your sense of humor can lead to a better life?"

"I remember, Laverna. And I wished from that day to this that you were my social worker. It would have made all the difference in my world. Not 'the world'."

"But I made it crystal clear to you that I only do investigations. I was but am no longer a social worker with an ongoing case load."

"Don't step on my wishes—I don't have blue suede shoes—Laverna. Someone once said 'What is life without hope'. Well I think there's a parallel there, with wishes."

"Lynn, I'm asking you to give Maureen a chance. To give yourself a chance. To give your children, your husband, your family a chance. Just follow the service plan for three months. What can you lose? It may make a significant difference in your life. Won't you please give it a try?"

"I will if you promise to come by for tea once every other week (and then imitating Laverna, perfectly). Won't you please give it a try?"

"I'll more than give it a try. I'll shake on the deal."

The Wynns left the building.

"Laverna, those with character disorders are very similar.

They have to compromise almost everything. You do this for me and I'll do that for you. Why do you suppose that's the case?"

"Maureen, I believe it's because of their emotional fragility. They want to have some control over their lives, their destiny because at some time in the past, something was taken from them forcefully, something that meant a great deal to them. So there has grown a protective distrust of the world around them and the people in it. I believe that's why we got on so well. I was up front. I answered every question honestly. I knew she was studying me. The C.D. people also have antennae that pick up vibes of deceit, which may be unknown or invisible to other people. And they know dishonesty within a very brief time, even if they're not Pisceans."

"How do you know so much?"

"Well I am a little older. . . ."

". . . . A little older.. . . ?"

"And don't come up with that waitress at the Last Supper bit. That's one of my lines."

"Do you think I'll know as much as you do when I'm your age?"

"Maybe. If you live, Maureen. If you live. . . ."

Don just received one of the shocks of his life. Red Bishop, one of the Court Officers, blew his brains out last night. Too much time in Juvenile?

Malcontent

Myrna Malcon, the new Commissioner, had been touring the state visiting Regional and Area Offices hoping to get acquainted with the staff. This morning at eleven she would visit the Cape and Islands Area Office. No supervisors or managers were to be present at the workers' meeting. The others would share in a dutch treat luncheon following the meeting.

"Has anyone here seen the new Commish?"

"I have. We had a legal staff meeting a few weeks ago at Central."

"Don! What is she like?"

"Well, she has the same initials as Marilyn Monroe."

"You mean—"

"And sandy blonde hair and blue eyes."

"Is she a Gemini?"

"I—don't think she has a sign."

"Everyone has a sign, Don."

"No-o-o. Not everyone. But you'll see and judge for yourselves. Her radiation of warmth will bowl you over. Maybe even fry you. I must away to Probate Court to see about finalizing the adoption of Cynthia Rottenbotham's twins. They've been living with the Learys for four years. It's one of Melinda's old cases."

"Does this mean you won't be lunching with M.M.?"

Don smiled. "You know I have a weak stomach."

His luck was about to run out. Cynthia was unable to afford the bus fare from Connecticut and wanted a continuance. Her court appointed lawyer, Mike Rock, insisted on preserving this wonderful woman's rights. He was going to appeal to the highest court if necessary. He wasn't aware that he had little or no appeal. For anyone. He tried to get the latest guardian ad litem to water down her observations and opinions. She was also a lawyer. Very, very strange looking. The day before she was to testify, she was arrested for shop lifting. Don insisted that they all go to the jail where the Court could take her testimony. Judge Harney, ever the gentleman, nixed the idea.

"Well, Mr. Goode, I see you're here and ready to go forward. However, I'm giving this mother one final chance. Is that clear?"

"Of course, your Honor. After all she's related to the Kennedys."

"I object to his using those words to belittle this wonderful person."

"Mr. Rock, they are her words. Stated here, under oath or were you not awake, again?"

"You see what he's doing your Honor? I don't believe this hallowed Court should stand for this!"

"If they let you in here, they should stand for anything."

"Why you, little. . . ."

"Gentlemen, Please. May we have some dates, Millie? See if we can come to agreement at least on those."

The new dates were given. Judge Harney assured both Don and Rock that this was the last continuance. If she failed to show again, the evidence would be closed, the case taken under advisement, and a decision rendered.

"May the record indicate N.F.C. you Honor?"

"Yes, Mr. Goode. No further continuances, Millie, on the record."

"Yes, your Honor."

"Don, I want to be your friend. Why do you take things so seriously? Come on. I'll buy you a cup of coffee, on me."

"Isn't that redundant? And aren't you redundant?"

"Aw, come on. It's just a case. Last case I had with you in Orleans, you drove by me like I wasn't even there."

"You weren't. And a case of what?"

"Envy? I think you envy my ability and legalistic maneuvering. Honestly."

"You don't know the meaning of honesty. And, when it comes to ability, you couldn't carry my jockstrap."

"I can't believe you're so wrapped up in your job."

"Believe it. It's true."

Don went around Rock, down to his car in the parking lot and headed for the office.

"Don, I thought you had a trial in Probate."

"I did, Noel, but the mother was a no-show. Now, if you'll excuse me, I have other fish to fry."

"Not fry, eat. I'm calling the Boston Fish House and making another reservation for you, for lunch at 1:00 P.M."

"Noel, I've already met the new Commish and she well knows who I am. Let her concentrate her energies on getting to know others. Like you."

"You're the area office attorney. You're also Deputy Regional Counsel for the Southeast Region. It would be a slap in the face, if you didn't show, especially, where you're not in Court."

"A slap in the face wouldn't do any damage. In fact, it might do some good."

"Now, now. . . . when it's time we'll expect to meet you at the restaurant."

From the moment the Commissioner entered the room, nearly every social worker used an inordinate amount of control to keep from laughing. Don's allusion to a comparative Marilyn Monroe was still ringing in their ears.

Myrna Malcon (one of the workers wanted to ask if she'd had

a tent named after her but didn't dare. No humor there), fielded questions beautifully. She was very bright and knowledgeable about social work issues. Two or three times she tried to elicit complaints about the legal services they were getting. There were no complaints.

After the luncheon, Don went to the Family Resource Unit to check on an address of a witness to be summonsed on one of his cases. Beth Casey, one of the new workers approached him.

"Don, I was just curious about something. Is the Commissioner married?"

"No, Beth. She was, however, engaged to a former client from the Guild for the Blind. He just happened to recover his sight three weeks before the ceremony. That was that."

"Don Goode! You're incorrigible. Absolutely incorrigible. But you're also very funny, and sometimes save the day for us poor social workers. Thanks."

Nola And Her Knife

Nola had just ordered a third 51B on a third 51A on the same child, same unknown perpetrator and same situation. And this, despite the Regulations of DSS, clearly stating 'that duplicate investigations are unnecessarily intrusive to a family and do not permit effective use of the Department's staff resources. In such cases, the screening decision shall be made by the Regional Director, Area Director or his/her designee'.

During the pendency of this situation, Don was going to one of the units for a conference. Sally from Intake called to him and asked a question about one of the regulations. As they chatted, Don's eyes fell on the screen in upon which she was working. He observed the name 'Valerie Quintal'.

"How can you be just writing that up when I already received a copy of the D.A. referral?"

"Two other 51As were called in."

"Were they separate or new incidents?"

"No."

"The regs don't require another screen-in, or investigation"

"That might be so but this is one case that's going to be investigated thoroughly. And I mean thoroughly."

"Why so?"

"Because of who is involved."

Two months prior, Jim Quintal, one of the brightest and most respected attorneys in Barnstable County appeared at the Area Office to meet with Noel and Keeshu Walker relative to many complaints filed by supervisor Neal Arthur and one of his workers, Mary Jane McKee, regarding Keeshu, at Noel's behest, coming into their unit, several times a day, claiming certain records were behind, visitations weren't being made on a regular basis and other invented complaints from unnamed people in the community.

The straw that finally caused both of them to seek legal counsel, came when Nola and Ruth Goldberg, her trusted ally and worker, manufactured and twisted an old allegation of a 51A to make it appear to be a brand new allegation. Mary Quincy, Regional Director came down to quell the potential riot. Shortly before her arrival, Manny was seen ripping pages out of the case record (which would have shown Mary Jane McKee's work was up to date), taking the record out to the parking lot and removing several sections while seated in his car. Laverna witnessed it and later came forward.

Nola had made the following entry in the case record: 'This supervisor strongly recommends that this case not be returned to current worker and supervisor assigned. Instead, case should be reassigned to a different worker and supervisor for case management of this difficult sexual abuse family situation.'

After Jim Quintal's visit and the dressing down Noel and Keeshu received from Mary Quincy, things calmed down considerably. Keeshu feared a lawsuit more than anything. Neal Arthur had provoked all of them by his pointing out their failures to follow regulations and basic unfairness in Nola's being permitted to give her workers all kinds of time off (Ruth had gone to California for nine days a year ago, with her former live-in abusive boyfriend who beat the shit out of her every other month, whether she needed it or not).

"That's the hardest working and most important unit in this office."

"Well, then, Noel, the rest of us should just go home."

"And, I suppose, you're going to make another complaint to Regional, Neal?"

"I wasn't going to but you've just given me a great idea."

A new directive from Regional. Another staff meeting.

"Why aren't they going to be penalized for the months they've already taken off?"

"Neal, you're never satisfied. You're so cerebral, unlike the rest of us. Here you've ruined a perfectly good set up for the Intake Unit and now you want more?"

"What I want, Noel, is something you've never been able to comprehend. Justice. Pure and simple. Like I'm pure and you're simple."

"Meeting's adjourned!"

Would the wounds start healing? No, they never would. Not until the rot was removed. And that would take major surgery.

The Dyke And The Kike

A few months after Jim Quintal's visit to Noel and Keeshu, when he exposed them for what they were, the first 51A on Valerie Quintal, Jim's daughter, came in. Nola was beside herself. What an opportunity. Her philosophy had always been if you can't attack last, get even. She called Ruth Goldberg into her office and told her the good news.

"Nola, I don't care if they do call us the dyke and the kike. This is heaven sent."

"It's heaven because we're going to send that rotten bastard of a lawyer to hell. The nerve of him to question our actions."

And so their scheme was hatched. It would be the fastest subbed case ever to go through DSS. They had to get the info out to the D.A. and the community as fast as possible. In case it was a mistake. And just because it might be you don't lose an opportunity like this. Drag him and his wife down to the office. Ask them all kinds of personal questions. Ask them about their sex lives. Natural, unnatural, ménage a trois? They would be pulverized into the ground. It might even destroy their marriage. Wouldn't that be just wonderful? Nola and Ruth never knew they could be so happy. And then when the multiple 51As came in, Nola twisted Noel around her finger—actually he had been there all along—and got him to approve the various investigations. It's too bad he was so weak thought Nola. Maybe if it were otherwise, we could have our own ménage. Wouldn't that be something? But I'd want Ruth in the middle. Don't let me get too near any man. Except to take advantage of him.

After they all had their way and were spent, the following letter was received at the Regional Office:

Ms. Mary Quincy

Department of Social Services

Regional Office

141 Main Street

Brockton, MA

Re: Copies of Records for 51A's filed concerning Valerie Quintal

Dear Ms. Quincy:

As Valerie's father, I hereby request copies of all file information, notes, records and reports, relating to the four separate 51As filed during the months of January and February. The first was filed by the Town of Yarmouth Police Department, the second by Doctor Howard Manners, the third was filed as the result of an emergency room trauma unit examination at Children's Hospital and the fourth by Doctor Howard Manners.

I hereby request copies of the paperwork provided to your Department from all sources, as well as all reports generated by the employees of your Department. From the information available to my wife and me, we are aware that the first case was substantiated with an unknown perpetrator; the second and the third cases were merged and then substantiated with an unknown perpetrator; the last 51A was not substantiated because Valerie was diagnosed as suffering from lichen sclerosus (et) atrophicus; that the disease exhibited the same symptoms that can exist with child abuse. The diagnosis was made by Doctor

Juan Pariso, a pediatric gynecologist. That diagnosis was confirmed by Doctor Ana Grist, a dermatologist from Massachusetts General Hospital.

As a result of this diagnosis child abuse did not occur. Therefore, I request that the records be amended and the substantiations be reversed so that the records reflect the actual diagnosis.

It is also important that you be aware that my wife and I both feel that we were treated as the perpetrators. Without being named we were kept in the dark about the activities of the agencies and departments.

I am aware of the statutory requirements of Chapter 119 and the theory behind the state agency's responsibility, but unless and until Social Services has sufficient training and staffing, as well as work places which provide confidentiality, follow-up and the elimination of hysteria which accompanies these matters, no one even considered that the situation had any explanation except child abuse. We never had any assistance in developing a therapeutic plan for Valerie. We all became victims of the system and have been damaged by the system.

When Valerie went to the doctor's office on Saturday, she was healthy and well adjusted. Now she is insecure because the system interfered with our lives and took away our control over her destiny.

While employees of your Department may well have in fact been working to assist us, because we were never advised of those efforts, they provided no benefit to us. If the state is going to create their power and responsibility and confer it on the Department of Social Services, then your Department has no choice but to provide the needed services or refuse the cases

Please re-assess the process and build in safeguards including mandated second opinions with a pediatric gynecologist in the case of children, to rule out any misdiagnosis as happened in this case.

Very truly yours,
Jim H. Quintal

"Don"

"Yes."

"Noel. Could you come down to my office?"

"Sure. Right now?"

"As soon as you can."

Don finished the correspondence and walked across the yard and down the corridor. He met James Blender outside the Intake Unit where he had recently transferred.

"What a tan! Been south or Tanorama?"

"Neither. I was doing the mountains in Colorado at the Claudine Longet Ski Invitational."

Claudine Longet? "It was dangerous but exciting."

"At least there were no spiders around, I bet."

"Not a one. But like what's green and has four wheels? Grass. I lied about the wheels, I lied about Colorado. I just saw that Invitational in the Boston Globe and wanted to share it. With someone. Anyone. Even you."

"What? The mountains or the Invitational sponsor?"

"Yes."

"See ya later, James. Maybe at Tanorama."

"Come in Don. Have a seat. I wanted you to see this."

It was a copy of Jim Quintal's letter to Mary Quincy. Don was deeply moved. He placed the document on Noel's desk.

"What do you think?"

"About what, Noel?"

"I mean this guy's been through quite a bit."

"He sure has. I can't believe Mary Quincy made such bad judgments about those multiple 51As. She seems so bright."

"What makes you think that? Not that she's 'so bright'!"

"Well the Regs say that the Regional Director or Area Director will make the screening decision when there are multiple 51As. I know you wouldn't be so stupid as to do that because it would be so obvious that it would be a revenge play. Why, a child could see through that. You could lose your home, savings, any other assets you may have."

"Why would I seek revenge, Don. I think Jim Q's a fine person."

"You didn't think so after you and Keesh met with him about a few months ago."

"You weren't there. Did he tell you?"

"No. He's so honorable, he wouldn't put me in a divisive situation."

"Then how did you know? Did you divine it?"

"No, I saw the three of you go into an unoccupied office. Then I saw the three of you emerge forty minutes later. Through amazing powers of deductions, I concluded you three had met about something."

"Why would you think I thought he wasn't such a fine person, after the deduced meeting?

"Because I was standing in a doorway — you didn't see me — and I heard Keesh say, "Man, I ain't getting mixed up in no mother fuckin' law suit. Got mixed up one time and thought I was lucky to escape with my black ass intact."

"Do you think Jim plans on suing?"

"I'm not the one to ask, but if you've assimilated the contents of his letter, it sure looks like it."

"What particular part?"

Don picked up the letter and quickly found the phrasing he sought.

"We become victims of the system and have been damaged by the system. Now she is insecure because the system interfered with our lives and took away our control over her destiny. From there you can go on to the part of Jim and his wife being treated as perps."

"You mean by the dyke and the kike?"

"Noel. You were warned eight months ago by Jim Blender that Nola was going to be the cause of your being fired. She fucked you over on the Antonia Marshall case. At least I think she did. Unless you were stringing me along, you asked me to go to the annex—the state police were here—and tell her you wanted Intake to take in a 51A to protect the children and Antonia from herself. I did as you requested. No 51A was ever taken in. A few months later, as you know, she tried to suffocate another baby. You couldn't explain your actions to the Death Squad, or inaction, I should say. Nola will still be here and you will be gonzo. All because you abdicated your position and power to her. She is the Area Director. She tells you what to do and how to do it. I have to conclude that that's the way you want it. But how are you going to support your family? She's laughing at you behind your back. If I were you, I'd start updating your resume and making applications elsewhere."

"You don't think I can ride out the storm?"

"Noel, your ship has already sunk in Barnstable Harbor. Its captain is going down within thirty days."

"Has someone told you this?"

"Yes."

"Who?"

"You. " And that's one for my friend, Melinda.

Together Again

They were lying in bed, having just completed the love act.

"Don?"

"Hmmmm?"

"Before you go off to dreamland as you always do, I want to thank you."

"Hmm. For what?"

"Not bringing your job home with you."

"Oh."

"I know you're dealing in human misery every day. Oh I enjoy the bizarre humor—like when you first started, you got one of those night calls from Falmouth Hospital and the social worker said the child's mother threw a hammer at her and could you meet him at Barnstable Court the next morning. You came back to the table and told the story. Then you began to laugh hysterically. And sing. 'If I had a hammer; I'd hammer in the morning; I'd hammer in the evening, all over your bod.' We were all laughing. I don't think Genie and Ave understood. I'm sure they didn't. But you know how imitative children are. What I'm really trying to say is. . . ."

"Think you'll get to it before breakfast, Hon?"

"You dirty rat. You shot my story in the back."

"You could never have been his stand-in"

"Wouldn't want to be. But Don, what I meant to say is thank you for not bringing the horror home."

"Actually, the Commissioner's a very nice person. I think we should invite her."

"Don! Your home should be a safe harbor. You're here to be refreshed, rejuvenated."

"After what happened tonight, I am."

"Good, Goode. If you shared those awful happenings, I'd be completely frustrated."

"Why?"

"Because I'm powerless to do anything. You know how much I love children. Can't stand seeing them suffering needlessly. There are so many sick people out there."

"You could open a clinic."

"Sure. Do you have a key to the door?'

"Well Mer. it's after one. And I have to hammer home another case tomorrow."

"Don, that was years ago."

"Oops! Right again. Tomorrow it's Orleans. Crazy uncle gave it to the dog, 'Whiskey', in front of little Mary, age 5. They're relatives of another case I have in Barnstable, where the father is accused of pornography with his own kids."

"Don, I said thank you for not sharing, so please count the number of hours of sleep you're going to get on your fingers and I'll go to sleep with gratitude."

"Shucks, 'tweren't nuthin'. Wait! I don't have enough fingers!"

"Use both hands."

REN

A Dog Named Whiskey

Little Mary Draper's mother, Doris, was in Pocasset Mental health after a severe psychotic episode. Mary was in the care of Granny Draper and her husband, Dan. Their son, Mitchell, 23, also lived in the house along with his dog, 'Whiskey'.

When Mary arrived at school a few days ago, she asked her teacher if she could visit the nurse's station. She showed the nurse bruises on her vagina and a discharge of blood.

"Has someone been bothering you, Mary?"

"Yes, Mrs. Lenox. My uncle, Mitch."

"Well, dear, how did it happen?"

"Uncle Mitch was showing me how he sticks his dink in his dog, Whiskey. The dog kept whimpering."

"Was anyone in the house?"

"Yes. Granny was there but Grandpa was working. Granny came in and saw what Uncle Mitch was doing and she said, "That's it children, play nicely."

Oh my God!

"Well what happened after that, Mary?"

"I told Uncle Mitch not to hurt the dog. That the dog didn't like it."

"And. . . ."

"He said, well if you're a Draper, you'll like it. He came into my room almost every night and got on top of me and kept touching me. I said it hurt and he said it was just his little finger and he was only trying to tickle me. One night, Granny said, 'Mitch, are you in Mary's room?' He said 'Yes, we're only playing' and Granny said 'Good'. I know it was late because I could hear the news with Natalie and Chet."

"Why don't you go back to your class, Mary. Or would you rather stay here while I go to the office?"

"Rather stay here. I feel like everyone's looking at me like I'd done something awful."

"That's the way a lot of children feel. That they're responsible."

"It happens to a lot of children."

"Oh, yes. But they're innocent. It's the adults who are responsible. You're fortunate that this came to light so soon. Many children keep it buried because the grown up said 'This is our secret'. Or I'll hurt you or your mother if you tell'."

"I forgot that part. He said it was our secret and if I told, something real bad could happen."

Mrs. Lenox left Mary and headed for the principal's office. If only 'Whiskey' could speak. But even anatomically correct dolls wouldn't help there.

She dialed DSS's number.

When Don arrived at Orleans District Court, he was surprised to see James Blender. He was with Mary Draper. Don had forgotten about James' transfer to Intake. He had little Mary sit on one of the benches in the outer lobby.

"Can you fucking believe it, Don? Giving it to a dog."

"Well I haven't seen all your old girlfriends, James, but . . ."

"Always ready with a quip, Don. Thank God."

"Otherwise, I might have the cell next to Lunie."

"How's she doing?"

Don told him about the pizza and beer party for her clients.

"And they let her out?"

"Just for the weekend. A trial furlough, I suppose."

"Did you call Bournewood?"

"That's not my responsibility. It was after hours. Strictly a social call."

"Her family there?"

"Nary a one. I suspect that's why she was using a credit card to pay for the pizza and beer."

"I don't know whether it's crazier on the inside or on the outside where we are. . . ."

"Perhaps fifty-fifty. So, it doesn't really make a difference. Jackie Mason says, If you don't think there's a lot of insanity out there, you're crazy!"

The case was called. Custody was given to DSS until the 72 hour hearing. Counsel was appointed for Doris and Mary.

"Your Honor?"

"Yes, Mr. Goode. Always nice to see you."

"Doris Draper is a patient at Pocasset. I have no idea when she would be in a position to assist her lawyer. I believe you appointed Mr. Rock for the mother. It might be a good idea to continue that 72 hour hearing generally. When Doris and Mr. Rock are ready, the Department will go forward. I would not limit them to the normal seventy-two hours."

"That's a sound idea, Mr. Goode. And a lot better than bringing everyone back for a hearing that's not going to take place. Will you see that Mr. Rock gets whatever copies he may need to adequately prepare for the hearing?"

"Certainly, your Honor. They'll go out in this afternoon's mail."

"Very kind of you. And I'm sure he'll feel the same."

"I wouldn't go that far, your Honor."

"Moderation in all things, eh Mr. Goode?"

"In all things."

"Oh, Mr. Goode. I had a call this morning. Marnie Lenz, Mary's aunt and her husband Ralph, wish to be considered as foster parents for Mary. Will you pass that along?"

"Absolutely, your Honor." Do cows fly?

"That all you have here today, Don?"

"In Court, yes. I have an appointment with a therapist who will testify in an upcoming case."

"Where's he/she located?"

"Family Counseling on Route 6 beyond the Visitor's Center on the right. Her name is Jan Sterling. Married to Neal Arthur, one of your old sups."

"Oh, yes, I've met her a few times. Well Mary's placement is off School House Road. Could we meet for coffee, somewhere?"

"Sure. I think Lori's is the closest she has new digs. Really nice. That'll work out fine. I was just about to go downstairs to the library and do some legal research. You've saved me from a fate worse than death. Thanks, James."

"Anytime, my liege. Anytime."

On the way to Lori's he thought of Uncle Mitch jumping off the Empire State building onto a bicycle . . . that had no seat.

Those Wedding Bells

Julie Harris had just finished taking an order from a customer when the booth phone rang.

"Kodak booth, Hyannis."

"Julie, Julie, Julie, do you love me?" It was Reardon. Singing. Sort of.

"What did you do with the money?"

"What money?"

"The money your mother gave you for singing lessons."

"In case you've forgotten, I've performed at policemen's balls."

You're not short enough for a performance like that. Julie Harris! You should be ashamed of yourself!

"Well, had you forgotten?"

She had the incredible urge to laugh hysterically but barely managed to control herself.

"Why are you calling? We agreed to three dates a week—spread out. I just saw you last night."

"And I'm still on cloud nine, Julie, I ache for you body, soul and mind."

"Have you nothing better to do? And why are you trying to

make love on the telephone?"

"Because that's the only kind you'll let me make. Haven't you realized we were made for each other?"

"I thought it was 'mad'."

"That, too."

"Listen, Rear, and I won't add 'end', I am working and you are not."

"I could come over and help you and then you could get off earlier."

"Nothing like that in my employment contract."

"You should have stayed at DSS."

"You'd be happier if we'd never met?"

"Oh, no! I forgot about that."

"Out of sight, out of mind, eh?"

"No. No. Honest, I didn't mean . . ."

"Do you want me to add 'end'? Why are you calling?"

"Well, the Lenz case will be coming up soon, and. . . ."

"That's funny. Marion never mentioned it and it's her case."

"Well, you know how reticent she is. I met Don Goode in Court this morning. He said he expects to have about twenty witnesses. So I thought you and I could start practicing . . ."

"Practicing what?"

"Our testimony."

"Oh. Where?"

"How about my apartment?"

"No way."

"How about your place when Marion's not around?"

"No."

"Where, then?"

"Someplace where there are a lot of people."

"Like the Windjammer? They already think we're fixtures."

"Good. Then they won't mind. We'll be like members of the family."

"Julie, I'm going crazy. I can't stand it when you're not around and when you are, I can't stand not being able to hold you . . . or . . ."

"This sounds serious. Have you seen a doctor? You know we've only known each other less than three months."

"It'll be three months tomorrow, Jule."

He's been keeping track. Good sign.

"If you're really serious, Rear, when is your next week end off?"

"Thank God! Then you will marry me?"

"No. I mean, no, that's not what I meant."

"I know you didn't mean you'd go away with me. Right?"

"Well, yes. That's exactly what I meant. To . . ."

Reardon was beside himself, ecstatic.

"To visit my parents."

"Do you really like to give people roller coaster rides?"

"Well, if we're going to get married in June, the least you could do is meet my parents. They're very nice people."

"Reardon, if you're packing to run away like a little boy, don't forget the string and the can of worms.

"Reardon, please speak to me!" She hoped he hadn't fainted or, worse, had a heart attack.

Two customers came. One with an order, the other a pick up. As she was counting out change, she felt someone behind her in the booth. She hadn't heard the door open.

Two strong arms came around her waist. Not a hold up. Please, not that. The arms turned her body towards him. It was Reardon.

"I love you and I accept your proposal of marriage for this coming June, three months hence."

"Oh, I didn't say which year, did I?"

' "No more of that—please. I'm off the weekend after this. Call your parents now. I want this thing solidified."

"I can't Rear. Company policy. No long distance calls."

"Here's my New England Tel charge card. Where do they live?"

"Right now they're living in Wellesley."

"Well you won't be able to call them then."

"Why not?"

"Those poor people in Wellesley don't have telephones."

"You should be so poor."

She dialed the number.

"Hi, Mother, Julie. Oh, you recognized my voice because you only have one daughter and you hadn't heard about any of the boys being in a sledding accident? I see." She looked at Reardon and shrugged.

"Like mother, like daughter," he said softly.

"Sometime Friday—not this Friday, mother, night. Want to give you time to slave drive the servants."

Reardon winced. What was he letting himself in for? Oh well, when they were married it would be their lives, not the parents! He wished June were tomorrow. Hey, he would have to tell his own family. They hadn't even met Julie. But he knew when they had, they would never forget her. They would love her as much as he did. Well, almost as much. No one else's love could approach his. He just couldn't live without her. Or thought he couldn't.

He waited out the remainder of the afternoon, sitting on a stool. He kept gazing at her, drinking her in. They were going to the Windjammer for dinner to celebrate. He hoped his dooky cooled down by then. All he had to do was look at Julie or even think of her, and up it came. It wasn't so noticeable sitting down, but it was getting to the restaurant table standing up that concerned him. He didn't want the hostess or waitress saying something like, 'Is that a gun in your pocket or are you just glad to see me?' I mean, it could be a gun. After all, he was a Barnstable police officer.

"What was that date in June, Julie?"

"Is that all you can think about?"

"As a matter of fact, yes."

"Well I liked the month of June. You know 'June Bride'. I'll call tomorrow to see what's available. Maybe they're booked up."

"Uh-uh. It's June. If not there, somewhere else. Your family have any connections with the church?"

"Sort of. My uncle is pastor of St. John's."

"And you think there might be a question? I don't care if it's two o'clock in the morning."

"Women are different from men, Rear."

"Viva la difference! " He wasn't used to drinking, and was on his fifth glass of champagne. He was getting silly. Drunk with love for Julie and almost drunk physically, from the champagne. One couldn't get more completely tight than that.

"Rear, don't you think we should order?"

"They sing, 'Food, glorious food' but I do not need it. One look at my Julie and I am filled to overflowing."

"You're filled to overflowing all right, but I am not going to say with what. I'm a lady."

"Hey everybody! My lady is from Wellesley."

"Rear, please. Shhh!"

The bar manager sent over another bottle of champagne. They all thought Reardon was a screech. Keep the customers entertained. They'll stay longer and spend more. Reardon began singing at the top of his voice.

"Julie, Julie, Julie do you love me?" Actually, he was a lot better than he was on the phone. His self-consciousness had been dissipated. The piano player picked up the tune and motioned Reardon to the microphone although, truth to tell, he really didn't need it. The restaurant wasn't that big. He would have needed it in the normal hustle and bustle, but everyone was listening, paying attention. Julie was starving. She ordered a cheeseburger—some celebration—and a pot of coffee. She knew who'd be driving. She'd alert Marion. She could meet them, have one drink to celebrate. Julie would drive Reardon home with Marion following. For a moment, she considered having Reardon sleep at their house. Certainly plenty of room. But when she saw the state of his emotions, she knew she'd be courting danger while he was courting her. Reardon was, as they say, in the mood for love.

When she returned from the ladies' room and her call to Marion, Reardon was into show tunes. He was taking requests from the customers. She didn't know he was the Cape's greatest advocate of Karaoke. That's how he had spent most of his free time before meeting Julie. A little shy at first. But after he got started, there was no stopping him.

"He's great, isn't he?" It was their waitress.

"He'd be even greater if he'd have something to eat. And I certainly would feel better."

"How many times in anyone's life, do they get a chance to fly like a star? Besides, who gets married every day?"

"Elizabeth Taylor."

"Okay, that's one. Name another."

They both laughed.

"Reardon is a wonderful guy. He's laid back but has a serious nature underneath and a good sense of humor."

"Are you his sister or his agent?"

"Neither. He used to date my roommate. That's how I got to know him so well. She knew he was a good catch but her problem was in pursuing him, relentlessly. A guy likes to do the chasing, or think he's doing it. When he was working this area, he'd drop in for a cup of coffee—always pay. And all he did was talk about you and how uncertain he was of your feelings. You played your cards right."

"I didn't play my cards. It was all very natural."

"That's even better."

When they got to his apartment, Julie expected some trouble from Reardon. She was wrong. He was as meek as a lamb. All that expressive singing had made him serene. He was just like a little boy on Christmas morning, still half asleep. But he had taken the unopened bottle of champagne home with him. He asked them in for a night cap. They refused.

"I never wear a nightcap."

"You don't wear them Julie; you drink them."

"Oh. Well give me a kiss goodnight, and I'll call you on the morrow."

"Romeo and Juliet. Parting is such sweet sorrow . . ."

"You never cease to amaze me, Rear."

He chuckled.

"You ain't seen nothin' yet."

It was the sweetest kiss either of them had ever experienced. Now they knew who they were and where they were going. Nothing was worse than not knowing. Right Reardon?

"I love you, Rear."

"What progress! And I love you, Jules."

"How much?"

"I love you a bushel and a peck, a bushel and a . . ."

"I thought you had done enough singing tonight to last a lifetime."

"Are you inferring that you never want to hear me sing ever again?"

"No, I'm declaring it."

"Jule!"

"Just kidding. Just kidding. I thought you sounded like a professional . . ."

"Thank you, my darling."

"Now don't get too puffed up. That was an incomplete sentence."

"Liar, liar. Pants on fire."

"They may be hot, but they're not on fire. Nite."

"Hey you can't make a comment like that and then walk away from me."

"Yes I can."

And she did.

"Julie, he's a wonderful person. You're very lucky."

"I know, Marion. But don't tell him."

"Don't tell him he's lucky, too? Well someone should."

"Marion, start the car before the sun comes up."

"But, it's only—"

They came out of Reardon's street and headed down route 28. Marion would wonder for days, why Julie didn't want anyone to tell Reardon he was lucky too.

Justice For The Thatchers

The Neilson twins did a very effective job of testifying at the trial of Mr. and Mrs. Thatcher's case for wrongful death against the state. When Mrs. Thatcher was describing Melinda and her upcoming marriage, her voice was cracking. There wasn't a dry eye in the room.

"We came here to give our best wishes to a bride. Instead we were handed a dead daughter. It's so unnatural for a child to predecease a parent. We would gladly give up our lives, so she could live."

It wasn't admissible and was stricken on the reluctant objection of the Assistant Attorney General who was defending for the state. What a loser case with which to be stuck. And talk about losers. The only witnesses she had—and she didn't want to call them—were Noel C. Peel and Manuel Gomes. It took Manny a full two minutes on direct examination to answer a question with his stuttering and feeble attempts to outguess the questioner. His cross-examination was deferred by Alan Browne until later in the trial. Noel had gone first and did everything but call for the Congressional Medal of Honor for Melinda. Posthumously, of course. Perhaps when you tell the same lie often enough, you become convinced it's true.

"Yes, and as I recall the outstanding courage of Manny Gomes, my brave friend, he even offered to drive into Roxbury with Melinda to get the twins. As I further recall, he even offered to go alone. But Mel—sometimes we called her that—she was adamant. It was her case, her clients. Even if she didn't know where Roxbury or Area B Police Station was—she would find it, on her own. She was dedicated to the very end."

"Mr. Coward . . ."

"Excuse me, sir, my name, my surname is 'Peel'. Coward's my middle name."

"What a pity. Mr. Peel, did you hear the testimony of Trudy Teller and Don Goode?"

"Of course. They were both good friends of Mel's. What do you expect? They're just trying to give a helping hand to the Thatchers. You know, mending fences instead of building walls."

"Why would either have to mend fences? Or rather, what fences would they have to mend?"

"Do you want one or two?"

"One or two what?"

"You asked two questions in the same breath, Mr. Browne."

"The simple thing to do, if that's not too difficult for you, is to answer one and then the other."

Noel reached in his pocket and took out the three lead weighted silver balls that Don had left on his desk a long time ago. As a joke. He moved them back and forth in his right hand. Too bad Jim Gavin, Noel's lawyer in his department difficulties, wasn't here. He had wondered about missing strawberries and keys. In this present case, since Noel and Manny were management, the A.G.'s Office represented them as well as the state.

"Mr. Coward—Peel—are you awake?"

"Yes. Yes. What's the question?"

"We'll try it again. Ms. Stenographer would you please read the last question to Mr. Peel?"

"Mr. Coward—Peel—are you awake?"

Are you awake?

"The one before that, please."

She read the question.

"We all have little repairs to make in our lives. I don't necessarily know in this case which ones, just that it's universal. They may, unconsciously, think that the Thatchers blame them for Mel's death, and are, therefore, trying to make it up to them by these preposterous stories. Now, mind you, I'm talking about unconscious thinking."

I think you think unconsciously all the time. Or are unconscious all of the time.

"Do you believe—I don't want to burden you with the word 'think'—that Trudy Teller or Don Goode would commit perjury to 'help out' the Thatchers?"

"Perjury? That's under oath, right?"

"Correct. Just as you are now."

"Well, not consciously, no."

"Have you known Trudy Teller or Don Goode to tell a lie, not under oath?"

"Well, I can't answer for the time before I became Area Director."

"Can you answer at all? Even for the time after you became Area Director?"

"Not consciously."

"Are you speaking for yourself or Ms. Teller and Mr. Goode?"

"Well, we're all in this together."

"Who all."

"All of DSS. I mean if I had done anything wrong or if people believed Trudy and Don, why wouldn't I be sued? I'm just a witness for the state, trying to get the truth out."

Manny winced. Those silver balls in Noel's hand were going fast and furious.

"You and Manny Gomes have been sued; you are a defendant in this case as well as Mr. Gomes as well as the state. Does that in any way change your attitude or your testimony?"

"I'll have to think about it. Your Honor, I don't feel well (it was past Heiniken time); could we take a break here?"

"Well, it's almost lunch time. I suppose a few extra minutes won't matter. This trial will resume at 2:00 P.M."

"All rise."

They were having a quick lunch at the Piccadilly Deli; seated at the counter. Or rather Manny was. Noel was drinking his Heineken.

"What the fuck were you saying up there? And do you think those jurors couldn't see those silver balls? I could see them from the back row."

You could've used your own if you had any.

"Now Manny, everything will work out just fine. The trouble with you is you worry too much. Get too nervous."

"You think I'm going to face Alan 'The Shark' Browne on cross examination with that story you cooked up? You should have left it simple, 'like we offered to send a male worker with her'. Instead you go into that bullshit 'Manny offered to go with her—he even offered to go alone!' For crissake, are you trying to skewer me?"

Noel laughed. "If anything is questioned, just say 'My memory must be faulty! I thought I taught you that a long time ago."

"Everything you taught me has gotten me into trouble. My transfer's been held up because of the Manzi-Roselli case that I tried to bag for a family friend. You always said it was simple, just brazen it out."

"Well I'm sure Joe Carnivale will bail you out."

"Bail me out? He's made a full confession to Judge Crownout. On tape! The Commissioner and Investigators have copies of the tape. That Bitch, the grandmother, called and told me all the kid had was a scratch."

"Why would she be in the hospital for a week or so, if all she had was a scratch?"

"I don't know. I wasn't thinking."

"If Joe saw her, why wouldn't he convey her true condition to you? He did see her, didn't he?"

"No. I told him not to bother. Besides, he had already unsubbed it. For me."

"Well, I doubt very much that I'm being terminated but should that be the case, we can both go and sign up together."

"What makes you think I'd want anything to do with you, Noel, when this is all over?"

"Manny, what a kidder you are. We'd better get back. You're on the stand."

"I'm not on the stand. You are. You don't think 'The Shark' is through with you, do you?"

"Now Mr. C. Peel, before the lunch break, you had just learned that you were a defendant in this case."

"That's correct."

"Does that put a different light on the situation for you?"

"What do you mean?"

"Do you wish to change any of your answers, to amend any by addition, subtraction or expansion?"

"You forgot the 'guzzintas'; you know: division? Just thought I'd inject a little humor into an otherwise somber situation."

No one laughed. Except Noel. And his laughter became maniacal. The jurors were shaking their heads.

"Mr. Peel, did you call a staff meeting after Melinda's death?"

"Absolutely."

"And did you and Mr. Gomes order Trudy Teller to go to a budget hearing at the MSPCC offices in Hyannis?"

"I don't know if you'd call it an 'order'. She was told to go."

"That would be an order, would it not? Told to go."

"It could be taken as such."

"Did you tell her she could remain for the tribute you and Mr. Gomes were planning for Melinda Thatcher with the rest of the staff?"

"No," Noel began to perspire noticeably on the upper lip.

He shouldn't have had those two Heinekens for lunch. A little food would have helped. He felt light headed and dizzy at the same time. He knew what was coming. He felt like Kevin Costner in 'No Way Out'.

"How many budgetary meetings had Ms. Teller attended at the MSPCC offices prior to this particular one?"

No answer.

"Mr. Peel, did you hear the question?"

"Yeah."

"Would you please answer it?"

"Yeah. None."

"How many meetings of any kind had Ms. Teller attended at the MSPCC offices as a representative of DSS?"

"None."

"How many meetings has Ms. Teller attended at the MSPCC offices since that time?"

"None."

"Whose function is it to attend such meetings?"

"Mr. Gomes."

"Is Mr. Gomes classified as management?"

"Yeah."

"So it was a management function?"

"Yeah."

"And you sent a worker, Ms. Teller?"

"Yeah." His answers were starting to sound funny. Even to him.

"Who called this meeting with MSPCC for this particular date and time?"

I wonder, does he know? Oh God, I'm going under.

"I guess they called it. But I'm not sure."

"You didn't arrange it? Insist on that and time change?"

No answer.

"Mr. Peel. I have a witness from the management of MSPCC, who will testify that you changed the meeting time from the following week at 3:00 P.M. to the morning of your staff meeting. Does that refresh your recollection?"

"Your Honor, I don't feel well."

"I'm sure you don't. Continue Mr. Browne."

"Yes!" He was standing up. "We sent her to MSPCC to spare her feelings. We all loved Melinda and the memorial was precious to all of us!" He started to cry. No one made any attempt to console him nor was any one empathetic. Least of all the jury. They were dry eyed.

"And was she more loved by you and Mr. Gomes than she was by Ms. Teller, her best friend?"

"Well, yeah. It's two to one. Get it? Two to one."

Again, that laugh.

"Did you and Mr. Gomes send Trudy Teller out of the office because you knew she had pleaded with you to send a male worker either alone or with Melinda, and you didn't want the rest of the staff to know?"

"That's a long question."

If this were a criminal trial and you were the defendant, I'd hope your sentence would be even longer. Much longer.

"Did you know of or hear Mr. Goode testify, that Melinda told him on the day before she was burned to death, that Trudy had asked about a male worker going with her and that she, Melinda, asked about the area, and that you and Mr. Gomes, assured it was a very safe area?"

"Same as above."

"What does that mean?"

"That's a long question."

"Nothing further of this witness, your Honor."

"Step down, Mr. Peel but do not leave the Courtroom."

'The Shark' made mincemeat out of Manny Gomes on cross-examination. He was shaking all over and the stuttering only made it appear that he was lying and trying to hold things back. It wasn't a question anymore of whether the Thatcher's would prevail. It was a question of arithmetic: By how much?

After the jury had filed out, the Court Officer called out, "The Court will see Mr. Peel in chambers."

"Have you been drinking, Mr. Coward—excuse me, Mr. Peel?"

"Only coffee, your Honor."

"Irish coffee?"

"No. No, Judge. I did have two valium to steady my nerves." He showed the Judge the bottle. He knew his speech was slurred.

"I see. Just wanted you to know I could put you in jail for contempt. If you were drinking, I'll accept your explanation. Dismissed."

He'd be hearing that last word again. Soon.

Trudy and Don went across the street for coffee.

"Look good to you, Don?"

"Sure does."

"How long you figure they'll be out?"

"No one has been able to determine what jurors do, why they do it or what seems to impress them most. Some years ago, a secret bugging of jury deliberations, supposedly for academic purposes, revealed such startling criteria that the law professor in charge of the project released the findings, publicly. The judge who had been talked into it was in deep shit. The jurors, and it was a capital case, talked about such deep issues as the prosecutor's tie not matching his suit, the defense lawyers shoes being scuffed and not shined, the good looks of the defendant, the judge's habit of holding or cupping his right hand over his ear and saying 'You don't say?' and many other extremely salient points. Guess we're better off not knowing how they arrive at verdicts. Generally, they're right on the mark. Other times, completely taken in. Like the guy who murders his kids and bludgeons his wife, so she won't feel the pain. Defense have two shrinks who swear the guy had a psychotic episode and couldn't distinguish between right and wrong. State brings in two shrinks who say he was depressed but not psychotic and that he knew exactly what he was doing. Kind of shows you Psychiatry isn't an exact science or not a science at all. Or you find beliefs in the practical old adage: 'You gets what you pays for.'"

It was a pleasant occurrence for the farmer and his wife. A six million dollar verdict against the state. One million each against Noel and Manny. The Thatchers did not intend to proceed on execution against either Noel or Manny but they didn't want them to know. Alan Browne told the Assistant A. G. but instructed her not to notify them just yet. They should suffer for what they had done.

The Thatchers thanked Trudy and Don for their help and then left the building. They would dispose of Melinda's belongings before they returned home. They arranged to meet Trudy that evening at Melinda's so she could select whatever she wanted.

"Well Trude, gotta hand it to the Commish."

"Not a mirror, I hope."

"No. About being up front. When we received the summonses from Browne we had to call Legal at Central, remember?"

"Oh yeah. Now I remember."

"She had that conference call with us and said she had reviewed the stories we gave to the Investigators on Melinda. 'Just tell the truth', she said. 'Let the chips fall where they may.'"

"Wait till she hears how many chips have fallen, Don."

"A million here. A million there."

"Here a million. There a million. Everywhere a million, million."

"How many is that, Trude?"

"Who's counting? By the by, how much longer do we got to put up with the A-hole?"

"Which one?"

"Noel- the -Coward."

"About ten days, give or take a second, or as the crow flies."

"Really? I don't know where you get your information, Don, but it's almost always accurate."

"I'm a cancer. People confide in us with the understanding that the confidentiality is maintained."

"But if you're telling everyone—and you are— how can you maintain confidentiality?"

"Because I never reveal the source. Never."

"Oh. I had the content in mind."

"Content is meant to be shared. People just don't want to be responsible for it. Anonymity makes life a little easier."

"Don, I have something I want to confide in you."

"See what I mean?"

"Yes. About six weeks ago, I stayed at the office one night to sift through that myriad of paper work we all have on our desks."

"Not all, Trudy. There is nothing on Noel's desk. He wouldn't even accept a copy of the new Regs. 'I don't need that shit cluttering up my desk', he said. Imagine. An Area Director who doesn't want to know what the governing regulations are for his office, for the Department. For him."

"Even if he had accepted them, he wouldn't be needing them much longer. To get back to my interrupted narrative. I half heard these voices coming from Noel's office which is next to mine. Then I distinctly heard Neal's name, 'Disobeys orders', 'fire him for that', 'that's grounds', 'he's nothing but a malcontent', 'let's get him good'. I didn't know what to do, so I continued working, with my ears perked. A little later, Manny went by my door and did his usual double take.'D-i-i-i-i—d-d- y-y-y-o-u j-j-j-u-s-t c-c-c-c-o-m-m-e i-n?' I told him I had been there all the time and reminded him that any attempted firing of any worker would meet with stern opposition from the union. Especially when the plot was hatched by management, secretly. Well almost secretly. He could barely talk for about three minutes. Then he went and got Noel and Keeshu, all of whom denied ever mentioning Neal's name."

"I hope you didn't wait until now to tell someone."

"I did like heck. Told Leona, the shop steward, the next A.M. She's such a thorn in their sides and elsewhere, they'll think they have the stigmata."

"Hooray for Trudy and Hollywood!"

They left the building and headed for their cars in the parking lot.

The next day Manny transferred all his real estate into an irrevocable trust for the benefit of his wife and children. This action would return to haunt him.

The Blessed Virgin Resigns

Mainly because she had been a nun for twelve years, her pastor, Colleran O'Malley, had selected Mary Jane McKee to be the Virgin Mary in the parish Christmas pageant. After three years of it, she had had enough. She knew from her religious training that that Mary was only about fourteen years of age when she gave birth to the Christ Child. She thought about herself, 'and you've come a long way baby'. She wasn't just 'in the world' now; she was 'of it'. Having left the convent four years ago, she was employed as a social worker in a New York state agency for one year. Three years ago, she came to work for DSS. She enjoyed the first two years immensely despite the pain and suffering in families. She felt she was making a contribution. Always having a good relationship with Noel, she was at a loss to understand how the past year had become such a horror show. Then she realized it was Nola, the evil one, who had taken over the office management. Noel was so weak that Nola could twist and turn him to get whatever she wanted. Whether it was directing management to torture certain workers, altering records, screening things out that should clearly be screened in, belittling her own workers in trying to meet deadlines, re-writing all of their investigations to meet her standards, threatening parents to either sign voluntary placements (to reduce her caseload) or go to jail. There was no end to which she wouldn't go to control the office. When she and her workers began to offend members of the community, schools, day care facilities and hospitals with comments like 'Do you realize it's four-thirty in the afternoon? How dare you expect us to take a 51A at this hour. Wait until 5:00 P.M. and call the Hotline. We're much too busy here', complaints just didn't go to the Regional Office, they went to Central, the Commissioner. As the old saying goes, 'Shit always floats to the top'. And it did.

Keeshu was in Neal Arthur's unit about five times daily. He tortured the four workers and Neal, almost constantly. He claimed their work was way behind the other units of the office. Actually, they were ahead. Mary went to Noel and explained the situation. Would he please exercise his leadership and help?

With his two arms and hands in the air,

"Not my department. Keeshu is in charge of managing your unit. If I told him what to do . . ."

He had already told him what to do.

After two more visits and having reached the highest point of frustration, Mary said, "What is your 'department', Noel? Do you have one? Do you have any function? You sit here with your feet up on your empty desk, picking your nose . . ."

"I could have you terminated for that . . ."

"No, you could not. Truth is an absolute defense. I would say you're not an Area Director. Perhaps more a Cruise Director, except they have pleasing personalities and serve to please others . . ."She left his office.

Now she was at the Rectory door, ringing the bell.

"Hello, Miss McKee." It was Madge, the housekeeper. She had been crying a great deal. Her eyes were red rimmed and her handkerchief was knotted around her fingers.

"Good evening, Madge. Is Father O'Malley in?"

Madge burst into tears and began wailing. Mary stepped inside the entrance hall and closed the door.

Madge went to the reception office and brought back the evening paper. It described how Reverend Colleran O'Malley had picked up a fourteen-year-old boy who was hitchhiking, took him to a motel, fed him whiskey and then raped him. Oh my God, thought Mary as she handed the paper back to Madge.

"The Diocese called. He's suspended indefinitely or at least until the Court matter is resolved. No ministering to the people. Such a wonderful man. You don't believe it, do you, Miss McKee?"

"I don't have all the facts. There are two sides to every story."

"Are you here because of this . . ."

"No, I came to resign from the pageant."

"Oh no! It's started. They'll all be deserting the sinking ship."

"No, Madge, no. I didn't know anything about this until you showed me the paper. I didn't want to be in the pageant even last year but was too shy to resign. It's time for new blood. A much younger person should play the role."

How about that fourteen year old boy with a wig? I'm awful!

"But the people are used to you. They don't want change. They don't like change."

"You're right there, Madge. People don't like change. But we all have to make adjustments in this life. Can't always have what we want. Or think we want."

With that, she said good night and turned to go.

As she drove towards Dennis Center she thought 'One less thing about which to worry. People would be better off if they did more divesting'.

Growing Fonder Of Wanda

Keeshu's wife, Wanda Walker, was a social worker for the Dennis-Yarmouth school system. She tracked the kids who were having problems along with their families, and tried to offer resolution. She was sincere, caring, and did a good job. She also resembled and spoke like Mrs. Huxtable on the Bill Cosby show. Everyone liked her. When the coach of a local elementary school was accused of sexual abuse of some young children, she investigated on her own and came up with clear, objective facts, which established his guilt. Not an ounce of injustice was involved in her report to the School Board. He was first suspended and then dismissed after it was learned he had a previous record of sexual abuse in Texas. These abusers will do anything; go anywhere to have access to children, thought Wanda.

She was in her office scanning the news items when her eyes fell upon one particular one. Ned Osco was being released from jail. How quickly time flies. He had sexually abused and molested two eight-year-old boys five years ago, on his school bus; before reaching their stop, he took a left towards the water and into a wooded area. Despite threats not to tell, at knifepoint, both boys disclosed as soon as they got home. Sometimes it's easier to tell if there is more than one victim. Strength in numbers.

Ten minutes later, the principal and guidance counselor came into her office. She was just finishing a second cup of coffee. It would help her brave the day.

"I can't believe it, Wan. I can't believe it."

"Can't believe what, Arturo?"

"Your husband's in this business so I'm sure you're more knowledgeable than I."

"I may be, but I'll never know and you'll never really know, until you tell me what it is you can't believe."

"You tell her Will."

Will handed her a handwritten note.

"Dear Mr. Rodriguez,

My son, Norbert, will be picked up today at school by Ned Osco, a family friend. I hereby give permission for him to do so. This may become a daily practice but I'll let you know. Norbie will be sleeping at Mr. Osco's residence tonight so he will probably be going to school from there.

Sincerely,

Mrs. Lydia Kambaugh"

Sonovabitch! And I'll bet she knows.

"I'll start calling DSS at 9:00 A.M. Make sure that the Intake Unit is in. And Art, don't feel bewildered. You're not alone. I can't believe it either. How about you Mr. Thomas?"

"I'll join the majority, Wan."

"Good. It's unanimous. Now if we can just light a fire under DSS. That Nola is one stubborn, mean bitch. And she affects some of the other workers that way. Too bad."

"Hello. May I speak to someone in Intake, please?"

Wish I could repeat Laverna Andrews or James Blender. Alas, no such luck.

"Hello. This is Sally Thistle. May I help you?"

Ugh. Oh shit.

"Hello, is someone there?"

"Hi. Yes, I just dropped my pencil. This is Wanda Walker over at D-Y."

"Yes, what is it?"

"We had a note from a mother this A.M. . . ."

"We don't answer mail here, Mrs. Walker. Perhaps if you . . ."

"I'm not asking you to. Believe it or not, I have an education and even though I'm black, I can write."

Score One!

"Well, you've already taken up five minutes of my time . . ."

"Because of your interruption. I'm trying to file a 51A. A convicted child abuser has a mother's permission to pick up her son, Norbert, age 13, from school and the child will spend the night at the convicted child molester's house."

"My supervisor has to approve all 51As and she's busy right now in a very important conference."

Nola was meeting with the Pebsco representative to discuss a retirement plan.

"You mean if 50 -51As come in while she's still in a meeting, you are not going to screen any of them?"

"That's correct."

"Okey dokey, Mrs. Thistle. My guess is that you'll be hearing from the Commissioner in about ten minutes."

"That's a laugh. Just because your husband's an APM here, doesn't mean you're something special or rate special treatment."

"Nice talking to you Mrs. Thistle."

Wanda had been on a panel with the Commissioner the week before. She hoped she'd remember her. When she called, she learned that the Commissioner was at a meeting but would get back to her. She gave D-Y's number and also the number of Barnstable Juvenile Court. Arturo, Will and she would be going to Court to appeal to Judge Cronout directly.

The judge was outraged. He called the juvenile D.A. in, outlined the case and ordered him to assist the school personnel in applying for an emergency C&P. He later granted it and custody to DSS in time to save young Norbie from the hands of Ned Osco.

He ordered the case on for the following Tuesday, when a 72 hour hearing would take place. When the lottery was drawn, Mike Rock's name came up to represent Mom with Peg Denmark for the child.

"Your Honor."

"Yes. Mrs. Johnson?"

"Important telephone call for Wanda Walker. They're holding it in the Juvenile Clerk's office. Laurie Hotchins says she can't hold it much longer."

"You're excused, Mrs. Walker. Believe me, you did a good job. Under the circumstances, most people having been rebuffed as you were by DSS would simply stew and let the matter pass. I, for one, am glad that you're aggressively protecting the safety of children. Same to you two gentlemen."

"Thank you, your Honor." In unison

Launching Ships After All

"Wanda Walker, here."

"Wanda! How nice to hear from you. I hope it's something with which I can help. And please call me Myrna."

"Okay, Myrna. Here goes."

She told the story. The Commissioner was baffled. It was incredulous.

"Thank you, so much. You can't have an effective department unless people share things like this with you."

Next Myrna called the Cape and Islands Office in South Yarmouth.

"They're in a unit conference right now, Ms. Belle—fatto doesn't tolerate interruptions, M'am."

"You ring through this instant or you'll be standing in the unemployment line."

"Listen you! Don't get up your rootin', tootin, high falutin' dander with me. I ain't paid enough to take that from someone who's got problems in her family and turns to us, expecting everything to be solved in the flick of an armpit."

"You won't be getting paid anything from now on. What in hell was wrong with the Cape Office, anyway? Let me speak to Mr. Peel."

"He's over at the Care Bears Bar. Having an early lunch. I don't think he'll be talking to anyone."

"Let me speak to Manny Gomes, please."

"That's better. You're finally learning. Say 'please' and you get a lot more than vinegar."

More than vinegar?

"Manny Gomes speaking."

"This is the Commissioner. The first thing I want you to do is go out and fire that vulgar and rude receptionist. The next thing I want you to do is to put Ms. Bellafatto and Mrs. Thistle on the phone. And I want it now!"

"Y-y-y-y-y-y-e-e-e-s-s-s, sir! Oops. I-d-d-d-d-d-i-i—n-n-t m-m-mme-e-a-n 'sir'."

"Just do it! Is there no one in that office capable of doing a simple thing, like following a direction or an order from the highest ranking person in the department?"

"Nn-nno. I m-m-e-a-n y-y-e-e-s."

"You really should have that fixed Mr. Gomes."

"Placenta, that was the Commissioner. She said to tell you, you're fired. As of right now."

"Oh Manny, you're always jishing. Wait till I tell my sariety sisters this one."

Jishing? She must have meant joshing. Oh well, no need to worry anymore about what she means. Or who cares what 'sariety' sisters means.

"She means it and I mean it. Where're Nola and Sally?"

"In Nola's office but don't go in there. She won't take any interruptions from anyone. I mean it, Man."

"Nola?"

"Get the fuck out of here! This time is sacred."

"It may be sacred, but the Commissioner wants you and Sally on the telephone."

She was at the height of her maniacal power. She had dominion over all things and all people.

"Fuck that ugly bastard and get your ass out of my privacy! I decide what calls I take."

Manny went back to his office and relayed the message word for word. Without stuttering.

"Now go over to Care Bears and get that poor excuse for an Area Director on the phone. I have one of his last assignments for him."

Goodbye Nola, Sally, and soon, Noel. She hadn't said anything about him. Yet.

Noel was in a daze. When Manny told him the Commish wanted him on the phone, he would just laugh and laugh.

"Oh Manny, you are the greatest kiddish in the world."

Sayonara Coward

Noel's hearing before the Commissioner was a disaster. His own attorney, Jim Gavin, wished he had been elsewhere. Nearly everything Noel had done had turned out wrong. But he kept smiling through as though nothing could ever harm him.

The next morning at 8:15 A. M., Mary Quincy drove into the parking area of the Cape and Islands DSS Office. There were five other cars already there. They belonged to the four day-a-week workers. She had phoned for a local caterer to deliver coffee and pastry at 9:00 A.M.

At 8:25 the workers started drifting in. Shirley, the secretary was at the receptionist's station.

"Placenta sick today or on a day off?"

"I have been advised to advise you, there is an emergency staff at 9:00 A.M. in the back building."

"So where's Placenta today, Shirl?"

She repeated what she had been advised.

When the available workers had assembled, Mary Quincy went to the podium. Directness was her forte.

"I'm here to tell you Noel has been relieved of his duties."

There was a loud gasp from the workers. Some of those to whom he had given extra privileges at the expense of other workers, began to cry.

"He will not be coming back. I don't want any of you to state to anyone else that he has been fired. Just say that he chose to resign."

"Did he really have a choice?" It was Ruth Goldberg who had received more time off than any six other workers combined.

"We-e-ll, yes. Presented with certain violations, judgments and habits, it was either resign or . . ."

"What are we supposed to do now, without a leader?"

You never had one so you really haven't lost anything.

"Eve Marden, Area Director of the Plymouth Office will divide her time between the Cape and there. Three days at this office and two at Plymouth."

"Is that going to be from here on out?"

"Oh no. Only until such time as a new Area Director is appointed or assigned here. For the most part, you have a good staff here. We hope to give you all the support you need. I have a few more people to meet with this morning before I return to Regional so I'm going to suggest you stay here for at least another hour. There's plenty of coffee; plenty of pastry. I want you to mix in and talk about what has happened. Catharsis. I'll return at the end of that time and see whether I can answer any questions you may have. As time passes, this will be easier to bear. Nola Bellafatto and Sally Thistle? I'll meet with you in Noel's office—old office—in fifteen minutes."

"What do you think is gonna happen, Nola?"

"Hey, what can I say? I lead a charmed life. Nothing's going to happen to me. I'm too valuable. You? Now that's a different story. I think you're going to get fired."

"Me? Fired? I only did what you told us to do."

"You must have misunderstood. We're in the business of protecting children. Why would I tell anyone not to take in a 51A? That defeats the very purpose of DSS."

Sally couldn't believe her ears. Perhaps for the first time she was seeing Nola for what she was. A totally corrupt person, yet smart enough to deceive her superiors and treacherous enough to intimidate her workers.

Then Sally remembered. The tapes! She was so afraid that she might misunderstand Nola's directives that she taped the unit meetings as well as the one on one conferences. With Nola's permission. It showed Nola how serious Sally was about her job. She went to the bottom right hand drawer of her desk. They were there. Every tape she had made. She felt a lot better as she went down the corridor to Noel's office. Old office.

Mary Quincy was seated with her back to Noel's desk. Beside her was Manny. The two chairs opposite indicated where Nola and Sally were to sit.

"Tell me Mary," Nola said shrugging her shoulders with the air of 'I've- got- better- things- to- do- and- other- fish- to- fry', "does there seem to be some kind of a problem here?"

"A very serious problem. You've instructed your workers not to take in 51As unless you first approve. That means when you're in a 'do not disturb conference', intake of 51As stops. The Commissioner said . . ."

"Whoa, right there. I never gave such instructions to any worker and anyone who says I did is a liar!"

"I've already talked to Rudy and Judy, two of your workers. And I think I may be able to add a third. Sally, your recollection?"

"What you've stated is exactly true. I have tapes in my possession saying the same thing."

"This is unconstitutional! It's against the law! You can even ask Don Goode, our lawyer. One cannot tape the conversation of another without their approval. Get Don in here, goddammit! Get him in here!"

"He happens to be in Orleans Court. Sally?"

"She gave her permission. It's on the tapes, several times. She said it showed how serious I was about my job. Personally, I thought she saw something sexually perverse in it. She thought I'd derive pure sexual pleasure out of listening to her voice, even after I had rejected a previous sexual advance of hers."

Take that, you dyke!

Nola's face was scarlet.

"You also failed to respond to the Commissioner's telephone call even though this APM told you to do so."

"Listen, Mare, I was in the midst of a very important unit meeting. I generally don't brook any interruptions. I thought Manny was talking about something else."

"If you did, why did you respond as you did?"

"Well, I really don't remember how I responded."

"I do," said Manny.

"I do," said Sally.

"Sally?"

"She said, 'Fuck that ugly bastard and get your ass out of my privacy! I decide what calls I take'. And it's on tape."

"Manny?"

"Ex-a-c-c-t-l-y-. I e-e-e-v-e-n wr-wr-oot-e it d-d-d-o-w-n f-f-for th-th-e c-co-m-i-i-s-h."

Mary was looking at a piece of paper.

"And that is exactly the way the Commissioner wrote it down from Manny."

"Nola, you are suspended for three months. Without pay. If during that time you are engaged in community services to a satisfactory degree, the Commissioner will consider removing the suspension. In addition, you are to write letters of apology to Judge Cronout, Wanda Walker and Don Goode."

"Why Don Goode?"

"You deliberately and intentionally made a false entry into the case record of Lydia Kambaugh stating that Don assisted the school personnel in taking out the C and P in order to cover yourself, by pretending there was, in fact, DSS involvement. The school personnel were forced to go to Judge Cronout because your unit, through your orders refused to take in the 51A.

"Mrs. Thistle. You shouldn't have followed orders of that sort. Common sense would dictate otherwise. In addition, you do not speak to callers from the community, schools, day care, and hospitals as though you were doing them a favor. They are doing us a favor. We are here to serve."

"Yes, Ms. Quincy."

"You are hereby suspended for two weeks without pay."

"Hey, how come I get three months and she gets ten days?"

"Because the Commissioner says so. She also said she may be ugly, but she's not a bastard and has the papers to prove it."

After Nola and Sally left, Manny turned to Mary Q.

"What about my situation?" How does it look?"

"Not too good. Probably a suspension of some kind. Maybe a demotion.

Maybe a transfer."

"But I'm already in for a transfer to New Bedford."

His twenty-two year old girl friend was there.

"And that may end up being where you'll end up being. Nothing definite until the investigation is complete and typed. You know, as a manager, you are responsible for that monster, Nola. You helped create her. You and Noel. All the carnage that's been done as a result, I wouldn't want on my head. Or in my face.

"If you'll excuse me, now, I'm going back to the workers in the conference room. Very little sadness there."

"How did Noel take it?"

"I suspect he knew it was coming but like the rest of us, thought somehow a miracle would come out of the blue and save him. Being a manager is not very difficult. You have to know what the agency's about, know your regs, and be fair to everybody. Noel failed in each of those categories. He fled responsibility. That's how Nola was able to take over. You were her supervisor; you must have seen what was taking place. Unless, of course, it was very insidious and she inched up on the power so as not to be too obvious. Maybe you woke up one day and she was on the top and you were on the bottom?"

"Mary! Please! Even I can't entertain that picture."

He ran towards the men's room making regurgitating sounds.

Mary Q. laughed and headed for the meeting.

All About Eve

It's noteworthy, the effort that good work habits can have on those who observe them. With her diligence, Eve Marden accomplished more in her three-day week at the Cape Office than Noel managed to avoid in six months. And she still found opportunities to pass the time of day with the workers. After their experiences with Noel's daily response of 'that's not my department', workers were reluctant to visit Eve's office. It quickly became apparent that she believed in the open door policy. If her door were closed it meant she was in conference or involved in a confidential telephone conference. Usually with the Commish. If it were opened, it was meant as an invitation to enter. It was an awkward feeling at first. And within days, she knew the full names of all the workers and called them by their first names. When you're dealing with fifty people, that's quite an accomplishment. Her work habits were contagious. People began to attack their daily chores with the same diligence she displayed. As Eve began to resolve some of the many problems in the office, the atmosphere became lighter. Radios could be heard even though they were played softly. There was a warmth and camaraderie that was non-existent during Noel's reign. No more "Don't reign on my parade' was ever heard or even thought of. The new mood affected even Ruth Goldberg, Nola's right hand man or woman. She began smiling at other workers, talking about their lives, doing things to please them. It's hard to believe people would be willing to forgive her for all the rotten things she had done to them but they were. Everyone seemed to want the healing process to succeed. Ruth was pleasant, they were pleasant in return. People began to joke at the staff meetings, which they, formerly, hated to attend. And they learned because they wanted to. As an Aquarian, Eve was a born leader as well as a teacher. Don soon learned that he couldn't tell her what to do or how to do it. Having been raised by an Aquarian mother, he pretended that's what she was. It was miraculous. That's what it was. He would suggest things to her in a very intellectual way in order to achieve practical results. He had been through a rigid basic training at home during his early years. Now it was pay off time. Remarkable how we can apply things learned. Thanks Mama. He could say that now because of the distance that separated them. Growing up, it always had to be 'Mother'.

One could feel a vibrancy in the air as soon as you entered the front door into the reception area. Vivian, the new receptionist, was the daughter of one of the older workers. She was efficiency personified. The workers were thrilled. Why should anyone be so happy to get a complete message? With Placenta you got either the number or part of the number or a number with no name or message.

Viv would remind you if you forgot to pick up your messages or remind you of an important conference or, in Don's case, she'd call him at Court to tell him about a witness he was supposed to interview that afternoon at the office.

Poor Placenta. As George Higgins has said, 'It's a hard life. It's even harder if you're stupid'. Too bad there wasn't a Schraft's on the Cape. She'd probably make a good chocolate dipper. Probably refuse to do it in the window though. Dip the chocolates.

Then the heavenly raises came through. It's as though they were waiting for Noel to leave, for all these wonderful things to happen.

Good Sam

Well, it couldn't last forever. Samantha Simpson, one the social workers, had a client named Tess Kringle, who had been evicted from her home. Sam invited her into her home to stay for a while, pending her obtaining other quarters. Tess' three children were in foster care. What Tess didn't tell her was that she had been in a long term affair with a dyke named Charlie Washington. Charlie had been sentenced to Framingham for six months for selling crack. At the end of her time, both the inmates and administration were glad to see her go. She had terrorized them for six months. She was six feet four and weighed three hundred and twenty pounds without an ounce of fat. She made sure you referred to her as 'African American'. Not 'black'. Never 'colored'. 'Everyone goes out with 'The Wash' they used to say. That is, if you wanted to live. There may be a lot of broken hearts on Broadway, but there are more broken bones on the Cape.

It didn't take 'The Wash' long to track them down. Sam—the beautiful one with the long strawberry blonde hair to her waist, went to answer the door. Tess whispered from the darkened living room.

"Don't answer it, Sam. It's my lover."

"Your what?"

"I'm sorry I never told you. I didn't think she was getting out until next month. I expected to be out of here by then. She . . . Tess isn't straight?

The bell rang again.

"I really didn't mean to put you in danger . . ."

"Danger! Danger of what?"

Sam was so fragile, so trusting, and so innocent.

"Being badly beaten up. Maybe even, death."

She ran down the corridor, followed by Tess, to the kitchen phone. She heard a window crash. She heard a voice, as she picked up the phone.

"And don't try to use the mother fuckin' phone, Toots. I've already cut the lines."

The phone was dead. Where to go?

The cellar.

They hid under the cellar stairs. They could hear the smashing and crashing of just about everything in the house.

"I know you fuckers are here cause I saw the car outside that you came in. I've been hiding across the street. You with the hair, you are goin' to have a lot of regrets."

They cowered and shook even more.

Then it was quiet. Then the cellar light went on. Footsteps. Heavy footsteps on the stairs. Then she found them in the dark at the bottom of the stairs.

When the ambulance carrying Sam arrived at Cape Cod Hospital, Sam was in hysterics. She couldn't talk. She couldn't even cry. They gave her a massive dose of painkiller for the pain she couldn't feel. Both arms and legs were fractured as well as her pelvis. She had bruises all over her body. Both eyes were black and four front teeth were missing. She looked like a frightened little boy who had had his first serious fight. Boy? Oh yes, the last thing 'The Wash' had done was cut off Sam's hair. And shaved her head.

But, 'The Wash' was able to walk away from it. Sam, who had resigned as a social worker, refused to go to Court to testify. Tess was in hiding somewhere in Hyannis. Waiting for 'The Wash' to come.

Goode Morning

"I thought I heard you out here. What are you doing up at five in the morning?"

"I have that Lenz hearing today."

"But you said it wasn't to start until eleven."

"I have other Court matters beginning at nine."

"So?"

"There are twenty witnesses in the Lenz hearing. I want to review their expected testimonies in the quiet of the office. There won't be anyone in the main building before 7:15 or so and no one in the back building until 8:25. No phones ringing, no one asking for answers or conferences. It's like heaven. Well, not like our heaven."

'Sounds like the opposite direction to me. So you've done this before?"

"Yes."

"Often?"

"No. A few times."

"Well you're not getting out of here with nothing but a cup of coffee and a piece of raisin toast. I see you've already showered.

Go do your thing with your Norelco and get dressed. I'll make some breakfast. Something that'll stick to your innards."

"Aw Mer. . . ."

"Don't you 'aw Mer' me. Do you think I want to be up for neglect. If it's a 51A for a child, for a grownup it must be 102A"

She got out a few pieces of low salt ham and one egg. She knew he wouldn't eat two. And one was better than none. She put a slice of raisin bread by the toaster. That would go in just before the egg and ham came out of the pan. Don had hardly touched his coffee. She put that in the microwave to heat.

"Feel better, now?"

"Mmmmm. Once over lightly. Just the way I like my eggs. And you're just the way I like my women."

"That's plural, Mr. Goode. Is there something you're not telling me?"

"I thought you might get upset so I haven't said anything before. I've got a harem. Every babe is just like you. In fact, the truth of the matter is I'm really going to service them now. I lied about the wheels. I mean the hearing."

"You can't service me as much as I'd like. How can you possibly service anyone else? And I'm not a babe. I am woman. And no one is just like me. I'm a unique individual. I'm asking no questions about the wheels. I don't even think it even qualifies as a Freudian slip."

"I don't wear slips. It's that old joke about 'what's green and has four wheels? Grass. I lied about the wheels'. Hey, I'd better get going. It's almost six o'clock. They'll be furious at the harem. I said no later than five forty-five."

Merrilee kissed him full on the mouth.

"Dream on, my darling, even though you're awake. I'll have a beautiful surprise for you tonight."

"What?"

"Me."

Permanent Custody

Don drove up route 6 to exit 8. He saw only one vehicle coming in the opposite direction. A telephone truck. No cars in the parking lot. The Lil' Peach was opened. He got a small coffee and headed for the back building. Ah peace, it's wonderful. He achieved everything he wanted to. Reardon (everyone was calling him that now) would bring the pictures. And, of course, Julie.

At eight twenty, he headed for the Courthouse feeling in control of his destiny and the Lenz case. So much comes from order. It's essential to well being.

"Don, can I speak with you in one of the conference rooms?"

It was Mike Rock.

"Certainly." With all this dynamite, he could afford to be gracious. As they say in basic training,' Give your soul to God because your ass belongs to me'. So long, Mike.

"You have any witnesses here?"

"Yes."

"More than the social worker?"

"Yes."

"How many?"

-BREN

"Twenty."

Silence.

"The state is supposed to appear with no witnesses."

"I'm not the state."

"Don, cut the shit. You can't have twenty witnesses."

"When we go to trial, it is customary for the Court to swear all the witnesses in at the same time. When they do, I'll ask the Court to permit you to count them. Okay?"

"I believe you. I was hoping you'd have none so I could convince my client that the road he's taken is foolhardy."

"Is he following in your footsteps?"

"Don, why do you hate me so?"

"I don't hate you. I intensely dislike your practice of convincing clients that they have done nothing wrong, that you'll get them off. All that's needed is a little manufacturing of evidence. Actually, you would have more success if you opened a business dealing with that. 'Evidence Manufactured Here'. Lawyers could submit whatever they hoped to achieve and a statement of facts. You would then manufacture whatever evidence was required to win the case. However, you'd be unable to take both sides of the same case because that might be a manufacturing conflict."

Don had promised himself he wasn't going to let Mike get him worked up like this. Another broken promise.

"Don, that's a great idea! We could be partners!"

Good God! What have I done? Does he think I'd be his partner? In crime?

"Well, what do you say?"

"Silence is not assent. Back to the business at hand. Pornographic Ralph."

"Do you take pictures of your kids?"

"If you take similar pictures of yours, you're going to find yourself before the Juvenile Judge."

"That aside, Ralph wants to agree to permanent custody in the state. Of course 'permanent' is not permanent. Is anything?"

"Death and taxes."

"So, are you going to excuse your twenty witnesses?"

If I trusted you, I would say, 'yes'.

"No. I think it will be a nice learning experience for them."

"Ever the teacher, eh?"

"That's better than listening to an Aquarian like you intellectualize the shit out of something, anything."

"Ouch. Almost partners one minute, the next you're driving sticks under my fingernails. Through my heart."

"Would you rather have a chink in your armor?"

"No. I just want you to be my friend."

Do cows fly?

"Mr. Goode, I understand there is an agreement in this matter."

"That's correct, your Honor."

"And who, might I ask, are all these people at the back of the room?"

"Witnesses for the state your Honor. I thought they deserved to view the process."

"Good Idea. Very considerate of you, Mr. Goode. Perhaps I can assist."

"You always do, your Honor. We're very fortunate to have you."

Pile it on, Don, even though you've already won.

Judge Cronout began laughing.

"If an agreement can put you in this frame of mind, I hope there are more of them, Mr. Goode."

"Actually, your Honor, I was doing an impression of Mr. Rock."

Rock leaped to his feet.

"Objection your Honor! That's a slur on my character!"

"Really? I thought it was meant to be a compliment."

"Goode compliment. . . ."

"Yes. Very. I'm glad you've seen the light."

"I was going to say G-o-o-d-e compliment anybody? That'll be the day. I want that remark stricken from the record."

I want him stricken. Now Don . . .

"Do you have a motion in writing?"

"No, Judge."

"Why not?"

'Because I didn't know it was going to happen."

"Mr. Goode. Would you have any objection if Mr. Rock submits a late Motion to Strike in this case?"

"Who is he going to strike?"

"You, you little—"

"Gentlemen, please. Whenever you two are together, I feel like a ref at a boxing match. In the present case, each counsel will receive a copy of my findings. In it, will be spelled out the course of action each of the parents is to follow if they expect to be re-united with their two children. They must—and I can't emphasize this enough—comply with the service plan of the Department. Ms. Lifka will keep accurate records to assist the Court in tracking the progress for these parents. Because of an earlier incident, visitation will continue to be under suspension until the Court can be assured that resumption of visitation would be beneficial to both parents and children."

"Are there any questions on this matter?"

"Now Mr. Goode, have you other matters pending before the Court?"

"No, your Honor. Some have been concluded, others have gone over until next week, having thought this hearing would take at least the balance of the day."

"Quite correct. Now I shall have the balance of the day to write decisions. And I wish to thank all of you witnesses for appearing today. These cases are very difficult at best, and some are lost, because of lack of witnesses. In those cases the children are the losers."

"Thank you again. Mr. Goode will see to your witness fees."

"I've already seen to that, your Honor."

"You have to get up awfully early to get ahead of Mr. Goode. Right Mr. Rock?"

No answer.
"I'll agree with that, your Honor."
"Thank you, Mr. Igo."
They filed out.

Lunch With The Lovers

"Don, I suppose if I invite you for coffee, you'll say no."

"You're learning Mike. It's not hopeless, after all."

"Listen you guys. I just heard you were getting married. After I call my office, I insist on taking you to lunch. How about Murph's Recession?"

Julie and Reardon nodded assent.

"Don?"

"Yes, Marion."

"Would you believe that that creep just asked if he could have the pictures back now that the case is over."

"Case isn't over, Police have custody of that evidence."

"I told him that."

"Brighten up a little. I'm taking the love birds to lunch. Won't you join us?"

"Can't. Have to work out a service plan for Mr. and Mrs. Creep. This one expires tomorrow."

They walked to the parking lot.

"Don, Reardon, dedicated as he is, is going back to the station to tell them what's happened with this case. Could I ride with you?"

"Of course."

She blew Reardon a kiss as he got into his car.

"Do you know the back way, Don?"

"Oh yes. Haven't been there for a while, though."

When they got through the entrance, Don whispered something to the waitress. Julie ordered a glass of Rhine wine. Don had a Kaliber.

"Imagine Julie, if I have nineteen more of these . . ."

"Twenty calibre. That's awful."

"It really doesn't taste bad at all."

"The joke. The joke."

"You look different, Julie. New hair-do or something?"

Actually, she was strikingly beautiful. How had Don missed that before?

"I'm in love. They say that makes a difference."

"Oh, the workers just got a nice raise. Why don't you come back? It's much different than when you left."

"A social worker never returns to the scene of the crime."

"Linda Ravioli did. She seems quite happy."

"She's in love. Got married in Hawaii, I heard."

"You seem to want to ask me something."

"I do. Will you come to my wedding? I know you hate to drive long distances. Marion said she'd be glad to drive you and your wife. The reception is at the Wellesley Inn. My parents are reserving a block of rooms there, so you can stay over. Marion will drive you home the next day. Talk about portal to portal. Are you familiar with Wellesley, Don?"

"Sort of. Lived there for two years."

"Really. Where."

"423 Weston Road."

"At the corner of Beverly Road? That beautiful house with all that nice shrubbery."

"That's the place. And where are your family?"

"The Cliff Estates, right next to Don Arnold who did the sports for Channel 5. But please don't tell anyone. They're loaded."

"Have they ever considered AA?"

"Literal Don. I have to know what you think of Reardon."

"He's a splendid person."

"Literal and succinct. Thank you. Why did you leave Wellesley?"

"This job came up. I had been an assistant D.A. and also taught for a while at a law school in the Boston Area."

"Don, I always thought you might be about Reardon's age. Now I wonder. You couldn't have done all those things . . . Are you thirty?"

"Thirty something, Julie. Then add six."

"My God!"

"Listen, it's not exactly middle-age."

"But you're so young looking."

"Family trait. When I was seventeen, I looked twelve. When I first started practicing in Boston, more Courts told me that the bar enclosures were for lawyers and could I please step outside . . ."

Julie was laughing. Out loud. Working that hard to get through law school and then passing the bar and being told to get our of the lawyer's arena.

Reardon came through the door. In civvies. More time off?

"This place is crowded. May I sit at your table sir, ma'am?"

"Sure. Pull up a chair."

Don signaled for the waitress who brought the champagne.

"Oh no, Don. You do not know what this does to him. He sang a hundred and twenty-five songs at the Windjammer the night I proposed to him."

"I didn't know you could sing, Rear."

"I can't. Just like to. What would like to hear?"

"The Sound of Silence."

"Now Jule. It wasn't that bad. Was it?"

"I mean every musical from 1920."

"But that was the second act. I thought you were limiting yourself to requests."

They were really made for each other, Don thought. Ain't love grand?

"Reardon, I invited Don and his wife to our wedding. And he accepted. Isn't that wonderful?"

"Well, I wasn't consulted. Why?"

"I had to find out what he thought of you first. And I couldn't ask him in front of you."

"You mean you went behind my back? What did he say?"

"He said you needed a lot of work."

"What is he? A dentist on the side."

"Refinement. Polishing. Manners."

"I don't believe you. If Mr. Michener doesn't mind, I'm going to ask the source. Did you cast aspersions at me, sir?"

"No. I said, 'He's a splendid person'."

Reardon threw his arms around Don, seated beside him.

"Thank God I found out in time. I'm marrying the wrong person. Don, do you like bridge, old movies, pizza and beer?"

"Those are a few of my favorite things," he sang, off key.

"Perhaps we could form a duet."

"Perhaps you should have something to eat before history repeats itself."

"Nag, nag, nag."

Don motioned to the waitress.

Sweet Delay

Reardon was driving Julie home. She had been given the day off by Kodak. It wanted to stay on the right side of law and order.

"Rear, I have a great idea! Why don't we go to Eastham and gaze at Nauset Light Beach. It's like standing on top of the world. Nothing but sea, sky and sand, as far as the eye can see. After that, we can go to Marconi. You know, stand on that platform where you can see both sides of the Cape merely by turning your head."

"Jule, stop. I'll go wherever you want. You know that."

"I know that."

They drove several miles in silence, savoring their propinquity.

"Are you afraid to be at your house, alone with me?"

"Yes."

"Jule, I love you. You know I would never force myself on you."

"I'm not afraid of you. Never have been."

"But you just said . . ."

"Think Reardon. Afraid to be at your house, alone with me'."

"Well if you're not afraid of me, then who?"

"Me. I am so madly, hopelessly in love with you, I don't trust myself. That's why I'm always suggesting outside activities. Haven't you ever been able to put it altogether?"

"Now I'm the one who's afraid. When we kiss goodnight I'm going to insist that you stay on one side of the gate and I on the other. I did read something a while ago that might help you. At least I haven't been able to forget it. We should always try to love others with a perfect detachment. You know, the way I love you, Jule."

"The way you love me, Reardon? If I were able to see you forty-eight hours a day, you wouldn't be content. That's perfect detachment?"

"Well, it's comforting to have you within arm's reach and never out of my sight . . . forever."

Now they were within seconds of Nauset Light.

"Pull the car over, Reardon."

"No. No. Police officer, help me! I'm being attacked by this lady."

On the way back from Wellfleet, they stopped at the Yardarm for a delicious meal of scallops, fries and the best spinach salad anyone ever tasted.

"Jule, I wish tomorrow were a certain Saturday in June."

"And I wish it were today, Reardon. Today."

It's Not Always Nice, Laverna

"Well, if it isn't Don Goode."

"Hi Lala. What's the good word?"

"There isn't one. Are you all set for the run down?"

"No. And I never will be."

"A security guard at that new home for mentally retarded children in Chatham was arrested on child pornography. Using the mails."

"If he's been arrested and no longer caring for children, is it necessary for us to become involved?"

"You'll have to check with your sup and the other powers that be. Screwball in Brewster, stripping and beating his thirteen-year-old niece. Made her shave her pubic hair so she wouldn't think she was a woman. The irony is, he videotaped the whole business. Has been going on for three years.

"A mother left her five kids, ages 12 to 2, off at the front door here, and then took off. Emergency C&P conference scheduled for noon.

"Father O'Malley picked up a fourteen year old boy, took

him to a motel, fed him whiskey and then raped him. No Bing Crosby, apparently. Even though he said, 'Going My Way?'

"Mother's boyfriend in P-.town raped her two daughters 12 and 10 years.

"Wellfleet police officer charged with felonious sexual assault of a fourteen year old girl. I know what you're trying to say, Don. But the 51A was called in. Perhaps you should meet with the D.A. See if this duplicity is necessary."

"Good idea, Lala. Let me make a note of that."

"An adoptive mother, returned two kids yesterday. Management is trying to decide if it's a C&P or not."

"Did she have her sales slip, La? Of course, it's a C&P. The children have been abandoned. So what was once considered to be irrevocable, no longer is."

"Looks that way doesn't it? Boy, two. Two years ago mother shattered his leg. Child was returned a month ago. Now she's twisted his arm out of its socket.

"Eight month old boy had his body blistered with second and third degree burns caused by parents throwing hot water on him.

"Four year old boy whose body was covered by more than one hundred wounds died this morning. He was disciplined to death by his foster mother in Centerville. She is said to have beaten, scratched, shook and pushed the four year old causing a concussion that resulted in his death. Don, we can cover the other new cases later. You'd better get your messages and get to that meeting. It's in Eve's office. She's sweet, isn't she?"

"Lala, anyone would appear sweet after Noel and Nola. But no, I don't think she's sweet. I believe she's very efficient and fair and that's just what this office needed. Especially after all that torture. God must love us an awful lot."

"To those he loves the most, the greater sufferings are expected. I say, I wish he didn't love us so much."

Strange Happenings

Todd Wynn had been in temporary custody of DSS for more than three months when the Care and Protection was marked for a full hearing. Then, strange things began to happen. Sid Silver, who represented the parents as private counsel, filed a Motion to Recuse all the judges in Barnstable District Court and all the judges who had ever sat on a Care and Protection matter in Barnstable District Court. That covered a lot of judges. Don objected strenuously but Mike Rock, Court appointed attorney for Todd, did not.

"What's the difference, Don, who tries the case? We know we're on solid ground. My God, the independent investigator's report, alone, is devastating. Parents left the children in care of ten-year-old Thomas. The three attempted drowning incidents, Todd walking down Route 28 stark naked. When the police brought him home, no parents. Not even Thomas. Off with his friends. Mother trying to chop off father's head with an axe while Thomas held him down and the two younger ones watched, as well as the neighbors. She kept yelling, "You fucking coward. I should have had them take you out a long time ago."

"Do you know who 'them' is?"

"I don't know what Kevin does during his many absences, but it fits in with criminal activity. Friend of mine at IRS says he has had no reported income for the past eight years. It fits."

"And you know about Sid Silver's son?"

"Yes. Oh my God! They're all involved with the Mafia! Do you think we're safe?"

"I don't know about that, Mike, but I sure as hell am angry at you, again, for letting the Mafia attempt to choose the judge in a case where we're all sworn to act in the best interests of the child. How could you stand idly by and let that happen?"

"Asleep at the switch, Don. I swear to you I didn't put it together until just now. Perhaps subconsciously, I didn't want to for one reason or another. What now?"

"The motion is going to be heard this afternoon at 2:00. It is not too late to record yourself as being against it."

"Okay. Okay. I'll make every effort to attend. Really, I mean it. Todd means a great deal to me. And so does this case."

He never appeared but had the audacity to call Don a week later. More nerve than an ulcerated tooth.

"Don! Mike Stone here. How are you?"

"I was fine until a couple of seconds ago."

"What time is that motion on for today?"

"It's not."

"Oh good. They postponed it then. What's the new date?"

"A week ago."

"If they postponed it, how. . . ."

"Don't play cat and mouse with me. Or is it rat? You are an asshole of Homeric proportions. And the day they make assholes bigger than you, they'll have to put 'em hindside to an elephant. I needed your help, not your dismantling of the state's case. I have a good mind to file a motion to have you removed as the child's attorney for non-compis mentis. You are totally underwhelming in your understanding of your function. To even claim you care is another fantasy trip."

"Don, I have a wonderful suggestion. It will really help you in your work. What you really need more than anything else is one of those courses in assertiveness training. I know you won't call me. But I'll call you in a few days after you've had time to cool off. Just remember: I was only trying to help."

Mike Rock did call back in a few days. Don called a truce. He had no choice. They had to agree on trial tactics, the order of witnesses to call, possible motions, closing arguments, which one could stress certain points so the arguments didn't seem repetitive. Eventually, they would find out it wouldn't make any difference what their strategy was. The decision had already been made.

She was as lacking in elegance as the old grey mare. There was nothing distinctive about her. No one was aware of any steps she may have taken in her toilette, but she was quite dusty. Dirt under her fingernails, hair not only uncoiffed, but dirty, oily and her face looked as though the front circle of it had been washed. It was gray on the sides and down through that portion of the neck that could be seen.

When she announced that she had never tried a Care and Protection case what were they, and so on, one side was very happy. The white hats were stunned. They never did find out who was responsible for assigning this eejit from Greenfield to this very sensitive case. Were they paying her? Oh, they'd be paying her very well, as it turned out.

The Defense called a psychiatrist, out of turn, because of his schedule, who testified that he had observed the family life (without Todd, of course) of the Wynns and while not perfect, it was exemplary. His name sounded very familiar to Don so he checked it out during the break. Bingo!

"Now Doctor Jacobs, you've given us your background and the various places you've been in your practice of psychiatry." Don looked up quickly at the judge. She appeared to be sleeping. Don didn't proceed. He waited. It was embarrassing. Fifteen minutes went by while Nellie Gray dozed and nodded. I'll bet her nickname in school was 'Dirty Nellie'.

"Any more questions of this witness Mr. Goode or Mr. Rock."

"Yes, your Honor."

"Well, what's the delay? We have to conclude this case expeditiously."

So you can get paid, right?

"Well things would proceed in that manner, your Honor, if the Court could stay awake." Please, a mistrial.

At this point, especially with his perception of things, Don didn't give a shit. Besides, he wanted it on the taped record. Or so he thought.

"I'll pretend I didn't hear that."

Why not? You haven't heard anything the State has said so far.

Two feet planted firmly ten feet in the air.

"Pretend away your Honor. As long as it's on the record."

"Continue Mr. Goode."

"Dr. Jacobs, there seems to be a three year gap."

"Really, Mr. Goode?"

"Really, Doctor. Where were you during that three year period?"

"You know. yo-o-u know, Mr. Goode."

"Well that may be, Doctor, but I want you to tell the Court."

Sid Silver let out an audible groan.

"Well, I was in prison for sexually abusing children in my practice."

"And now you want us to believe you are capable of telling us what is best for children?"

He didn't answer.

"Well I have a question."

It was Dirty Nellie.

"And you served your time, Doctor Jacobs? You paid your debt to society. Isn't that correct?"

"Excuse me, your Honor. Are you co-counsel in this case?"

Please, please. A mistrial.

She ignored Don.

"Well if he's paid his debt, I think it's wonderful of him to come in and testify of his own free will, knowing his past may be thrown back in his face by a certain kind of lawyer. Proceed, if there are any more questions." Don was stunned.

"Excuse me, your Honor, did you want to render your decision now? I mean you haven't heard any of the state's witnesses as yet. You know, people who care about this child. They—don't you move Dr. Jacobs—have observed certain behaviors which gave them grave concerns for the welfare of this child. They—not Doctor Jacobs—are the ones who come and testify of their free wills because they care."

"Dr. Jacobs resume the stand please."

"What is the meaning of this?"

"Your Honor made a completely unilateral statement which shows bias on the Court's part. I wish to rebut that."

"Doctor, were you paid to come here today?"

He was afraid not to answer truthfully.

"Yes, Mr. Goode. As an expert witness."

"And what were you paid?"

"Fifteen hundred dollars."

The self-satisfied smugness left Dirty Nellie's face.

"Mr. Goode, I agree that my comment could be misinterpreted, in some circles as bias. Therefore, I'm going to strike it from the Court record."

"How are you going to do that? Splice the tape?"

"Well, I'll simply disregard it."

As you would, the entire case for the State.

Twenty-Five Grand Reasons

The Court Investigator was the first to testify for the State. She was excellent. Her report was timely and telling. She was fair also. Because of the complexities in the family make-up, the report was thirty-two typewritten pages long.

The witnesses came and went. Dirty Nellie thoroughly cross-examined each one, demeaning each of them and what they had to say.

During the break, they spoke with Don and Mike. Said the judge made them feel like they were criminals on trail for murder. All they had done was come forward because they cared about the welfare of the child.

When the foster mother brought Todd to the Judge's chamber for private viewing, Dirty Nellie said the child didn't look abused to her. In fact, he looked "fit as a fiddle". When the foster mother tried to clarify the situation by saying she had had exclusive custody of the child for more than three months, Dirty Nellie said no foster parent could provide care that would make a child look like that. That must have come from the natural family.

The foster mother found Don upstairs in a conference room. She was fighting back tears.

"She is going to send him back. And I can understand why you call her Dirty Nellie. Even her soul is dirty."

"Please, please, Sarah, beautiful and short. There are at least two more days of trial. Then she has to sift through the evidence and render a decision within ten days."

"Don, she's going to send him home. And I wouldn't be surprised if it's forthwith."

"Forthwith? Sarah, you wouldn't give a dog away like that. It requires planning, separation techniques. Please, don't make me feel any worse than I already do. I know you're a woman and I'm always amazed at your intuition. You don't have to slave through logic like men. You just intuit, go right through or over what's in the way. Especially when it comes to other women. What am I saying? I'm bolstering your prediction."

"Don. Mark my words."

"My mother used to say that a lot."

"Mine, too. Glad it wasn't wasted on you."

More witnesses came and went. The Wynns, Sid Silver and his assistant seemed abnormally smug. No matter how damaging the evidence that was going in, they appeared totally unaffected by it. When the testimony concerning Todd in the altogether went in, even the part about no adult supervision, dirty Nellie invited counsel into her chambers. Don thought of that old vaudeville number about which he had read. 'Don't go into the lions' den tonight, mother, the lions are ferocious and they bite.' He'd use Mike Rock as a shield. Well, he had to be good for something.

"Gentlemen, I really don't see how a child running about nude is important in a care and protection proceeding. I, myself, have been in that situation, many times."

"Were you arrested your Honor?"

"No. Mr. Goode."

"Pretty common out there in Greenfield, eh?"

"No, Mr. Rock." Mike's awake!

"I think what the Judge means is that she has seen lots of children running around bare-ass. Right Judge?"

"No, Sid, I mean—Mr. Silver. And I'm confiding this to you four. It's not for general consumption. Strictly confidential. I have a child who got out of the house without a stitch on. Several times. I was so embarrassed."

"I thought it was your child who was nude."

"It was, Mr. Goode. And stop trying to twist my words."

It's the only way they'll ever be straightened out.

"If it wasn't important, why were you embarrassed?"

"Well I, I . . . don't know. It's just that . . ."

"That you like to get embarrassed over unimportant things?"

"Mr. Goode! I can see that this is getting us nowhere."

"Funny but I feel the same way about this whole proceeding."

"Shall we resume gentlemen?"

Resume what?

Motion For Mistrial

Don told Mike Rock what he intended to do the following day, and asked for his support. Rock assured him that he would support him. In fact, he would bring a similar motion in behalf of the child.

The next day, Don arrived at the Courthouse at 8:20. He liked to have a second cup of coffee in peace and quiet. Coffee gone, he went in search of Sid Silver to give him a copy of the Motion for Mistrial. He was unable to find Sid until just before the session was about to begin. He gave Mike Rock a copy and asked for a copy of Mike's motion. He didn't have one. Couldn't afford to offend a judge. Never knew when he would run into her again. Don wished someone would run over both of them. No such luck.

When Dirty Nellie read the motion, she started to cry.

"And I confided in you, Mr. Goode. Now you've taken my confidence and turned it against me. How could you do this to me? I feel exposed.

"And further on you claim I'm biased. You claim I cross-examined all the government witnesses. Well how do you expect me to get at the truth. Do you honestly believe I have no right to ask questions?"

"For clarification purposes. To understand what the issues are, what the testimony means. A judge is supposed to be objective, fair, and impartial. Not the devil's advocate that you've demonstrated during the entire proceeding. You even acted as the Governor, granting a full pardon to Dr. Jacobs. The Wynn's attorney should have mailed in his defense so you could rubber-stamp it. He and his assistant haven't had to do a thing during the trial. It is their function to cross-examine the state's witnesses. But they didn't even have to do that. Because you are their co-counsel."

Mike was proud of him. A lot of things were much clearer in his mind.

"Do you have anything to say Mr. Rock?"

"While not being the moving party in this motion—Mr. Goode is—, I would have to agree with some of the allegations. There has been a partiality shown by this Court and I ask the Court to examine its conscience before acting on this motion. Thank you."

I don't thank you, Mike Rock.

"Very well, we'll take a short recess before ruling on this motion."

She went off the bench and closed the door. She must have counted to three and came right out again, almost propelled.

"Do you have any more evidence, Mr. Goode?" Would it make any difference?

"No. That's the Commonwealth's case in chief, your Honor."

How that word, Honor, stuck in his throat.

"Excuse me, Judge."

"Yes, Mr. Rock?"

"The purpose of the break was to give you time to think about the state's motion."

"Oh that thing. I denied that."

When? Before the trial?

"Mr. Rock, do you, as the child's attorney, have any witnesses to call?"

"No, your Honor."

"Good. Now if you gentlemen wouldn't mind, I'd like to talk with Mrs. Wynn in my lobby. It has nothing to do with this case."

"Just a minute—do you two know each other?"

"Of course not, Mr. Goode."

"Well, Judge, have you ever met before?"

"Absolutely not! What are you trying to imply?"

"If you don't know each other and you've never met, how would either of you know you'd want to meet during a pending trial where you will, allegedly, make a fair determination regarding the future of her child?"

"Women's intuition, Mr. Goode. Women's intuition. Any objection?"

Don was too stunned to object. But he'd never seen anything like it. It was so blatant; he didn't know what the objection should be.

They were closeted for forty minutes. For people who had never met, they had a lot to say. Or do.

"Mike, it must be in ones."

"I wouldn't be surprised. Did you see the size of Mrs. Wynn's handbag? It was as big as a suitcase."

"Try money case. The Judge is as fine a politician as money can buy."

"I hope she uses some of it for soap, shampoo and deodorant."

"Mike, don't forget mouthwash."

"Toothpaste!"

"Dentist!"

"Home perm!"

"Shit, at this rate the dough will be gone in no time."

The newfound friends finally emerged from chambers. One richer, the other poorer, no doubt.

"I really don't think it should be necessary for either of the Wynns to take the stand. They've been terribly shaken by this whole ordeal."

They're the Wynners, we're the losers. And they're not as shaken as I. No sir. Not as shaken as I, thought Don.

"Why don't you just find that the state has failed to prove their unfitness, today? I mean, like right now."

"Oh, can I, Mr. Goode?"

Mike, the Aquarian, to the rescue. The judge's rescue.

"No, you cannot, your Honor. The law requires that you reduce your findings to writing within ten days. Further, the Department, according to Santosky v. Kramer, 455 U.S. 745 or 102 Supreme Court 1388 or 71L. Ed. 2d 599, must prove parental unfitness by clear and convincing evidence. The test applied prior to that decision, was by a fair preponderance of the evidence. So this Court, I'm certain, can see the giant steps that have been taken by the Supreme Court of these United States to take family life seriously, to preserve it whenever possible. Even the state does not treat it lightly. It very reluctantly will move to intrude on family life because it knows that the state is a poor parent. I could go on for hours, your Honor . . ."

"Please don't, Mr. Rock."

"I did neglect to mention your Honor, that you must carefully consider and weigh all the evidence on both sides."

There are two sides?

"For the sake of brevity, I'll just ask a few questions of the Wynns."

Don was beside himself.

"Don't you think that might be better left to their counsel? You don't want to appear to be even more obvious than you are, do you? I mean, they are paying Mr. Silver. Say, come to think of it . . ."

Dirty Nellie's face was flaming. Even under the dirt, you could see it. A deeper red perhaps.

"Mr. Silver?"

"Yes, most Honorable Judge," he bowed to the east.

Now we're in Japan. Maybe that explains why we're being japped.

The Wynns told what wonderful parents they were. Mr. Wynn only slapped Todd around because he had his head in the toilet bowl. The several bruises on his face and body causing Doctor Hand to find a flat affect representative of the battered child syndrome, was all a mistake. Mr. Wynn worked in a coin collector's shop. Later, when Don checked, the business had gone out of operation three years before.

Mrs. Wynn was the ultimate mother . . . if one could add just one little six-letter word.

There was very little cross-examination because the Wynns' lawyers would take turns objecting so that the question or answer or both, would diminish in meaning. After all, they did have three lawyers representing them: Sid Silver, his assistant, and Dirty Nellie.

"Closing arguments, gentlemen?"

"Just a minute, your Honor. There does happen to be such a thing as rebuttal in trials." Good for Mike.

"What could you possibly rebut?"

"You mean you've already decided what you believe about the parents' case?"

"Why do you make reference to that, exclusively?"

"Because I don't know of any lawyer, hereabouts, who tries a case and then wishes to rebut his own case. Now I've never been to Greenfield and don't think I ever will, but I am going to call a witness in rebuttal."

"Not if I say you're not."

"Whether you say 'yes', 'no' or 'maybe'. I shall call the witness. The child calls Molly Slader."

The witness began to approach the witness box.

"Don't come any further."

"Yes, your Honor."

"Mr. Rock, I am not going to allow this witness to testify. Why I've never even heard of rebuttal."

Did she think they'd take the money back?

"Under the circumstances, I shall make an offer of proof."

"If I say she is not going to testify, what good will it do to tell the Court what she would say?"

"I don't know how long you've been a member of the bar, but in order to protect rights of parties, this state has an Appeals Court and a Supreme Judicial Court. They review the findings of lower Courts, where people claimed to be aggrieved. And from what I've seen here, these last five days, I can more fully understand why they're so busy. Now are you going to take an offer of proof on what Molly Slader would testify, if allowed, or am I going to file a formal complaint with the Judicial Misconduct Commission?"

Mike, too bad you didn't come alive in the beginning.

Dirty Nellie was shaking. She looked, furtively at Sid Silver and his assistant, but they kept looking to the left of her.

"Very well,' she was speaking very softly." Make your offer, Mr. Rock." He turned up the volume on the microphone as loud as it would go.

"This witness, Molly Slader would testify that she is a day care provider; that after a January visit home Todd's behavior was bizarre; that he told her it hurt too much to see his parents, that he didn't want to scream and cry; that his brother, Thomas, had told him that the next time he saw him he would drown him and then he'd be out of the way for good."

"And you think that's pertinent, Mr. Rock. I don't."

"Do I get the opportunity to answer?"

"No. Closing arguments, gentlemen, in this order: Mr. Goode, Mr. Rock and," she smiled, "Mr. Silver."

"No. In this order: Mr. Silver, Mr. Rock and Mr. Goode."

"Mr. Goode! I'm an experienced judge. . . ."

"You could have fooled me. It certainly doesn't show."

"Are you trying to say you know more than I do about the law and procedure?"

Doesn't everybody?

"In the procedure governing this type of case—and you have said you knew nothing—and that hasn't changed—the attorney for the parents go first, the attorney for the child goes next and, finally, the attorney for the state—just like in criminal cases—goes last."

"This isn't a criminal case . . ."

It isn't?

"Are you going first or not, Mr. Goode?"

"Not!"

Don put his folders in his attaché case and left the Courtroom.

"Mr. Goode! Mr. Goode! You can't leave. Get back here!"

He kept walking. He went downstairs and made a call from the office of one of the probation officers. Good. His friend, who had more balls than he did, took the info and did as he was told.

Please Come To Boston

When Dirty Nellie left the bench for the lobby, she found a call waiting.

"Judge Gray?" a voice thundered. She almost jumped out of her seat.

"Y-e-e-e-s?"

"You will appear tomorrow morning at 9:00 A.M. before the Appeals Court to determine whether a most serious charge against you shall go beyond the preliminary stage. Is that clear?"

"Ye-e-e-s, sir. For whom shall I ask?"

"Judge Homer Julius. And remember, 9:00 A.M. sharp!"

"Ye-e-e-s-, sir."

She started to cry again. She left an urgent message on Sid Silver's line. But he didn't call. She went home and took a warm bath, and washed her hair. It had been so long she had forgotten how nice it felt. Well one good thing came out of this mess. From now on, she'd do this once a month whether she needed it or not. Well maybe not every month. But she still couldn't sleep. She was frightened. She couldn't quite understand. In her neck—dirty neck—of the woods, if a lawyer wanted to thank a judge—even before the trial—nobody seemed to mind. I mean she had a house, kids to educate. Couldn't do that on a judge's salary. So you help people and they help you. Tit for tat.

Next morning her phone rang at 7:00 A.M. It didn't have to ring more than once. She was still awake. And exhausted.

"Hello."

"Nell, Sid. Forgot to check my messages last night."

"In the office, now, at 7:00A.M.?"

"Always. What's up?"

She told him. He roared laughing."

"You think it's funny."

"Yes. The call was a joke. There is no Judge Homer Julius. Besides, the whole investigation process is very involved. Certified or registered mail, sixty days notice—not of any hearing—just so a judge can get a lawyer, examine the charges. It takes tons of time."

"Who do you think is responsible?"

"Well, the obvious. It's either Goode or Rock. I would say Goode. Rock's too cautious. He'd enjoy listening to the story but I doubt that he would institute it. Of course, you treated all those government witnesses like pieces of shit. The suspects grow and grow."

She believed him, but she didn't. She couldn't chance it. She dressed hurriedly and drove to Boston. That drive, alone, would take ten years off anyone's life.

There was no Judge Homer Julius. Yes, the clerk was positive there was nothing involving a Judge Gray. Did she have the registered letter with her? Never, never by phone. She left and paid the outrageous parking fee at the garage on Somerset Street next to the new Court House.

Why hadn't she listened to, and believed, her co-counsel?

It Paid To Pay

A group of neighbors, who had testified in the Wynn case, were standing in the driveway of one of the couples. The six stood there on a Saturday morning, discussing the case and the judge and their suspicions.

Kevin Wynn came running across the street waving a sheaf of papers and an envelope in his hand.

"I won! I won! And it only cost me $25,000 to get this decision."

"May I glance at that Kevin?" It was Esther Livingstone.

"Sure." He handed her the papers. She was really interested in what she thought she saw on the envelope. It had been mailed from Brockton, but the return address was taped over. Interesting.

"Wait'll Lynn gets back. My lawyer says 'forthwith' means right away."

Esther felt she had to speak up. If you were going to hell and not back, you should be given the opportunity to prepare for it.

"Do you think that's wise, Kevin? He's been away almost four months. Don't you think it would be kinder to let Todd prepare to separate from his foster parents—and I hear they're very nice people."

"Yes, they are nice. Very nice. I'll talk to Lynn—oh, there she is now, throwing daggers this way. Try not to catch any."

He showed her the decision.

"Go and get the little fucker."

He told her about the neighbor's comment.

"They go into Court and try to cut your balls off. And now you, you asshole, you're going to take their advice about what is the best way of re-integrating our son back into our home?"

"Gee Lynn, you sound just like a social worker. Not the 'balls' part but, you know, about coming back into the home."

"I said to go and get the little fucker!"

"I can't. It's Saturday. DSS is closed."

"I don't give a good shit if it's Easter Sunday and DSS has gone out of business. Go get him!"

"I'm waiting till Monday. I'll call DSS first thing."

"Coward! Fucking coward."

"This is Mr. Wynn. Could I speak with Marion Lifka?"

"One moment, please."

"Marion Lifka."

"Kevin. We want him back right away."

"I don't know what to tell you, Kevin. Don is very good about furnishing us with Court decisions. Even lets us open his mail in search of them. Could I call you back in about ten minutes? A new number? Yes. Okay."

There was no report from the Court. Marion called the Juvenile Clerk.

"Laurie, Marion Lifka. Do you have or know where I could obtain a copy of the Wynn decision?"

"Don always picks them up directly. And we get a copy for our folder here. Let me check, Mar."

"Not in the folder. What's the rush? From what I hear, that's one decision you'd want to delay."

"The father called. Said he got a copy of the decision Saturday morning. It's—or he says it is—ordering a return of Todd, forthwith."

"The plot sickens."

"Our position is awkward, at best. Here's a parent claiming to have a Court decision which orders a child returned 'forthwith' but we don't have a copy. Are we in violation if we don't comply?"

"Marion, leave the legalistic worries to the lawyer. I don't see how there can be non-compliance if you haven't received the order. Imagine returning a child who has been in care that long, 'forthwith'. I wouldn't give an animal away like that. What the hell did Dirty Nellie think of the other judges who found the Wynns unfit? If she found them incompetent, it's a classic case of Freudian projection. Listen Mar, I have another call. If I see or hear anything, I'll give you a call."

"Thanks."

"Mr. Wynn? Marion Lifka. There is no decision here and even the Court - has no record of having received one. Maybe yours got through and the others were held up. Was yours mailed from Greenfield? I believe that's Judge Gray's home Court."

"I think I threw the envelope away. No. Wait. It's right here on the kitchen counter. Mailed from Brockton."

"Brockton? How is that possible? Unless the judge mailed a copy to your attorney, Mr. Silver and he mailed it to you or made a copy and mailed it to you. Those things are usually dated, as I recall, on the last page above the judge's signature. Do you have it?"

"But Kevin, that date is the day before the last day of the trial. What? It was supposed to end the day before but Mr. Silver was sick and the case went over? This way, Mr. Silver received the decision before the trial was over. You say it's unsigned?"

"I don't want to cause any problems. Just glad I'm getting my kid back."

"About Todd. I checked with the Juvenile Session. They feel we needn't comply until we have the order in hand. I could see the difference in time being a day apart but not like this. I'll call the foster mother and alert her of the possibility—I think she already suspects after her experience with Judge Gray—of Todd's return 'forthwith'. In that way, she can prepare him to separate. If it's to be, so be it. I hope things work out for all of you."

"Thank you, Marion. I hope I've learned."

"I'm sure you have."

Different Postmarks

Three days later, the decision with copies were received at Barnstable Court. The envelope was postmarked 'Greenfield'. 'Brockton', 'Greenfield'. What gives?

Don was upstairs in the Court's library. Laurie came and got him.

"Bad news. On the Wynn case."

"You wouldn't have to be an Einstein to figure that out."

The decision decimated Don, DSS, Mike Rock, and all of the witnesses. Like we should be hung without a trial. We were.

The phone rang.

"For you, Don."

"Thanks Laurie. Who. Oh, hi Esther. Really? Maybe he meant his attorney's fees. No. For the decision? No. I'm just reading it now. If it's true, he sure got his money's worth, I'll tell you. It's like something out of Kafka. Yeah, thanks, Esther. Be talking to you. No, not for myself. I just feel sorry for Todd. 'Bye."

"Laurie, that was a neighbor of the Wynns. She said, on Saturday Kevin came running over to a group of them waving something in his hand, and said he'd won his case and it only cost him $25,000 for the decision."

"Oh my God!"

"Do you have Mike Rock's telephone number on that appointment list?"

He telephoned Marion first and gave her the bad news. Could she call Sarah?

"Mike, you sound awful. Flu, probably. Lots of it going around."

Filled him in on every detail. Appeal? Certainly worth looking into.

"Don, you were right."

"About what?"

"It must have been in ones. That's why it took so long to count. Well I hope she does something about her toilette."

"Listen, I want to read you two paragraphs. We'll arrange to meet when you're better. In the meantime, I'm going to order tapes of the trial." What trial?

"Better send a notice to Silver. That's required procedure."

"Right. Now listen."

He read.

"Isn't that from one of the memoranda that Silver submitted? I thought you were going to read from the decision."

"Mike. I am reading from the judge's decision. And I'll tell you, for someone who has never had any experience with Care and Protection cases, she cites every case known to man. And, the decision is dated the day before the last day of the trial."

"Well, she could, conceivably, have written or started to write it . . ."

"And had it researched and typed so that Kevin received it two days later. From Brockton?"

"Holy shit! That means Silver and his assistant wrote the decision. To prove how good they are, to their client, they rush to mail it from Brockton. The ones for the Court and us go to

Greenfield. It's a weekend. Dirty Nellie's unavailable. Finally gets around to signing it on Tuesday or Wednesday.

"Wait a sec, Don. How could Kevin get a signed copy, if what you say is true?"

"His wasn't signed."

The Silent Tapes

It took five weeks to receive copies of the trial tapes. The originals are sent to the office of the Chief Justice of the District Courts. The reason for the length of time is that tapes from all over the state are channeled there for copies.

Mike and Don arranged a mutual time to meet after Court hours, at the DSS office, which had a beautiful machine that could pick up a pin dropping on a rug.

In that final horror, it didn't make any difference how excellent the machine was.

All the tapes were blank.

They went next door for a beer and commiseration. When everything can go wrong, does it?

DSS required that permission be granted from Central Office for any appeals. One had to go through a legal supervisor. The supervisor, in turn, contacted the legal deployment at Central Office. A checklist, of an internal nature, was compiled to assist in the determination of whether an appeal was feasible and justified. Next came the consideration of the chances of success.

What that had to do with justice, Don never understood. But you played by the rules, or else.

Don's first telephone conference with his supervisor, Charlie Coyne, lasted an hour and fifteen minutes. Coyne couldn't believe it. 'You mean to tell me . . . ' was used over and over again. At the conclusion of the second conference, Charlie told Don not to get his hopes up. Don didn't like the sound of it.

Mike Rock received a letter from Sid Silver threatening to sue him. Don was called by Mary Quincy to give a full explanation of the case, in writing. Lynn Wynn had sent a heart-rending letter to Senator Edward M. Kennedy decimating Don and DSS, for trying to separate a loving mother from her son who was bonded only to her. And thus it went. They were pulling out all the stops to prevent an appeal from taking place. Would they succeed?

No Appeal

"Don . . . Charlie Coyne. I want you to know you've been doing a great job. . . ."

Oh-oh. Bad news. Like when a judge who 's bagging a criminal case says, 'I want to commend the assistant district attorney who's done an outstanding job in this case. However . . . '

" . . . A really great job. So many people have written or called because of the way you've handled things . . ."

"Chuck, how long is it going to take before you get to the bad news?"

"Now, I didn't say it was bad . . ."

Yes you did.

"It's just that the General Counsel and his deputies don't believe an appeal can be justified in this case. Even if you could reconstruct the record . . . Mr. Wynn's comments to the neighbors is not in evidence. If Mrs. Wynn carried a trunk—and I understand from what I hear about her size, she could—into that lobby, that would not be evidence of a pay-off."

"You mean a judge sitting on a case who calls in one of the

parties and meets secretly, behind closed doors for forty minutes, and then rules in their favor, can't be called into question?"

"Well, even the General Counsel thought that was a bit strange, to his way of thinking."

"But not strange enough to challenge via appeal?"

"Don, you know I don't make these decisions. Quite frankly, I believe you and if I had my druthers, I'd say go ahead and good luck. But the fact of the matter is I'm just a conduit through which information passes, going up and then coming down."

"Maybe you should be a can-do-it, Chuck."

"Please don't be angry at me, Don. You've always made my job a lot easier. All those times when I'd be at Regional and the phones would be ringing off the wall from the field attorneys needing emergency help and guidance, I knew it was never you. And that meant a great deal to me.

"And I'll confide something in you, you Cancer, even though I didn't intend to. Do you always drag things out of people?"

"I haven't asked any questions."

"I'm leaving."

The next thing I'll hear is that the world's ending.

"When?"

"Two months. Would you be interested in my job? I'd be glad to recommend you."

"To paraphrase an old song. 'Take that job and shove it'."

"Not in a good humor, man."

"Do you see me wearing an ice-cream suit, riding a bicycle attached to a freezer chest, and doing a one-ring-a-dingy?"

"Okay. You don't have to come to the next two meetings in Brockton. Now do I hear the smile?"

"No I wasn't planning on going anyway."

"You know it's required unless you're on trial or otherwise in Court."

"I know. What I do, is get the list of dates of meetings ahead of time and then schedule Court dates to coincide."

"Why the hell didn't I think of that? You are one smart son of a bitch."

"You couldn't do that because you chair the meeting."

"I mean when I was like you. Not chairing.

"Can we have lunch or dinner or even coffee, just the two of us, Don?"

"You can if you're able, you may if you wish."

"I believe I'm going to miss your correction of my syntax; and everyone else's come to think of it, more than anything else."

"Should you send me a note from time to time, I'd be glad to correct it and send it back, graded, with comments."

Charlie had been saving this protraction for a long time

"And then I'd answer back, 'Dear Don, your continual correction of my syntax is something up with which I shall not put."

"Samuel Johnson! Charlie you've returned to the classicists. I guess those Xaverian Brothers knew what they were doing."

"They always did, Don. They always did. Well, most of them."

Two weeks later Kevin Wynn was arrested by the F.B.I. It soon developed that he and his partner would spend three or four days at a time breaking into the homes of the wealthy in various sections of New York and New Jersey. That would account for all the gold rings and chains Lynn was wont to wear. They would take their booty—or most of it— to the Mob's fence. Financially, the great part of it was that it was not taxable. Until, of course, you got caught. Then they wouldn't even take the taxes, federal, state or local. They'd just take you.

Typical coward that he was, Kevin turned state's evidence and exposed the Mafia. Now his life wasn't worth two cents. The feds gave him a new identity, including social security and a completely fabricated background. Under his old identity, he was sentenced to three years in Danbury. After being a second story man and scoring for seven years, he thought he'd never be caught. And the good news was he'd be away from that no-good bitch, Lynn. He should have stayed divorced the first time. To go back for more pain, emasculization to the point of dehumanization proved that there was something wrong with him. He did love his children. Well, not Thomas. He wasn't his. Kevin thought of him as being the Omen. And he was evil.

After ten months, Kevin was in his cell playing solitaire when he heard the turnkey. He looked up. It was one of the agents who had made the deal with him.

"Time to go Mr. Collins."

"There must be some mistake. I've been keeping track of the time. Sentence: three years. Time served: ten months."

"When you have the power behind you, you can make the figures come out any way you want."

"Believe me, I'm not complaining. Just didn't want to leave and then get hauled back in."

As they approached the personal property area, the Turnkey excused himself and went into one of the small offices. There was a pay phone on the wall. He picked up the receiver.

The Wynns divorced again and Kevin took Todd with him on several trips to New York and New Jersey. He figured if he got caught, with his new identity, he'd be a first time offender. At the most, suspended sentence and probation. He sure didn't want to do no more time. Small or big. And he didn't want to have to share his booty.

In a way, the Mob had been good to him. Supplying those lawyers at no cost to him. Selecting the judge. He did have to borrow the $25,000 from them for Lynn to give to the judge. How could a judge be so brazen to call in someone involved in a case, being tried, and meet with them thirty minutes or longer? I guess the difference is, he thought, I admit I'm a crook.

Don called Mike Rock to tell him the bad news.

"Mike Rock, please. Don Goode calling."

"Just a moment. I'll see if he's available."

"Sorry. He's in conference right now. If you'll leave your name and number, He'll make every effort to get back to you."

That's funny. He could hear Mike laughing in the background. Sounded like a party going on. I wonder what they have to celebrate.

Anyone trying to figure out an Aquarian, has a lifetime of work set out for him. Don left his name and number.

When he got to Orleans, Don got a space as close as possible to the Liquor Loft so he wouldn't have to lug his order too far. Although lately, some new young clerks had been offering to carry one's supplies to the car. Maybe he looked older than he thought.

A Robe For The Misbegotten

One of the brandies that he wanted was not on the shelf. A clerk went back to check the supply. Maybe he'd try Town Center in Eastham. As he waited, Don picked up the latest edition of the Cape Cod Times. He was so used to the Boston Globe, despite certain reservations, that another paper seemed almost foreign to him. There it was on the front page, lower left.

Governor Dukewell Nominates Cape Attorney to Head Juvenile Courts Today, Governor Dukewell nominated Cape Cod lawyer, Michael Rock, as Chief Justice of the state's Juvenile Court System to fill the vacancy caused by the retirement of Sidney Snodgrass two months ago. The governor predicted that his appointment would be hailed all over the state. "Although young, Mr. Rock has had a vast amount of experience with the juvenile system. His caring attitude for both parents, juveniles and society, in general, is legend. Most of his practice has been in the Juvenile System which explains why he is looked upon as an expert and besieged by those organizations that wish enlightenment. "The Boston Globe claims to have conducted a telephone survey of 1500 lawyers all over the state. Not one of them has ever heard of Michael Rock. The Executive Counsel is expected to vote on the appointment two weeks from next Tuesday, the 22nd.'

An Affair to Remember

He had reached his retreat from the world, which was his world. Taking the key from his pocket, he inserted it into that door which would allow him entrance to Love. Turning the key, he stopped in wonderment. Of course! Why had he not seen it before? But then—the obvious always seems to elude us. "The forest for the trees," he thought. Through this simple action, he saw all that was symbolic of the union between man and woman and God. It must be the same the world over. The right key was an admission ticket to Love. But only if one found the right mate to the key. How astonishing were all the tools men fashioned from the beginning, which were subconsciously conscious expressions of this mysterious union. So many of these began to flood his mind that he was unable to keep their numbers. He was rushing in to tell Merrillee of his new discovery but: he restrained himself. It would not be important to her. These things which he used to tell her were not important. She needed to be told of no symbols or substitutes because her love was very real to her. He was love to her. Once she had told him during the preliminaries leading to that ultimate expression of love, to please not speak with words, words, words. They were only that: words. Tell me with yourself of your love and I shall tell you of mine and we shall be one. How deep she was! He would never understand the marvelous grant of mystery which had been given her and all women. And—sometimes after—he would ask her how she came to know so many, many things. And she would tell him she really didn't know how she knew; that it didn't make any difference how. And he would tease her: It isn't fair! We men have to reason things out to their logical conclusions, while you—his loveliest creatures—need not bother! She knew he loved her. That was enough.

"Merrilee? Hello? Anyone home?"

"Don! Mmmmmm—"

"Wow! Watch out. Remember what you're always telling me?"

"I never tell you anything. No one does. Besides, I know something you don't know."

"I know that. More of that mystery you say you have to keep about yourself?"

"Well you said it was a woman's most important asset."

It's anyone's most important asset. Once someone knows all about you, you're not as interesting. Men aren't smart enough to realize it. Too open.

"Yes. But so much in one woman?"

"You flatterer. Mmmmm."

"Merilee!"

"What? I can't even kiss my own husband?"

"Honestly."

"What? Mmmmmm."

"Please hon. I think I'm swooning."

"Mmmmm—"

"You mean—"

"I mean that kind of trouble I can stand more of."

"The children?"

"I sold them"

"Wait a minute! You should have consulted me!"

"You didn't want me to sell them?"

"Oh I don't mind that. It's just that I wanted to make sure you got a good price. After all . . ."

"Oh. Listen, I don't think we should rush into anything. I mean we should get to know each other better, don't you?"

"Absolutely. I'll go mix the drinks. Martinis for you, dry Bourbon Manhattans for me. And I'll make that cheese dip we like so well."

"Don, I don't think you should."

"Really? Why?"

"Because I already have."

"Are you trying to polish my apple?"

"Not your apple, no."

He turned away so she couldn't see his Kevin Costner smile.

"Well, may I serve the drinks and whores' ovaries?"

"Don Goode!"

"What? The kids aren't around. Been sold into slavery by their uncaring mother."

"You don't want me to do anything?"

"I sure do. That comes later. They also serve who only lie and wait."

"What has gotten into you?"

"No one. I do the getting into."

"My sweet, darling husband has become a raving sex maniac."

"I'm not sweet."

"Get the drinks, waiter."

"Aye, aye, Ma'am."

Don returned with a grin much larger than Kevin's.

"You look like the cat that swallowed . . ."

"This is so funny Mer, Carly Simon was singing 'Anticipation' in the kitchen. Isn't that remarkably coincidental?"

"No, it's not. I did not invite that woman into my home. Now you tell her to leave instantly or I'm not going to be responsible for what I do."

"Mer, Mer. She was singing on the radio."

"Even worse. That's practically brand new! She'll ruin it."

"Have you touched your drink yet?"

"I've tried to, but there are eight olives in this little cocktail glass. What's the significance?"

"In the time of the Caesars, they were considered a sex food."

"Then why don't you have any?"

"Well, they don't go very well with dry Bourbon Manhattans. Twists of lemon do, though. Here. Give me your glass. I'll remove them."

"Well, not all of them Don. I won't have any sex appeal or drive left."

"You're not supposed to look at them. You're supposed to eat them."

She popped three in her mouth while Don replenished her martini.

"Has she gone?"

"Yeah. She overheard what you said, so the bitch took the radio with her and stormed out the front door. Didn't you hear the last strains of 'Anticipation'?"

"With teeth like those, I don't want to anticipate. When she asks for a hunk of lip, she means it. Literally."

"Merrilee. You can certainly be a bitch."

"All women have that potential." Like, she could rent those teeth out as condos.

"But why? You're God's loveliest creatures."

"In your mind's eye."

"No, in His."

The music and the drinks were very soothing. They both had a very warm feeling, inside and for each other.

"Don?"

"Mm."

"I love you."

"You have remarkably good taste."

"I know. Don't you really want to know about the children?"

"Gone, but not forgotten."

"Don. My mother was concerned about you last week. Thought you looked rather peaked and that you were working too hard. Much too hard."

"So?"

"Well I think she has a crush on you, which is neither here nor there. Anyhow, she called this morning and said she would take the kids today, tonight and for the weekend."

"How much did you charge her?"

"For taking our children, off our hands? I should pay her. Anyway, she arrived for lunch; I had everything packed—thank God I had done a load of laundry yesterday. I helped pack the car and off the three of them went to Wellfleet. My father was—guess—golfing. Likes to push the season a little.

"Don? Don? Don!"

He jumped up off the sofa.

"What happened?"

"I never met anyone who could fall asleep as quickly as you. I'm surprised you haven't done it in Court."

"Have."

"Have what?"

"Have fallen asleep in Court."

"Oh. Listen, since we can sleep late, do you want to take a nap now—I mean both of us—and have a late supper, watching the late news and the late show. It will be heaven."

"I had something else in mind. And I was thinking . . ."

She went up to him and threw her arms around his neck.

"Listen, my husband, stop thinking and spontane."

"Spontane? Spontane?"

"Oh—Don. Mmmmmm

"Oh, oh. My darling!" He carried her to the bedroom.

"You know, Nicky, you don't *have* to carry me. Because . . .

"But I do. I do. Besides, my dear T. McKay, the doctor said

you should get lots of exercise and I'm taking you to a place where you'll get it. Get it?"

" . . . Because if you can paint, I can walk! Oh my darling Nicky, I was looking up!"

"And you'll be looking up for a long, long time. At me."

"You're not *that* tall."

"I wasn't talking about height."

"Well then, how . . ."

"Position."

"Oh. But what does your being a lawyer have to do with it?"

It was the closest thing to heaven because both of them were there. Theirs would be an affair to remember.

Eat your heart out *Sleepless In Seattle*.

Epilogue

Julie and Reardon were married at St. John's Church in Wellesley on Saturday, June 19, at 4:00 P.M.

Two months after leaving DSS, Noel appeared on a local radio show to explain his departure from DSS. He said he had been there three years and had taken the office as far as he could. It was time to move on to bigger and better things. He became a shoe salesman at the Fayva outlet in the K-Mart Mall, Hyannis.

Manny was suspended for two months, without pay. He transferred to New Bedford, left his wife and children to live with a social worker fifteen years his junior. When he asked his wife to dissolve the irrevocable trust on his real estate, she refused.

Nola never returned to DSS. She had a miscarriage and got a job as a counselor in a residential home for wayward and emotionally troubled teenaged girls. A week after she was suspended from DSS, she received in the mail a package, containing a hard hat, a foot long cigar and a note which said, 'Nola, you're every inch the man your father is.' Some of the staff suspected Don.

Lunie was released from Bournewood. Three weeks later, she

sold her house in Hyannis, resigned from DSS and moved to Arizona.

Mr. and Mrs. Thatcher, who had fallen in love with the Cape, returned home, sold the farm and returned to the Cape. Trudy had three houses selected for them to see.

Trudy became an APM in the office.

Keeshu Walker resigned after one of his private clients accused him of sexual abuse.

Joe Carnivale went to work for a landscaper. No one has seen him since.

James Blender left DSS to become an investigator for the Department of Mental Health.

Reggie Case became the Chief Probation Officer at the Orleans District Court.

Tony Cesspo was arrested for attempted murder of his girlfriend in Hyannis. She testified and he was found guilty and sentenced to 5-7 years at Cedar Junction.

Chai Chiocco, changed her name, attained sobriety and sees her daughters once a week.

Charlie Coyne left DSS to go into private law practice.

Judge Rachel Daniels retired from Barnstable Probate Court.

Jerome Dunbar, Ruth Diamond-Gold's attorney, successfully obtained her divorce from China and also the suspension of all visitations with Becky. China is awaiting trial on sexual molestation.

Tonto East went to live on a reservation in the Southwest.

Florence and Ralph Fenwick divorced—Subsequently, Cindy was returned to Florence's care.

Amanda Faye disappeared from the face of the earth. Her son, Arthur, eventually went on to independent living.

Hy Flambeau became a fire-eater with the Circus. They did not want him to change his name.

Judge Arlo Fassbinder was found murdered in his bed. There were so many suspects, the police were unable to solve the crime.

Don Goode rejected a promotion to Regional counsel and

continued to work as area attorney out of the Cape Office.

Ruth Diamond decided to stay on the Cape with her daughter, Becky. She completed the renovation of all the Nickerson Cottages and because of their connections, now has a thriving interior decorating business called 'An Old Testament to Ruth—Off with the Old, On with the New'.

Jim Gavin tells people that it was another Jim Gavin who represented Noel.

Ruth Goldberg married Kevin O'Malley who was as totally accepted by her family as Ruth was by his. At the request of her family and because of tradition, she was to be known as Ruth Goldberg O'Malley.

Placenta Harris got a job selling chocolates at Brigham's.

Noreen Hartman became a supervisor at DSS.

Judge Harney retired from Barnstable Probate Court.

Amos Haskins was found murdered in an alleyway in Hyannis.

Judge Holden was elevated from the Orleans District Court to the Massachusetts Appellate Court.

Lynn Holster had her third child.

Judge Horatio Hensley retired and became a dog fancier.

Laverna Andrews became supervisor of the Intake Unit.

Laurie Hutchins became secretary to Judge Kelly at Barnstable District Court.

Aubrey James replaced Keeshu Walker as APM of the Cape Office.

Gina Johnson was made assistant Chief Court Officer.

Although a new pastor was assigned to her church, Mary Jane McKee still refuses to participate in the Christmas Pageant.

Myrna Malcon resigned as Commissioner of DSS. No reason was given.

Dr. Nicholas Nicholai was convicted of several counts, over one hundred, of sexual assault on children under fourteen years of age. He was sentenced to the state prison in New York for 80-100 years.

Griselda and Nicky Nickerson purchased a block of fifteen more cottages and employed Ruth Diamond to redecorate them.

Father Colleran O'Malley was sent to a home for troubled priests in the Southwest.

Mary Quincy resigned and went to work as an investment counselor for the elderly.

Jim Quintal and his wife successfully sued the state and DSS and recovered 2.3 million dollars, in the Federal Court for violation of Civil Rights.

Rose Rappucci of Martha's Vineyard did not marry Senator Edward Kennedy. Somebody else did.

Robert Reed, attorney for Arthur Faye, became the youngest judge ever appointed to the bench at Edgartown District Court.

The State of Connecticut, which removed Cynthia Rottenbotham's three children for gross neglect, has placed them for adoption.

Samantha Simpson returned to western Massachusetts to work in a dress shop.

The five abandoned Sheinfeld children were all adopted.

Warren Slaw was sentenced to 5-7 years at Cedar Junction.

Lydia Kambaugh married Ned Osco and petitioned Probate Court for Ned to adopt her son, Norbert, whom he had sexually abused.

Missy and Bobby Lenz were adopted without strenuous objection by their parents, Ralph and Marnie.

Tess Kringle and Charlie Worthington were married in a quiet ceremony by a lesbian minister.

Neal Arthur became an APM in the Plymouth office.

Hal Ambrose was sentenced to 8-10 years at Cedar Junction.

Bill Appetito, abductor of Katie Sears, is still awaiting trial. Katie continues in foster placement.

Conchita Bonana started her own business, making Mexican hats.

Mary Draper was adopted by her biological father and moved

out of state.

Maureen Dubin resigned to work full time in the underground to save children.

Maheet Jones was returned to his parents (adoptive) who satisfactorily completed the required number of classes in parenting skills.

Mrs. La Mer, Edna's mother, died of cirrhosis of the liver. Edna went to live with a wealthy aunt in Rhode Island.

Maureen Lifka transferred to the Intake Unit.

Louise Lou of DMH was fired.

Eve Marden went on to become Regional Director and then Deputy Commissioner.

Antonia Marshall will be released in two months from Gaebler, which is closing.

Abby Gilday and Sergeant Mason of the Nantucket Police are engaged.

Sid Silver, attorney for the Wynns, was found dead in his car. Foul play was suspected but, to date, no hard evidence has been found. The body of his son has never been recovered.

Jan Sterling, wife of Neal Arthur, gave birth to triplets, all boys.

Prudence Valentina married a Brazilian Nationalist who wanted to remain in this country. A week after she gave birth to a daughter, he disappeared.

Lynn Wynn was driving at four o'clock one morning without a license and drunk. She drove down the wrong side of Route 3. Her daughter, Bridget, was thrown clear of the accident and miraculously escaped with minor injuries. Her new baby, Trip, was severely injured. It is not known whether he will survive and, if he does, whether he'll be able to walk or talk. A few weeks before the accident, Todd, was found abandoned by his father in a motel on Long Island, New York. He was returned to Massachusetts and resides in his first and former foster placement. An adoption petition is pending.

Characters - 51A

Officer Alnut - Barnstable Police - Sheinfeld C&P
Bill Appetito - Abductor of Katie Sears
Hal Ambrose, s.w. - Sexual abuser of Ginny and Cissie, DMH clients, formerly
DSS clients.
Laverna Andrews, s.w. - DSS Intake Worker
Dr. Arnold - Falmouth Hospital - one of Cindy Fenwick's doctors.
Neal Arthur - Supervisor of Lunie Nelson
Luigi Avanti - Attorney for Maheet Jones' parents (Allah and Miriam)
Nola Bellafatto, s.w. - DSS Intake Supervisor
Alan Browne – The Thatchers Attorney
James Blender, s.w. - DSS
Conchita Bonana, s.w. - DSS
Lisa Brown - Barnstable police officer
Joe Carnivale, s.w. - DSS Intake worker
Carla Carlsburg - Former teacher - seduces boy 12
Reggie Case - Probation Officer, Orleans D.C.
Tony Cesspo - Chai Chiocco - Unmarried parents of Lola, Marie

and Tony, Jr. L

Ellen - friend of Chai's who witnessed beating.

Paul Cronout- Juvenile Judge, Barnstable

Cathy Crosby - cowboy Tex boy friend

James Callas - Attorney for Amos Haskins

Charlie Coyne - DSS, Don Goode's Supervisor

Rachael Daniels - Judge, Probate Court

Doris Draper - mother of Mary, 5

Granny and Dom Draper - parents of Doris

Maureen Dubin, s.w. – DSS

Jerome Dunbar - New York attorney for Ruth Diamond-Gold

Enid Evans, s.w. - DSS Supervisor

Tonto East - Boy Scout Leader and foster parent

Mr. Fenton - Clerk for Judge Daniels

Ralph and Florence Fenwick - parents of Cindy

Amanda Faye - Mother of Arthur

Heinz (Hy) Flambeau - client of Chris McLean, s.w., DSS

Arlo Fassbinder - Judge visiting Barnstable D. C.

Don Goode - DSS Attorney

Ruth Diamond - Gold - mother of Becky, wife of 'China'

Jim Gavin – Noel Peel's lawyer

Abby Gilday - Witness in Maheet Jones, C&P, Nantucket

Ruth Goldberg, s.w. - Intake, DSS, Haskins case.

Manny Gomes - Area program Manager, DSS

Nellie Gray - Judge from Greenfield in Wynn case

Placenta Harris - DSS Receptionist

Noreen Hartmen, s.w. - DSS

Julie Harris - Former DSS s.w. Booth operator for Kodak

Dr. Hayes - Surgeon at Falmouth Hospital

Gene Holston - father who shakes baby to death

Judge Harney - Probate Court

Amos Haskins - father of Lavinia, 4, & Antone, 3

Eugenie – mother of same

Harriet Haversham - mother of boy named 'Sue'

Judge Holden - Orleans D. C.

Mrs. Holton - Becky Gold's baby sitter in New York
Lynn Holster, s.w. - DSS
Miss Holmes - Nurse at CCH
Judge Horatio Hensley - Barnstable D.C.
Laurie Hutchins - Clerk, Barnstable Juvenile Court
Arlene Hunter, s.w. - DSS Jones case - Nantucket
Chuck Igo - Attorney for Lenz children
Jeff - Former s.w. —Mike Pompeo
Aubrey James, s.w. - DSS
Dr. Jacobs - psychiatrist
Gina Johnson - Court officer, Barnstable D.C.
Dr. Jonas - Nantucket hospital, doctor for Maheet Jones
Miriam and Allah Jones - parents of Maheet
Katrina Jospeh - Mother of Karen Roselli, grandmother of Tanya Manzi
Judge Homer Julius - friend of Don Goode's posing as Judge to Judge Gray
Karo Karlyle - Mother of baby she kills
Marge and Bill Kenyon - Foster-then adoptive parents of Lola and Marie Cesspo
Judge Kevin Kelly - Barnstable D.C.
Lydia Kambaugh - Mother of Norbert, 13
Tess Kringle - Client of Samantha Simpson, lover of Charlie Washington
Marnie & Ralph Lenz- parents of Missy, 5 and Bobby, 3.
Leona, s.w. DSS - also shop steward
Juan Leonardo - Probation Officer, Barnstable Juvenile
Mrs. Lenox - school nurse for Mary Draper
Evalinda Lindall - Bio. mother of Maheet Jones
Mrs. LaMer, daughter Edna
Esther Livingstone - Neighbor of Wynns
Lou La Penta - DSS Attorney for the Berkshires
Marion Lifka, s.w. - DSS
Louise Lou - DMH worker who sends letter of complaint against Lynn Holster.

Mary - Barnstable, Clerk's office, handles paperwork on C&Ps
Elvira Madigan - Noel's choice to foster Katie Sears
Madge - Housekeeper for Rev. Colleran O'Malley
Ted Manzi - father of Tanya
Eve Marden- Area Director for Plymouth and Cape after Noel's departure
Antonia Marshall - child on dismissed C&P
Bertha Marshall - Mother of Antonia
Sgt. Mason - Nantucket Police - Jones case
Rocco Martini – Juvenile Judge - Wareham
William Melley - Day care provider
Millie - Judge Harney's clerk
Ted Mitchell - psychologist specializing in sex abuse cases, sentenced 40-50 years for sex abuse of patients.
Mary Jane McKee, s.w. - DSS - supervisor is Neal Arthur
Dr. Murphy - Lunie's caretaker at Bournewood Hospital
Myrna Malcon - New Commissioner DSS
Lunar Nelson, s.w. - DSS and Hotline Worker
Dr. Nicholas Nicholas - He runs a clinic for victims of sexual abuse in New York
Griselda and Nicky Nickerson - Owners of Irish Village Motel who befriend Ruth
Diamond-Gold and Becky
Nella and Neila Neilson - Runaways, clients of Melinda Thatcher
Rev. Colleran O'Malley - priest
Ned Osco - Convicted sex abuser involved with Lydia Kambaugh and son, Norbert
Kevin O'Meara - former General Counsel for DSS
Debbie Payne, s.w. - DSS - LaMer, C&P Orleans - Edna the child
Noel Coward Peel - Area Director for DSS
Enrico Pinza - Judge, Nantucket - Maheet Jones case.
Michael Pompeo - 16, adopted at birth from Korean agency by Brooklyn cop and wife.
Imelda Preble - Aunt and caretaker for Lavinia and Antoine Haskins

Mary Quincy - Regional Director of DSS for Southeastern Region
Jim Quintal - Attorney - father of Valerie
Rose Rappucci - Mother of C&P case in Martha's Vineyard
Arturo Rodriguez - Principal D-Y
James Reardon - Barnstable Police officer
Robert Reed - Attorney for Arthur Faye, Amanda's son, Martha's Vineyard
Karen Roselli - Mother of Tanya
Cynthia Rottenbotham - client of Melinda Thatcher
Ivana Rossi - Emergency caretaker for Karen and Abel Sheinfeld who were abandoned by mother with three other children represented by: Antoinette Perry
- parents represented by Mike Rock
Sarah - Todd Wynn's foster mother
Katie Sears - 9 years of age
Samantha Simpson, s.w. - DSS
Mr. and Mrs. Sheinfeld - abandoned five children in an unheated house for three months.
Sid Silver - Attorney for Wynn Family
Warren Slaw - Owner of Tony's Restaurant
Molly Slader - Todd Wynn's day care provider
Jan Sterling - Therapist, 6a No. Eastham - Witness for DSS
Jack Smithers - Chief Probation Officer - Orleans D.C.
Jim Smythe, s.w. - Supervisor
Tony Spiro - Live in boyfriend of Karo Karlyle
Dr. Talbot - Falmouth hospital - Took care of Tanya Manzi
Trudy Teller, s.w. - DSS supervisor of Melinda Thatcher
Will Thomas - Guidance Counselor D-Y
Melinda Thatcher, s.w. - DSS
Mr. and Mrs. Thatcher – parents who sue for 10 million - Atty Alan Browne represents them.
Prudence Valentina - former client of Melinda Thatcher and James Blender.
Vivian - New receptionist replacing Placenta

Lynn and Kevin Wynn - parents of Thomas, 10, Todd, 4, and Bridget, 8 mos.

Keeshu Walker - DSS - New Area Program Manager

Wanda Walker - D-Y school social worker

Charlie Washington - Lover of Mrs. Kringle, a client of Samantha Simpson